HARD TRUTH

Secret of the Back Row

HARD TRUTH

Secret of the Back Row

A Megan Montgomery Novel

Patricia Bortz

www.patriciabortz.com

TATE PUBLISHING
AND ENTERPRISES, LLC

Published by Tate Publishing & Enterprises, LLC
127 E. Trade Center Terrace | Mustang, Oklahoma 73064 USA
1.888.361.9473 | www.tatepublishing.com

Tate Publishing is committed to excellence in the publishing industry. The company reflects the philosophy established by the founders, based on Psalm 68:11,
"The Lord gave the word and great was the company of those who published it."

Book design copyright © 2013 by Tate Publishing, LLC. All rights reserved.

Cover Designer: Karin Sterling

Published in the United States of America

ISBN: 978-1-62746-972-2
1. Fiction / Christian / General
2. Fiction / Christian / Futuristic
13.08.30

Acknowledgements

HARD TRUTH (Secret of the Back row) has been a labor of love for me for the past five years, but maybe not for those around me. I need to thank my many patient friends who, despite this drawn out affaire, have faithfully continued to pray for me. (Please, Lord, let her finish this book?) I especially want to thank my daughter Mandy Greene, my sister Theresé Haley and my long friend Margherita McElwreath, who gave me tremendous moral support and invaluable input.

Special thanks go to my dear friend Anita Kallam, who spent countless hours editing and polishing my feeble words. Without her help I never would have had the courage to follow through with this endeavor.

God bless Karin Sterling for the awesome cover! She has more talent and dedication than she will ever know.

I have to thank Elizabeth Graham for her inspiring lyrics. They instilled a passionate heartbeat throughout the book. Also, thanks to Lynda Amundrud, whose precious poem summarized it all!

From the bottom of my heart I thank my husband, Robert, for all his work on this project. How many times did I say, "*This* is the final version," only to have him read it *one more* time? He had more patience than I ever dreamed possible, especially at the end of long arduous days, when preoccupation kept me glued to my computer. Would I ever think about dinner (or even lunch for that matter)? But, Robert never faltered. He always encouraged me, asked the right questions and made fabulous suggestions. Where would I be without him? Still writing it?

Finally, it was God who inspired me with incredible scriptures and phenomenal scenarios. He answered my questions and I followed His lead. By His divine will, I, a lover of numbers and spreadsheets, have become a writer. He is my ultimate Hero! Super big thanks to Jesus, my Lord and Savior!

In memory of my loving father,

Al Adams

Prologue

A message from the demon Satan:

I, Lucifer, speak to you who read this book. You must understand that mortals think their battles are between people made of flesh and blood or, at the very least, against natural forces within the world. But their real battle is against those without bodies – the mighty wicked beings and great evil princes of darkness who rule this world. In reality, humans fight against huge numbers of controlling spirits in unseen dimensions. Mortals only hear what they want to hear. They only believe what they want to believe. They don't seek the truth but find it easier to accept my lies; therefore, they remain falsely secure in themselves and forever under my power.

A message from the angel Gabriel:

It is not an easy task to be a mortal on the earth today. Michael, God's great Archangel Prince, stands guard over God's saved people. However, I must urge all who read this, all who are humble, to seek the Lord. Seek righteousness and humility and perhaps God will protect you from the day of His anger.

<>

"Then war broke out in heaven. Michael and his angels fought against the dragon, who fought back with his angels; but the dragon was defeated, and he and his angels were not allowed to stay in heaven any longer. The huge dragon was thrown out – that ancient serpent, named the Devil, or Satan, that deceived the whole world. He was thrown down to earth and all his angles with him ... But how terrible for the earth and the sea! For the Devil has come down to you, and he is filled with rage, because he knows that he has only a little time left." (Revelation 12:7-9, 12 GNT)

PART ONE:

The Abomination

Chapter One

Day 1290

The Archangel Michael and three-thousand of his host hovered within the sixth dimension, where demons and angels usually dwell. In this illusive dimension, light-rays, more like sound-waves, encircle objects. They reflect off microscopic mirror-like particles which makes it possible, from one single position, to see completely around an object (though not through it).

The sixth dimension surrounds the three physical dimensions and is separated from it by an impenetrable veil. Invisible yet strong, the veil filters out all color, feeling and scent, which reduces the vast sixth dimension to a sense-deprived world. Sometimes, however, the spiritual beings exude such powerful energy it permeates the veil and invades the physical world beyond. Sound also passes from spirits to mortals when specifically directed.

Michael's angels occupied the dome. They were poised for action. He knew that after the horrible thing was worshiped the remaining days were numbered.

High above Jerusalem ten-thousand demons descended. They gained speed and gathered strength from each other. They converged on the gold-domed edifice and clamored for a great battle.

xxx

Reb steered his way through the jeering crowd which had created mayhem all around him. Atheists and skeptics threw stones and rotten fruit at everyone who approached the magnificent structure. He kept in stride behind a man who towered over him which protected him from frontal attacks at least.

Reb's back caught a rock but he did not flinch. His rebellious nature would have responded with retaliation had it been any other day. Today, however, he had a greater purpose. Today would mark a turning point and he would be the catalyst. He checked the bundle tied next to his body. Thankfully, it was still secure.

The line to enter the Dome was long. He stood still for longer periods than he moved. It gave him time to think ... to doubt ... to pray. Finally, he reached the security stations. Deliberately he slowed his breathing. In ... out, in ... out. He forced his facial muscles to relax. There were three check points – three guards to pass, three guards to fool.

The first one stopped him, asked his name, checked it off his list and waved him on.

The second stepped out and blocked his path, a machine gun clutched across his chest. Reb's heart began to race. *Keep breathing and relax, relax, relax.* The guard leaned toward him with the typical 'you're dead meat expression' as he barked, "Haven't I seen you before?" The smell from his sweat saturated uniform slapped Reb in the face. The guard's mirrored sunglasses glared at Reb, whose jaw began to tense. *Relax, relax. I know this man but from where?* The recollection came back and he forced a smile. "Yes, your son is in my history class." His son was not a good student. Reb had called this parent in more than once. Sheepishly, the guard backed off. "Oh, yeah, that's right. Enjoy the ceremony professor."

"Thank you, I'm looking forward to it." Reb moved on to the next station, wiping his sweaty palms on his robe. Would his slim stature be enough to conceal the extra bulk he carried? Undaunted he continued. He stepped into the scanner manned by the final guard. No bells or whistles. No, "Step over to the side, please." He was through.

His breathing slowed as he entered the outer octagon. He stopped until his eyes adjusted to the dimmer light. The overwhelming silence and pungent incense both penetrated him at the same time. The ceiling, as high as the room was wide, magnified his insignificance. *What am I doing here?* The walls were covered with priceless golden tile murals. Gold covered everything. It was more gold than He had ever seen before! Amazed, his left hand automatically went up. *Praise God for the Biblical grandeur of this place!*

Back to task, he circled around the outskirts of the room to the back row where he exchanged glances with his solemn fellow Christians. His gaze shifted from one to the other searching their faces for a reason to stop, to walk away, to abandon the cause. Everyone was serene, at peace. They were all on board. Silently he took his place among them.

The man to his left pointed to the center of the room, the Holy of Holies. In Solomon's Temple it was the most sacred of sacred places. In this edifice, disguised to bring Jews, Muslims and Christians together, it encircled the Sacred Rock with a thirty-foot high purple velvet curtain suspended from an interior gold dome. This dome was supported by imposing pillars draped with bronze chains. *What will become of it all?*

Sixtus was Satan's man. He would surely not allow God to be worshiped in this majestic place. It was true that Sixtus had authored the peace treaty but he was a beast, despite his apparent compromise. Reb knew that Sixtus was determined to destroy them all, but he would control them no longer. Reb would see to that.

The hunched over elderly high priest stood next to the regal curtain. He addressed the people.

"We are here to dedicate this holy place to the God of our forefather Abraham and to celebrate the peace we now enjoy between Israel and the Islamic world. I proclaim King Solomon's words." The entire audience of three-thousand stood as he read from the Holy Scriptures. "When Thy people Israel are defeated before an enemy, because they have sinned against Thee ..."

The priest's voice faded as Reb focused his attention on the man seated next to the Holy of Holies. He sat erect on his ivory throne. Its long legs resembled lion paws. *You think you are a lion, Sixtus, but you are not. You are a coward hiding there between your armed guards.* Sixtus was a notorious liar, swindler and power monger. Reb couldn't understand why women often swooned and fainted when Sixtus passed by them. But they did. He could not control the churning in his stomach.

"Thou dost know the hearts of all the sons of men that they may fear Thee all the days that they live in the land which Thou hast given to our fathers." Reb's attention came back to the clergyman. "Amen," echoed throughout the room. The audience shuffled into their seats.

"Now let us hear from the distinguished man who made this day possible, President Sixtus III."

The man on the throne took his time. He stood once all eyes were on him. Tall and pompous, he began to speak.

"We are here to dedicate this holy place to the god of the universe. I give tribute to the dedication and sacrifice necessary for this outcome."

As he spoke, Reb's attention went to the royal curtain that surrounded the Holy of Holies. Without a sound it opened inch by inch, exposing the twenty-foot statue behind it. Isolated gasps exploded from the audience. The icon, molded to the exact image of Sixtus III began to speak.

"This is a momentous occasion, a new beginning. Today, we celebrate three and one-half years of peace and unity among all nations and religions throughout the entire world. Right now, every knee must bow and every tongue must declare that I am lord."

Reb clenched his fists. This sacrilegious sight was not a momentous occasion that molded and mended cultures. This was an outrage that would desolate Jews and Christians alike.

"On the contrary, this triggers Israel's isolation and defeat," Reb whispered to his neighbor.

Reluctantly, the attendees obeyed and shifted from their seats to their knees to worship the icon and the man it represented. Defiantly Reb stood up along with the other one-hundred and fifty back row observers. Their long white robes, a statement of peace, were a stark contrast to the black tunics of the worshipers on their knees.

Reb crouched behind the rebels and removed the three plastic cylinders and powerful scope that was hidden under his cloak. Carefully he assembled them. Finally, his steady nimble fingers expertly clipped a handmade trigger to the barrel. He had practiced this repeatedly. He could do it in the dark. He pumped the air gun three times, and then slid a curare filled dart into the clip. He only had seconds to find his mark and shoot. He had been practicing that too, however, he had never killed a man before. Doing so would seal his fate. It would seal the entire world's fate.

He seized the moment when all eyes were on the icon. With great care, not to draw attention, he placed the gun barrel on his back row accomplice's shoulder. He searched through the scope for Sixtus. The light that came through the windows was distorted, artificially magnified to enhance visibility. He second guessed his aim and lost precious time. He took a deep breath and blinked away the sting in his eyes produced by sweat that dripped from his forehead. Finally, he zeroed in on his target's head. He lowered his sight to the man's neck. Sure of his mark, he took one more deep breath and gently squeezed the trigger.

Father, forgive me.

The lethal dart propelled from his gun and passed silently over hundreds of kneeling worshipers. It successfully pierced his prey's jugular. A slight prick and the man's face froze. His eyes opened wide, panic stricken, as the poison entered his bloodstream. Horror gripped his face but he could not speak. Reb watched intently. *Paralysis has already engulfed him.* His body slumped slightly, which caught one guard's attention. He spotted the dart. Immediately, a fully automated shotgun arsenal cut down all the standing protesters in the destined back row. Like slow motion they fell in front of Reb, a crested wave on a bloody sea. Within seconds, several bullets painlessly pierced his body. He too began to fall forward. *In one horrifying instant, the long sought after precarious peace treaty is broken.*

"Sixtus III is dead, assassinated by a revolutionary dissident." The report flew around the world. A tall stately gentleman watched the shocking video clip for the third time. Sixtus III mused. His decision to heed her warning was a good one. His muscular jaw pulsed as he closed his eyes and let his head drop back onto his chair. He did not have her clairvoyant powers, nor did he want them. But just once, he would like to prove her wrong. Today was not that day. He would be in a morgue right now, killed by a poison arrow, if she hadn't advised him to send his double to the dedication ceremony.

He flicked his right thumb against his forefinger. It was a habit he had developed as a child artfully flicking tiny paper wads in every direction. If he wet them, sometimes they stuck to the ceiling. It had incensed his mother. He did so love to irritate her. It gave him power over her. It was that sweet taste of power that propelled him to where he was today. Now thumb flicking was the way he released tension and controlled fear.

He wanted to phone Ashtoreth but knew he should not. When the time was right, she would contact him. *Ashtoreth, why haven't you called?* He started the video again and then hurled the remote across the room. He clutched his fine wineglass so tightly it popped. Bordeaux and blood spilled onto his desk. *Why does she have such power over me?*

Sixtus concentrated on his next step. He, after all, was the commander. He had the ultimate power. He was the master of his own destiny. The world played right into his hands. They witnessed his death today. Now he must plan his resurrection. *What a miracle it will be. What a miracle indeed.*

<>

"And from the time that ... the abomination of desolation is set up there will be 1,290 days." (Daniel 12:11 NAS)

Chapter Two

Day 1150

In the seventh dimension (better known as the Seventh Heaven – God's home), a great burst of light flashed from the Father who sat on the throne. A scroll, sealed with seven seals, was in His right hand. Then the Lamb, baring wounds that once had caused His death, approached the throne. Millions of angels burst into song. Slowly the Lamb broke the first seal and began to unroll the scroll. Then a voice like thunder, said, "Come!"

xxx

Sixtus III sat in his private New Babylon office. He gazed out the window at the Euphrates River. He loved the heat but this unrelenting, ninety-five percent humidity, suffocated him. A perpetual fire blazed behind him which kept his office dry but was still not enough. The air was thick. It had been nine months since the last rain and his mood reflected it.

His two top advisors, Helmut Dethloff, a small man with an even smaller head, and Conrad Fowler a huge man with a heavy beard and a shaven head, sat before him like Mutt and Jeff. They were perched on the edge of their seats. He hadn't told them why he summoned them. Beads of sweat formed on their foreheads, not solely from the room temperature. He loved to see them squirm.

Sixtus shifted in his seat. He leaned his chair backward, balancing on the two back legs. He controlled the silence. The fire behind him crackled and popped. He was partial to that sound – like the breaking of bone. He had broken his arm once as a child. He recalled the pain. An inner refreshing calm swept over him. He was pleased. Nothing made him feel more alive than pain. He had not experienced much pain since Ashtoreth had "miraculously" raised him from the dead. When the media released this "fact," they coined him the White Horseman. He loved that title above all others.

Abruptly Sixtus' thoughts turned back to the meeting at hand. *How can I gain perfect loyalty from the masses?*

"Be a savior," The evil voice whispered into his ear.

"I want to create the need for a savior. Helmut, what do you suggest?"

Helmut Dethloff, silent for a moment, tilted his dwarflike head to one side. "Since you have regrouped the former top one-hundred and thirty nations into ten protected states, and have removed all borders within and between them, the people have been reluctant to accept all your modified laws." Sixtus impatiently tapped his pen on the desk. "A humanitarian act would stir the people's hearts. If you were to show compassion on those hit hardest by the ..."

"Ah, yes, the starving children in Africa," Sixtus interjected. That was a ploy he hadn't used yet. "Set that up immediately."

Dethloff smiled and sat back slightly in his chair. "I'll have your administrator schedule the trip for next week."

"No trip" he almost yelled. "I have no intentions of actually going to that godforsaken place. That's what studios are for. Sometimes I think your head is made of wood, Dethloff. We'll film something in the studio and then you can interpose whatever in the background." Without skipping a beat he turned to his chief military advisor. "Conrad, what do you have in mind?"

Conrad leaned back in his seat, crossed his arms and stated, "President Sixtus, your troops control peace among the states. You police practically the entire world. This, I believe gives the people a feeling of security."

Dethloff shifted back and forth in his chair, ran his fingers through his hair and added, "In addition, economic growth is on the rise. You have taken steps toward developing world peace, social progress and human rights for all."

"Yes, indeed the New World Order has arrived." Sixtus barked his interruption and waved his hand in the air to dismiss the obvious. "But I want more. I want the people to believe that I am their White Horseman, their savior, their god."

Both advisors were silent. Sixtus continued to tap his pen searching their faces for a response. Three minutes passed then Dethloff spoke.

"Well sir, people crave a savior to rescue them from some hardship; a war, a sickness or a disaster. We could create any one of those conditions; it just depends on the amount and the severity." Quietly he added, "What did you have in mind, Mr. President?"

Considering Dethloff's proposal, Sixtus agreed. "Let's start with a little of each. Whatever the problem, I of course, will be the one to save them from it. Make it real and pervasive.

The covert name will be Red Horse."

Chapter Three

Day 1100

Demon activity shook the sixth dimension. There was a deafening cacophony of fluttering wings.

xxx

"This is Frank Haven, reporting to you live from Mogadishu, Somalia. Again, President Sixtus III has been instrumental in rescuing still another country from the ruinous affects of terrorists, militants and mercenaries. All day people gathered in the streets chanting 'Sixtus saves. Sixtus saves.' Again, he proves to be the great leader we have all been waiting for ..."

<>

"Then the Lamb broke open the second seal; and I heard the second living creature say, "Come." Another horse came out, a red one. Its rider was given the power to bring war on the earth, so that the people should kill each other. He was given a large sword." (Revelation 6:3-4 GNT)

Chapter Four

Day 970

Satan and his cohorts flew excitedly around the room. His favorite mortals were sinfully playing below and he blessed them. This was a momentous day. Sixtus needed all the confidence and karma Ashtoreth could give him. Satan had given him clear direction, planted every scheme and developed every angle. All Sixtus needed to do now was sell it to the people.

xxx

She reared her head and arched her back. Her long black hair fell recklessly onto his face. The scent intoxicated him. He wished she wore her magnificent hair down not only when they made love. Her sleek graceful body arched over him. Ashtoreth – was she a goddess or a witch? He could not decide. She was a prophet, he knew that for sure, and she captivated him. She was the only woman he desired past the first night and at that very instant, he was putty in her hands.

A buzz came from his ear phone. He engaged it. "Sorry to bother you, Sir. You have fifteen minutes until the press conference."

Recklessly Sixtus grabbed Ashtoreth's cascading aphrodisiac and pulled her face down to his. He caught the breath that her beauty took away then wildly kissed her full lips. The moment was intense. He knew if he didn't push her away immediately he would not, could not leave her. The force of his arms almost pushed her to the floor. She did not resist so he turned over on his side. Like a black cougar, she pounced on his back and held onto his chest.

"It is time," was all he said. Her long black-painted nails cut deep into his skin before she released him.

Sixtus entered the bathroom and stepped into the shower. The cold water brought him back to reality. He let it run until it became so hot it burned like the fire inside him. When he stepped out onto the cool tile floor she was there. Her bronze body glowed as if rubbed with fragrant oil. Her smile was alluring but she did not speak.

He dressed quickly. This presidential suite was his New Babylonian haven. He was especially thankful for the bedroom that was conveniently situated between two offices; his private office on the right and the Unity Office on the left.

Ashtoreth followed him to the door. On the other side was a room full of reporters. Sixtus turned to face her. Her eyes glowed. He took one step toward her and ritualistically placed his hands on her shoulders. Immediately the power passed from her body to his until a metallic taste filled his mouth.

Chapter Five

Within the sixth dimension a legion of demons followed Sixtus from the bedchamber through the slightly cracked-open side door into the Unity Office. Their presence permeated the room and rendered an oppressive atmosphere. It was only three-hundred and twenty days since the countdown began and the direction of the world had changed forever. These demons were here to insure that Sixtus maintained control. One perched on each reporter's shoulder. In unison they chanted and cheered, "Praise to Satan, the Prince of Darkness. Follow him to the end ... follow him ... follow him!"

xxx

Electrified, Sixtus squared his shoulders and held his head high. His stride was strong and confident. His enhanced charisma elicited great expectations in every eye. He reveled in it. He needed to convince the public that they still had control, even though ultimately he controlled the entire world. Domination over their pockets was the ultimate sway. Inevitably it was the only way. This moment was critical to his future. The metallic taste in his mouth turned sweet and he smiled at his audience. He began in his typical, persuasive tone.

"It is not insignificant that I address you today from the Unity Office. No other disaster affecting our time has done more to unify us than the computer meltdown the entire world experienced ten days ago. The world has been immobilized as computer memories have been erased; bank records, business records, personal records even worse transportation, communication and alarm systems – all affected."

The memory of his loyal but gullible scientist made him smile. He supposed the man to still be somewhere deep in the ground surrounded by the control panel he had designed to discover the so called "life" element. Instead it had erased every computer program, every data file, and every memory chip. Nothing pleased him more. He came back to the present.

"I could go on and on but to enumerate all our woes serves no purpose. We must resolve to move forward. This calamity will not defeat us. Instead it is the catalyst that propels us forward. We must develop fortitude. We must forsake old disagreements and grievances. There must be harmony to avoid splits in the New World Order, splits that would eventually destroy us. I urge you to be of one mind. Let us unite our thoughts, our purpose. Then we will march ahead, stronger than before. One goal aligns us – to survive and prosper." He raised his hands into the air. "Civilization as we know it must be reborn. Then it will spring forth hope for the future, a bright future, a fruitful future where you and your children will thrive and flourish once again."

You could hear a pin drop ... then, one by one, the reporters began to clap. Sixtus punched hardened fists into the air. Great enthusiasm and acclimation filled the room. He had them!

With his most commanding voice he unfolded his plans. "This is to inform you that within the next sixty days every man, woman, and child must report to their local polling place and register. Please bring all hard copies of identification, birth certificates and licenses. Also, bring any proof of ownership, titles, deeds, registrations, etc. The United World Commission (UWC) will issue you a temporary smart card called the Secure Personal Identification & Detailed Existence Record Card referred to as a SPIDER Card. It will contain all vital information, history, insurance, medical records, income including all finances and ownership of any kind. In the future, all transactions and information will pass through this card and this card only. It will automatically update on an ongoing basis. I repeat this will be a temporary card. Every person must replace it after a two to three year period.

"I know all your cars and trucks are currently immobile. For each vehicle you own, bring the title and you will receive a new computer board that your local auto mechanic must install. The UWC will reimburse all expenses for this. Computers at the gasoline pumps are being restored as we speak. This plan will soon get the world up and moving again." Applause spontaneously ignited the room, followed by a standing ovation.

"Thank you." He stepped away from the podium. It had gone well. They were eating out of his hand and into his plan. They were convinced. They responded to the call. Oh how he loved the applause!

<>

"... I heard the third living creature say, "Come!" I looked, and there was a black horse. Its rider held a pair of scales in his hand. I heard what sounded like a voice coming from among the four living creatures, which said, "A quart of wheat for a day's wages, and three quarts of barley for a day's wages. But do not damage the olive trees and vineyards." (Revelation 6:5-6 GNT)

PART TWO:

The Escape

Chapter Six

Day 366

Within the sixth dimension, the guardian angel Kasha followed his mortal Nadia Lyudmila Lichtenstein. He was a small quiet angel so quick with a sword he put most others to shame. Kasha remembered Nadia as a child, born to Russian immigrants. He had enjoyed her curiosity and impetuousness as she scrambled through her younger years. He had worked overtime to keep her safe but it pleased him. As she grew, she became more levelheaded, but her candor often caused her to throw caution away. However, she did nothing without purpose and resolve. She was headstrong, trust-worthy, and compassionate. She defended the weak. Nadia was totally honest, totally sincere, totally straightforward and confident.

Even as an angel, Kasha could feel her drive and passion. His pure and immeasurable bond to this mortal was like no other. It was as if she was becoming him or he was becoming her. He secretly wondered if somehow, he was slightly human or she was slightly angelic. Her aura compelled faithfulness and servitude from him. So much so, he desired her presence almost more than Yahweh's. Currently Nadia was in grave danger. Kasha did not trust anyone else to guard her, so to leave her side, even for a moment, was perilous.

xxx

Nadia hated to go back but she was at the end of the line. She just didn't have enough. She tossed her head back to dislodge the wispy bangs that tickled her lashes. The rest of her hair danced around her face as she flew down the street. She strained every muscle in her legs, arms, shoulders and back. She worked hard, pumping – pushing – pushing. Soon it would be behind her.

She entered the Katonah Shopping Center. It was a small strip-mall of only about seven stores, mostly vacant, and the Post Office. She pulled her bike up onto the sidewalk, chained it. She proceeded alongside a well-manicured flowerbed edged by diagonally cut red bricks. The bricks reminded her of the toasted wafers Herb always put on top her ice cream when she was a child. That was a world away, a lifetime away. O for those days.

Pink, purple and blue zinnias overflowed the narrow garden. She lingered past them as long as possible. Mr. Adams had the only flowerbed around which still bloomed in September. The Hamlet of Katonah was a peaceful place to grow up, but that had all changed. Many suffered from the economical crash. Crime increased. Many stores closed. Families moved away. Thankfully, Al Adams still owned Fancy Florals.

She inched up to the front door of the little flower shop, held her breath then charged through it. The potent floral scent assaulted her senses. Uncontrolled tears spilled over, dotting her shirt.

"Hi, Little Princess," Mr. Adams greeted her with a familiar smile. "Have you come to collect some money?"

She wiped her face as if the tears never existed. The store was empty except for the heavy fragrance of roses and carnations. She approached the counter. She heard herself whisper as if someone might be ease dropping, "Yes, Mr. Adams, I was able to get the windmill at a reduced price but I'm still short. I'm really sorry to come back to you again."

He flashed another big smile. "Will five-hundred dollars help? I have to itemize my monthly expenses. Contributions outside the UWC are banned."

"I know, Mr. Adams, are you sure you can do it? That's quite a lot."

"Yes, I'm sure. Someday soon I will benefit from it too I suspect. We all have to do our share."

"You have done more than your share, Mr. Adams. God bless you." Would he ever know how much he had done for her? He had been like a second father. He was more a part of her everyday life than her real father had been. She would miss him tremendously.

"I know He will, Little Princes, I know He will." Mr. Adams took her SPIDER Card and ran it through the store Point of Sale (POS) terminal which downloaded the funds to her account.

"Thank you so much. We all thank you."

"You are all quite welcome, Nadia. Now wait right here, I have something for you." Mr. Adams disappeared into the back room. She looked long and hard around the small shop. It drew her back to her childhood. It was here that Mamma taught her how to prune plants and keep an eye out for aphids and other pests. Mamma checked on shipments, manned the counter and processed special orders. The store came to life around her. There was something magical about her fingers. Miscellaneous cut flowers and ten minutes was all she needed to produce a magnificent arrangement.

She never saw Mamma idle, yet she never ignored or neglected Nadia. Her mother always had time to encourage her or answer intimate questions. *Oh, Mamma, I wish you were still here.* She fought back tears. The sweet memory of her childhood could not overcome the more life changing memory those flowers brought back – her mother's death.

Mr. Adams reappeared. "Here," he held out Mamma's tattered work apron. Seeing it caused her tears to spill over again, warm on her cheeks.

"I'm sure your mother would want you to have it."

She closed her eyes and held it close. Mamma wore this apron every day since she first started to work for Mr. Adams. She recalled the day she painted her own handprints on the two front pockets. Mamma said that way her little hands would always be there helping her. Scissors, clippers, colorful ribbon snippets and doodads always filled the pockets. They were empty now. Would Mamma want her to stay and fill them again?

"Mr. Adams, would she want me to leave? To run away? Alex thinks I'm crazy."

"Would she want you to be safe?" Leave it to Mr. Adams to answer with a rhetorical question that brought her peace.

"What is your goal?" He continued.

"That's easy – to teach."

"There you have it. What are you running off to do? You are not running away. You are chasing your dream." She had never wanted to be anything but a teacher. This was her only chance. He was right. She must go.

"And don't worry about Alex. He'll eventually come around."

"Thank you, Mr. Adams ... for everything. And remember, when it's your time, I hope you will join us." She threw her arms around his neck and he bear hugged her practically lifting her off her feet. She did not want to let him go.

"To be sure I will," he answered and kissed her forehead.

Heart nearly broken, she left his store for the last time. She stood motionless outside the door. *Good-bye, my dear friend, good-bye.*

It was finished. Another chapter closed.

New doors would open. Move on. Don't stop.

She redirected her attention, checked the total on her SPIDER Card. Close to the goal! If she could get a similar amount from Herb, she would even have several dollars leftover to fill a propane tank. Who was she kidding? They were not really dollars any more. There were no more actual dollars merely compensation, transferred from one account to another. Just how many people out there believed the cashless society was a success she didn't know. All she knew was, she didn't.

She bicycled through town. The wind fought her but she pushed back. The physical strain eased the emotional pain. Early fallen leaves twirled in spirals across her path and drew her to the abandoned Esso station where they pelted noisily against the dirty windows. She rode up to the front door and peered inside. Hard work and oil smells had formerly filled its walls, but not now. It was eerie and quiet. Times were grave. No one had heard from the Barkers since they close this service station and moved away. Her heart gave way to a distant flutter as Tommy Barker crept into her mind.

When they were little he once chased her down Bedford Boulevard. She giggled and ran as hard as she could, past huge oak trees, that cute pink house and the big stone church where he finally caught her and threw her to the ground. Without a struggle, knees planted on either side of her waist, he pressed her shoulders to the ground. Then Tommy leaned over her, slowly closed his eyes and landed a wet juicy kiss right on her unsuspecting lips. After a quick smile, he got up and ran away. He left her breathless. She recalled the sweet smell of grass beneath her head. She always suspected Tommy did it on a dare by her older brother Alex, but she didn't care. After that, she had a crush on him that lasted through the tenth grade.

She wanted to cry – tears for her mother, for herself, for Tommy, for the world – but instead she prayed. *Lord, be with Tommy right now, wherever he is. Keep him safe. Draw him to you.*

She crossed the street and headed home. Her pace slowed, her body cooled down and her muscles relaxed. She loved her brother even though at times he wanted more control over her than she liked. Tommy was the first boy that Alex influenced but certainly not the last. She remembered dating several of her brother's high school friends. All of them feared they might lose her brother's valued friendship. They were also afraid to get too close, afraid to go too far. He warned them often enough so she couldn't blame them. She laughed at the thought.

But then there was Todd. Todd had been Alex's best friend for as long as Nadia could remember. Since Todd was his best friend, he was her best friend too. Then she went away to college. When she came back, somehow everything changed. Todd's smile was different. It was as if he was seeing her for the first time – a woman, no longer a child.

Light, passion, and love had grown between them every day since. His love entrenched all that she was and ever hoped to be. Todd introduced her to life, love, truth and peace, a peace that went far beyond all understanding. A giggle erupted from deep inside her. Soon Todd would be her husband. It was more than she ever could have asked for, best friend turned to lifelong mate, however long that life might be.

She turned left down Parkway and circled around behind The Marketplace. She parked her bike and approached the building. Something dark and hairy scurried under the steps so she ascended on tiptoes. She was glad she had Faith, a small rat terrier who lived up to her breed's reputation. With her around, the rats that infested the whole town never enter their building, at least not for long.

She opened the back door. A familiar bell chimed over her head as she entered the dimly lit hallway. Her nose crinkled at the slight smell of fresh fish and seafood. *Herb must have just gotten in a batch.* She walked past the locked door on the right that led to her apartment and stopped at the partially opened door on the left. She knocked briefly and entered.

Herb sat at his desk, shoulders rounded, engrossed in paperwork. He had sandy blond hair slightly peppered gray that was balding on top. His slate blue eyes softened when Nadia entered. A big warm smile that probably melted many hearts when he was younger welcomed her.

"Hi, Herb, I need to bring Faith down the back stairs again. Something ran under the steps as I came in."

"I've been meaning to tell you about that. There may be a nest under there." Herb was the best tenant that she and Alex could have. He kept The Marketplace clean, organized and well stocked. "Herb?" she said reluctantly.

"Yes, Nadia, is everything alright?" His concerned for her safety was written all over his face. She wished she could tell him her plans but, for his safety, it was better that she didn't.

"For now it is, but I have to go away for a while. There are some children that need a teacher and I have agreed to take the job." She had told him she lost her teaching job but she hadn't told him the reason. She suspected he knew she was "unmarked" but he didn't press the issue. She continued without hesitation, "I will be living in a place that doesn't have electricity so I need to buy a windmill. I don't have quite enough to pay for it and I was hoping …"

"To borrow some money from me," he cheerfully interrupted. "Don't think twice about it. Would three-hundred and fifty help you out?" She knew her parents had waived his rent more that once when hard times hit. Their compassion and friendship saved the store many times.

"But don't you dare think about paying me back. It will be my wedding gift. When is the big day by the way?" Nadia couldn't help but smile.

"No date yet. We'll do it soon, though, very soon. Oh, Herb, I can't thank you enough!" He entered the amount onto her POS terminal and she downloaded it immediately onto her SPIDER Card. She gave him a big hug and a kiss on his cheek.

"Herb, do you by any chance have any fresh cherries?"

"No, sorry darlin', but I will let you know if I get some."

"Thanks, Herb, you're the best!"

He winked. She waved and then bounced from the room as if on a cloud. She unlocked the door marked "Private" and bounded up the stairs to her apartment.

Chapter Seven

Nadia's prayer for her first love, Tommy Barker, went up to the seventh dimension. As a result the Ancient of Days commanded the heavenly beings in the sixth dimension. They ignited into furious activity. The guardian angel of Thomas Barker gathered an army of the most powerful angels. They arrived only minutes before an extremely poisonous, powerful demon, and his bloodthirsty cohorts descended on Barker's house. A battle between the spirits raged out of control.

xxx

Tom Barker watched through sheer curtains as the sheriff and his deputy approached the house. He was an auto mechanic and a specialist in computer board installation. Since the computer meltdown people had come to him from miles around with new computer chips provided by the government. Although it grieved him deeply, he was obligated to report every chip he mounted. By law he recorded the chip identification number, the owner's name and registration number. Each chip contained a GPS and a vehicle locator. As a consequence, the ever more vigilant government tracked every car and truck on the road. It identified exactly where each was at any given moment. A monthly report was required to justify every unusual outing. As a result, people drove less and stayed closer to home.

Barker however, had rigged his own car to operate without a chip. He could easily slip through the radar with it, but he had to drive at night or during the day, very cautiously, on back roads. The car was ready to go whenever his SPIDER Card expired. Today was that day.

The officers uneasily looked from side to side as if expecting something dangerous to jump out at them. Did they know Tom was unarmed? The deputy circled around the back of the house then reappeared in front. Shades blocked each window. The sheriff rang the bell. Then the deputy pounded hard on the front door. Barker feared the glass would break. He didn't dare move or make a sound. He knew why they were there.

"Let's break the door down. You know he is in there." The deputy insisted.

"Barker, open up!" The sheriff battered even harder.

His heart throbbed wildly. He hated to break the law and Sheriff Winslow had been his friend. But the time had come. Seconds dragged like hours. He hunched over and scurried to the kitchen. He grabbed his almost full backpack and a bottle of water from the counter as he scurried to the back door. It squeaked when it opened. *I should have fixed that a year ago.* He pushed in the lock as he snuck out. Every second was an advantage.

The front door crashed open behind him.

Like lightening he darted across one-hundred feet of open yard. *If I can just reach the trees before they see me.* Dusk covered him like a shroud. He disappeared into the dense woods, twisted and turned, careful not to break branches or leave a trail. There was no path.

As of this moment he was an outlaw. His worldly possessions consisted of his car, a toolbox, limited provisions previously packed in his trunk and an address – purportedly of a "protected haven".

Finally he made out the black Ford Fiesta in the distance camouflaged by cut branches. It was a great little car that his father had given him when he turned eighteen. He patted the hood as he cleared the branches. This little baby had been his only friend at times. The engine purred to the turned key. Slowly he maneuvered, with headlights still off, between trees and underbrush. Night was dropping fast. He could barely see ... had to trust his instincts. Branches crunched under the tires. One caught the chassis, a thud made his heart sink. *Must have been a tree trunk.* He'd check for damages later. Now he had to get to ... Yes, there it was, the gravel road. His journey to safety had begun.

Chapter Eight

Serpentine, a sleazy shrimpy demon had a rat's head and a lizard's body. His black piercing eyes were set so close together that his coarse spindly brows overlapped. His long pointed tongue hung over his sharp teeth as if it savored the smells surrounding it. Each protruding lick dripped saliva. Within the sixth dimension, he hung over Megan Cameron Montgomery's shoulder and slobbered by her ear. His high-pitched voice coached her every move.

Megan's guardian angel, Hakah, was powerful and majestic. His muscular arms and legs were so solid he appeared to be wearing armor. He warned Megan constantly to no avail. Serpentine cackled. "Don't waste your breath, Hakah. You know she never listens to you. She probably can't even hear you anymore. You are powerless to help her when I am around."

Sadly Hakah knew he was right.

xxx

It was almost impossible to get a cab at LaGuardia Airport. Megan focused on one thing only – taxi … taxi … taxi. She hoped for enough karma to make it happen. Crossing her fingers she stepped through the baggage claim doors into the muggy dusk air.

"Yes," she whispered to no one in particular. She thrust her hand into the air, "Taxi!" One cab left on the stand and it was hers. Slowly the car maneuvered up to the curb. Red letters on the side displayed the word "Restricted." *Oh, no, an "unmarked" driver. Why me? I really don't need this right now!* Maybe it wouldn't even matter. Restricted, after all, meant different thing to different people.

The trunk popped open and the driver moved so quickly to her side that it caught her off guard. Before she could think twice, her bag disappeared into the trunk and the driver held the passenger door open. He stood next to her now. She wore heels but he was at least six inches taller. Their eyes locked briefly and her heart skipped a beat. She sensed his large hand on the door as it almost touched her face when she slid into the seat. He gently closed the door behind her. She was not only curious now, but desired to yin with his yang.

Immediately he was behind the wheel, "Where to Miss?" The rearview mirror reflected his intense eyes and engaging smile. She pulled out her iPhone and checked the address, "1625 Katonah Avenue, in Katonah."

"I am sorry, Miss, but that is out of my jurisdiction. I'm restricted."

"I know you're restricted, I saw the sign." Irritated, she glanced up at his identification card and read his name – Jeremiah Walker. "Jerry, I promise I won't report you. Yours is the only cab left and I'm already three hours late." She dropped her voice a notch. "I will make it well worth your while, believe me I will." She smiled her most alluring smile, but he didn't take the bait.

"I'm sorry, Miss, your offer is very tempting, but I just can't."

A cabby had never turned her down before. What was wrong with him? Accusingly she demanded, "Well, what am I suppose to do now?"

"I'd be very happy to take you to Grand Central Station. You can easily get a train from there that will take you right into Katonah." His voice was low, soothing and composed.

"Alright," she crossed her arms over her chest and glared into his mirror.

When he turned the wheel to pull into traffic his strong forearms flexed. Out of nowhere excitement surged through her. Her heart and mind raced. The reckless feeling irritated her to no end. Frustrated, she pulled out her phone again and began to dial. She had no clue when she would arrive at Nadia's house but wanted her friend to know she was still on her way. Nadia's voice announced, "Sorry, we can't pick up right now. Please leave us a message."

"Hey, kiddo, I am in New York but can't get a cab. I'll be coming by train. I'll call you later when I know which one. I can't wait to see you. Bye-bye."

The drive to Manhattan was quiet. She settled into her seat, which was measurably more comfortable than most. The car was clean and the air-conditioning refreshed her. Chicago colleagues told her that New York cabbies were slobs, so she was pleasantly surprised. She trashed her favorite skirt due to her last Dallas cab ride and its stained seats. She couldn't afford any damaged clothes this trip; she had packed too quickly and sparingly. Before she left home this morning it was like fifty-two pickup, throw everything up in the air and whatever lands inside the luggage goes. Barring everything else, she was sure she had her favorite red gabardine suit and the white lace-trimmed top. That combination often got her the spotlight, which she desperately vied for on this assignment.

"Your cab has a pretty smooth ride." Megan said sincerely.

"It's my cousin's car. We like to keep it running as effortlessly as possible. That makes it more economical to drive and provides sophisticated fares like you a more comfortable ride."

She studied the back of his head. His curly brown hair was pulled back into a tight ponytail. He was probably in his late thirties. His massive frame exuded strength, but a gentle spirit dominated him. He was very polite, very courteous, almost gentle, when he had refused to take her to Katonah. What a strange bird. This was the first taxi driver that she could not pay enough, or otherwise convince, to drive her to her final destination. She must be losing her touch. Automatically her eye dropped to his left hand on the wheel – a gold wedding band. That might be the reason. But it didn't answer her other questions. Someone "unmarked" is a rebel. *Why would someone who rebelled against the government stick to the restrictions, refuse to go beyond the city limit, and not take me where I want to go? Why does someone remain "unmarked" anyway? How difficult is it to take the "Chip"?*

"Why are you a restricted driver?" She condemned.

"I don't want to take the Chip." He hesitated. A sheen of secret knowledge invaded his eyes, but then he merely stated, "It's that simple." *That's simpleminded and ignorant if you ask me.* Even a cab driver should be smart enough to figure that one out.

Jerry smiled. His dimples, accentuated by his five o'clock shadow, deepened. Again, her heart melted. *How can he be doing this to me?* She shifted her weight, re-crossed her legs and pulled her skirt down around her knees. Defiantly she crossed her arms again. He continued to smile as if he remembered a private joke.

Megan deliberately diverted her attention. She was thrilled to be in the Big Apple at last. As they crossed the bridge from Long Island to Manhattan, her anticipation intensified. The lights sparkled on the horizon as if stars drew the skyline against a scarlet haze. She was captivated, immediately relaxed and at home. She was born to be here. This city was her heart. And right now it beat hard inside her. The car took on the city rhythm – the atmosphere was electric. This is where she belonged. It was her dream – New York City, Day Break anchorwoman. T*hat* dream she wasn't living of course. Not yet. But *that* dream had pulled her through countless hours of grunt work research for Matt Haven. It inspired her to do her best at all the human interest crumbs that Matt would throw her when they bored him. They whet her appetite for the big stuff. This trip was the big stuff and she was ready for it. But, how to get there – for real? Who knew? Maybe this trip was the first step in that direction.

Sooner than she liked they pulled up to Grand Central. Between the front and back seats, a POS terminal registered the fare followed by a line to add the gratuity.

"Will this thing provide a receipt?"

"No, Miss, I am not permitted to award a receipt. I am very sorry. I will hand write you one if you like."

"No, thanks, it won't do me any good." *No receipt, no tip. That should teach him a lesson.* She pressed "yes" to accept the charge and waved her wrist over the pad. It bleeped, "Thank you." "You're welcome," she mumbled automatically. The driver was already outside retrieving her luggage.

"Straight through those doors, Miss, you will see a monitor. Look for the Southeast train on the Harlem Line. It will indicate the time of departure and the track number."

Awkwardly she maneuvered her luggage through the doors. *You'd think the doors would be automatic.* When she entered Grand Central her eyes opened wide, surprised to find it little affected by the world economy. On the contrary, it was amazing! On either side of the huge walkway small boutiques sold everything from hats and sunglasses to cell phones and laptops. She considered getting her nails done but decided she couldn't afford the splurge, every penny saved went into her "new car" fund.

The Grand Concourse suspended oval shaped chandeliers over the north and south balconies. Each had seven tiers of lights. Ten side windows had sculptured arches over them, which curved into a grandiose domed ceiling containing six green, star constellations. She carefully studied and identified each one. Her all-time favorite stood out – two children sitting next to each other – the Gemini Twins! They hadn't crossed her mind in years.

When she was young though, experiencing them was an annual festivity at her grandmother's. Mid-December was the time when her whole household stood on the front porch, bundled up in blankets, hands cupped around hot chocolate and eyes glued to the yellow hued Gemini meteor shower. Every year Bomi would say, "See the shower? Now trace its path across the sky. There you go. It points right to the Twins! That's God showing off His brilliance." Excited, Megan would jump up and down.

That was so long ago, but that's when the desire to be a star was born in her. She dreamed of sparkling and shooting across the sky, of lighting the world with knowledge and news. She wanted to be the best, most well known newscaster of all times. That's what would cause her to jump up and down now.

"Hand luggage may be subject to security checks, thank you for your cooperation." An authoritative voice boomed through loud speakers.

Reality check. She was in New York.

Everything in Grand Central mesmerized her but something was odd. At first she couldn't quite put her finger on it. Then she discovered the rhythm was off, or at least not what she expected. The sights and sounds made sense but the passers-by were lifeless, as if in a daze. No big metropolis hustle and bustle. For the first time since she arrived in her dream city she was disappointed. She chalked it up to flight fatigue.

She found the monitor the cabby promised. *Cursed man.* Two Southeast trains were posted, one on track forty-two, which left in twenty minutes. The other on track thirty-five left in forty-five minutes. At least the trains had a rather regular schedule. If she didn't get the first she would grab the second. She followed the signs to tracks thirty-one through forty-five, passed under the arched walkway and stopped at the ticket machine to purchase her ticket. That was easy enough.

The smell of cinnamon rolls teased her nose and made her raw empty stomach groan enough to scare any pickpockets away. She must find the Cinnabon before she did anything else. Megan followed her nose down the "Dining Escalator." Sure enough, it led her straight to the tiny shop.

The woman behind the counter had dark, greasy, peppered gray hair. Her wrinkled face was sunken and sallow. Harshness pulled her mouth downward. She picked the crust from a sore on her wrist and snapped, "What do you want?"

Megan, not sure she really wanted anything after all, answered, "A tall cup of regular coffee and a cinnamon roll."

"All we got is regular coffee. If you want fancy coffee you have to leave town," she barked. She produced the hot coffee and a warm roll that dripped with icing. Thankfully, the wretched soul bagged them. Megan quickly passed her wrist over the POS terminal and at the same time noticed her leather watch band was fraying around the clasp. *I've got to replace that as soon as I get back to Chicago.*

Ten minutes to departure for the first train. She could make that easily, but her wobbly suitcase and extra goodie bag were a pain. She took the escalator back up to the main floor, turned left and headed for track forty-two. On her way, she passed track thirty-five and slowed down. She was tired and desperately needed to refuel. *I might as well just take the later train. It will give me more time to unwind and update the office. Besides, my feet are killing me, I need to sit down. And I need to eat this divine roll before it gets completely cold.*

Her green plaid suitcase wobbled back and forth, as she turned the corner to descend into the tunnel. *If this flight bag gives me any more trouble, I am going to ditch it when I get back home.* The concrete ramp heading down to the train was about six feet wide and much steeper than her high heels liked. Once on the platform, she entered the third car. It was empty. She pushed her suitcase toward the window seat next to her. Thankful, she sank into the seat. Oh the relief when she slipped her shoes off! Careful not to spill, she juggled the coffee and cinnamon roll on her lap. The sweet smell coaxed her to smile.

Chapter Nine

Jeremiah Walker's guardian angel, Justin, was not only strong, but also steadfast and unwavering. Once during a deadly battle, Justin disarmed five-thousand demons, one at a time. He never tired, never gave up, and obstinately continued until help arrived. He vowed to hang on to this mortal until the end. He believed the end was in sight.

xxx

From Grand Central, Jeremiah Walker pulled his taxi back into traffic and sped up to meet the pace. He headed west on 42nd Street. The beautiful woman from the airport would be his last fare unless he could pick up one around the theater district. He slowed as he approached Broadway. He hoped someone would be lingering at the Times Square pedestrian mall. There were several graffiti-laden benches and tables between Broadway and Seventh Avenue but the only lingerers were two gang members. Walker recognized their colors; black for the night and red for the blood they often shed. Walker sped up. He didn't need a bullet through his window.

He headed north on 8th Avenue then went east again on 44th Street. One more sweep past the Majestic, Broad Hurst and Shubert theaters. No luck. He crossed Broadway just north of Time Square. The once bustling street was almost empty. Sadly, there were only about ten theaters still in production. He turned left and headed north again. It was just about a year ago that they changed this street name from Avenue of the Americas to Sixtus Avenue. Walker was fed up with Sixtus. The man held very little regard for America or its people, except of course for its natural resources which he appropriated for other "more needy" nations. There were many other ways New York City had changed too – more subtle ways. Walker could tell the citizens were no longer the cutting edge breed they once were. He was sure it was due to chemicals that poisoned the air. It was time he got out.

Still no fares. He made a nostalgic turn west onto 51st Street. He remembered the last time he had seen a Broadway show. He slowed down and passed their favorite pre-theater restaurant, René Pujol. The steps were slightly broken but the sidewalk was clean. *I wonder if Francois is still the maître d'.* Walker liked

Francois. He always treated Sam as if she were a queen. To Walker she was a queen. On that particular night Walker ordered the duck. He could always judge a restaurant by the duck. They either did it right or they didn't. René Pujol always did it right – crisp on the outside, rare on the inside. He could almost see Sam's green eyes sparkle and tilt up over her crazy horn-rimmed glasses. She had pondered her choice, salmon or sea bass. It was always one or the other. Her long blond hair swished around her face and draped haphazardly over her slender, bare shoulders. That night she chose the bass and the goat cheese salad to start. Sam laughed when Francois refilled her water glass. She always said, "One glass of water for each glass of wine." Her playful wink as she sipped her merlot promised an amorous evening after the show.

This memory was more vivid than most. His loins ached as his heart wrapped around it. Sam was unmistakably beautiful. Sam was bold. Sam was strong. Sam was the light of his life, or had been. The woman tonight at the airport was very much like her. *Why didn't you tell her the reason you refused to take the mark? It was an open door, a perfect opportunity to be a witness.*

"Lord, protect that pretty woman. I wish I could have taken her safely outside the city. Please, guide her, get her there quickly and unharmed. And Lord, forgive me that I didn't tell her about You. Please send someone who will."

From 51st Street, Walker turned right on 9th Avenue. The farther north he went the fewer the cars. He often played a little game as he drove, to see how many green lights he could catch non-stop. One… two… three… four… five… six... His mind, fixated on the road, distracted him from the stark reality around him. The reality that at one time this area was very populated. Kids laughed and raced skate boards, friends met for drinks, shoppers dallied at store windows and lovers strolled without a care, wrapped in each other's arms. Many neighborhoods had totally disappeared – wiped out by the epidemic. Others were ruled by gangs who haunted the streets and alleyways. They taunted those brave enough to venture out into the night. The lifeless deserted sidewalks made his stomach churn. The city he loved was no more.

He parked by Docker's Pharmacy and slid his SPIDER Card into the POS terminal mounted between the front and back seat. That mechanism represented his final lifeline to the financial world. He keyed his password and pressed his thumb against the screen. The day's fares downloaded onto his card and the readout registered "complete."

"It is finished." He sighed and sat there unable to move. *I must go on.* Not much of a pep talk so he tried again. *That airport trip was a sizable amount. I'm sure it was enough to cover the supplies I'll need.* With resolve, he pulled a pad and pen from the glove compartment and scribbled down a prescription. He tore off the top page and slipped the prescription pad in his backpack.

A two-toned alarm beeped when Walker entered Docker's. The dimly lit store had only three narrow aisles separated by six-foot high, overly stuffed, metal shelves. Each contained various items that ranged from cold remedies, to baby formula, facial tissues and laundry detergent. When the grocery store down the block closed down, Randy Docker had added dry goods, canned goods and miscellaneous toiletries to the pharmaceuticals. The store was clean but not well organized. When new items arrived, they were jammed into spaces vacated by older items. *I can only guess how Docker keeps track of anything. Or maybe he doesn't. That suits me fine.* The less accurate his inventory the better for Walker's purposes tonight.

He went straight to the back counter which stretched the store's full width. Not much had changed since he had been there last. It was a typical pharmacy counter. Candy, gum and magazines packed its front shelves. Nail files and clippers and hand sanitizer lined up, one after the other on top. The only free space was a separate, three-foot cutout section next to the register, attached by several hinges and locks. It gave access to the area behind the counter and a hallway that led to the back rooms. That's where Walker needed go.

The boy named Jordan Crane sat behind the counter reading a comic book. He was a young man that Docker had rescued off the street and trained to manage the store.

"Hey, Doc, how's it flyin'?"

"Oh, pretty good, how about you?"

"Pretty slow tonight. People need lots of things but don't have any money to pay for them."

"I know what you mean. How is that rash your mother had?"

"Oh it's much better thanks to you."

"That's good. Please give her my regards." He breathed slowly and off handedly added, "Can I get this prescription filled for Rachel Berk?"

Instantly the boy named Jordan closed his comic book and stiffened. "I'm really not supposed to fill any more prescriptions for you, Doc, since you're not legal anymore and all."

"I know, but she's pretty sick and I don't have any more samples." Rachel's rapid pulse and high fever confirmed her need for strong antibiotics. The only accurate way to know if this medication was appropriate would be to analyze a blood sample. It was beyond his current status to request one. Only time would tell if she would die from this new deadly strain.

"Is she that young boy Kirk's aunt?"

"Yes, that's the one."

"I like that kid. He's just like I used to be; reckless, mischievous, but mostly innocent. I think he is headed down the wrong path." The boy named Jordan looked down at his comic book and pushed it to the side. "All right then, but just one more time. I'll leave it for the pharmacist to fill tomorrow when he comes. She can pick it up then."

"I want you to let me fill it for her tonight. She has an extremely high fever and I'm afraid without it she might infect the whole building. Diseases like that spread very quickly. I wouldn't want you to be responsible for fifty other people getting it." Fifty people *was* a stretch, but the boy needed to know the seriousness of the situation. What this neighborhood didn't need was another pandemic.

"Wow, Doc, you put me in an awful spot. I could lose my job, or worse be arrested." Walker was counting on the boy's naivety hoping to persuade him, but the boy named Jordan had been on the streets too long. His allegiance was primarily to himself. *Lord, help me convince him.*

"I know what I am asking you to do. I know it's a risk. Please, Jordan." He said in a soft but powerful voice. The boy looked away and shifted back and forth. Walker remained quiet.

"Ok, Ok," the boy named Jordan mumbled, practically to himself.

Jordan's tall lanky body stiffened as he lifted the counter top. He motioned to the back room where the medicine was stored then turned his back.

Walker quickly maneuvered down the hallway. It was almost too dark to see. When his eyes adjusted to the light, he turned left and entered a small room. He easily found the light. Drugs filled the shelves from the ceiling to the floor, all clearly labeled and stacked alphabetically. *Fortunately, Docker is not the pharmacist.* He found what he needed and put them into an empty receptacle. Just seven little pills, they would not be missed. He hoped. He turned off the light and quietly closed the door behind him.

The two-tone beep startled him. An elderly woman entered the front door and walked straight up to the counter. Walker pressed himself against the wall. He hoped she hadn't seen him.

"Can I help you?" Jordan's voice shook. The counter top opened then quickly clicked down again. *Jordan, Jordan, don't let her see me back here.*

"Yes, Jordan, remember that cream you sold me a few weeks ago? It worked really well for me and I want to get some more for my sister. Which shelf was it on?"

"Right this way." They moved to the front right of the store.

"You're such a nice young man, Jordan. How long have you been working here?" she babbled on.

Walker's heart raced. Careful not to make a sound, he slipped under the counter. He inched over to the left side isle. His head towered over the soda, snacks and chips rack. He didn't relish this sneaking around like a criminal, but he had just broken the law. He was a criminal now.

"Dr. Walker, is that you?" He exhaled slowly. He hadn't even realized he was holding his breath. "Yes, Mrs. Miller, how are you this evening?"

"Oh, just fine. My sister, Greta, has a nasty rash on her arm though. Last month, Jordan here sold me this cream he said you recommended for his mother. It worked for me when I used it and I hope it works as well for her. Would you mind stopping over to check her out?"

"Well, what kind of rash does she have? What does it look like?"

"Oh, just a regular rash I guess."

"Is it red or purplish?"

"I think it's more purplish, like three circular globs."

Almost afraid to ask, Jerry Walker added, "Is there a faded yellow ring around each?"

"Why, yes, Dr. Walker. I think you have described it perfectly."

He walked over to the aisle where Mrs. Miller Jordan lingered. This was not the same rash Jordan's mother had. He gave a cursory glance over the topical remedies on the second shelf, then pulled out an aloe-based cream and handed it to the little woman.

"This should work better than that other one. Her rash is similar to a superficial burn but may be the symptom of a deeper, more serious problem. You need to get her to a doctor as soon as possible."

"You're the only doctor she has."

"Then take her to the emergency room at the hospital."

Her eyes widened as fear crept into her tired wrinkled face. "At her age they will probably turn her away. You know how they run things these days."

Indeed, he knew only too well how things were run these days. He scribbled a doctor's name and address on his prescription pad and handed it to the worried woman.

"This is my friend. He works at the Columbia University Medical Center in the Lawrence Kolb Research Building on West 168th Street. His name is Richard Houston. Ask for him and tell him that I sent you. He will be able to help you."

"Thank you, Dr. Walker, thank you very much. Can't you stop by to see her?"

"Yes, I will try to come by tomorrow," he lied. Tomorrow may not even exist for him, certainly not here. "It's getting late tonight and I still have my rounds to make."

Her shoulders slumped, more forlorn than ever she answered, "Oh, I understand, Dr. Walker." She quickly followed Jordan to the counter then turned again to him. She sincerely stated, "You are such a blessing, Dr. Walker. Don't know what the neighborhood would do without you."

His spirit waned but he mustered up a weak, heartfelt smile, "Yes, Mrs. Miller. Thank you." Her sister's fate was most likely already sealed. Not many people survived this mutant bacteria strain. So far, there was no treatment, there was no cure. There was only pain, fever and death. This lethal bacterium causes the white blood cells to mutate until they accept the foreign matter. Once they do, the rash fades and the body begins to burn from the inside out – no stopping it. Only recently had he linked the rash to the syndrome. The three-ringed inflammation signals that the body is infected but once it disappears, after three or four days, it's too late to arrest or stop the deadly bacteria from multiplying and killing the host.

Richard Houston, Walker's research partner, discovered that the airborne microorganisms were concentrated mostly over Manhattan. The air north and west of the city contained very few traces of it. No one knew its source. Public concern grew daily as new outbreaks occurred every week. Los Angeles, Dallas, Paris, London and Madrid had similar cases. He couldn't stop the panic no matter how hard he tried.

Walker discovered what might have been a vaccine for it. But, three days after he recorded his findings, he received his termination papers and the United World Peace Forces (UWPF) escorted him from the lab. He hoped his colleague continued the research, but he had not heard from him since.

That was over three weeks ago. It was not safe for Houston to speak to an "unmarked" person. Walker understood that, but still missed his friend's companionship. He wondered if the research continued or if they halted it altogether. He mournfully suspected that all his work had been nullified and secretly swept under the table.

He continued down the food aisle and picked up a few essentials; beans, dried fruit, beef jerky, power bars, trail mix and nuts. He rounded the corner, passed a small greeting card selection and toothpaste display then picked up a bar of soap.

When Mrs. Miller left the store, he walked back over to the counter. "Jordan, may I see one of those knives that you have up there?" The boy avoided any eye contact. His friendly manner was gone, replaced by an unforgiving wall. Without a word, the boy named Jordan climbed up a stepladder and retrieved a Swiss army knife from a red cardboard box on the top shelf. Walker opened the blades; large knife, small knife, scissors, wood saw, curved blade – *must be for gutting*, wire stripper, and a magnifying glass.

"I'll take it."

Jordan scanned all the items except for the pills. Walker waved his SPIDER Card over the receiver. It registered "insufficient funds."

"Sorry, Doc, do you want to take off the knife?" Walker fought to contain his frustration.

"No, I'll put back two cans of beans."

"OK, that does it. What do I tell Mr. Docker if he finds out about the pills?"

"Tell him I held a gun to your head."

"He won't believe me."

"Tell him that's what I said you should say."

"Well, ok, Doc, but I don't want to get into trouble for this."

"Trust me, you won't." Walker didn't know that for sure. After tonight, it wouldn't make any difference. The trouble he headed for now was worse.

"Thanks, Jordan." He stuffed his purchases into his backpack. Except the knife, that he slid into his front pocket. Almost as an afterthought he added, "God rewards those who seriously try to find Him." Jordan glared at him as if he had three heads. Walker just darted him a grateful smile and left the store.

Out on the street relief washed over him but the guilt remained. "Thank you, Lord, thank you." The rush of a passing subway car rattled below the grate he stood on. A surge of hot air streamed into the already steaming night air.

A police cruiser pulled up next to him. Walker didn't recognize the driver. *He must be new to this precinct.* The officer's face was gaunt, pockmarked and scarred. He had a large two-headed dragon with flaming red eyes tattooed on the back side of his left forearm. His hat, pulled down low on his forehead, hid his eyes but his scowl was in full view.

"Are you driving this vehicle?" He pointed to Walker's car.

"Yes, sir, is there a problem?"

"Yes, there is. This is a "restricted" vehicle and I don't want "unmarked" drivers parking their heaps on my streets."

"Sorry, officer, it won't happen again." Hoping their conversation was over Walker stepped off the curb.

"Just hold on a minute." The cop busied himself in his cruiser, probably running Walker's plates. "Looks like you're about at the end of your line, Bub. I can't wait to see you tomorrow. I'll be eager to arrest you." He gave Walker a killing stare, then loudly laughed and drove away.

If all goes well you won't see me tomorrow ... Bub. Walker was back behind the wheel. A minute later he headed west on 81st Street to his cousin's garage.

He drove up the narrow concrete ramp, stopped on the third floor and parked at the south end. He pulled a black leather bag from the floor. He stashed bandages, pills, disinfectant pads, syringes and vials into his backpack's outer pocket. His grabbed a titanium baseball bat that was clamped under the driver seat.

Heaviness filled the air. Was it paranoia or had he seen something move behind his car? He glanced around the entire lot. It was too dark to see anything. *Should I wait or should I go?* His heart pounded. Suddenly he opened the door and slung the backpack over his shoulder. White knuckles pulsed around the bat.

There was no one around.

Focused, he jogged toward the north exit door. Should he walk down the ramp and risk exposure or take a chance on the stairs? The stairwell had a light, but once inside he could easily become trapped. This was the last night. His SPIDER Card expired at midnight and someone was bound to know. He opted for the stairs.

He quickly descended five, six, eight steps and, suddenly, the second floor door flung open. One by one, three young men sprinted onto the landing. They knocked into each other, bantered back and forth, and howled their excitement. Finally, a younger boy silently slipped out and eased the door shut behind him.

Walker had seen this group many times before. Their gang name was SOS, short for the Serpents of Sheol. Their colors were purple and black. They shaved their heads all except for a black spiked row that started at their temples and wrapped around their ears resembling ram's horns. The boys shaved their eyebrows also, and replaced them with crescent piercings. Their job was to torment any and all who refused to obey and support the local government.

Tonight their bodies moved as if a drug pumped through their veins. They were wild. Walker had seen it before, boys with no fear, the power of darkness on their side. They shuffled from side to side, their feet pounded the steps. The leader flipped a switchblade back and forth between his hands completely in control.

"Hey, hey, wha' ya' say, old man? We gonna git ya t'night." He gestured toward the younger boy, "This here kid wants ta carve his initials in your forehead."

Chapter Ten

Within the sixth dimension, twenty demons flew in rhythmic patterns three feet over the street gang. They all followed their mighty leader. He had a black ram's head. The conic horns curled down to his shoulders. His body, however, resembled a horse. Six legs pawed, pranced and punched the air, restless as he pursued his defenseless prey. They had a mission to accomplish and finally it was time to strike.

Jeremiah Walker's guardian angel, Justin, was mightier than most. His iron arms wielded a sword like no other. His strategy included an element of surprise, which caused most demons to back down without a skirmish. He had been assigned many outstanding saints to guard. Among the most famous were Moses, Paul of Tarsus and Francis of Assisi.

The huge demon stumbled backwards when Justin suddenly appeared. He brandished his sword and roared his warning like a lion, "Dare you come against me, you pitiful bitter goat without a chance? My mortal will not break to the pressure you make. Tell your Prince of Darkness this man belongs to the Ancient of Days, who reaches down from above and holds him. He will rescue him from his powerful enemies, and from those who hate him. They may attack him, but the Lord will protect him. This human delights Him. Take your cohorts and flee. You have no power here."

An even more ominous demon came up the rear, Foreboding. His size made him slow so he only moved when driven by purpose and determination. He carefully eyed the young boy, Kirk McCartney, and then climbed onto the boy's shoulders. His low voice slowly and forcefully declared, "That man is a traitor. It is your duty, your civil and moral duty to execute him. That is your job. You can do it. You must do it. That is your destiny."

Then Justin whispered into Walker's ear, "I urge you, live a life that measures up to the standard God set when He called you. Be always humble, gentle and patient. Show your love by being tolerant."

xxx

Walker froze and clenched his bat. They were just boys, no older than fifteen maybe sixteen at the most. That "kid" was only about ten or eleven.

"Kirk, is that you?" The young one-stepped back into the shadow.

Walker towered over them, tall and strong. He knew this was not a random mugging. They targeted him and they probably would not stop until they killed him.

He offensively raised his bat to strike if a boy came too close. Then he thought better of it, turned around and sprinted up the stairs. Only four strides brought him to the top. He flung open the door, then slammed it behind him and jammed the bat between the handle and the doorframe.

One of the boys yelled, "We know where you live. We'll get you yet!"

Minutes later, Jeremiah Walker careened down the parking lot ramp. Above him loud thunderous bangs echoed from the door he had blocked. Then he heard the boys clamber back down the stairs. Their excitement swelled as they shrieked wolf calls, signaling other gang members to gather for the hunt.

He darted around the corner, then jumped a railing and dropped down into a stairwell. He hit the ground hard but his heal landed on something soft. He automatically shifted his weight, lost his balance and then rolled onto his side. A pair of lifeless eyes stared at him and a foul rotten stench filled his nostrils. He clutched his hand over his nose and mouth so as not to gag and reveal his location to the gang members who rushed past him on the street above.

Once he had a patient who had been stabbed seven times then was left when his assailant realized he was not on the "Rogue List". Fortunately a neighbor found the injured man and called an ambulance. This poor young woman could have been one of these, left to rot because no one could redeem her body for the reward. Was her soul redeemed? Walker clenched his fists but there was no one to punch. This once beautiful person simply wasted. *Why, Father, why?* His only recourse was to pray for her murderer. Her murderer – very few murders were investigated these days. The authorities claimed there wasn't time. Their top priority was finding Rogues. That's where the money was.

Walker would become a Rogue before the night was over. He wasn't a fighter; he was a mender, a healer. What would he do if he actually were caught? He didn't know and he didn't want to find out. His plan was to run, before they came after him. He hoped it wasn't too late.

Chapter Eleven

A messenger angel flew to Hakah's side. "A prayer for Megan went up, Hakah, you may act now." Hakah, Megan's guardian angel, was dedicated to her protection. He had not seen Yahweh's face since Megan's grandmother died twenty-three years ago. It had been that long since someone had prayed for his human. Without prayer, Hakah could only warn his mortal, he had no permission to intervene.

Hakah commanded, "Go detain that other train. I'll get her off this one." the messenger had three sets of wings, one set over her arms and two sets on her back. Her wings, stronger and broader than most angels, lifted her like a gazelle over the tracks and through the twisted tunnels toward track forty-two.

A conductor walked on the platform right next to track thirty-five where Megan had boarded. Hakah whispered into his ear, "Walk through the door." Immediately the sixty-year-old man stepped from the platform onto the train. Megan occupied the first seat across from the door. The demon Serpentine sat relaxed on her shoulder. Slime dripped from his mouth. The angel Hakah flew to Megan's side and commanded her, "Find out where this train goes."

"You have no power here." Serpentine screeched to Hakah through sharp, clenched teeth. "I have always had the power and now I have the authority too." Hakah answered.

xxx

Megan spoke to the conductor, "Does this train stop in Katonah?"

"No, Miss, this is an express train. The local leaves from track forty-two in about …" He looked at his watch matter-of-factly. "Three minutes. It's the last train to Katonah tonight."

Panicked, she fumbled to find her shoes that had slipped sideways under the seat. She located them, shoved them onto her aching feet, jumped up and pulled her suitcase toward her.

Of all the crazy things to do. Why now?

In a flash she was off the train, up the ramp and headed deeper into the tunnels of Grand Central. *There it is.* Katonah was clearly marked on the roster of track forty-two.

A short round conductor stepped out of the train and onto the platform. He walked the entire length of the train, eyes glued to the tracks below. She tore down the steep ramp. The little man shook his head and looked up just as she pulled her suitcase onto the last car.

Megan's heart pounded. She gasped for breath and collapsed into an empty seat next to the window. *I can't believe I made it. Why did I wear these shoes? There must be someone upstairs who likes me.* Suddenly her hand reached for the precious elephant shaped ivory comb that secured her thick locks away from her face. *Thank God, I didn't lose it.*

One hour until the train would arrive in Katonah. That gave Megan a little time to unwind. She ate her desperately desired cinnamon roll. By then it was cold and a big disappointment. The coffee was still drinkable and she savored every drop. She put her head back on the vinyl seat and closed her eyes. It wasn't comfortable but she didn't need comfort. All she needed, at that moment, was rest.

For the last twenty-four hours, she had forged ahead non-stop. She got the call only last night that she would represent UWBC (United World Broadcasting Center) at Sixtus III's press conference tomorrow and the meetings that followed throughout the week. She often dreamt about covering a top story but this exceeded every expectation. After all, Matt Haven always handled the truly big stories.

Poor, smug Matt had covered the twenty tornadoes that touched down in Tennessee. Unfortunately, a rabid squirrel bit him. Matt was alive but full of pain. Megan chuckled to herself because she never liked him much. She found it comical that a tiny mischievous animal survived such a terrible force when so many people did not. What a bizarre twist of fate that landed her this opportunity of a lifetime. *Maybe it's not so comical after all.* But she still giggled once more.

Her mind raced. There were so many details that she finalized before she left home this morning. Not the least was this side trip to see Nadia. Again, Megan pulled out her iPhone and dialed Nadia's number. Again, she left a message on Nadia's voice mail. She reported her new ETA. Nadia was not the best at answering her phone, but she was the best at everything else.

Megan caressed the elephant comb that secured her hair. It was smooth and warm to her touch. It always brought her good luck and was the only thing she owned that had belonged to her grandmother, Bomi. Bomi, the only "mother" she ever knew, was an adventurous and intriguing woman. Megan longed to be just like her.

The elephant comb had an amazing story behind it. One fateful day, when Bomi was young and lived in the Natal Province of South Africa, she risked her own life to pull a Zulu child from the middle of the road just as a jeep careened around the corner. The child's mother was the tribal witchdoctor. She believed that Bomi had thwarted an evil spirit who had intended to steal her daughter's life. She assumed Bomi came from the gods. The witchdoctor appealed to the creator god and asked for his blessing. She then bowed down on her knees to the white goddess, her daughter's savior. The native woman removed from her own thick hair an elephant comb hand-carved from the finest ivory. It was deemed to have mystical powers. The woman pressed it into Bomi's reluctant hands. Bomi humbly tried to decline the gift but the Zulu mother insisted.

Megan rubbed the comb again, confident it had saved her from additional peril this evening. *Yes, Bomi you really were a hero that day. And you were my hero almost every day of my life.* No one ever protected her as much as her Bomi. Megan swore no one ever loved her as much either. She never cried more than the day her dear Bomi died.

The rhythmic hum of the train lulled her into a much needed sense of rest. She tilted her head toward the window. Outside, concrete and skyscrapers transformed into trees, small towns and open spaces. Amazing! This is not how she pictured New York. She began to envy Nadia all over again.

Chapter Twelve

Megan's guardian angel, Hakah, flew hard and furious, the atmosphere swirled around him. As he left the sixth dimension and entered the seventh, his body revitalized. He was no longer transparent. A shimmering film gelled all over him to form elastic breathing skin that sparkled like gold dust and tingled slightly as he moved. Or was the tingling only his imagination? He didn't remember feeling it before but he welcomed the new skin just the same. Several times he had taken on a human body on earth, but his seventh heaven body was far more comfortable. He was exhilarated! He had forgotten what it was like to be "home."

Eagerly Hakah approached the throne room of Yahweh, the Ancient of Days. The Father sat on a lofty throne, His glory filled the temple. Mighty, six-winged fire creatures hovered about Him. One was like a lion, one was like a bull, the third had a human face, and the fourth was like a flying eagle. Two wings covered their faces; two covered their feet, and two they used for flight. The great antiphonal chorus sang, "Holy, holy, holy is the Lord Almighty; the whole earth is filled with His glory."

The Master's face gleamed, like pale blue translucent quartz. It had a wax like luster. All around the throne was an emerald colored rainbow. Lightning flashed, and rumbles echoed from the throne. As always, He took Hakah's breath away. A brilliant light emanated from His body. The warmth from it soothed and beckoned Hakah closer. As he drew near the throne, a sweet aroma welcomed him – cinnamon, cloves, ginger, lilies of the valley, roses, honey suckle and more. They combined into an indescribable bouquet yet somehow remained separate and distinct.

"Hakah," God's voice bellowed, "I am so happy to see you once again face to face."

"Yes, my Lord, I have longed to be in Your presence. Thank You for sending Your messenger to report the prayer that went up for my mortal."

"Ah, yes, your current charge, Megan Cameron Montgomery." His voice rippled when He said her name.

"She desperately needs Your help, Lord."

"Oh, does she now?"

"Well, yes, Lord." Apologetically he replied, "I know they all need Your help but this one needs some special help. I know she hasn't chosen the Way the Truth and the Life but she has had a hard life, harsher than most, and she has done many good deeds."

Yahweh's eyes pierced Hakah as the angel brought forth his petition. The Ancient of Days rose slowly to His feet, leaned down into Hakah's face and bellowed, "Cursed is the one who trusts mortal man and turns their heart away from Me. Megan is like a stunted desert shrub that has no hope for the future; she lives on a salt-encrusted plain surrounded by a barren wilderness; goodness will pass her by forever."

The air thrashed around The Ancient of Days as if a storm were eminent.

"Megan relies only on the talents and abilities I gave her. She trusts only herself. Sixtus, that pseudo-world ruler, commands her confidence."

Hakah took a slight step backward and weakly protested, "But she doesn't know You, my Lord."

His eyes burned wild and His voice reverberated in Hakah's ears, "The truth about Me is known to her instinctively. Her heart contains this knowledge. I also carved a space there, a royal space that only I can fill."

Yahweh stood straight and tall. He towered over Hakah, stretched out His arms and continued, "Since earliest times men have seen the earth and sky and all I made. They have known My existence and great eternal power." He pointed a strong accusing finger at the angel and exclaimed, "So she has no excuse! I gave her the Word. If she would but read it, I would speak to her. Blessed she would be if she trusted Me and made *Me* her hope and confidence."

His angry words were slow and deliberate. "My beloved Son died a shameful death for her. He shed His holy and precious blood to buy her redemption. Should I accept her if she has not accepted Him? No, Hakah, the only way to Me is through Him."

"But You love her Lord."

"Yes, but I hate the sins she has committed." Again, He pointed at Hakah. "You are out of line. You may not come here to intercede for your mortal."

"I know You are a just and impartial God."

"And because I am, should I deliver her over to Satan when he comes to claim her? I am fair," His mighty hands clenched into fists and stiffened. "I will treat you and Satan the same, the good and the evil."

"But, my most powerful Lord, Satan could only ask Your permission to test her faith. If she has none he cannot come." Conviction gave Hakah the courage to straighten his stance.

"That indeed is true, but that does not excuse or pardon your behavior. The only One permitted to intercede for any mortal is My Son, Jesus. He, and only He, has permission to plead her case. He is the key to her destiny. He has knocked countless times on the door of her heart but she has not opened it. If she does not open to Him before her earthly body dies, He will be the Judge at her door. Then He will lock her soul in the fifth dimension until the final Day of Judgment."

Yahweh sank back down into His throne. His eyes softened. "If she refuses My grace and My eager and perpetual desire to welcome her into My kingdom, I cannot force her. She has free will, Hakah. I have given her the choice to go to heaven or to hell. If she does not choose Me, she has chosen the other route. She is rebellious." Hakah wanted to protest but instead listened. He looked at the ground. His stance waned.

Yahweh's voice softened even further. "The human heart, Hakah, is very deceitful and desperately wicked. No one can really know how bad it is. Only I know. I search all hearts and examine the deepest motives so I can give each person his just reward. You do not know how I long to open heaven's floodgates and pour My love, forgiveness and mercy into Megan's heart. My desire is to do immeasurably more than all she could ask or imagine, according to My power. But she has shut Me out."

"Hakah let Me show you Megan from My perspective." The Ancient of Days pointed downward and unlocked a portal that spanned fathoms, through the seventh dimension, past the sixth dimension and into the fifth. Up until now, the existence of a fifth dimension was only a rumor to Hakah. What he now witnessed was not what he wanted to believe, yet he could deny it no longer. God opened the gateway to a wretched black tar mass. It was penetrated by crusted stones which dripped waste and oozed puss. The stench of rotted flesh immediately reached his nostrils. Reflex caused him to recoil and hold his breath. Could this actually be my beautiful Megan's space? He turned away, regretfully ... disgusted.

"But, my Lord, where are all her good deeds?"

"Look again. Do you see those faded white spots?"

Hakah reluctantly peered once more down the long portal. "Yes, Lord." He saw under many stones a white wash that, over time, had turned a lifeless gray.

"They simply cover, for a time, her deeds of mind and heart. I guarantee that underneath it all it is cold, dark and rank. Her spirit is dead – everything that is death is collected there. Life only runs through blood. Her soul, Hakah, has no blood, therefore death prevails. No soul has blood until it is washed in the blood of the Lamb. When she is cleansed by His blood, her spirit will spring to life and the rivers of living water will flow from her innermost being forever. Cleansed or not, eventually she, like all mankind, will one day stand before My Son for judgment."

Hakah gazed again at the fifth dimension. He searched the deteriorated heap that made up Megan's space. "Where is the light?"

"You refer to the light of My Spirit." The angel nodded. "She has no such light. One must first be washed in the blood before the Spirit can be born within them."

Vanquished, Hakah searched the unsightly mass once more for some slight hope. He watched three aphid-type creatures that undulate thousands of spindly legs, searching around the mass until they found each other, merged, and then morphed into a glob of rank gooey tar that fastened its grip onto a jagged stone. It was securely cemented to her space.

"What just happened?"

Yahweh explained, "Evil thoughts do not become sin until they accumulate. If the mortal dwells on them, eventually they adhere to each other and become sin. As a result that sin inhabits them. At that precise moment, when the inadvertent thoughts became her focus, she sinned. In this particular instance she cursed again the one who prayed for her."

Oh, please, Megan, no more. The horrific smell and grotesque sight was too much for Hakah to bear. He could no longer peer at her wretched soul and instantly the portal closed. Hakah despaired and hung his head. "Will you tell me who prayed for her?"

"His name is Jeremiah Walker. He has long been a valiant and faithful warrior who listens to Me, follows My command and desires to do My will."

"And who is his angel?"

"Justin. We see him often." was the compassionate reply.

"Thank you, my Lord." Justin was an angel Hakah admired greatly. Silence haunted the atmosphere for a moment seeming like years to Hakah.

"Hakah, do you smell the soothing fragrance that surrounds My throne?"

"Yes, my Lord." Hakah breathed deeply to eradicate Megan's disgusting odor.

"Do you know from where it comes?"

"Yes, my Lord, from the sacrifices of your people."

"You have answered correctly." The Ancient of Days shifted and put both hands on the throne armrests. He leaned forward and spoke close to Hakah's face. "Go back to Megan. You are dedicated and strong, one of My very best. Continue your diligence and be vigilant, Hakah. The enemy is relentless."

The Father sat gently sat back again and continued, "You have My permission to alter her circumstances. You must remember Hakah, I long for all to enter My kingdom, but I am on one side and all people are on the other side. My Son, Jesus, is the only one who can be the mediator and bring us together."

"Thank You, my almighty powerful Majesty. Your kindness never fails me. You are just and true." Hakah bowed low then sprang into the air energized by God's presence and gentle admonition. He knew what he must do and he was prepared to do it.

Chapter Thirteen

Satan, the mightiest most beautiful demon, stood tall and proud. He had strong strikingly symmetric facial features. His piercing eyes had a yellow glow. His pupils were as black as coal. There was no other like him. He commanded all attention.

He snarled at Serpentine. "So where is she?" The slithering serpent did not follow directions well, either out of defiance or sheer stupidity. Satan didn't know which, but he suspected the latter. The weaker vessel clearly lacked the backbone to blatantly disobey orders. Satan debated; should he assign another demon to Megan Cameron Montgomery? His plans for her were becoming too great.

"She is headed to Katonah." Serpentine reported hesitantly.

"Where is Katonah? She needs to be at the New York City press conference tomorrow. Why is she going to Katonah?"

"To visit an old classmate from college."

"Follow her. I don't want any more mishaps. Do you understand?"

"Yes, sir, your majesty. I will be at the station when she arrives."

"See to it that you are." No one could tell what kind of trouble Serpentine would get into but most likely there would be trouble, and then he would have to pay.

xxx

Two cans of tuna fish, two cans of chicken soup and a peanut butter jar fit into Dr. Jeremiah Walker's backpack center pouch. Three small boxes of matches should be enough. He closed the cylindrical tin's lid over them. It fit easily into the side pouch. What else would he need? Nothing more from the kitchen, there was very little food left.

Next Walker glanced around the living room. His eyes settled on a small photograph of Sam. He had taken that picture in Central Park about four years ago. She had been particularly proud of herself that day. She managed to climb to the top of a rock formation, but made a funny face when he snapped her picture. He loved that crooked smile.

He slid the picture from the frame and then removed a small Bible from his shirt pocket. It was Sam's Bible. She had always carried it. Now it was his and he always carried it. She diligently referred to scripture whenever she had a question or dilemma. She glowed when she read a passage that truly spoke to her heart. Those passages she underlined. Whenever he read them he tried to imagine how God had used them to minister to her. He had memorized most of them. Sometimes he imagined she was there, reading the words to him. Her Bible was his last real connection to her. Without it he was lost. He opened the book to her favorite passage, Romans chapter eight, verse twenty-eight. Walker slipped the picture between the pages, then slowly closed the book and put it on the credenza next to the front door.

He went into the bedroom stripped and headed for the shower. The cold water refreshed his tired body. He dried himself then pulled on a clean pair of blue jeans. He took an extra pair of briefs from the drawer and stuffed them into his backpack. Then he went to the closet and took out a long-sleeved, hunter green, cotton chamois shirt. He slipped his arms into it buttoned the front and rolled up the sleeves. It was soft and comfortable but that was not why he loved it. He loved it because it was Sam's favorite. She would sit next to him, place her head on his shoulder and gently rub the supple sleeve.

"You're so strong," she would say when she squeezed his bicep. He was built more like an athlete than a doctor. He had played sports in high school and turned down a football scholarship at Tulane for an academic scholarship at Columbia. People always looked at him twice when he told them what he did for a living.

He closed his eyes and tried to imagine Sam there next to him now. Her image faded. He chided himself for not remembering her every detail. He could no longer hear her laughter, once a mysterious elixir to him that magically turned sadness into joy. She had been gone for over a year, fourteen months and twenty-one days to be exact. But who was counting?

You've got to get out of here so move! Walker shook himself free of the nostalgic moment and abruptly went back to the living room. He walked over to the window and closed the sheer curtains. This apartment held so many wonderful memories for him. Sam had been the one to find it advertised in the New York Times. They went to see it together for the first time and they both loved it instantly. It was a small, one bedroom, but it had a spectacular Hudson River view. They had spent countless evenings on the sofa, arms and legs entwined, as they watched the sun go down.

He envisioned Sam's legs. *Oh those legs.* If he didn't know better he would swear they went on forever. She always complained that they were too thin, but for him they were just perfect. In fact, everything about Sam was perfect. She was the best thing that had ever happened to him. Why she loved him was a complete mystery.

Walker went to the door, picked up Sam's Bible and slipped it into his chest pocket. He took one last look around, then turned out the light and locked the door behind him. He walked five flights down and out the front door. On the front stoop a ragged old man sat with his head down. His arms rested on his knees until the door opened behind him.

"Hey, Doc, how are you tonight?"

"Not too bad, Ray, how about you?"

"Oh you know me, Doc; I got nothing to complain about. As long as it doesn't rain too hard I'm fine."

"There's some milk and cheese in the refrigerator and a loaf of bread on my kitchen counter. Why don't you go up and have a bite to eat? You can sleep there too. I won't need the bed tonight."

"Got a hot date, Doc? It's about time you spent some quality time with a woman." Ray gave Walker a playful wink.

"Yea, well, I guess you're right."

Ray Saunders was homeless but it never seemed to bother him. He always wore a smile and offered a warm greeting. Sam liked Ray very much so she often invited him for dinner. Afterward he would spend the night on the sofa. He never asked for anything, but thankfully accepted anything they offered him. He was not a proud man. He would be quick to tell you that the war had stripped away his pride. Instead, he was honorable, kind and gentle. He told Walker that what he treasured most was character; honesty, decency, goodness and ethics. As a marine, he had fought for the moral principles our founding fathers established, liberty, freedom and justice for all. But none of that existed any longer. America didn't exist any longer. According to Sixtus III, there were no more Americans, only citizens of a higher, greater world nation.

The Purple Heart pinned to Ray's chest was all that remained from his old world. Fortunately, he had fallen through the cracks. Walker was amazed that the street gangs, other than the occasional annoyance, left him alone. There must not be a bounty on his head. Walker handed Ray the key to his apartment.

"Gee thanks, Doc, but you don't need to give me the key, just open the door for me."

"No, that's all right. I am in a bit of a hurry. I'll buzz you tomorrow when I come home," *If I do come home.* It made sense. Ray needed a place to stay and the rent was not due until next month.

"Well, okay if that's what you want. See you tomorrow."

Walker walked south on 11th Avenue, then immediately turned east onto 89th Street and accelerated his pace.

Chapter Fourteen

Ray Saunders' guardian angel coaxed and encouraged his mortal. The man's time was short, his body was weak but his mind was strong. The angel had his charge in the right place at the right time. His plan would play out perfectly.

xxx

Ray Saunders entered Jeremiah Walker's apartment building. Doc told him that at one time the building was completely occupied but now it only had a few tenants on the top floors. When he closed the outside door the quiet haunted him. His eyes focused on the floor as he groped down the hallway toward the staircase. Suddenly, something scurried across the floor past him. He jumped and lost his balance. His shoulder collided against the wall and his hands began to tremble. A hairless tail ran into the shadow. He suspected it was a rat. He hated rats. *Why God made rats, I'll never know.* A rat had bitten him once and it was hell. In record time the infection passed from his ankle all the way up his leg. That's actually how he met the Doc. Doc had saved his life from that bite and continued to help him survive ever since. So that evil little varmint had brought him a salvation of sorts. But he still hated rats – with a passion! He rubbed his shoulder like Sam would have and kept his eye glued to the floor until he reached the stairway.

Ray owed his life to the Doc. Come to think of it, he really owed him much more than that. Doc truly became his friend. He never had a friend before. Not a real friend like the Doc and his wife, Sam. They treated him as if he actually was somebody and not just a dirty old bum. Yep, Doc and Sam were real friends. He would do anything for them. He wished he had something to give them, but he didn't. He was tired, old, and worthless.

He had to stop and wait on every landing to catch his breath. Each step became more strenuous. He couldn't count the many times he had been up to Doc's apartment but the ascent was never as difficult as tonight. He legs were heavier than usual, fatigue overcame him. *I'm really getting old. Once I have a bite to eat, I'll feel a whole lot better.*

He dropped Doc Walker's keys into a basket on the small table next to the front door, the way he had seen Doc do so many times before. He crossed the room to the couch and sank into the overstuffed seat and sighed. It was nice to be back in their apartment. Doc and Sam always made him feel so welcome and at home. Their apartment was clean and warm. Bookshelves occupied most of the walls and those shelves contained books, books, and more books. *I don't know how two people could possibly read all of those books.* But Doc said that they had.

The center shelf on the left wall was saved for photographs. The largest was a wedding picture of Doc and Sam. *She was so beautiful. They were so happy. It's such a shame she died so young.* He remembered especially her voice. It was soft, always happy, and calm. It reminded him of his own mother although Sam was young enough to be his granddaughter. When Sam spoke, he slipped back into time, curled up on his mother's lap safe and secure. She faded all his worries away. Sam also sang sometimes after she and Doc had retired into their bedroom for the night. Ray would fall asleep on the couch to her soothing melody, although he never really understood the meaning of its words. *Maybe I'll ask Doc about it tomorrow morning. Good ol' Doc. I sure hope he's having a great time tonight.*

Ray pulled on his knees to get himself up from his seat. The only problem with a soft couch is trying to get up after a much needed rest. He slowly moved into the kitchen and straight for the refrigerator. He made a cheddar cheese sandwich, poured milk into a tall glass and shuffled back to the couch. This was his only meal today. He wanted to sit comfortably and savor every bite. *Too bad Doc isn't here to share it with me.*

When he finished his strength returned. This time he stood up easily, made a quick trip to the kitchen, put the glass in the sink, and then headed for the bedroom. He didn't remember the last time he had slept in a real bed. He stripped down to his underwear and slid between the sheets. They were cleaner and softer than anything he had ever slept on before. He reached to turn off the light but noticed a Bible next to the lamp on the bed stand. Curious, he opened the book and began to read. As he read, Jesus spoke the words quietly to his heart.

"I have loved you even as the Father has loved Me. When you obey Me, you are living in My love, just as I obey My Father and live in His love. I have told you this, Ray, so that you will be filled with My joy."

I must be hearing things. Did you just speak to me, Jesus? He continued to read and Jesus spoke again. "Yes, your cup of joy will overflow. You must love each other as much as I love you. And here is how to measure it – the greatest love is shown when a person lies down his life for his friends; and you are My friend if you obey Me. You didn't choose Me. I chose you!"

The words almost jumped off the page so he read them again. "You didn't choose Me. I chose you!" Jesus announced to him, "I love you more than you can ever know. I died for you, My dear, dear friend." How could this be, Jesus called him, friend? His heart began to beat so fast his chest could hardly contain it!

What must I do?

"Confess and believe." The soft voice urged. *Confess and believe.* His mind raced back over the years, too much to confess, too late to believe.

"It is never too much and never too late. Just confess and believe."

A friend ... a friend who died for me. His heart raced as never before. He couldn't catch his breath. There was a deep pain in his chest.

I'm sorry, Jesus, that my sins caused you to die. Thank you for being my friend.

Chapter Fifteen

At the very moment Ray prayed, a burning flame pierced the fifth dimension. The sacred blood of the sacrificial Lamb poured out and spilled over onto Ray Saunders' space. It was washed completely clean; no more puss, no more rot, no more sin. A perpetual light pervaded his heart's empty space as the Holy Spirit entered it. A choir of angels began to sing a celebration anthem in the seventh dimension. A smile graced The Ancient of Days' face.

"Well done, My Son." He said, "Well done."

xxx

Ray thought his heart would burst, this time with unexplainable joy, peace and love. He never experienced more peace than he did at that very moment. *Thank You, Jesus, my life is Yours. I want to do Your will.* He closed his eyes savoring the moment. Then Sam's song began to run through his mind. Now he understood and hummed as he remembered the words.

> You gave Your hands to the piercing nails
> You gave Your feet to walk in my pain
> You gave Your breath to breathe forgiveness
> You gave Your life for me, for me
>
> Jesus, Lord Jesus! What You gave means everything to me
> I did not deserve Your sacrifice; but You gave yourself for me
>
> I give my hands to Your works of kindness
> I give my feet to bringing Your love
> I give my breath, to speak of Your glory
> I give my life to You, to You
>
> Jesus, Lord Jesus! What You gave means everything to me
> Jesus, Lord Jesus! What You gave means everything ...[i]

Ray drifted off into a deep, deep sleep. It was the first time in many years that he went to sleep without pain, without regret, and without guilt.

Ray never heard the living room window break. Nor did he smell the smoke that slowly crept under the bedroom door.

Out on the street below two SOS gang members jumped and shouted at the explosion!

"That was an exact hit. You're totally amazing! Doc is a dead man now."

"Stick with me, and you'll go places," answered the leader.

They didn't skip a beat, but harassed and chided two young women who walked past them. "Hey, hey, hey you wanna' get laid?"

Chapter Sixteen

The sixth dimension exuded electricity. Powerful, noxious demons were exuberant about Sixtus' conquests. Their celebration intoxicated both the man and the spirits that soared around him. Satan mightily declared, "This is my son in whom I am well pleased!"

xxx

Sixtus' Spanish leather straight back chair pushed against his spine which forced the tension from his back. Before him was the United World Commission's (UWC) official progress report. His popularity had skyrocketed. He locked his gaze on the roaring fire behind his desk. The fire drew him, inspired him. He closed his eyes and imagined the fire pulsing through his veins, burning into his very soul. *Victory is mine.* The atmosphere around him was kinetic as Sixtus pondered his next move.

Alex Lichtenstein hunched over his computer. He needed to complete his article tonight to meet the deadline. He wondered how much of it would be censored. Laughter from downstairs and his sister's voice briefly interrupted his train of thought.

"Alex, we're here. Are you coming?"

"Just a minute," he muttered. A growing amount of statistics pointed to the sun's rapid deterioration. If it lost all its energy it could become a black whole sucking the earth into it. Most astronomers and other specialists considered it merely speculation and highly unlikely. Alex considered it quite plausible and in this article he completely backed his theory.

He moved to his telescope to verify one more calculation when music began to filter up through the closed door. His head immediately popped up. Bewildered, he ran down the stairs. Shock momentarily froze his step. A tall thin blond stood with her back to him. She scratched out a quasi tune at best, on his father's violin. *What is she doing in my living room handling Papa's violin?* His blood boiled. This could not be forgiven.

"That was my father's violin!" The woman jumped and spun around. The instrument flew to her side.

Nadia entered from the kitchen carrying a tea tray. "That was beautiful, Megan. I didn't know you could play."

"I don't really. I took a few lessons when I was young." She backed away from Alex.

Without a word, he jerked the violin from her hands and examined it from top to bottom. *She better not have damaged it!* It was a Stradivarius. The monetary value was great, far greater than even he could believe, but ... it was Papa's.

"My father played first violin for the New York Philharmonic. He also taught music at Julliard," he barked.

"I'm sorry, I ... I didn't mean any harm." Alex was thrown off by Nadia's reproachful glance. He ran his fingers back and forth through his hair.

"No harm done," Nadia said. "Alex is an accomplished violinist but unfortunately has not played since Papa died. You must play longer next time, Megan. This, as you may have guessed, is my charming brother, Alex."

Incensed, Alex watched his sister put the tray down on the coffee table and hand the woman a cup of tea.

"Alex, this is my old roommate, Megan. Remember this morning when I mentioned to you that she was coming?" He didn't remember any such conversation but was sure it did not include this woman's obvious lack of respect or musical talent.

Nadia and Megan reminisced about college days but Alex shut out their chitchat. He took out a microfiber cloth to clean the magnificent instrument. Four gentle strokes and the rosin she deposited under the bridge disappeared. He examined the back, the neck and the front once more. His fingers glided gently over the smoothly polished wood. It almost had a pulse of its own. Convinced it was perfect, he returned it to its proper place within the glass cabinet.

No one had touched his father's violin since the day he died. To do so was almost sacrilegious. Papa never even let *him* play this priceless instrument. Papa's sharp words echoed in his brain, "Practice, boy, practice. You are still not worthy to cradle her graceful body or play her delicate strings." Alex stiffened at the memory of his father standing over him for hours, beating out the timing between two sticks. "G he would scold, or B-flat. What's the matter with you boy, are your fingers made of wood?"

Alex could feel his cheeks burning red. He went over to the wet bar and automatically poured a much needed drink. It didn't take long for the vodka to do its job – his body slowly relaxed.

Laughter burst from the two women behind him. It broke his concentration.

"Nadia, you haven't changed one bit. You still can make me laugh at the drop of a hat."

"And you are even more beautiful than before." Nadia turned to Alex, "Every guy I ever dated in college, Megan dated first. They were like moths to a flame." As if he really cared.

"But they always dated you longer." Megan responded. Alex could understand why. Nadia was not only smart and funny she was kind and good. He envied her passion. It erupted from her like an exploding geyser. Alex stared at his sister. Her chocolate brown hair shimmered in the light. Her high cheekbones and squared jaw made her tanned face striking. She had a natural style that most women these days covered up. She never wore makeup so the freckles stood out across her nose. He loved those cute freckles. He used to tease her about them when she was little. Teasing never bothered her much.

If she wasn't his sister he would marry her for sure.

The woman continued, "All I can say is they never dated me more than three weeks."

Alex turned away from them again. *All I can say is I wonder why?*

"That's because you never let them get to know you, the real you." Nadia chimed.

"I like to laugh, I like to have fun. What more did they need to know? No reason to divulge any secrets that they could use against me, right? No partiality, I didn't trust any of them."

Scratch scratch, pick pick. Was she a barnyard hen? This Megan person was clearly a typical blond absent of any meat on her bones. Alex had no use for their conversation. He poured another glass of Gray Goose. The tumbler had no time to sweat before he took the first swig.

Chapter Seventeen

Chaos ruled the sixth dimension. Demons pressed down on mortals. Their guardian angels warded them off. The harder the angels pushed, the harder the demons pushed back. Evil was rampant on the earth. The angels were losing ground.

xxx

Jerry Walker spent the last hour and a half visiting patients. He had changed bandages and doled out painkillers, medications and encouraging words. All the while, he couldn't stop thinking about his bat. Should he go back to the parking garage for it? Fire engine sirens clamored to the north. *That should draw the kids away from me.*

He walked south on 10th Avenue headed toward 81st Street. The smell of garbage cooking in the heat wafted up from overfilled trash bins. It probably hadn't been collected in weeks. No one wanted the cleanup jobs. It was just one more reason to get out of the city.

The garage was up ahead. *No apparent activity but why is it so dark?* Or did it just seem darker than usual?

He passed the vacant guardhouse. Each step silent, each step guarded, he ascended into the unknown. He kept close to the railing. He squatted down and peered under parked cars as he approached each level. The steel barriers, heavily graffiti marked, posted harsh warnings from the street gangs. The tenseness in his body heightened when he read the fresh red paint "Death for Rogues"! Would he survive the night?

Finally he reached the third level and spotted his cousin's car parked right where he left it. He glanced toward the exit door. A kid clenched his bat and fidgeted back and forth. It was Kirk. Walker took slow, deliberate steps toward the boy who hadn't spotted him yet.

"Kirk," Walker said his voice steady and tranquil. The boy took a stance and swung the bat around his head. "Kirk, I don't want to hurt you. I just want my bat." Walker held out his hand. He hoped Kirk would just give it to him.

"I don't want to hurt you either, but I gotta."

"Why?" The boy was too young to have gotten this idea on his own.

"'Cause if I don't they won't let me join the SOS."

"Why do you want to join their gang? Evil companions will corrupt you. "

"I'm already corrupt, Doc. And if I don't join them I won't eat, and if I don't eat I'll die like my mom did. A kid can't work unless he joins a gang."

The boy was only about four feet tall. His face had small features except for his large deep blue eyes. He had straight dark brown hair which looked like it had been cut with a bowl on his head. Walker knew he had recently run away from home. Walker wondered if the fresh scar on his face was a clue as to why he ran away or the result of a street gang scuffle.

"Aunt Rachel was great to take me in, but she'll die too before very long. You know she will, Doc. So, I got no choice."

"You do have a choice, Kirk, come with me. I'll watch out for you..." The boy's face cringed. "We'll watch out for each other."

"With all due respects, Doc, you're a dead man too."

Gradually Kirk began to lessen the swing on his bat. Finally, he dropped it down to his side and leaned on it slightly. Walker could easily grab the bat away from the boy but he wanted the boy to trust him. *Kirk, just hand me the bat.*

"What if I told you I had a plan," Walker tested the waters.

"What if I told you the plan was to kill you tonight. That sort of cancels out any plan you might have."

"Not if you help me. We would make a great team. We could do it together and then you wouldn't have to hurt me." The boy tensed his grip on the bat again. Walker tried another angle.

"Why don't you hold onto the bat for now and come with me. I am going to your Aunt Rachel's house right now. That way we can talk a little more about it and you can make your decision later."

"Well, ok, but I keep the bat."

"Sure, you hang onto the bat." Walker rested his arm around Kirk's shoulder as they walked together down the ramp.

Kirk put the key in the lock and entered his aunt's studio apartment. A damp musty smell greeted Walker as he entered behind the boy. Rachel Berk's home was very small, dark, and cluttered. There were dishes piled high in the sink and on the counter. Dirty clothes overflowed a basket at the foot of the bed. A blanket draped from the sofa to the floor, a bed pillow next to it. A wheeze came from the bed in the corner.

Rachel called out, "Kirk, is that you?"

"Yes, Aunt Rachel, and Doc Walker is with me too."

"Oh, thank God you've come, Doctor Walker. I had a very hard day today."

Walker crossed the room greeted by his dying patient's pale green watery eyes. She tried to raise her tiny frame up onto her right elbow but couldn't quite make it. "It's all right Rachel, just rest." Walker pulled a can of chicken soup from his backpack.

"Kirk, go wash out a pan and warm up this soup for her."

"But, I ..."

"No buts just do it." Kirk followed Walker's order and went over to the stove.

"And while you're at it, wash those dishes in the sink and those on the counter too." Kirk did as he was told but mumbled all the while.

Walker didn't need to take her temperature. Her tormented glassy eyes revealed a high fever. He lifted her frail wrist to check her pulse – slow but steady. She winced even at that slight movement. He rose to go to the bathroom.

"Please don't leave, Doctor Walker. I need help."

"Yes, I know. Lie still. I want to get your temperature down." He opened the medicine chest behind the mirror. *She has nothing, not even an aspirin.* He had witnessed this hopeless state too many times in the past few months. It ate at his core. He grabbed a washcloth from the towel rack next to the sink and wet it from the cold tap. Next he filled a toothpaste crusted plastic tumbler with water and returned to her bedside.

Rachel pulled the sheet up to cover her mouth as she coughed. Phlegm and mucous erupted. "Here, you should spit that out," he pulled out a clean hand-kerchief from his front pocket.

"Thank you," she muttered, and coughed again. He found the medication he had taken from the pharmacy, removed one pill and handed her the glass of water. She took it without question. The rest of the pills he placed on the small bedside table. Gently he pressed the cold washcloth on her burning forehead. Her eyes closed and some of the tension left her face.

Walker closed his eyes as well. *Please, Lord put your healing touch on her body. I know you can. Please!*

The Master Healer answered, "My power is unlimited. My touch is divine. I will choose the healing. I will choose the time." It was not what Walker wanted to hear.

"I don't think I'm going to get through this, Doctor Walker." Rachel whispered. "What will happen to Kirk?"

"My wife's favorite Bible scripture says, "All things work for good for those that love the Lord and are called to His holy purpose."

"What does that mean? I don't believe all this could possibly have a happy ending. Look at my life, Doctor Walker, and then you tell me that God hasn't turned His back on me."

Her bitter voice alarmed him. "Let me read you something else from the Bible." Walker took out Sam's pocket version and flipped through several pages. He searched for a specific verse. He found Psalms 31:22-24 and hoped this would sway her. He began to read. "I spoke too hastily when I said, 'The Lord has deserted me,' for He listened to my plea and answered me. Oh, love the Lord, all of you who are His people, for the Lord protects those who are loyal to Him, but harshly punishes all who haughtily reject Him. So cheer up! Take courage and depend on the Lord."

Through worried eyes she responded, "I don't know what to do. I'm so tired I can't even think."

"Give her the Bible," responded the gentle voice in Walker's head.

I can't, it belonged to Sam. It's my final link to her!

"Give it to the dying woman. My grace is sufficient for you."

He fingered the precious book's soft worn cover. He brought it to his nose and smelled it one last time. *I died with Sam when she breathed her last breath. I live again because of you, Lord. You are all that I need. I desire no one on earth as much as you. My health fails, my spirits droop, yet you remain the same. You are the strength of my heart. You are mine forever.* He removed his sweet wife's photo and reluctantly handed the book to the seeking woman. He spoke ever so softly to her, fearful that the heavy beat of his heart might emerge if he spoke any louder.

"God showed how much He loves us by sending His only Son into this wicked world to bring us eternal life. It is not our love for God, but His love for us. Read this book. Start here." His hands trembled as he opened to the gospel of John. "Listen to what God has to say to you and follow His plan. Then you will understand and know what to do."

She eyed the book and flipped uninterested through the pages.

Would she live long enough to read it? Walker slowly got up and moved toward the door, his heart held loosely in Rachel's hand. He couldn't bear to think about the book, his last intimate tie to Sam, left behind.

Kirk came over to the bedside carrying the hot bowl of soup. Rachel put down the Bible and began to drink the warm broth. She managed a slight smile, "Thank you. Thank you so much."

Kirk picked up the bat. "So what's your plan?"

Walker checked his watch – eleven fifteen. It had been a long night but it wasn't over yet. He and his new sidekick Kirk descended the subway steps, one at a time. They constantly looked out for someone who might recognize them. Thankfully, the 103rd Street station on the 1/9 line was empty. Walker checked out the ticket booth. A young woman sat inside the metal enclosure surrounded by bulletproof glass and iron bars. She twisted the end of her long greasy ponytail around her finger, chewed gum and fumbled with her iPod. Gum and iPods were contraband in a ticket booth. Lucky for them she didn't seem to care. Kids were happy these days if they lost their jobs. They preferred Welfare.

Walker and Kirk waited motionless in the stairwell, their backs pressed against the graffiti-laden wall. Walker's heart raced again. He had no means to pay for two subway tickets to the Bronx.

Out of the silence, a northbound train rattled. Kirk motioned to Walker that they must jump the turnstile. Instantly, the boy crossed a twenty-foot span of open space and effortlessly bounded over the three-foot high barrier. He never looked back. The train screeched to a halt at the edge of the platform. Walker briefly glanced again at the ticket booth attendant. Still occupied. This was his last chance. He darted across the room. When he reached the stile, he placed his left hand on the center bracket and lifted his legs as high as he could to clear the arm. In his younger days, he never would have worried about the leap, but after tonight's great chase, he no longer trusted his agility. *Lord, please help me.* Walker's feet landed firmly on the concrete platform just as the train doors opened. Three people got off the train and the two fugitives slipped between them through the open doors.

Kirk sat silently next to him. They were headed for ... where? The rapidly moving subway car was empty except for a young couple clearly engrossed in each other.

Panic struck Walker! He reached frantically for the loop in his backpack. The bat was still there, cool to his touch. He let out his breath and closed his eyes. At last he began to breathe more easily. He was not cut out for this outlaw stuff but he was now, indeed, an outlaw. Before they got off this train he would become illegal. He was sure Kirk had no papers either. When they ran together they became criminals together. He hoped it had not been a mistake to bring the boy.

The subway car jostled them back and forth. The lights flickered off and on as the train clacked over the rails. He contemplated their next move. Head north was all he was told. He heard that a community of the "unmarked" lived in the Catskills, a small upstate New York mountain range. He didn't know how to get there, but he was determined to try. God would lead the way. If it were His will they would make it. If it wasn't then God had a better plan.

What is the boy thinking? Will he stick by me or turn me in the first chance he gets? At least for now they were both safe but conviction swelled again inside him. He began to pray.

Come, Lord, quickly
My spirit is fainting
Come, Lord quickly to me
For I am sinking down
Let the morning bring me word
Of Your unfailing love
For I trust you
For your name's sake, O Lord
Preserve my life
In your righteousness
Deliver me
Let the morning bring me word
Of your unfailing love
For I trust you

Show me the way I should go
To You, I lift up my soul
Teach me to do only your will
For you alone are God
And I hide myself in you
Come, Lord, quickly
I need you, I'm calling for you.[ii]

He drifted into a deep sleep ... or was it a trance? He was not sure, but the Lord God Himself visited him.

"Jeremiah," Jesus' voice demanded his attention. "You are My witness and My servant. I have chosen you, because you know and believe Me and understand that I alone am God. There is no other God; there never was and never will be. I am the Lord, and there is no other Savior. The great day of My return is near. How bitter is the sound of that day, the day when I shout My war cry. A day of wrath, that day, a day of distress and agony, a day of ruin and of devastation, a day of darkness and gloom, a day of cloud and blackness, a day of trumpet blast and battle cry. I am going to bring such distress on men that they will grope like the blind because they have sinned against me; their blood will be scattered like dust, their corpses like dung. No money will have any power to save them."

"On the day of My anger, in the fire of My jealousy, all the earth will be consumed. I intend to destroy, yes, to make an end of all the earthly inhabitants."

Walker woke with a start. Panic gripped him.

Kirk tugged on his arm, "We are almost at the last stop."

The dream left him horror stricken. *Lord, what must I do?*

"Warn them," was the only answer. Walker determined in his heart to do so.

<>

OH, SAY CAN YOU SEE BY THE DAWN'S EARLY LIGHT

Chapter Eighteen

Day 365

Serpentine kept Megan awake, way into the early morning hours. Enthusiastically he poked and prodded her body, just enough to keep her from falling asleep, just enough to peek his pleasure. He harassed her and loaded negative thoughts into her mind. That was his favorite past-time. Mortals were so gullible and worried over many useless topics, mostly scenarios that would never happen. He loved to fuel their insecurities and create havoc in their minds. Eventually the fun wore off. He let her fall asleep. He decided to create a longer lasting havoc.

The demon flew off into the starless sky and in minutes approached Bergner's Hardware store. It was here that Nadia hoped to buy the windmill. He would see to it that her plan would be disrupted and impossible to complete. With the touch of a finger, he set fire to some oil rags in the storage room. That ought to do the trick. A sinister chuckle turned into menacing laughter. He bounded up into the early morning sky elated. His scheme was sheer brilliance.

Satan summoned Baleful. He had the body of a wild boar, the head of a hyena and two sets of wings, one on his shoulders and one on his back. His cunning whit often excused his lack of ambition. Satan disliked him intensely because Baleful was not a demon that could keep his mouth shut, nor could he keep his eyes on his own business. This annoyance did however, come in handy at this particular point in time. As Baleful approached, Satan demanded, "Do you know the mortal that Megan Cameron Montgomery has gone to visit?"

Apparently eager to please the master he adored, the snoop reported, "I've had my eye on her for some time now."

Satan's impatience showed. "Well, your eyes are not my eyes. From now on I want a detailed report on every move she makes."

Baleful, seemingly oblivious to Satan's distain of him remarked offhandedly, "You can't own Nadia Lyudmila Lichtenstein. She already belongs to Je ..."

Satan exploded and grabbed his underling by his throat, "Do not say His name or I will gladly, and with great pleasure, rip out your tongue." Fire flashed through his clenched teeth sending smoke up Baleful's nostrils. "I can own whomever I choose." The devil loosened his grip and tossed the demon to the side. Satan's mind reeled and he began to pace, mumbling almost to himself. "Everyone can be bought. It's just a matter of price." When he looked up, Baleful was watching him with admiration. Satan waved his hand to dismiss him. "Do as I say, you fool, and get out of my sight."

Baleful beamed. His new assignment sent him to the skies as the sun began to rise.

xxx

Megan awoke with a start. Was it a dream? No the alarm! At first she was disoriented then she remembered the exciting day ahead. *I wonder what it will be like seeing him in person!* She reached over and turned the alarm off. Six-fifteen sharp! It was early but she was ready to go – bathroom first. She brushed her teeth in record time then grabbed her robe. Someone was already buzzing around in the kitchen. The wonderful aroma of coffee teased her. She was eager to follow it.

Megan entered the kitchen and immediately embraced its hominess. The room was clearly a remnant from the past. It was a good size by apartment standards, but very cozy. Hand-painted flowers adorned pale yellow walls. Several of the white wooden cupboards had glass inserts which displayed pretty vases and bowls. On the broad windowsill sat four ceramic pots. Colorful flowers spilled over their edges. Parsley, basil, dill and cilantro grew in rectangular trays between them. Cookbooks galore filled numerous shelves on the far wall. The large oval table donned a bright yellow tablecloth. A potted African violet was in the center.

She could easily imagine the countless hours Nadia must have spent here with her family. She loved to visualize what Nadia was like as a child, what she did, where she went, and what her family was like. This morning she tasted that "normal" life and wanted more.

"Good morning, Megan, did you sleep well?"

"Yes, but I had a rough time getting started. I kept thinking about the press conference this morning. I am so nervous. I can't believe this is actually happening!"

"Well believe it. It is happening and you'll be fantastic! Meg, you were always good at interviewing. This is not much different than that."

"Oh, yes it is. Most people never get a chance like this. I may actually have the opportunity to ask the most powerful man in the world a question!" Last night in bed, she rehearsed and re-rehearsed exactly what she would say. She played out every possible scenario.

Nadia poured her a cup of coffee. Megan put two spoons of sugar in her cup and stirred it while Nadia added just the right amount of milk. Nadia always made the best cup of coffee. In college, she used hazelnut cream when they could get it. It was to die for. She closed her eyes, pulled the cup to her nose, drank in the sweet aroma and savored the moment.

"There are certainly a lot of questions that I would like to ask him too." She jumped at Alex's peeved voice behind her. "It seems he is trying to control more of our lives every day." He crossed the room and poured himself some coffee, then joined Nadia and her at the table.

Megan quickly defended the man. "Well of course he has control, he's President of the UWC (United World Commission). Don't you see? In order to pull the world out of financial destruction, he had to elevate performance and efficiency. He had to restructure on a global basis, and that is naturally a painful process. If he didn't have control where would we be?"

"A whole lot freer for one thing," Nadia added as if treading on eggshells. "The UWC is Big Brother personified. Everyone needs to believe in someone, something to give them hope. Granted, Sixtus exudes charisma and much of the entire world buys the hope he claims to offer. But he is a liar and a fraud."

Megan, frustrated by Nadia's narrow-minded view, stiffened in her seat. She also saw the judgment in Nadia's eyes. She wanted so much for her friend to see why Sixtus acted so severely.

"Restrictions are necessary when there is a crisis. Who was it that pulled the whole world out of total financial ruin after the computer meltdown literally erased the memory of every computer? And who was it that organized the distribution of over forty-million tons of food in the last three years since floods, fires and earthquakes destroyed most of the farmland in the Western Hemisphere? And who is it that has kept the terrorists at bay for so many months?"

She could not understand why Nadia made it so complicated. Sixtus clearly was the redeemer of the world. "Sixtus III made order from confusion. He is the one who brought peace between nation after nation even between Israel and the Islamic nations." She never remembered Nadia looking so sad and strained.

"He says, 'Peace, peace,' but there is no peace among God's people, Megan. Look how many of the Israelis had to flee Jerusalem to save their lives these last two and a half years since the treaty was broken."

Alex shook his head. Was he still angry from last night? He looked straight at her. "What I find so appalling is that Sixtus set up an icon to worship himself right inside the holy temple walls."

She pulled her hair away from her face and tied it in a knot in the back of her head. Her beautiful morning filled with so much promise was crumbling around her. "Well, maybe he should be worshipped. Remember he actually arose from the dead! How much holier can you get than that? All I can say is that Sixtus III has done tremendous things for this world ever since he came into power."

Aware of Alex's undivided attention, she raised her head, cocked it to the side and put on her sweetest smile hoping to taunt him and teach him a lesson. "Besides, Sixtus III is very good looking. He is probably the most desirable bachelor of all times." Then she redirected her attention to Nadia. "You, my dear friend, are too political."

Alex, obviously oblivious or otherwise ignoring her blatant flirtation immediately became defensive. "She's not political; she just stands up for what she believes. Now it's not only a mandatory SPIDER Card it's a mandatory "Chip." And Nadia…"

Megan interrupted. She hoped to diffuse the animosity, "But only for Federal employees and welfare recipients."

"Teachers are Federal employees. Nadia was fired last week," Alex shouted back.

She was shocked. She hadn't considered all the ramifications before. She looked from Alex to Nadia then reached over and took her friend's hands. "Oh, Nadia, I'm so sorry. I don't understand why you make such a big deal of everything. Why didn't you just take the "Chip"? It's just a transponder, a microchip the size of a grain of rice. It's no big deal. They easily implant it under the skin with a syringe. It is just like the SPIDER Card, except it's better. You can't lose it and it can't be stolen or falsified. It keeps everybody honest." With a big smile, hoping she had smoothed things over she added, "It's a really great idea!"

Nadia looked long and hard at Megan as if she desperately wanted to give her something. "When you take the "Chip" you are required to pledge allegiance to Sixtus III and the UWC. It's the mark of the devil, Megan. In taking it you will suffer the eternal consequences."

Chapter Nineteen

Hakah, Megan's guardian angel, sat himself in the middle of the kitchen table and spoke directly into her face. "Those who worship the beast and his image and whoever receives the mark of his name, will drink the wine of God's wrath, and the smoke of their torment will go up forever and ever; and they will have no rest day and night."

Serpentine laughed and tugged at Megan's hair causing it to tumble out of the bun and fall haphazardly around her shoulders. Gently he stroked her as if to pet a favorite cat. This delightful woman was his responsibility and he intended to take charge. "Save your breath, Hakah. It is utterly useless to warn her. Mortals will do anything these days to satisfy their fleshly desires. If they can't buy food or entertainment for a week, you'll see they will come crawling for the "Chip." It is only afterward that their conscience will be tormented." He gave a hearty laugh. "But then it will be too late. Soon everyone, the small and the great, the rich and the poor, the employers and the laborers, will be given a mark on their right hand or on their forehead. Satan will make sure that no one will be able to buy or to sell, except the one who has the mark."

Hakah stood up. He towered over Serpentine and forced the slimy demon to step away from his charge. "The woman Nadia speaks the truth." Serpentine shrank back and flew to perch on an empty chair next to Nadia.

Baleful, who had been sitting passively in the corner, desired to be the center of attention, "Yes, but if she refuses the mark she will get no more benefits or legal funds. She will not be able to buy food, clothing or anything. In fact, without it she cannot live." He smiled menacingly, wagged his head, shrugged his shoulders and rejoiced, "As a matter of fact, that makes it all rather simple."

Baleful moved slowly and deliberately toward Kasha, Nadia's guardian angel, and then hissed into his face, "Without the "Chip" Nadia is illegal and completely broke. That's perfect! She's exactly where I want her."

Kasha carefully wrapped his mighty wings around Nadia and whispered gently into her ear, "Do not be afraid of those who can kill the body but cannot touch the soul; you must fear Him who has the power to destroy the body and damn the soul to hell. Two sparrows aren't worth much, and yet not one falls to the ground without your Father knowing. He has counted every hair on your head. So there is no need to be afraid; you are worth more than hundreds of sparrows."

Baleful changed his point of attack and mounted himself onto Alex's shoulder. "She is continually talking about the Bible and that Prince of Peace."

Jonathan quick to come to the aid of his mortal stood up and put his sword to Baleful's throat.

"Temper, temper," Baleful jested.

Serpentine whipped his pointed tail around eager to enter again into the fight. He attacked Alex from the other side slurping into his ear, "The world is not being destroyed; it is just changing through natural forces. There is scientific proof for it all."

Baleful snarled, "You can preach all you want, Kasha. Mortals don't want to know the truth. The truth is that Satan has not yet begun to fight. Just wait and see what these birth pangs bring forth. You all fail to remember that he has the power to destroy!"

xxx

The atmosphere in the kitchen had grown tense. Megan looked into her coffee cup and wondered why her dear friend was so adamant. She wanted to understand. She really did, but it made no sense. The devil had nothing to do with it. Her shoulders slumped as she rested her forehead in her hand. Then she looked up and asked.

"Since when have you become so religious?"

"Since I have been reading the scriptures and comparing them to all the chaos that's been going on in the world."

"Personally, Nadia, I think you've been taking this "Jesus" thing much too seriously."

"I shouldn't take the destruction of the world seriously?" Nadia's eyes shrank into slits and she began to pace like a caged lynx.

Megan had never known Nadia to snap at anyone, least of all her admired brother. Passion clearly flew through Nadia's body, her back straightened, her arms swung wildly around her head and her hands tightened into fists.

Alex was quiet for a moment. He relaxed his stance. "Well, I'm not so sure that the world is in danger of being destroyed. It may be that nature is just asserting itself with a vengeance."

"Well you don't have to be a rocket scientist to know that the world is drastically changing. Every week you read about the destruction caused by another earthquake and the number who die each month from continuous swings in the weather. First droughts and insects, then floods and mudslides, not to mention all the crops that have rotted away in the fields. Mutations of bacteria and viruses are causing diseases we can't control let alone cure. In the last two years one fourth of the world's population has been destroyed by drought, famine, murder, disease, insects, wild beasts…"

Megan, not wanting to be left out of this conversation jumped in, "And rabid squirrels." She thought about it further and added, "I did a piece three months ago on that strain of killer bees that keeps invading the Southwest. And the mad dog packs are still not completely under control. But Sixtus III has all of this under control."

Nadia's face relaxed and tears welled up in her eyes. "I don't want to fight. This is my last day at home." She picked up her coffee cup, walked over to the sink, set it down and then slowly turned around. With true compassion in her voice she said, "Megan, only divine intervention can save us from the direction everything is going. There is much worse yet to come."

The room fell silent.

Nadia refreshed Megan's cup of coffee. A bird chirped outside the window. Faith's dog tags tinkled as she crossed the kitchen to her water bowl. Then Alex got up and went to the refrigerator. "Anyone up for toast and jam?"

Megan ruffled her fingers through her hair, stood up and carried her cup to the door. "I would love to stay and join you, but this reporter has got to get dressed. I can't afford to be late!" Megan gave her friend a reconciliatory smile and immediately headed for the shower. The strain of the morning had left its mark.

Megan occupied the front row seat that was reserved for United World Broadcasting Communications (UWBC). She turned around, noticed the packed room and pinched herself to make sure she it wasn't all a dream. The Communications Office was a large room that accommodated about one-hundred padded folding chairs. Many paintings from contemporary artists lined the walls, all composed of brilliant colors except for one, the one hanging behind the lectern. Megan was particularly drawn to it. The artist used only bold black, white and gray strokes to depict a warrior astride a white horse. The rider triumphantly brandished a fearsome bow. A victory crown graced his head. His reared steed trampled emaciated bodies. Anguished faces cried out for help. The tone was ominous and foreboding. It was aptly entitled "The White Horseman."

She scooted to the edge of her seat, mesmerized by the man who stood before her. His dark eyes captivated her. They had looked straight into hers when he first entered the room. What charisma. His charming smile and sincere laugh swept her away. Sixtus III's gray Armani suit camouflaged his thin muscular frame. He stood relaxed. She admired the way he always had complete control of the crowd. The reporters never raised questions that embarrassed or stumped him. This morning had been no different.

"We must continue to unite all peoples and all nations. World-wide economic growth is of the utmost importance to resume the standard of living we all enjoyed at the turn of the century. I assure you, the distortions which have resulted from the strict currency controls, are temporary. They make way for economic recovery."

The first ten questions had been related to the economy. His answers were evasive as usual. Then suddenly the questions took a sharp turn when Sixtus called on a reporter from the back row.

"President Sixtus, regarding the two men dressed in long robes that walk barefoot on the streets of Jerusalem." He checked his notes then continued. "For nine-hundred, seventy days they have warned the world of a returning King and admonish everyone to repent. Is it true that you have arrested them?"

All eyes shifted to the President. Megan caught her breath and wondered how he would answer. Sixtus straightened his stance.

"No, of course not. Why would I arrest them? They are completely harmless, disillusioned men. They are homeless so I merely offered them shelter out of harm's way."

That same reporter continued, "These men, who the people call the risen Elijah and Moses, claim that the three-year drought in the Middle East is a warning from God for all nations to repent. Do you see any validity to their claims?" Sixtus chuckled quietly.

"These two men have no prophetic powers. They only seek fame and glory for themselves." Another reporter interjected, "But, Mr. President, last month they actually predicted the death of all the fish in the Mediterranean Sea twenty-four hours before it happened."

"Next question please." Sixtus averted his eyes and scanned the crowd.

Megan's hand shot up with the others. Sixtus smiled and called on her. Immediately her mind went blank and her heart began to race. *Question, question, what was my question?*

She took a deep breath, gently rubbed the ivory elephant pinning back her hair and began, "Mr. President, you stated earlier that as of January first, the "Chip" would become mandatory for everyone around the globe regardless of occupation or social status. What will be the repercussions for individuals that are not in compliance?"

Sixtus seemed to enjoy her question. "We must all work together for the good of society as a whole. When you consider all the world-wide calamities that have struck over the past several years, you see we have no other alternative. Sometimes this may mean an individual must compromise so that all may survive. Each person must do their part for the better good, even if they are asked to make some personal sacrifice. If they do not wish to work with us then they have chosen to be against us. That is an act of treason." Sixtus smiled as if the idea excited him.

Disillusioned by his answer, she prodded further, "Punishable by death?"

Straining to read her nametag he casually remarked, "Ms. Montgomery, each offender will be granted a fair trial and sentenced accordingly." There was lunacy in his cold calculating eyes. Sixtus checked his watch. Every reporter except Megan raised their hand again.

"No more questions. Thank you." He left the room as quickly as he had entered it.

She sat in her seat stunned. What had she expect him to say? What he did say was not what she wanted to hear. And the way he said it, so matter of fact, with no regret or remorse, almost with relish. Her friend Nadia was truly in trouble.

Chapter Twenty

Hakah greeted Nadia's guardian angel Kasha. "Thank you for your mortal's constant prayers for Megan. She is in dire need of them all."

Kasha responded from his vast experience. "Human prayer silences the seventh heaven. The Ancient of Days waits for them, longs for them and enjoys them. It is the most powerful tool mortals have. I will remind mine to pray for yours more often."

"Thank you Kasha, I am eternally grateful."

xxx

When Megan arrived at the Katonah train station Nadia was standing on the platform. *Ever-faithful Nadia is so naive and innocent.* The whole train ride back from New York City she had tried to think of some way she could convince Nadia to take the "Chip" before it was too late. Sixtus made it very clear that the consequences for not taking it were grave.

Nadia slipped her hand into hers and gave it a gentle squeeze. Like school-girls, they walked hand-in-hand down the steps. The harsh words from that morning dissolved away. Nadia broke the silence. "I have to go on an errand. Would you like to come?"

"Sure. What's up?"

"I have to go to Hawthorne to buy a windmill."

"A windmill, what on earth are you going to do with that?"

"I am going to move to a place that has no electricity and we thought a windmill would work the best for us."

"Why, for Pete's sake, are you moving to a place without electricity?"

"It's rather a delicate situation," Nadia began slowly. Megan could tell her friend was holding back information.

"Just tell me, Nadia, I won't spill the beans."

"Neither Todd nor I will have the "Chip" so we won't be able to have a utility account." Megan started to interrupt but caught herself. She didn't want Nadia to be on the defense like she was this morning.

"We want to live in a place that will give us the freedom to come and go as we please. You must understand the direction our government is going, Megan." Nadia dropped her head. "I watched Sixtus' press conference this morning." Her tone became upbeat. "You, by the way, were fabulous as I knew you would be."

Megan looked at the ground. Guilt and betrayal haunted her, though she knew she had done nothing wrong. "As long as you have your SPIDER Card you have time." She hoped it would be enough time to change Nadia's mind.

"My time is up, Megan. My card will expire at midnight tonight." They waited for three cars to pass then crossed over Katonah Avenue and approached a delivery van. Big green letters were painted on side "The Marketplace".

"This is Herb's truck. Get in. We can talk as we ride."

No matter what she said, she could not persuade Nadia to take the "Chip." She should have known it was no use, once Nadia's made up her mind she rarely changed it. This whole situation was so bizarre. Why would she unnecessarily put herself at such risk?

They rode for a while lost in their own thoughts. She was determined to try another angle. *I have nothing to lose. She knows already but maybe she will learn from my experience.* She looked at her hands sweating in her lap and took a deep breath. The words came out in a whisper.

"Nadia, do you remember our first year at Miami when I got pregnant?" The wound was so deep she barely lived a day without feeling the pain ... forcing it out. The thought of it was bad enough but to speak the words made her weak.

"Of course I do, my dear sweet friend. I wanted so much to help you. My heart broke for you. If I could have taken some of your pain I would have."

"I know, Nadia. You tried to convince me to keep the baby, but I knew Evan would leave me if I did. He didn't want a child just then and I could understand that. I loved him so much. I couldn't bear the thought of losing him."

Evan Swanson was the most handsome man she had ever known. In the beginning, they spent hours together. They walked on campus and studied at the student union. He helped her pass her first speech class. He gave her pointers and became the perfect "critic." He was a senior, wise and confident. He educated her on many things; all the ins and outs of campus life, the ups and downs of physical intimacy, and finally, the guilt and pain of losing a child. He had an apartment off campus which made all the girls in their freshman dorm jealous. All except Nadia.

Nadia knew from the start that he was trouble. She had a sixth sense about those things. When Megan found herself pregnant, she only had to look at Nadia and her sensitive friend knew her secret. She had the abortion as he wanted, but afterward he no longer seemed to have time for her. Three weeks later, he walked hand-in-hand with another girl down the center sidewalk on campus. He never called her again after that. No matter how hard she begged him, he just pushed her away. His last words to her were, "I need to throw the baby out with the bathwater." She was not a baby anymore. For nine weeks, she had been a mother but she wasn't that anymore either.

Every man after that lied to her in some way or another. They broke promise after promise. Now, she no longer expected the truth and trust flew out the window. Convinced she had a target painted on her chest, she kept moving. She had gotten very good at dodging bullets and in the process built a very high wall around her heart.

Nadia had remained a friend, a true friend to the end; even after Megan had gotten rid of the baby, even after Evan had gotten rid of her and even after she had gotten rid of the countless others that followed him. Now it was her turn to be that friend.

"Nadia, you gave me some very good advice back then that I didn't take. I have regretted that decision every day since and I don't want you to live with the same regret."

"Megan, I know you want to help me. And you are a dear friend for trying, but I have made my decision based on my love for God and my desire to obey Him. He will protect me. Because my love for Him is greater than any love I could have for a man, it's a much easier decision to make and I am at peace."

Megan pressed her fingers against her lips to keep them from quivering. Rage, that had built up over the years, poured out, "Where was your God when I needed Him? Why didn't he protect me?" Silence haunted the truck.

Eventually, very gently, Nadia responded.

"I don't know why they were allowed to wound your spirit,
I don't know why you had to suffer for so long;
I can't explain why some are spared and some endure,
And how some still go on.

I don't know why some are gone before their time,
I don't know why for some, the pain goes on and on;
I cannot see the bigger picture, how it all can work for good,
But just one thing I know –

God is good, God is faithful.
He was there and held your hand,
When you could not understand.
He is here, He is the Healer,
When the tears seemed to overflow,
Love was there, never letting go.

I don't know why the questions never seem to end.
I don't know why, I'm called to trust Him once again;
I cannot see the bigger picture, how it all can work for good,
But one thing I see and know and I will always confess –

God is good, God is faithful.
He's right here and holds your hand,
When you cannot understand.
He is here, He is the Healer.
When tears seem to overflow,
Reach out for love, He won't let you go.

My faith is strong, I still believe
In the goodness of God, and His care for me.
I don't need to know every reason why
All I need to know is that He hears my cry!

God is good, God is faithful
He is with you now, was with you then
Poured His love again and again.
He is here, He is the Healer;
Hold onto Him and don't let go.
He loves you more than you will ever, ever, ever know.
God is good."[iii]

Tears spilled onto Megan's cheeks and she turned her face toward the window. They passed the Hawthorne train station where three girls laughed and talked together as they climbed the stairs to the platform. They must have been around ten or eleven; just about the age her daughter would be, had she not aborted her. *I killed her; I killed my baby before she even had the chance to take a breath.* She bit her lip and stroked her elephant comb. She suppressed the sobs that threatened to overcome her.

Chapter Twenty-One

Hakah, Nadia's guardian angel received a warning. He must delay their return. He turned every traffic light red and put three school busses in their path.

xxx

More than seventy-three percent of the USA is now in a drought. That's a record for this nation. The southern dryness is due mainly to the La Nina climate pattern... Alex's fingers sped across the keyboard as the doorbell rang. He didn't hear it at first but tuned in when it was repeated quickly three or four times.

"I'm coming, I'm coming. Hold your horses." He bound down the stairs taking two at a time and pressed the monitor a little out of breath. "Yes, who is it?"

"It's Officer Sandler. May I come up please?"

"Sure, Bernie." He rang the buzzer and opened the apartment door. Bernie Sandler was a lean man, fit and well groomed. He seemed too shy and passive to be a police officer, but Alex didn't know another man with a greater desire to serve the community. He was a year younger than Alex. When they were kids, they had played soccer together. Alex shook his hand and slapped him on the back.

"Hello, Bernie, come on in. I haven't seen you for a while. How's Katherine?"

"Oh, she's fine. The kids keep her busy but that's what she lives for."

"Can I offer you something, iced tea or water maybe?" Alex noticed a reluctance and coolness in this usually friendly man. "Bernie, what's wrong?"

"I'm sorry, Mr. Lichtenstein." He cleared his throat. "I need to speak to Ms. Lichtenstein. Is she here?"

"Mr. Lichtenstein? What is this, Bernie? Nadia is not here. May I help you?"

"No, I'm sorry... This is official business and I need to speak to Nadia ... to Ms. Lichtenstein."

"Well, as I said, she isn't here, but I will let her know that you stopped by."

Bernie heaved a huge sigh of relief. "Well, all right then. I'd better go now, but I have to come back later." He gave a gentle, almost whispered warning, "Tell Nadia to take the "Chip," there's a warrant out for her arrest. Alex, be careful. Everything you do is being watched."

Nadia and Megan drove the rest of the way in silence. Megan continued to stare out the side window. She was at a complete loss for words. Nadia was certainly doomed and there was nothing she could do to help her. As soon as Nadia pulled into the parking lot she jumped out and ran to Megan's door. Megan gave her only friend a long hard hug. She held onto her as if her life depended on it. The spell was broken. It was like old times. They were sisters again. They clung to each other until another truck pulled up beside them. The driver stepped out, glanced past them and pointed to Nadia's tires.

"They're bald, lady."

"But not as bald as you, Prince." Megan responded under her breathe as he rounded the back of the van. She pointed to the sign painted on his truck.

"You clog it. We clear it."
"Call Prince Plumbing"

Megan and Nadia looked at each other and burst out laughing. Megan needed that. She searched her bag for tissues, took one and passed one to Nadia. They continued to laugh, wiped their eyes and walked into the store.

Nadia went straight to the counter and asked for Mr. Murphy. The young clerk behind the counter made a brief phone call. He explained that Mr. Murphy was in the back storeroom where a fire had broken out early that morning. It was a smoke filled, water-drenched disaster.

Nadia immediately took Megan's hand in hers. "Let's say a quick prayer. I'm afraid that the windmill may have gotten damaged." Megan smiled at her friend and listened as Nadia whispered, "Lord, you know what we need and you have provided the funds to buy it. Please, Lord, may your perfect will be done. I love you. In Jesus' name, I pray. Amen."

"Good afternoon, ladies, may I help you?" Mr. Murphy approached them more like a sumo wrestler than a store manager.

Nadia looked up and smiled brightly. "We have come for the windmill. Remember last week you agreed to sell it at a discount since it had been in your store so long and was an outdated model?"

Mr. Murphy was a huge man, about three-hundred and fifty pounds worth. A roughness about him made Megan uneasy. She gave him her prettiest smile too, hoping to improve the situation, whatever that may be.

"I am sorry, the discount is off. I need the full price now. I've got a storeroom under water and I have to cut my losses. That windmill is in great shape so I need the full price. It's unfortunate but there's no other way." His voice was sharp and gruff. He tried to avoid eye contact but both women looked straight at him. Then he crossed his arms and stared at Nadia.

"Please Mr. Murphy, I only have $3,000 and we will not be able to survive without that windmill."

"I'm sorry, Miss." He shook his head, "I've made my decision and can't go back on it. I've already lost too much money."

"Don't sell it. I'll be back." Nadia insisted. She gazed at Megan who read the desperation in her eyes.

Chapter Twenty Two

From the seventh heaven, the Prince of Peace heard Nadia's prayer, saw the need and bestowed the grace where he saw fit. As a result, a flame coursed through a sleek syringe. It pierced the fifth dimension and bore into Megan's heart. He had designed her heart especially for giving, but over the years it became hardened by circumstance. The beacon infused grace, which resembled white liquid fire, into the rigid surface. Grace, the unmerited divine assistance, meant to stimulate and soften the heart. It only penetrated a small portion of the outer crust, but it was enough to move Megan to action.

Hakah whispered into Megan's ear. "Do it, Megan, do it. I know you can. I know you will. You have given so much just give this one more time. She needs you. Your dear friend needs you. If you do it the scent of your sacrifice for God's people will permeate the air around Him. He will be well pleased."

xxx

"How much money do you need?" Megan inquired not really sure what difference it made to her. "$1,850" Nadia said. Tears welled up into her eyes.

Megan thought of the beautiful car that she had been saving up for. Every extra dollar went into her "new car fund." This would deplete that and then some. What was she thinking? *I want to help the only real friend I ever had. I need to help her. It would be the only truly heroic thing I have ever done.*

"I will pay the difference," she said looking deep into Nadia's forlorn face. She then turned to Mr. Murphy, "Ring up the sale."

"I can't let you do that, I'll think of another way."

"Yes, you can, Nadia." It was a done deal.

Driving back to Katonah, Nadia smiled at Megan and said, "You are the answer to my prayer." Megan smiled back. No one had ever said *that* to her before.

Quietly the tall perfectly shaped woman entered his New York office from the adjacent chamber. Her body beckoned him. She wore a crisply ironed, sharply tailored, turquoise blouse and a pair of black sleek fitting slacks. Ashtoreth's blazing black hair cascaded down her back almost touching her tiny waist. He watched her as she skillfully twisted it into a knot on the back of her head. She went to the bar in the corner of the room. Invitingly she poured herself a glass of merlot.

Sixtus III needed a distraction. He chose a Cuban Cohiba from the humidor that sat under the window. Ceremoniously he brought the cigar up to his nose and inhaled its sweet aroma. He crossed over to the fireplace and picked up the poker. The handle, intricately carved into a cobra, had two rubies inserted as eyes. Its head rested firmly in his hand. The protruding tongue pressed against his wrist. Sixtus added two new logs and stoked the fire until the blaze satisfied him. He watched the red hot iron glow then used it to light his cigar. He took a long satisfying puff. He was ready to begin the meeting.

"The general destruction of principles and morals has been instrumental in overthrowing the nations, more so than the entire force of a ruthless enemy. While the people were virtuous they could not be subdued. But I am delighted to see that once they lost their virtue, they were ready to surrender their liberties to their internal invader. I am satisfied with the results.

"Now that their mental health has disintegrated I want to concentrate on their physical health. What is the result of the PC3 Project?" (Population Control – Third Edition, a form of eugenics or the "science" of human improvement through controlled breeding). The PC Projects involved the addition of a genetically altering biological agent to standard flu shots. All male non-Islamic participants under the age of forty received this special serum.

Helmut Dethloff sat on the edge of his chair opposite the president. Sweat dripped from his forehead. He fidgeted back and forth as if he wished to be anywhere but there. Sixtus disdained the weasel but recognized he was the most adept chemical engineer in the world. When Dethloff finally spoke his voice shook.

"The most recent study indicates that seventy-five percent of the injected male population is now sterile. That drops the population growth to one point seven percent. Once the growth rate goes below one point three, extinction for that nationality is inevitable and irreversible."

"Increase the dosage. I want that one point three rate achieved. Now let's focus on our next objective. Can we start another plague?"

"If you want to control it, I would suggest something more subtle." Conrad Fowler wore his military uniform. He sat straight as if at attention and reviewed his notes. "We could start off by weakening the overall population. I suggest we increase the bacteria we have already been using to pollute the major cities. That would kill many more people in the selected isolated areas. It would create a huge hysteria and the populations will clamor to be saved."

Dethloff added, "The bacteria we began using nine months ago was formerly used by the insurgents. Its existence is classified, so we could introduce it to the population as a new strain. People are used to seeing contrails in the sky. We could continue to drop the chemical in larger amounts on the designated targets."

"Perfect," Sixtus reasoned. "Let's mildly saturate the general public worldwide. Then choose an isolated spot in, say, the Western Americas and somewhere in Asia to introduce the lethal doses. That should do the trick.

"I want you to target several large areas that will destroy roughly two million people. The covert name will be Ashen Horse." Fowler and Dethloff raised their eyes and stared in disbelief at the man behind the mahogany desk.

Dethloff sputtered, "You can't do that. It will have profound repercussions!"

At this impudent outburst, Ashtoreth's eyes widened. She poured a glass of sparkling water and moved toward the two men sitting across from Sixtus. Her gait was so smooth she appeared to glide across the room. Cold and without emotion, she handed the glass to Dethloff and placed her hand on his shoulder. Immediately he gasped for breath and clutched his chest.

Ashtoreth stated calmly, "I think he is having a heart attack." Sixtus shot a piercing glance toward her and engaged the device in his ear.

"Get EMS here immediately!"

Within minutes, the room was cleared of all except Sixtus and the powerful sultry prophet. Sixtus used that moment to rebuke her actions. "He was a valuable advisor. Please stop eliminating people that I need."

"I didn't like the way he spoke to you. He should have had more respect." She came to his side and ran her long fingers through his hair. "Besides, I am the only one you really need." Sixtus became breathless at her touch. She took advantage and challenged his earlier decision.

"Do you know what you have just set in motion? I saw it in the crystals this morning. Dethloff was right. Not only will the earth be plagued by disease but also a chain reaction will trigger famine. Then wild beasts will evolve. Over one quarter of the earth will perish."

Wild with excitement he met her eyes. "So be it."

Chapter Twenty-Three

Michael the Archangel looked down from the seventh dimension and saw an ashen horse; and the rider's name was Death and Hades followed behind him. They had authority over a fourth of the earth to kill with famine, deadly disease and wild beasts.

xxx

Megan sat cross-legged on the living room sofa making some phone calls and returning a few important messages until she couldn't stand it any longer. She had to follow her nose into the kitchen where Nadia prepared an inviting meal on the stove. Nadia hummed and almost danced as she made her way between stove and refrigerator. She wore a tailored linen apron with two small handprints painted on the large front pockets. Pink straps secured it around her waist and neck. It suited her perfectly.

"What a beautiful apron."

"Thanks. It was my mother's"

"Well it looks beautiful on you. Can I help you with anything?"

"Sure, would you like to set the table? There will be four of us for dinner tonight. I can't wait for you to meet Todd. He should be here in about ten minutes." Nadia opened the cupboard that contained the plates and bowls, and then pulled open the drawer of silverware. Megan immediately got to work.

"I'm excited to meet him too. It sounds like you two were made for each other. I sure hope he appreciates the catch that he got."

"Oh I'm the one who was blessed. Last weekend he packed a scrumptious lunch – wine, cheese and French bread. He even brought a tablecloth and picked wild lilies for a centerpiece. We drove to Bear Mountain and ate in the park. We have a special spot there where we can see the mountains for miles. He is such a romantic!"

"He sounds perfect to me. Does he have a brother?"

"No, but he considers Alex to be his brother."

"Yes, Alex," Megan's heart sank. "But he doesn't seem to even know I exist. Or maybe he does and just hates me."

"He doesn't hate you, Megan. Let me tell you a little bit about my brother." Nadia hesitated briefly before she began. "He had a girlfriend many years ago who he wanted to marry. He was building a life around her. He even planned to move to Florida so that she wouldn't have to leave her family. Then, when he dropped out of school, she dropped him like a hot potato during an extremely volatile time in his life. She claimed she could never marry a man without a college education."

Nadia added the last of the sour cream to the beef stroganoff and turned the fire down low. She set the timer then continued. "Alex is probably the smartest person I know. He is a very gifted writer that many publications seek out when they need a scientific article. He not only knows all the technical stuff but can put it in a language that the average reader can understand. He is always working on something."

He's smart and very capable. Megan didn't get it. "So why did he drop out of school?"

Nadia lowered her eyes and her voice, "Because of me."

"What do you mean?" She had finished setting the table and sat down to hear the story.

Nadia put her hands in the pockets of her mother's apron then sat down next to her. "You know that my mother died when I was young."

Megan nodded, "Yes, but you never said how and I didn't want to pry."

"The reason I didn't explain it to you was that Alex told me never to tell anyone the details surrounding her death."

"It must have been a painful experience for both of you." Megan was sincere and compassionate. Nadia continued.

"I'm telling you now because I want you to understand him." Nadia rubbed her forehead with her fingers and slowly began. "Alex was going to a fantastic astronautical university in Florida. Mama was driving him back to school his sophomore year and fell asleep at the wheel. She died in the ambulance on the way to the hospital. He claimed responsibility for the accident even though it wasn't his fault." She repeated the words and emphasized the fact, "It was no one's fault." She dropped her eyes again.

"I was only in middle school at the time so Alex came home to help take care of me. Papa worked twelve to fifteen hours a day in the city teaching and practicing with the New York Philharmonic. He also traveled with them around the country every two or three months."

Megan said nothing, not quite sure how to respond. Her friend's sad face paralyzed her. Bereaving people handicapped her. Unable to help, she never knew what to say. But Nadia didn't fall into the "people" category. She was in the "best friend" category. Suddenly, Megan regretted terribly that she hadn't come to New York when Nadia's father died two years ago.

She took both of Nadia's hands in her own. "I'm so sorry, Nadia. It's such a sad story." She tried to refocus and summarized. "So your brother gave up a career as an astronaut, left his fiancée, and moved back home to help raise you."

Nadia shrugged her shoulders and mustered up a little smile. "Yeah, that's pretty much it in a nut shell."

"Wow, he *is* amazing. I can see why you admire him so much."

"Yes, well that's why he doesn't show a lot of interest in women. He still feels a certain responsibility for me, and on top of that, he doesn't want to get burned again. Allie left him when he needed her most."

"Well, I can identify with that. I guess he and I have a lot more in common than I thought. And he really is pretty cute too." They both laughed.

"Be patient with him, Meg. He may just come around after all. But don't let him know we discussed all this. He would kill me if he knew I told you."

"My lips are sealed," she dramatized with two fingers passing over her closed mouth. The front doorbell rang interrupting their conversation.

"That's Todd. Let me go buzz him in." Nadia ran to the living room and pressed the buzzer to open the door on the street, one floor down. Then she unlocked her front door and ran back to the timer ringing in the kitchen.

The street was dark; the sun had just dropped behind the building. The man who rang the bell opened the door and entered. He was not Megan's fiancé Todd.

<>

WHAT SO PROUDLY WE HAIL AT THE TWILIGHT'S LAST
GLEAMING

Chapter Twenty-Four

Day 364

Kasha hovered over Nadia's bed. The two women lay serenely beneath him. Both wrestled with the consequences of their actions. "Wait for the Lord's return, be patient, like a farmer who waits for his precious harvest to ripen. Yes, be patient. And take courage, for the Lord's coming is near."

xxx

Nadia lay silently in her queen-sized bed thinking about the reunion last night with Tommy Barker. His arrival thoroughly surprised her. She never expected to see him again and there he was, back in her life; her first crush, her first kiss. Long lost emotions stirred up inside her. *It's over. I can't hold onto to these feelings.*

Tommy was never one to mince words. He no sooner got into their apartment when blurted out, "I'm looking for a butterfly. Someone told me I might find one here."

Dating back to the first century, Christians secretly identified each other by drawing a fish in the dirt. Now that the underground had formed, the sign became a little more subtle, a little less known. A butterfly was a believer who had not taken the "Chip."

Nadia was overjoyed to tell him he had come to the right place. Tommy's eyes were just as bright as she had remembered. His smile was just as charming. Alex had given him a bear hug and patted him repeatedly on the back, so happy to have an old buddy return. But Todd, usually eager to fellowship with a believer, was reserved and almost rude. Nadia couldn't figure that out.

They had chatted over dinner and into the night about old times and all that had transpired since Tommy's family left town. He couldn't have arrived at a more strategic time. Alex planed to drive Nadia and Todd to a safe community using Herb's van. Disappearing with Tommy before sun up was a much better solution, but Todd questioned Nadia's reason for "hooking up" with this unknown Rogue. It made perfectly good sense to her. It eliminated Alex's exposure to danger and the need to log an unnecessary excursion. *Why was Todd so reluctant to agree?* Had he sensed something she hadn't seen? She tried to shake it off.

Nadia checked the clock next to her bed once again. Three AM. There was no more time for sleep even if she could get some. Carefully she pushed back the covers not to disturb Megan who was asleep next to her. Noiselessly Nadia crossed the familiar room and entered the bathroom. She turned on the light and gazed at her reflection in the mirror.

She had spent little time taking care of herself in the past few months and it showed. She touched her tight face and examined the small circles forming under her eyes; too much sun and too little sleep. Her eyes stared back at her, tired and pale. She always described them as the color of straw but Todd insisted they resembled deep golden pools. This morning they were definitely straw.

Nadia washed her face, and then smoothed on some cool moisturizing cream, the last from a jar that Alex had given her. She wanted to pack the empty jar for sentimental reasons but decided against it. There really wasn't room in her bag and even less room in Todd's old farm house where they were going. She brushed her teeth and turned off the light. When she returned to her room, Megan was sitting up in bed waiting for her.

"So, were you just going to sneak off and not say good-bye?"

"Of course not. I just didn't want to wake you until the last possible minute."

"I couldn't sleep." Megan crossed her legs under her as if she expected a long conversation. Nadia knew there wasn't time.

"Is there anything I can say to make you stay?"

"No, my dear friend I'm afraid not." She extinguished the brief light of hope that had been in Megan's eyes.

"I didn't think so. In that case I have something for you." Megan got out of bed and walked over to the corner dresser. Her slippers flip-flopped on the bare floor. She picked up the elephant comb that her grandmother had given her and cradled it gently in her hands. Briefly she closed her eyes. Then she held the comb out to Nadia. "Here, I want you to have this."

Nadia was astonished that her friend offered the delicately carved artifact to her. She knew the sense of security it gave Megan.

"No, Megan, I can't take it. I know how much it means to you."

"That's exactly why I want you to have it. It has brought me good luck and maybe even saved my life on several occasions. I was told it has magical powers. You're headed for trouble, Nadia, and need all the protection you can get. Besides, you are closer to me than any sister and I don't want you to forget me."

"Trust me, Megan even without it I wouldn't forget you."

"Maybe so, but I still want you to have it." Megan dropped her gaze and sheepishly added, "Maybe if you think of me now and then you will pray for me."

Nadia accepted the priceless gift and attempted to twist it into her short limp hair. Three times she tried and three times it fell out. They both laughed. Instead, Megan secured it to the colorful cotton scarf that was loosely knotted on Nadia's chest.

"Oh, Nadia, I wish you weren't leaving. I feel so totally lost at times, utterly and totally lost."

"I promise to pray for you every day if you promise to do something for me."

"Sure, anything."

Nadia took her Bible from the bed stand, opened it and flipped through the pages settling on a Psalm. "King David prayed this to God when he was being threatened by those who hated Him." She began to read, "I have heard that everything has limits; but your commandment is perfect. How I love your law! I think about it all day long. Your commandment is with me all the time and makes me wiser than my enemies . . . Your word is a lamp to guide me and a light for my path."[iv] Nadia slowly closed the book and handed it to Megan.

"This is God's word. If you read it every day God will help you to find your way and you will not get lost." Megan stared at the book and stroked its soft leather cover. "Promise me, Megan, that you will read it every day." Pleading, she looked deep into her friend's eyes and recognized hesitation. Would she do it?

"I wouldn't even know where to begin," was her excuse. Then she blurted out, "All right, I promise."

"Here, I'll show you where to start." *Thank you Lord.* Nadia opened it towards the center. The page was entitled The Gospel of John. Nadia placed a leather marker there.

"Megan, when you hear His voice please don't harden your heart against it."

"Ok, I'll start today. Thank you so much." Megan took her hand and started for the door and then gave her a final hug.

The poignant moment was broken by a conversation heating up in the living room.

Chapter Twenty-Five

"Your mortal is weak and wayward; the perfect mix for destruction." Serpentine poked at Jonathan, Alex's guardian angel. "You have been with him all these years and have nothing to show for it. Jonathan, you are just as weak as your mortal."

"That isn't true. He is kind and smart and loving." Jonathan wondered why he let himself get sucked into such a conversation with this demon.

Serpentine flew down to rest on Alex's shoulder. His long tongue slurped and spat as he spoke. "I agree he is very smart. That is why he does not believe his sister's illogical preaching."

"Logic tells everyone they deserve to be free and Jesus makes them free."

Serpentine laughed. "Satan freed man from the tyranny of The Ancient of Days. He freed them all to become self-made gods. What more freedom could any man want?"

Jonathan fumed over Serpentine's reaction. "Satan's so-called freedom is, in reality, slavery. It fosters pride, envy, anger and lust. This freedom leads to death and eternal damnation. What greater slavery is there? Satan wants to bring every man down with him to the depths of the bottomless pit."

"He will do whatever is necessary, Jonathan."

"His demise is inevitable. His power is short term." Jonathan pushed Serpentine away from his charge.

"No, Jonathan, you are wrong." Serpentine strutted as if on a stage. "Look! God is overturning the land and making it a vast wasteland of destruction. Priests and people, servants and masters, employees and employers, buyers and sellers, lenders and borrowers, bankers and debtors, none will be spared. The land will be completely emptied and looted."

Serpentine breathed hot into Jonathan's face and proclaimed, "You know yourself what God has spoken. You see the clear evidence that the land suffers and it suffers because the people have sinned. The earth cries out, the crops wither, and there still is no rain. Crime has defiled the land; the people have twisted God's law and broken His everlasting commands. Therefore, God's curse is upon them; they are desolate, destroyed by the drought. Few will be left alive."

Jonathan, simply yet with authority responded, "But those enduring to the end will be saved."

xxx

"We can't take the "Chip," Alex, because it's the mark of Satan. We can't pledge allegiance to Sixtus III. It would be like pledging allegiance to the devil himself." Alex paced back and forth trying to diffuse the tension building between them. Todd's voice softened.

"Come with us, Alex. You don't back Sixtus."

"Yes, I know, but at the same time I don't know where I stand with God." Alex had many heartfelt conversations with God in the past but they were all one-sided. He never got an answer, at least not one that he recognized or asked for. He didn't expect that to change any time soon.

"Alex, you can know. Obviously, we have not seen God yet, but His own Spirit dwells in our hearts. That proves to us that we are living with Him, and He is living with us. God sent His Son to be our Savior, Alex. Anyone who believes and says that Jesus is the Son of God actually has God living in him."

It all sounds like mumbo-jumbo. How can Todd believe this? Alex moved to the bar, clinked three pieces of melting ice into a tall glass and poured himself a vodka. He downed half of it in one gulp and then He gestured the bottle toward his friend. Todd declined.

"You are only cheating yourself of all that Christ can do for you."

"That may be so but it is my decision to make." Alex finished his drink then refilled the glass. "I'm sorry I just can't go with you. But if you guys need anything, anything at all, let me know and I'll get it to you."

"Thanks, Alex, but for right now we should be all right. The community there works together to help one another. Besides, I intend to replant the fields and hunt in the woods by the lake. Remember going boating the last time you were out? What a storm we had that night."

"Yes, I remember the lake very well." The horror of that outing was forever seared into his gut. Even now at the mention of it Alex began to sweat.

There was an uneasy silence between them. Alex broke it.

"Take good care of her, Todd, will you?"

"You know I will. I love her more than my own life."

Nadia entered the living room and both men stopped to stare at her. "Have you been talking about me again?"

"Let me get that." Todd took the suitcase from her. "Tom loaded all your school supplies into the car and is waiting for us. Herb said we could pick up a few groceries from his store so I am going to do that now. See you downstairs." The two men gave each other a final bear hug and then Todd disappeared down the back stairs.

"Alex, Megan went back to bed. You don't mind if she stays for a week or so do you?"

"No, Nadia, that's fine. Even in your absence, you take care of those you love."

"I love *you*, Alex, and I don't want to leave you behind. Please come with us. It's all coming to an end soon. You know it yourself. It's all around us."

"I don't know anything for sure, except that I don't believe in your Prince of Peace. I can't, Nadia. Don't you see how foolish it is to rebel against Sixtus? There is no one else like him. No one is able to wage war with him or his government ... and still live."

"Personally, I would rather die than follow Sixtus,"

"Nadia, you don't know what you're saying."

"I know very well what I'm saying. The world is crumbling around us and Sixtus is taking full advantage of it. He is exploiting us all. Papa could never trust the man, and I don't either."

At the mention of his father Alex drained his drink and slowly walked over to his father's magnificent violin. He poured himself another glass of vodka and downed it in one gulp. Carefully Alex took the instrument from the shelf and closed it in its case.

"Here, Nadia, I don't want it any more. I am sure he would want you to have it. He loved you so much more than me."

"Alex, that isn't true. You never gave him a chance."

The alcohol took over. He rubbed his fingers through his hair. He couldn't contain his anger and pain. His mind reeled and he heard his voice babble, "He never gave me a chance. Nothing I did was ever good enough for him. He blamed me for Mama's death. I know he did."

"You are wrong, Alex. First, Papa loved you very much. Here, let me show you something." She went over to the bookshelf and picked up the Russian Bible. She opened it to a page that was marked by a well worn letter.

"This is a letter that Papa wrote to Mama when the Philharmonic was performing in Chicago one year. He wrote about you. You can tell it came from his heart. Read it then look at the passage it marks. Mama even underlined it. She knew about the Prince of Peace, Alex. Before she died she told me He was the Messiah. I only believed it myself after Todd and I began to search the scriptures together. Read it for yourself."

"I can't read the Scriptures. I am too far away from God. I don't know what I believe any more."

"Read the letter from Papa and the passage Mama marked. Find out the truth for yourself. Alex," she took his face in her hands, "I pray that your heart will be flooded with light so that you can see the future God has for you. I pray that you will understand how incredibly great His power is ... far above any earthly king or leader. It's that same mighty power that raised Christ from the dead. He uses that power to help those who believe Him."

Alex could not respond. A great silence generated miles between them.

"Alex, do you remember being on the lake the last time we went to Todd's farm? Do you remember the storm that came up so quickly? When I was swept overboard, you dove into the water to save me. We never talked about it."

Alex knew exactly what she was talking about. It was that very event that constantly haunted him. He had promised to live for God if He would save her. A promise he hadn't kept.

"Papa would have beaten me senseless if he had known we were on the water that night. I dove to the bottom three times before I found you. I remember my lungs burned and my arms were numb, but I couldn't let you go. I had to save you. It was just after losing Mama, and I couldn't lose you too."

"You didn't save me, at least not all by yourself. You pulled me up from the bottom of the lake, but as we bobbed up and down in the waves, I saw an angel in the water holding you from behind. When I saw that angel, I knew God had a special plan for your life. Ever since that day I have looked to you for guidance and support. Now I ask you to look to God for wisdom and strength."

A great silence engulfed them. He didn't know what to say.

"I love you, Alex." He locked his arms around her. His love for her knew no bounds. He was sorry he could not embrace her beliefs as easily as he embraced her body. But that was over now too. Soon she would walk out that door and their lives would change forever.

"You had better go now, Nadia. Todd is probably waiting for you in the car."

"Please, Alex, promise me you will never take the "Chip.""

"But I don't ..." Alex looked into her begging eyes. The memory of similar eyes flashed back at him, the eyes of his dying mother. He had pulled her as gently as possible from the twisted wreckage of the car and had held her broken body in his arms. She looked at him expressing that same forever good-bye. She wheezed a whisper to him, her words barely audible, "Take care of Nadia. She will need you more than ever now." Her eyes pleaded for his answer.

"Please, promise me." Nadia brought him back to the present.

"All right, I promise." He answered weakly. Nadia gave him a look of doubt.

"I promise!" he repeated strongly with a laugh.

"You'll see, my dear precious brother, the Lord will take care of you."

"I just hope He takes care of *you*."

"He will, I can guarantee you that. Good-bye Alex."

"Good-bye, Nadia, and if you need anything, anything at all."

"I know, I know. I love you."

"I love you too."

Nadia left the apartment with her father's violin, never to return.

Chapter Twenty-Six

On a bare hill, a flag waved to signal the onslaught of battle. It beckoned soldiers to come. The Leader, fierce strong and mighty, issued orders to His sacred warriors. He summoned His knights, His proud champions, to gratify His anger!

A voice shouted, "Listen!" There was a rumbling in the mountains like a great crowd. "Listen!" The voice repeated.

All around kingdoms clamored, nations mustered. It was Yahweh. He marshaled the troops for battle. Yahweh and the instruments of His fury came from a distant country, from the far horizons to destroy the whole earth.

"Scream in terror!"

The Lord's time had come, the time for the Almighty to crush the nations. At this, every arm fell limp; fear paralyzed the heart of each man. Pangs and pains seized them, and they writhed like a woman in labor. They looked at one another, helpless, as the flames of the burning city reflected upon their ashen faces. The day of the Lord had come, the terrible day of His wrath and fierce anger.

The land was destroyed, and all the sinners with it. The heavens were black above them. No light shone from the stars or sun or moon. He had punished the world for its evil, the wicked for their sin; He had crushed the arrogance of the proud man and the haughtiness of the rich. Very few survived.

Terrified, Walker awoke from this dream; sweat saturated his clothes.

xxx

Tommy Barker pulled his car slowly out of the alley behind Nadia's apartment. She had driven to the farm on Round Lake many times before when she transported Rogue families to safety. Now it would be her refuge as well.

From the backseat Nadia took one last look at her kitchen window above them. The light was on. *Alex must be getting something to eat.* She saw the flowers on the windowsill bidding her good-bye. She was leaving everything behind; her parent's memory, her childhood, the home that she loved, but most importantly her dear brother, Alex. As they drove around the corner, she closed her eyes and with resolve prayed.

Dear Jesus,

I will not turn to the left or the right
I'm gonna face ahead, standing firm in your sight,
I'm gonna follow you
Your way alone is true
Temptations come and distractions go
I'm gonna hold my ground, in this life that I know
Will bring me home to you
Your love will pull me through

I have cast my lot, I have entered the race.
I'm gonna run it long, I'm gonna keep my pace
Leaning hard on you, and your saving grace
'Til I see the end and behold your face.
O, God – that's what I'm longing for.

I could not stay if I didn't believe
That you are here with me and you'll never leave
For I depend on you
In everything I do.
Sometimes it's hard to be true to your heart
I want to walk by faith, wanna do my part.
You'll keep me strong for you.
Your grace has seen me through.

O, God – that's what I'm longing for.
I'm longing for you
O, God – you're what I'm longing for.
Jesus, just to feel your warm embrace
Just to see your face..."[v]

Nadia's folded hands dropped into her lap. A deep calm swept over her. Just a few blocks away a lightening flash, closely followed by a thunder clap, broke the stillness of the morning sky. A tremendous storm brewed.

When Walker woke his body ached as if he had been in a fierce fight. Heaviness weighed on his chest. At first he didn't know where he was then a truck rumbled on the highway above him. In a fog, he finally remembered. They had taken shelter under a bridge not far from the railroad tracks they had followed all day.

His eyes shot open as three rats climbed up his leg; a fourth, the size of a woodchuck sat on his chest, whiskers moving back and forth just waiting for the right moment to strike. Walker's hand clutched for the bat he laid next to himself the night before. Wham, he got one!

Kirk jumped up when the rodents squeal. Four gray creatures with long pointed tails scurried away from around his legs. Walker, still swinging, shouted, "Kirk, are you okay?"

"Yeah, let's get out of here. This place gives me the creeps."

Walker let the bat slip to the ground as he approached the dead animal. "Not before we eat. Go get some wood so that we can make a fire." He needed to work quickly if they were to have meat for breakfast. Though the sun had not quite risen he could see the clouds thickening. Rain would put out any fire he started.

Kirk McCartney eyed the heap of dead fur on the ground next to Walker. "You've got to be kidding. I ain't eatin' no rat."

"That's fine with me. You can open a can of tuna if you prefer." He knew Kirk hated canned tuna.

"So where do I find wood?"

"There are some trees on the other side of the railroad tracks. Look there."

He had never skinned an animal before let alone a rat, but he surmised it was big enough to feed them both amply. He opened what he determined to be a gutting blade on the Swiss army knife that he bought just two days earlier. *Is it possible we have been on the run only two days?* It seemed more like a week of Sundays.

He estimated that they were making pretty good progress though they had to keep off the main roads. His plan was to follow the railroad tracks north until he found a way to safely cross the river. Then they would continue north until who knew what. *God will show the way. He has done it before, he will do it again. I just wish the boy had a little confidence in me. I guess it's not gushing out my pores. Lord, increase my faith.*

Chapter Twenty-Seven

"You have food for your body, Jeremiah Walker. I will provide direction as well." Jesus was sitting on the throne next to His father in the seventh dimension. "His prayers are so honest and direct. It is really quite refreshing. I will send him a challenge, and then his faith will increase." The Ancient of Days nodded and smiled at the growth of Jeremiah Walker.

Satan was waiting impatiently when Baleful finally arrived. "So what happened this time," he demanded.

"I got the cop there ready to arrest her. They were within blocks of each other but just at that precise moment, Kasha caused the lightening to strike a power line. Obviously, the stupid cop got distracted and Nadia got away."

With indignation Satan growled, "Obviously, just like that, she got away. So where is she now?"

"She's on her way out of town." Baleful tried to move away from his master but Satan pinned his wings to the ground.

"And where is she going?"

"Well, that I don't know. Somewhere in the mountains I suspect."

"You suspect," he disdainfully condescended. "So why aren't you following her?"

"Well, you said you wanted a report."

With hot fiery breath, Satan spat into his subordinate's face. "I said a detailed report. You have not given me details. You, Baleful, are worthless. Go and find her. She will lead us to the others!"

xxx

Kirk followed Walker down North Water Street Park into a town named Ossining next to the river. The tantalizing smell of pasta sauce mingled with cheese drew him to the door of a small Italian restaurant. A green and white awning shielded him from the late afternoon sun. The rain that morning hadn't drive out the muggy air. The cool shade brought him back to life. He leaned his head against the storefront window and longed to go inside. *A big plate of spaghetti would be really great!* He noticed some of the tables had already filled up for the evening meal. A man came out the door. Kirk's mouth watered at the delicious smell. The cold puff of air-conditioning was like ice-cream on the top. He had real ice-cream once and loved it!

He and Doc Walker had walked all day and Doc still never told him exactly where they were going. He was positive the man didn't know. Kirk was also sure he had made a mistake joining up with Doc. Although, he had to admit that he *was* an interesting traveling partner. He knew something about everything, from where squirrels live to how long it takes a spider to build a web. Doc didn't actually talk much but when he did, Kirk discovered it made sense to listen.

Doc ruffled the hair on Kirk's head. It annoyed him.

"Sorry, Champ. I wish we could go in." Then with an optimistic tone he added, "We can go and sit down over there and open a can of tuna." There was a wooden gazebo across the street with white painted rails and benches inside – not a bad spot to stop and rest awhile. But Kirk did not intend to eat tuna for the rest of his life nor rat ever again. If that was his fate, he was certain he wouldn't live much longer.

Doc started to cross the street when suddenly a ruckus arose at one of the tables in the restaurant. A woman slapped the back of a boy about his age.

"Looks like he swallowed wrong," Kirk said. Doc came back to the window, looked for a second then ran into the restaurant faster than a car trying to beat a yellow light. What a piece of luck for Kirk. He followed Doc inside.

"I'm a doctor. Does he have something stuck in his throat?" The boy's eyes were wild and his head bobbed up and down. His mouth was open wide. He looked like someone had pushed a baseball down his throat.

Doc went up behind the kid and jerked him to his feet. The woman started to yell at Doc but stopped. It seemed unreal. Doc grabbed him around his waist and squeezed hard five times. Nothing happened. He did five more. Then pow! A small piece of bread flew out of his mouth like popcorn in a street machine. The poor kid coughed then sucked in with a gagging sound. *I hope he doesn't puke.* Everyone in the restaurant gawked at him. Then on top of it all his stupid mother yelled at him.

"Blake, I told you never to talk while you are eating. Now thank the kind man." Blake looked like he wanted to climb under the table.

"Thank you, sir."

"Yes, thank you very much. I am Mrs. Pierce ..." She acted as if that should mean something to them, which it didn't. She went on, "... the mayor's wife ... And this is my son Blake." She reached out to shake the Doc's hand and suddenly her happy thankfulness changed. Her eyes became like slits as they moved up and down his body and then at Kirk. Her hand went limp in Doc's firm grasp. As soon as she pulled away she wiped her hand over and over on her napkin. She made Kirk feel like dirt.

Doc didn't seem to notice. He was always trying to change the world. And right now he had that same look he always had when he saw someone down and out. Kirk never would understand him. She looked rich. Her husband probably owned half the town. They probably had more money than they could ever spend. But he had that silly "I feel sorry for you" look again.

"Who are you?" She demanded gruffly. Maybe she misunderstood his puppy face.

"My name is Jeremiah Walker. I am a retired doctor. I am sorry if our appearance offends you. We have been traveling all day and have not had the opportunity to refresh ourselves."

Kirk's stomach began to growl. "Come on, let's get out of here."

"No, you and your son must stay and have dinner with us. I owe you for saving my son's life." The tenderness and kindness in Doc's voice must have changed her mind. He had that effect on people.

"That isn't necessary, ma'am. You owe us nothing; your good fortune and health come from God." Kirk couldn't believe Doc turned down a real meal.

"I insist." Without waiting for an answer, Mrs. Pierce ordered the waiter to set two more places at the table. Thank goodness somebody had some sense!

Kirk devoured a big plate of spaghetti, a salad and lots of garlic bread. He sat next to the other kid, not saying a word. Walker and the mayor's wife were yakking away, something about the blessings that come from God and the warnings that had haunted Doc's dreams.

The woman said, "So what must I do to be saved?" This seemed to demand all of Doc's attention. Kirk, bored with the conversation, zoned out until a police officer entered the restaurant. The officer walked up to the take-out bar across from the restrooms.

Kirk pushed his chair away from the table and asked to be excused to go to the men's room. Doc nodded his head. He clearly hadn't noticed the cop. Or maybe he did and didn't care. Maybe he trusted Kirk that much. He looked at the ground as he passed by the uniformed man. Guilt washed over him.

Chapter Twenty-Eight

A voice thundered from the sixth dimension, "Foreboding, do your job. Do not let this mortal get away." Foreboding, angered by the terror that the voice instilled in him, harassed Kirk, "This is your chance; it will be very easy, walk over to the cop and report what you know about Walker. He is a fugitive so you will be doing your duty as an upstanding citizen to report him. Your gang leader will come after you if you don't complete your mission."

Foreboding grimaced at the sound of the angelic choir resounding with jubilation above the newly saved woman's table. "Your time is short, Jeremiah Walker. You have prayed with too many pitiful wretched beings. Your death is eminent. Your head will be mine and your soul will burn forever."

xxx

Kirk remembered an older boy that had not killed when the SOS leader told him to. That boy had lost three of his fingers to a pair of hedge cutters. Loyalty to Doc or loyalty to the gang?

Doc and the woman's heads were bowed when Kirk came out of the restroom. He stopped and spoke to the officer then pointed toward Doc. The woman was now blubbering.

The officer told Kirk to go outside and wait for him on the sidewalk. Kirk obeyed.

The Mayor's wife and her son pushed their chairs away from the table and got up to leave. She hugged Walker and thanked him again profusely. Blake shook his hand. Walker glanced around the restaurant searching for the restrooms. He just realized how long Kirk had been gone when he saw Mrs. Pierce smile at a police officer on her way out the door.

"Good night, Officer McGuffey is it?"

"Yes, that's right, Mrs. Pierce. Have a nice evening."

Then the officer stared at Walker and their eyes connected. Walker knew exactly what Kirk had done. His first reaction was to bolt. When the policeman turned to the register to pay Walker seized the moment and dashed toward the kitchen door.

An inner voice whispered, "You live safely within My shadow. I alone am your refuge, your place of safety; trust in Me. I will shield you. I order My angels to protect you wherever you go. Be at peace, I am always with you. Just wait. Help is at hand." He recognized that voice but fear and instinct drove him toward escape. Fight or flight?

Neither. He returned slowly to his seat and looked out the window. Kirk leaned with his back against the wall.

Walker began to pray with all his heart. *I trust You, Lord, for protection. Keep me safe from this trap. I put myself in Your hands. I know You will save me. You are faithful. Guide me and lead me as You have promised.*

Walker remained seated. He finished his cup of black coffee.

The busboy did his job.

Time seemed suspended.

Officer McGuffey approached the table then sat down next to Walker. McGuffey began the conversation. "Do you know that boy standing outside the window there?" Walker looked up and acknowledged.

"Yes, officer, we have been traveling together."

"Do you know what he told me about you?"

"I can imagine, sir."

"Why aren't you running then?"

"Sometimes it is wiser to take the route of least resistance. Besides, I know where my fate lies and it's not under my control or yours." Walker affectionately touched the pocket that his wife's Bible used to occupy. Deep in his gut a desire burned; a desire to be near her, to touch her, to smell her hair and feel her breath on his neck. Apparently he would join her sooner than he thought. His battle was coming to an end. But then what would happen to Kirk?

Chapter Twenty-Nine

Thirty demons usually swarmed around Officer Leo McGuffey. They always were relaxed, completely at home around him, until he talked to a Rogue. When McGuffey sat down with Walker they took their cue and immediately flew to Katie Westerly's house. There they surrounded Katie. They pressed down, chided, urged her to end her life and do it quickly. She always made trouble for them and they wanted it to end.

Victoria, Katie Westerly's guardian angel, fought a losing battle. She shouted to Katie above the demon roar, "He who began a good work in you is faithful to complete it."

Laughing, a demon reminded the mortal, "Your sins are too great. How could He ever use you?"

In a final act of desperation, the faithful angel pressed herself against her charge, engulfed Katie with her wings, and took the brunt of the attack. All the while she chanted repeatedly, "Victory in the Lord. He is mighty to save."

xxx

Katie Westerly sat on the bathroom floor next to the tub. It had Edwardian claw legs, the old fashioned freestanding kind. She had rescued it several years ago from an abandoned farm house that was being demolished. It was her favorite place to relax and unwind after a stressful day.

Tonight was different. Tonight she placed her arm over the tub and held a utility knife against her wrist. The blade was extremely sharp and very thin with a pointed tip. There would not be much physical pain, certainly much less than the unutterable emotional pain she now experienced. She tried to remember the last time she laughed. It didn't make any difference any more. The pain of life was too great to ever feel joy again.

Katie decided to move into the tub. That would make the clean-up easier. She had spent the day cleaning the whole house. The more work she did the less left behind for her brother to worry about. Leo was such a good kid and now a terrific police officer. *Lord, keep him safe.*

And be with Gary. Forgive him. She closed her eyes and saw his handsome aging face. His new young wife was not anything like Katie. He was happy. Katie was devastated.

Suddenly the phone rang.

Oh, please hang up. Two, three, four rings. *Hang up, hang up.* Five, six, seven rings. "All right, all right, I'm coming." She cursed under her breath and stumbled from the bathroom to her bedroom.

"Hello," she said in despair.

"Hi, Bunny," It was her brother, Leo. He had saved her life more than once, but this time she wished he hadn't.

Chapter Thirty

A company of demons entered Alex Lichtenstein's apartment lead by Satan himself. He desired to see this woman, Megan Cameron Montgomery, first hand. Her moral decay delighted him. He was told that she followed the stars. "That's my girl."

Jonathan, Alex's angel, challenged him immediately, "What makes you think she is yours? She is a good person."

Hakah sadly instructed Jonathan, "You know that Jesus is the only way, the ultimate truth, and the everlasting life. No one comes to the Father except through Him."

"See, Jonathan, rules are rules," Satan mocked. Sheer pleasure oozed from his pores. "I am the Prince of Darkness and until they become children of the Light, they are all mine. Including that man she is playing with right now. Let her be distracted by the answers she finds within. As long as she only searches inside herself, she will never discover the truth about God and be forgiven."

Hakah swore that if he had a heart it would be bleeding. He remembered looking through God's portal into the fifth dimension at the state of her immortal soul.

xxx

"I'm sorry, Alex, I feel like an intruder."

The chip on her shoulder was gone so he decided to be civil. "No, it is okay, really. Come and sit down. Can I get you something to eat? Nadia mentioned something about cherries in the refrigerator. Herb brought them up this afternoon. She said ..."

"Cherries, Nadia got me cherries? She is such an angel. Yes, please, I would die for cherries!" He chuckled at this childish reaction.

She followed him to the kitchen chatting all the way. "My grandpa had this huge cherry tree in his back yard. I used to climb it, hide in the branches and eat cherries until my stomach would practically burst. Oh I can't remember when I had my last fresh cherry." Alex found a small bag of the precious fruit in the refrigerator and offered her the bowl.

"Thank you so much." Like a kid with a box of chocolates, she popped three in her mouth at once. Her cheek stuck out like a chipmunk storing up for the winter.

"They are divine. I feel like I have died and gone to heaven."

"I guess Nadia was right, you do like cherries."

They went back to the living room. Megan curled up on the recliner with the bowl of cherries on her lap. Alex went back to his book.

Ten minutes later Alex looked up. The bowl was empty, her eyes were closed and her head was dropped back on the chair. If he hadn't seen her jaw moving he would have sworn she was asleep.

"Boy you ate those fast."

"Oh, I'm sorry. Did you want some?" She looked up as if surprised he was still in the room.

"No, it's okay." He didn't care for cherries much so couldn't imagine eating so many at one time. She was a little crazy and for some unknown reason he found that charming.

"I wanted to save some for later but couldn't resist the temptation to eat them all." Her smile was distracting.

"Nadia told me you have a telescope. May I see it?" The question came out of the blue and with such exuberance he couldn't say no. She really could change the subject fast. Silently he led her up to his room.

"Oh, wow, a Newton Reflector!" Megan's face brightened. "Does it have an equatorial or Alaztmuth mount?"

Maybe he had underestimated her mental capabilities. He looked at her, as if for the first time. There was grace in her movement. Her hands were delicate, her fingers long and thin. Her thick blond hair was pulled back into a ponytail which made her look eighteen at the most. She had a beautifully sculpted oval face, and startlingly beautiful pink lips.

He stammered a moment and then explained, "It has an equatorial mount motorized with a clock drive. How did you ..."

She clasped her hands together and interrupted, "It's huge! It must be at least fourteen inches around. I bet it cost a fortune."

"Sixteen inches and it didn't cost too much." Not sure he should add, "I made it myself."

"You're kidding, I don't believe it. So when did you do this?"

Alex never heard someone so energized about a telescope. He barely admitted to himself how thrilled he was when he had finally finished it. Was she sincere or making fun of him?

"I started grinding the lens when I was about sixteen. It took two years before it was fully operational."

"This is so amazing." She motioned toward the eye-piece. "May I look?"

"Of course, first I have to open the hatch." Alex went to the wall next to his bed and pressed a button. Slowly the window in the slanted ceiling began to disappear like a car sunroof.

"Wow and the skylight opens. I suppose you just made that too." Megan appeared more amazed every moment.

Blood rushed to his face. Normally he didn't like attention but right now, a childlike pride bloomed inside him like the first time he impressed his second grade teacher.

"Well sort of, this used to be the attic. My father engineered the hatch. I pretty much did the rest."

"I can just imagine all the time you two must have spent here together." Megan settled herself onto the stool in front of the telescope.

"The two of us?" Alex thought about that for a moment, "I suppose we did." He remembered the stiff criticism he received from his father when he had measured the hole in the roof incorrectly. That lecture went on for days. Unfortunately, it overshadowed any positive feelings he might have had about the entire experience.

"After it was finished he never came up here again." She ignored his comment and looked with wonder into the mammoth telescope. The sky, previously cloudy, was crystal clear and full of stars.

"Here let me find Polaris for you." Megan leaned back only slightly forcing their arms to touch when Alex bent forward over the lens. He smelled her hair and momentarily stopped breathing. He was sure she could hear his heart pound so he quickly found the star and backed away.

"This is so fabulous! I seek guidance from the stars, you know."

"I don't believe much in astrology." Alex admitted flatly.

"Well, what do you believe in?" Megan was clearly miffed by his disinterest and looked as if she was about to pout.

"I believe in God, I guess."

"Now that's a pretty broad topic."

"Well, the more I study science and all its aspects the more I'm utterly amazed. I'm convinced that only some amazingly brilliant creator could have caused the galaxies to exist with such precision. I suppose that must mean God."

Megan paused for a moment then remarked matter-of-factly, "I think that if there is a god he doesn't know what's going on, or at least he doesn't care. If believing in God works for you, then fine. All I can say is I'm a good person and whether He exists or not makes no difference to me. If I continue to look into myself searching for answers, I will always remain true to myself and that's what really counts. To me it's a matter of logic; clean cut, mathematical, scientific."

"You mean God could exist for me but not for you?" It made no sense to him. Beauty, brains but way too crazy.

"Well if there is a god, he knows what I mean." She huffed and puffed and pushed the stool away from the telescope. Alex didn't believe this was really coming from her heart.

"Could it be that your view of life stems from a desire to run away from your past? We must all suffer the consequences of our actions. The bottom line is can you really live with yourself? I mean, does your philosophy give you some sense of inner peace?"

"I don't know." She snapped back. "How can I establish perfect peace when there is so much chaos in the world? That's where the fault lies. Besides, my past is just that, in the past. I don't like it and I don't want to think about it. I surely can't change any of it."

Was she shifting the guilt or was it the dumb blond syndrome? Alex thought about it for a moment then walked away. He tried to flesh her out. "There is a lot about my past that I wish I could change. When I was young I made a promise that I failed to keep." The day he fished Nadia out of the lake pressed on his mind.

She softened. "Don't be so hard on yourself, Alex. A promise made when you're young is difficult to keep for a lifetime."

"Megan, you can't heal a wound by merely saying it's not there."

"I can do whatever I like." She crossed her arms and definitely began to pout. She got under his skin in more ways than one. She drew him and repelled him at the same time. How could one woman do both to him? The bottom line ... she really irritated him.

<>
WHOSE BROAD STRIPES AND BRIGHT STARS,

Chapter Thirty-One

Day 363

Justin, Jeremiah Walker's angel, had seen the black cloud of demons as he approached Katie Westerly's house the night before. He had flown fast and furious to the aid of her angel Victoria who had managed to keep them circling above. But Justin's reputation had preceded him and they had taken off without a fight angrily vowing to return.

Katie Westerly's guardian angel rested lightly on her shoulder. They had come through another fierce battle together and she was so proud that her dear treasured mortal survived. Once again she gently wrapped her wings around Katie and whispered in her ear, "It is time to celebrate because the Lord's joy is now your strength. You must not be discouraged or sad."

xxx

Katie woke when the sun just barely began to rise. For the first time in months, she actually looked forward to getting out of bed. After a quick shower she brushed her short gray hair straight back off her face. There was no time to blow it dry. She wanted to prepare a big breakfast for her guests that arrived unexpectedly last night. She pulled on a light blue tank top and a pair of her most comfortable blue jeans.

September was generally cool although the past few years had been much warmer than usual. It was predicted to go over 100° today. September was actually one of her most favorite months. She loved it because it was a month for new beginnings; the first day of school (though she hadn't been to school in over thirty-five years), new books, new clothes, new teachers and the possibility of doing a better job than the previous year ... a brand new start. Today she captured her childhood again. This would be a new beginning; the beginning of a new walk, a new outlook, a great expectation.

Leo McGuffey had grumbled when he drove up in his police cruiser with Jerry and Kirk in the back seat. This was the fourth group she had helped. He was her brother but he, like her ex-husband, didn't understand why she risked being arrested by hiding and helping complete strangers. She knew that her brother loved and respected her. Because of her he never arrested a Rogue or whispered to anyone where they went.

Kirk had been especially troubling to Leo. The boy had turned the doctor in, yet both Doctor Walker and Katie forgave the kid and insisted that he stay at her house too. Leo had candidly referred to the boy as a weed that needed to be cut out and burned. Katie remembered as a child being for hours on her knees with a spade digging up dandelions in their parent's backyard. With a tired heart she had answered her brother. "We may call them weeds. But who knows, God may call them wildflowers."

"There is no reasoning with you," her brother had said. "Christians will always remain a mystery to me." Then he just shook his head and drove away.

That was last night.

They had spoken only about fifteen minutes before the two exhausted visitors retired for the night but it was long enough to change Katie's outlook forever. Just before closing the guest room door behind him Jerry Walker said, "Thank you for being willing to do the good works that God prepared in advance for you to do." Those words pierced her heart and kept going over and over in her mind. She knew they came from a scripture but couldn't remember which one. It had taken her about forty-five minutes to find the reference but when she did she was elated.

She began at Ephesians 2:8. "Because of His kindness you have been saved through trusting Christ. Salvation is not a reward for the good we have done. It is God Himself who has made us what we are and given us new lives through Christ Jesus; and long ages ago He planned that we should spend these lives in helping others." There it was, "and long ages ago He planned that we should spend these lives in helping others." She read it three times before closing the book. God had a plan for her. A plan that He designed for her ages ago, a plan for her to help others. Hope reigned in her heart, hope that had not been there for months. Her faith again began to soar. She was happy, so happy, reminded that God had made her what she was. Jesus had died for her and actually had a plan and purpose for her life, a purpose far beyond what she could imagine.

Katie had spent the rest of the evening planning for the next day. *I'll make them a big breakfast, pack them a hearty lunch and drive them to the northern Ossining border.* Going any farther would attract too much attention from the officials; too many check points and too many questions. Katie found her map of New York and circled the destination. She had showed that same location to the other Rogues that had passed through her doors. She placed the map on the kitchen table and turned out the light. One day she would also be running for her life but in the meantime, she was determined to help others get safely away.

Katie washed Jerry and Kirk's clothes, folded them and left them outside the door where they slept. The stars were bright outside her window when she finally put her head on her pillow but that didn't keep her from getting an extremely good night's sleep.

Now the morning birds were calling and the sun shone bright through the sheer gingham curtains at Katie's kitchen window. She was frying bacon and mixing pancake batter when Doctor Walker entered the room.

Kirk McCartney had not said a word since Katie Westerly dropped him and the Doc off near the Ossining train station. He couldn't understand why they had forgiven him. He almost wished they hadn't because it piled heavy coals on his guilt-ridden shoulders. He had betrayed Doc but, for some reason, he and Katie had said it was a blessing. Kirk didn't know what to believe anymore except that this man was not like anyone he had ever met before.

Doc smiled. They walked for a while in silence, and then Doc put his arm around Kirk's shoulders. "Smile, we have full bellies, a clean shirt on our backs and two sandwiches for lunch."

"You certainly don't need much, do you?" Kirk said sarcastically.

"Nothing we have is necessary to our happiness but God. The most important thing I have is right here." Doc patted his pocket where his wife's Bible used to be. His smile faded.

"Kirk, let's say a little prayer for your Aunt Rachel." He closed his eyes and mumbled a few words Kirk could not hear. *Why does he talk that way to a god that doesn't even exist?*

Chapter Thirty-Two

God was delighted to answer Walker's prayer immediately. He had been waiting patiently to saturate Rachel Berk with faith. But it was only at *her* request that He would enter the fifth dimension and breathed His Holy Spirit into her space. When it happened it would ignite a raging fire that would burn away all the decay and waste that her sins had produced. Jesus spoke ever so gently.

"Rachel, I want your roots to reach deep into the soil of My marvelous love for you, so that you are able to feel and to understand how spacious and how extensive, how bottomless and how soaring My love for you really is. You are My beloved child. I will protect you as I would the pupil of My eye and hide you in the shadow of My wings."

A magnificent chorus of angels stood close by waiting to rejoice at the birth of Rachel's spirit.

xxx

Rachel Berk sat on her sagging couch reading the pocket-sized Bible that Doctor Walker had given her. She had read it constantly for the past two days. Each time she picked it up she seemed to gain more strength.

This morning she started a new chapter in Colossians. She read the words silently, "You have been raised to life with Christ, so set your hearts on the things that are in heaven, where Christ sits on His throne at the right side of God. Keep your minds fixed on things there, not on things here on earth, for you have died, and your life is hidden with Christ in God."[vi] She read it again.

"I desperately want to hide, but I feel as if I am already dead. Lord, how is it that my life can hide in you? Take me, Jesus. Take my life and do with it what you want. My eyes are fixed on you."

Rachel Berk closed her eyes and pressed the Bible to her heart. It was miraculous, but finally she felt safe and secure. She could tackle whatever would come.

Chapter Thirty-Three

Serpentine joined the thousands of demons congregated in the conference hall. It was delightful to feel the evil power they emanated. His eyes searched the sea of mortals. There she was beautiful, cunning, smart and cold. *Oh, she's just like me.*

xxx

Megan regretted wearing such high heels. Her feet ached terribly and the day was only half over. She couldn't wait to sit down. When the first session finally came to a break, she turned to her cameraman, Frank. The light on his camera blinked red. She tugged on the corner of her red suit. It must line up perfectly. She smiled and squared her shoulders. Her sore feet forgotten, her energy pumped – she stood completely relaxed and at home. Megan lived and breathed the reporter role – her ultimate high. Frank's light turned green and without notes she summarized the morning's events. She turned her microphone off and told Frank to get something to eat. Already people were lined up at the buffet table so she opted to go to the restroom before lunch.

She checked her watch for the time and noticed the band had worn practically through. She removed it from her wrist and placed it in the zippered pocket of her handbag. The watch lost a minute each day but she didn't care. It housed her most prized possession. She had bought the watch in a secondhand shop when she was fourteen. The unique filigree hands initially caught her attention, but when the salesperson showed her the secret compartment behind the base she knew she must have it. Every day she visited the shop to make sure it was still there. Five months later she had saved enough from her lunch money to buy it. Megan hid her mother's picture in that little compartment. Aside from this precious photograph she had no memory of her mother at all.

She had sneaked the picture out of the house the day her father's girlfriend went on a rampage and destroyed all the old family albums. Funny how, after all these years, she still kept it behind the watch. Perhaps, it was the power that it represented. The power she obtained that day when she defied her father's lover. On that day she became emancipated and took control of her life.

Megan had exactly twenty-three minutes before she needed to be back to set up for the next session. She quickly headed down the north corridor towards the elevators. *There must be an unoccupied ladies room somewhere – maybe on the second floor.* She had just pressed the elevator button when …

"Ms. Montgomery, it is so nice to see you again. I trust that the conference has been enlightening you."

Megan recognized his voice immediately. She spun around and smiled, her heart beating wildly. President Sixtus III approached. Two military uniformed guards followed close behind.

How could he have remembered her name? She had fantasized about having an impromptu encounter with this amazing man of her dreams but never believed it would actually happen. She wanted to sound sophisticated and coy but she could hardly speak. With all the eloquence of a third grader, "Yes, sir," squeaked out. *You bumbling idiot. Why not expound upon the inspiring morning I just experienced?*

He smiled slightly and glanced down her body. *He loves my red suit.* It was fast becoming her lucky charm.

"I'm sure the restrooms are crowded on every floor. Why don't you use my private quarters? I am headed there right now myself." He seemed completely sincere. *Well he really is just a regular guy.*

"That would be great! Thank you, Mr. President." *That would be great? Couldn't I have said something a little more intelligent like, I would love to accompany you? No, that would have been stupid. Oh, I am so stupid.*

When the elevator arrived Sixtus motioned for her to get in, "After you, Ms. Montgomery."

"Thank you," popped out.

One of the guards scanned his wrist against the security eye and pressed the button for the fifth floor; the same floor where she had seen the President in person for the first time, the floor of the Communications Office.

When the elevator doors opened, she immediately stepped out. She remembered the excitement she experienced yesterday entering this floor. It was nothing like the excitement that coursed through her veins right now.

"I heard your summary of this morning's conference. I think you pulled all the important parts together quite nicely. Your comment on keeping financial matters balanced was exactly what the session was all about. Do you come from a financial background?"

"No, I don't, but the main point I was trying to make was that all Americans have the right to see for themselves the balance, if and when it comes. The transparency is what is important."

He apparently did not want to address her point. Instead he redirected the conversation. "Ms. Montgomery, as I am sure you know there are no more Americans. We are all now citizens of one greater nation."

"I ... well ... I do know that," she stammered like a scolded child.

They passed the Communications Office on the left and continued down the hall. At the far end were two mahogany doors marked "Restricted." She read the quote over the doors, 'In the truest sense, freedom cannot be bestowed; it must be achieved.' She pointed to the inscription.

"Who said that?" Megan inquired. The guard in command approached a screen, swiped his wrist, and then gazed into it for retina verification. Automatically the doors parted.

"It is a quote by Franklin D. Roosevelt." Sixtus answered.

She was impressed and hoped to redeem herself, "I believed that wholeheartedly."

"Good, then you agree that for one to enjoy that freedom one must perform one's duties otherwise that freedom must be revoked. Did the Hebrews of Biblical times not stone a stubborn rebellious son? Freedom is not a gift. There is a price to be paid by every citizen." A chill crept down her spine. His eyes pierced though her. "Sacrifice makes us stronger. Do you believe that too, Ms. Montgomery?" He did not wait for her answer. "What you sacrifice today you gain tomorrow."

The mammoth doors silently closed behind them like the doors of a crypt. He smiled at her. She must have misunderstood him. Eventually they stopped at a nondescript door. The guards unlocked it and stepped inside.

"All clear," one stated when they emerged again. They took their post outside, rifles held tight against their chests.

The door opened directly into the sitting room. Megan stepped across the threshold and immediately became Cinderella entering the king's palace. The silk carpet was so lush she was tempted to remove her "glass slippers." Prince Charming took her hand and led her into his castle.

Chapter Thirty-Four

There were just the two of them; Hakah on the defense, Serpentine on the offense. Hakah rested lightly on Megan's shoulder. Serpentine flew circles around both of them occasionally grazing his wings against the ceiling. Every time he tried to move closer to the mortal Hakah forced him away. Eventually he perched on Sixtus.

"Everyone who calls upon the name of the Lord will be saved." Hakah shouted at Megan.

"The Lord is not here, Megan. Don't waste your breath, my darling." Sinister cooed. "Though your voice may be louder, Hakah, she only listens to mine."

Sadly, Hakah saw the truth in it.

xxx

Megan had only been five minutes in the powder room. When she returned Sixtus handed her a large glass of red wine. He had removed his suit coat and tie and had unbuttoned the two top buttons of his tailored shirt, just enough to expose the dark hair on his chest. She smiled at him trying to be demure. She sipped her wine and watched him from over the rim. She was not sure what her next move should be. He obviously intended for her to stay a little while, but his hungry eyes made her uncomfortable.

"I really should go now. The afternoon session will be starting soon."

"Please sit down and at least stay long enough to finish your wine." Reluctantly she sat down on the large chaise lounge that he indicated in the center of the room. It was so low that she almost spilled her wine. Her purse slipped off her shoulder. The cushions were lusciously soft and upholstered with hunter green velvet. She imagined a crown on her head, a princess preparing for an afternoon nap.

"Stretch out your legs. Those high heels must make your feet ache." She was mesmerized by his confident caring tone and so she lifted her legs and scooted back dangling only her feet over the edge.

"Why don't you remove your shoes?"

His eyes devoured her.

She wanted to hide.

Her head dropped down and her long loose hair fell around her face. *I wish I had my elephant comb to protect me.* For the first time she spoke to God with a sincere heart. *Oh, Lord, what should I do?*

Instantly Megan's phone began to ring. Instinctively, she pressed the receiver in her ear and whipped her feet back to the floor. "Hello."

"Where in the world are you? The conference is about to resume," Frank yelled at her.

"I am having a private interview with the President. I will be there momentarily." She spoke loud enough for Sixtus to hear hoping to create an accountability factor. Megan clicked off her phone, raked her fingers through her hair, pushed it back off her face and raised her head.

Her strategy had failed. The president, his two thumbs wedged into his belt and his hands cupped loosely around his zipper, stood only about a foot away from her.

"I would like to show you the bedroom. I have something for you there." He had thrown her completely off guard. He was shockingly brazen and had more than enough power to overtake her. She did not know the source of her confidence but it stopped her knees from shaking as she rose to her feet. He did not step back. Her legs pressed against his. The subtle aroma of Gucci Guilty Intense filled her nostrils. She used to like that cologne. Gently she stroked his fingers with her left hand and raised her right hand to his cheek.

"I am sure what you have is very beautiful but my camera man is waiting for me. I know you understand." She slipped away from him and flew to the door. It was locked. *You bloody vulture.* It took only a moment to open and close it abruptly behind her. She stared at the ground as she passed the guards then bolted down the hall, through the massive wood doors to the elevator. Her hands trembled. She pressed the down button.

She stepped back from the wall and looked up ... seventh floor. She shook her hands back and forth as if that would stop the trembling. *Why are these elevators so slow?* Finally the down arrow glowed green. The doors took their time, but eventually opened. She dashed in.

Inside, three gentlemen commented to each other about the conference. The conference floor button was already lit; safety was a few moments away. She moved to the corner and envisioned them examining her through x-ray vision glasses. One of them sported the same cologne as Sixtus. *Get me out of here.*

She glanced down at her wrist to check the time and immediately froze. Fear again swept over her. Her watch was in the outside pocket of her purse and her purse was on the couch in Sixtus' suite. She had to go back. She had to get her mother's picture.

The elevator slowed but that's not what caused her stomach to flip flop up towards her mouth. When the doors opened, the men got out. Megan immediately pressed the button for the fifth floor. She wouldn't think about it. She just had to do it. She had no other choice.

I won't say anything to him. I'll just go in and get my bag. Maybe he'll be out of the room, in the bathroom or something. The elevator stopped on the fifth floor. The door did not open. A voice came over the intercom and she glanced up at the surveillance camera. Sixtus' guard said, "What is the purpose of your return?"

"I left my purse in the president's apartment."

"One moment, please." That one moment seemed like forever. Then the door opened. She approached the two mahogany doors. They opened also. When Megan arrived at the suite, she nervously glanced at the guard.

"He is expecting you."

She straightened her skirt, pulled her hair back off her face and twisted it into a knot at the back of her head. She squared her shoulders and the guard opened the door. Resolve and determination pushed her inside.

What she saw when she entered shocked her more than anything she had anticipated. She stopped short, frozen momentarily. Her head reeled; her mind raced back ... back ... Déjà vu assaulted her.

In the beautiful Cinderella room, Sixtus stood bare-chested. In front of him was a slim woman wearing his blue silk shirt, her shapely legs exposed. Her bare feet pressed into the lush carpet. Her dark hair cascaded down her back. Their light chatter brought Megan back to the moment. Incensed that he already had a half naked woman with him, Megan marched right over to the chaise lounge where she immediately spotted her hand bag's gold chain.

Sixtus handed the other woman a glass of red wine and only then did she turned to look at Megan. Ashtoreth, Sixtus' guru! Megan had never seen her before with her hair down. The open shirt exposed hints of black lace. She was magnificently beautiful! Their eyes locked. Her cold stare immobilized Megan. If looks could kill, Megan would be dead.

Sixtus broke the connection. "So Ms. Montgomery, you have returned. Have you decided to join us after all?"

Hotly she retrieved her purse and said nothing. Her trembling fear exploded into uncontrollable rage. She became irrational. No one in their right mind would march over to Sixtus and slap him hard across his face. But that's exactly what she did.

Ashtoreth's blood chilling eyes bore through Megan as she lunged toward her. *She's going to strangle me.* Suddenly Ashtoreth stopped. Megan followed her gaze to Sixtus' face, that stunned "I can't believe she slapped me" face. Ashtoreth burst out laughing. Megan flew to the door and by the time she closed it behind her, Sixtus laughed too, a laugh so deep she knew he laughed at her.

Chapter Thirty-Five

Michael the Archangel bowed low before the Ancient of Days. Michael came to request that more of his troops might be sent to protect the inhabitants at Round Lake.

The Lord Almighty said, "I know the plans I have for them. They are plans for good and not for evil, to give them a future and a hope. When they pray, I will listen. When they seek Me they will find Me. I hear there every word. Yes, send more of your valiant warriors. Their battle has just begun."

xxx

Nadia's thoughts went to yesterday morning. She and Todd had arrived at the old farm tired but excited to begin their new life together. The farm had been in Todd's family for generations. He had spent many summers there as a boy learning how to tend the fields and feed the animals. He had told Nadia how much he loved working the land. He always dreamed of one day being a gentleman farmer. His dream was now coming true.

Yesterday Nadia had aired out the farmhouse. She opened each window in every room; five bedrooms (Todd assigned her the master bedroom), the living room, eat-in kitchen and family room. A huge fireplace separated the large kitchen from the even larger living room. It used to heat the whole house during the winter months. About fifteen years ago, Todd's father installed a wood burning furnace that heated not only the house but the water as well. There had been plenty to keep Nadia busy; dusting, sweeping, rearranging kitchen cupboards. By evening she was tired but satisfied that the house was ready.

The farm also had an old barn. It was in a beautiful location past the house, behind the east field and about twenty feet from the edge of the woods. Over the years, the barn had been used for everything from housing chickens and farm equipment to celebrating family reunions and community activities involving the whole town.

Now it would be a school for "unmarked" children. Last spring the Monroe School Board renovated Wilton Lake Elementary School. They auctioned off most of the classroom supplies. One of the Round Lake families bought all the materials and donated them to the new little school. Yesterday morning Todd prepared the barn. He hauled all the farm equipment to the shed up by the house. The only thing that remained was a huge stack of chairs, several tables and an extremely large collection of cobwebs. Yesterday afternoon the whole community helped move in a blackboard, a desk, several large carpets and four tall cabinets filled with text books, pencils, paper and many other classroom essentials. It was no longer "the barn." From now on, it was the Round Lake Schoolhouse.

Today Nadia would set up the tables, arrange the chairs and decorate the walls with posters and signs. It was not ideal, but it was sufficient to give the children a high-quality education.

Nadia was so happy finally to find herself immersed in her passion again. She loved children and was thankful for the opportunity to teach them. For her it was not a job but rather a special and precious gift. So far, there were twenty children in the small community of Rogue and "unmarked" families. They lived in homes clustered around a large lake (Round Lake) located outside Monroe, New York (formerly the United States of America).

Several years ago, when the town celebrated its one-hundred, twenty-fifth birthday the four walls of the barn had been roughly insulated and then paneled. The floor was still all dirt, however, except for a large wooden door leading to a root cellar toward the back of the building. The cellar was about four feet deep, three feet wide and six feet long. It was not much more than a crawl space but big enough for great-great-grandma to store shelves and shelves of apples and potatoes over the winter months.

Nadia unrolled a heavily worn area rug woven with deep red, chestnut brown and charcoal black threads. As she suspected it was just the right size to conceal the root cellar door but she could easily pull it back in an emergency. There were many emergencies she needed to prepare for.

Lost in her thoughts, Nadia turned around then jumped in her skin. Tommy Barker stood right in front of her smiling from ear to ear.

"Oh, Tommy, you scared me to death."

"Sorry, Miss Nadia, I have come to help." He lifted his tool box as proof. He leaned over and kissed her cheek. Nadia looked up into his eyes. He was taller than she remembered, or maybe he had grown since his family moved away. Suddenly aware of how close they were standing; Nadia stepped back and took a deep breath. Old familiar feelings crept up again. She refused to dwell on or encourage them.

"I was told you have a blackboard that needs hanging."

"Yes, as a matter of fact I do." Tommy followed her over to where the blackboard sat leaning against the wall. Together they lifted it up off the floor. Doing so exposed an opening in the barn's exterior wall. It was large enough for a child to crawl through. Heavy, four-inch wide plastic strips hung down from the top to keep the elements out. It was a hen door intended for the chickens to have easy access to the small barnyard behind it.

"Tommy, do you think you could build a cabinet to go in front of that opening?"

"I sure can. Just tell me exactly what you want and I'll get right on it. In the meantime let's hang this blackboard."

Nadia and Tommy spent the rest of the afternoon working. They rearranged tables, set up folding chairs and found places for all the supplies. She enjoyed their light festive conversation. Time had regressed. They were back in middle school. It made the work a pleasure.

"Tommy, will you help me with one more thing?"

"Sure, anything for the teacher," His smile warmed her heart. She was so happy to be here; so happy to be a teacher once again. He followed her over to a large metal cabinet that filled the wall to the right of her desk.

"Could you help me take this bottom shelf out?"

"Sure," his eagerness overflowed. "But don't you need it for those books that are on it?"

"No, let's take them out. It's a set of encyclopedias that I want the children to have access to at all times. I'm going to put them on the cabinet you're building me. In the meantime let's stack them over here." They pulled, pushed and heaved all the boxes out of the cabinet.

"That's it I think." Nadia said as she sat back on her heels resting her hands on her hips. She needed an open space large enough for one adult to hide.

"Let's pull that shelf out now." When they did, they exposed a cardboard box on the floor way in the back. Tommy, on all fours, pulled it out and passed it to Nadia. *What could this be?* Packing tape tightly secured all the edges. Tommy used his pocket knife to slit it open.

"Be careful, don't cut the contents." When she opened the box she couldn't believe her find; a perfectly folded, wrapped in plastic, American flag! A note written in big bold green letters sat on top demanding their attention. Nadia read it out loud. "For whatever is born of God overcomes the world; and this is the victory that has overcome the world – our faith."[vii]

Nadia flung her arms around the flag, drew it to her chest and closed her eyes. She held tight and clung to what it represented; freedom, victory, honor and truth. The American flag; she never imagined she would ever see one again.

She remembered the first time she experienced its importance at her pre-school graduation. She stood straight and tall next to the flag at the front of the assembly hall beaming from ear to ear. Her right hand pressed her heart as she led her classmates in the Pledge of Allegiance. Her parents were in the audience. They had fled from Russia so that Nadia could be born an American citizen. Her father could not disguise his pride. Tears crept down his cheeks. He had never cried in her presence before ... or since.

Tommy got back down on his knees and checked the bottom of the cabinet for a pole. Sure enough, all the way in the back a pole and a stand hid in the shadow. He pulled them out and put them together. Nadia carefully unfolded the precious flag. She fought back tears. She would always be an American citizen no matter what Sixtus III said.

Together she and Tommy reverently hung the flag and placed it in the corner. Nadia put her hand to her heart and said the words that she no longer could legally teach her students.

"I pledge allegiance to the flag of the United States of America." Tommy squared his shoulders, pressed his hand to his heart and joined her. "...And to the republic, for which it stands, one nation, under God, indivisible with liberty and justice for all."

They stood in silence not moving, not taking their eyes off the long lost symbol of their beloved nation, heartlessly torn from its roots.

<>
THROUGH THE PERILIST FIGHT

PART THREE:

The Getaway

Chapter Thirty-Six

Day 362

A ferocious wind encircled Jeremiah Walker like a tornado. The force ripped at his body. Then he rose above the wind and saw all the nations below him. The Lord, enraged against the nations, stormed against their armies. God utterly destroyed them and lead them to slaughter.

Using all his strength Walker dragged himself closer to the ground. Dead bodies littered the stark and bloody land. Blood even flowed from the mountains. There were too many to bury and the stench of rotten flesh overwhelmed him. He found no one alive to help him.

Suddenly the sky began to melt away and disappear. Burning ash covered the earth – debris from fallen stars. Walker wept. He could not stop the destruction.

Someone in the distance shook him. "Doc, Doc, wake up, wake up, Doc!"

Walker awoke unashamed of his tears. "The world is coming to an end," he groaned. "The world is coming to an end."

xxx

Todd pulled a NY Giants T-shirt over his head, combed his hair and bounded down the stairs eager to start another day. He had decided that Thanksgiving was the day that he and Nadia should get married. Yesterday he cleared the matter with the minister. Today he would announce his intentions to Nadia and the rest of the world.

He stopped short when he reached the kitchen. Nadia and Barker sat at the kitchen table chatting over coffee. His mood immediately changed.

"Good morning," he abruptly interrupted their conversation.

"Good morning, my love." Nadia answered. "Isn't it a beautiful day?"

"Looks like it might be," he answered with no real hope that it would. "Tom, I could use some help today building a chicken coop. One of the neighbors offered to swap two chickens for a bale of hay." He had baled hay all day yesterday and was glad to have already bartered some of it. Everyone in the Round Lake community jumped at the opportunity to help each other. Survival required it. He walked over to the stove and poured himself a cup of steaming hot coffee.

"Sure, I'd be happy to help. But first I want to walk into town. I want to talk to the owner of that service station. You know the one on the corner of Main Street. It has a minimart attached. I'm hoping they'll hire me in exchange for gasoline and other supplies."

"That sounds like a terrific idea," Nadia was too chipper.

"Well let me scoot out of here. I'll be back in about an hour."

"Bye and good luck!" Nadia said.

Why does she care? Todd mustered up a weak smile and waved him away.

"You two certainly got an early start together today."

"We didn't actually start together." She slowly added, "What are you saying, Todd?"

"I'm saying I got up this morning wanting to share something really great with my fiancée and I see her already chit-chatting over breakfast with a total stranger."

"Tommy isn't a total stranger and we just happened to come into the kitchen at the same time. What is the matter with you, Todd?"

"I don't know. I see you with that guy and it makes me crazy."

Nadia sat on his lap and put her arms around his neck. "Todd Philips, you are down-right silly. Now give me a kiss and let's start the morning over." Her kiss was sweet. He melted under her touch but still questioned Barker's intentions.

"Now what was it that you wanted to tell me?" He had lost his enthusiasm for everything.

"Let's discuss it later. Right now I want to eat and then start plowing the upper field. I think it might not be too late to plant some peas. I also want to get some garlic in the ground for next year."

"That's a great idea. I have some last minute things to get together before the dedication ceremony at the school tonight. Then I want to check out what your grandparents stored in the attic. I have a feeling there may be lots up there we can use or else share with the neighbors."

"It sounds like a plan. How about we meet back here for lunch?"

"Ok, my darling." She kissed him and left. He continued to stew.

Barker and Todd had been working on the chicken coop for about thirty minutes in silence. Barker knew Todd had something serious on his mind, something that had been eating at him all morning. He relaxed when Todd finally spoke. "You were in the barn all afternoon yesterday with Nadia. Did you get a lot done?"

Barker smiled, "Yes, I hung the blackboard for her and then helped her move all the tables and chairs around. Boy, when that woman knows what she wants there's no stopping her."

"So you think you know what she wants?" Barker stopped stapling wire to wood beams, stood erect, surprised by this attack from a man he genuinely admired.

"I know she wants you, if that's what you mean."

"And just how do you know that? Did you discuss it with her?" Todd stood up also, legs wide apart, his fist clench around a hammer.

"No, she has never talked to me about her relationship with you. But I can see how she looks at you. Even a dummy like me can recognize love when I see it."

"So does this mean you are not pursuing her?" Todd leaned into him. Barker stepped back but looked Todd square in the face. He thought of yesterday in the barn with Nadia. He had cherished every moment even though he knew she didn't share his feelings. Barker constantly got flustered around women and blurted out stupid things at inappropriate times. Except around Nadia. Even when they were kids she had a look in her eyes and a sparkle in her smile that made him feel as if he were someone special. When he talked to her the butterflies in his stomach disappeared. He sprouted wings instead and flew. He would always love her even if only from afar. The answer he gave Todd came directly from his breaking heart.

"I have loved Nadia every single day of my life for as long as I can remember. But she has clearly chosen you, Todd." Barker stopped himself from completing his thoughts out loud. *And because I love her, I love you, because you are the one who will protect her, provide for her and love her the way I never can.*

A moment passed. "Well, Tom, under the circumstances I would like you to move out of the main house. The guest cottage by the lake is empty. I am sure you will be quite comfortable there."

Chapter Thirty-Seven

In the fifth dimension Jesus waited patiently. His perfect will regarding two of His friends was about to come full circle. "Just a little while longer, My sweet apple blossom, then I will take your hand and bring you home."

✗✗✗

Rachel, Kirk's aunt, sat cuddled up on her sofa in the tan fleece blanket that her sister had given her many years before. Fever scorched her inside but constant chills made her outside shiver. Her chest ached as she coughed into a clean towel. She didn't need to look at it. She knew it was full of blood.

Her hungry stomach began to growl but she tried to ignore it. She had eaten the last piece of bread this morning and planned to save that last can of beans for dinner. The New Testament Dr. Walker had given her, was propped open on her lap to the second last page. She began reading silently with a smile in her heart, "Listen, says Jesus. I am coming soon! Happy are those who obey the prophetic words of this book."[viii]

"I am ready for you, Jesus!" She whispered.

The doorbell interrupted her peaceful thoughts. Exerting extreme effort she got up and made her way to the door. Visitors came rarely, especially since her sister died.

"Who is it?" She called weakly.

"Jordan Crane," the man's voice proclaimed. "I work down at Docker's. I'm looking for Kirk McCartney. Does he live here?" Rachel rose on her tiptoes and looked through the peep hole. It was that nice young man who worked at the pharmacy around the corner.

"Yes, Kirk lives here but he isn't home now."

"May I come in? I'd like to talk to you."

"Just a minute." Rachel decided it might not be a bad idea to speak to the man. He might know where the boy had gone." She unlocked the door and opened it wide.

"Thanks, Ms. Berk. Doc Walker told me you were Kirk's aunt."

"That's right. Do you know where Kirk is?"

"No, I was hoping you might be able to tell me that. I haven't seen him around the past few days and I thought maybe he was sick or something." His short cropped hair hid beneath a Yankee cap. Kirk used to have a cap like that. She wondered why he never wore it any more … Her mind drifted.

The boy named Jordan put his hands in his pockets. *Should I invite him in?* He looked like he had no intentions of coming any closer. Probably better if he didn't. She might be contagious.

"Kirk is a real good kid. He used to come into Mr. Docker's pharmacy every day but it's been almost a week since I've seen him."

Why does he look so worried? She tried to reassure him and herself, "Kirk hasn't been home lately but I haven't been well ... He's probably been in and out while I've been asleep ... The last time I saw him was several nights ago when Doctor Walker brought me my medication ... Kirk left with him." She had a new thought, "Maybe he's living with Doctor Walker. He's such a nice man that Doctor Walker."

"Well, okay, I'll be going then." His shoulders slumped and his hand dug deeper into his pants. "If you see Kirk, tell him I was looking for him." Clearly the information she had given this young man hadn't put him at ease. She knew what would.

"Wait just one minute, I have something for you, Doctor Walker gave it to me but I won't need it any longer and I am sure he would want you to have it." She rambled and found it hard to think.

Rachel clutched her sweater to her neck. Her worn quilted slippers shuffled over to the sofa where she left the precious little Bible. She picked it up and held it to her heart. *God bless Doctor Walker wherever he is.* She returned to the young man. He fidgeted back and forth in the doorway.

"Doctor Walker told me to start right here." She showed him the place. She was lucid again. "But I read through the whole book twice. God spoke directly to me you know. You've got to read it," she commanded with conviction. "He'll speak to you too." The boy named Jordan jammed the book in his back pocket and left.

"Doctor Walker was right." Rachel said as she closed the door, "All things do work for good." She didn't bother to lock up. And she never ate that last can of beans. Twenty minutes after she passed the Bible to Jordan Crane, that nice young man who worked at the pharmacy, Rachel Berk died. She was cuddled up on the sofa with a warm smile in her heart, wrapped in the tan fleece blanket that her sister had given her many years before.

Chapter Thirty-Eight

Megan's angel Hakah hovered over her. He was glad the week was over. She was beginning to listen to him and he was proud of her. He had a feeling her biggest challenge was yet to come.

xxx

Megan let herself into Alex's apartment with the key Nadia had given her. The reality of her encounter yesterday with the most powerful man in the world still haunted her. She had repeatedly washed her hands trying to remove the filth. Like last night, she headed straight for the shower. Megan dropped her head down as the water drenched her body. *What is the matter with me? Can't I have a normal relationship with a normal man? Maybe there aren't any normal men out there. Or maybe that is normal for men. Never again – never ever again will I trust a man.*

Alex had just pulled out some leftovers when Megan, without a word, entered the apartment. He heard the shower running and wondered if she had had dinner yet. He waited to eat until the shower stopped and she emerged from Nadia's room, pristine. Her jeans fit her like a glove. She wore a red and white plaid blouse unbuttoned at the top, which exposed the nape of her long slender neck. She had white towel wrapped turban style around her head. Next to her beautiful ivory skin it made her look like an alabaster statue of a goddess. Even with no makeup she was gorgeous. He had to catch his breath before he could speak.

"So, how was your day?" He offered, sensing a lingering steam. Last night she returned from the City boiling. She stormed into the apartment, slammed every door and huffed, without a word, to her room where she crashed around all night. Tonight he hoped to spend a little quiet time with her. Maybe even go for ice-cream later. "This evening on the 5:00 news I caught your final conference day report. You were awesome!"

"I'd rather not talk about it." She remarked sharply. "Have you heard from Nadia?"

"I got an e-mail from our contact at the lake. He is the only one in town that has a computer, the only one with a computer that we can trust, that is. We code every correspondence otherwise your big friend in high places would discover their little haven."

"Sixtus is not my friend," she bit off his head. "Please, don't ever say that again."

"Well... sure... sorry." He couldn't understand her sudden change in attitude about the man she adoringly talked about only two days ago. But he wasn't going to argue with her about that one.

"It's okay. I've had a rough day," she softened.

"So, anyway, Nadia and Todd got there safely and Nadia is already setting up her school. The town's people have apparently been expecting her for a long time. They are anxious for her to start teaching."

"That's really great. So what's the next step?"

"What do you mean?"

"I mean when are you going to go and join her?"

"Not me. I still have so much work to do here. Besides, I don't really fit in there."

"Here we are a couple of misfits."

Her lips surrendered a brief smile so he eagerly returned it. Silently they sat side by side and ate the delicious meal leftover from Nadia's last night home. That night seemed so long ago...

"Are you going to get it or are you still in la la land?" The doorbell rang.

"Oh I guess I didn't hear it the first time." He excused himself and went to the front door. "Who is it?" He asked through the intercom.

"We are looking for a butterfly." A timid masculine voice answered. Immediately Alex pressed the buzzer. Megan dropped the towel from around her head and pulled her hair back into a ponytail securing it with the elastic hair tie she had around her wrist. Many feet shuffled on the stairway and Alex opened his door. Two women, a man and six children stood before him. He saw fear mixed with hope in their eyes.

"Come in," he invited quietly.

Chapter Thirty-Nine

Jesus quietly said, "Jeremiah, though you are tired and worn out I will give you power and might. I know even the boy is exhausted and tempted to give up. Wait for Me and I will renew your strength. You will mount up with wings like eagles; you will run and not tire. You will walk and not faint."

xxx

Tonight Walker hoped they would have safe passage over the river. There must be a checkpoint up ahead but in the darkness, they might be able to sneak past, undetected. *Oh, Lord you have been with us this far. Please, keep us safe tonight.*

The road up the mountain was narrow and winding. It was carved out of cliffs on the right side and then dropped off sharply on the left. They kept as close to the outside of the guardrail as possible. Walker caught Kirk by the shirttail once when he stepped on some loose rocks and almost slipped down over the edge.

The trek up the mountain had drained Walker's energy and weakened his legs. He needed some nourishment and, though Kirk never complained, Walker knew he needed to rest too. They stopped at an overlook to eat the last of their provisions and to wait for the sun to set. The higher elevation reduced the air temperature. It sent a refreshing breeze over the trees and several scarlet leaves fluttered down on the stone wall where Walker and Kirk sat.

Bear Mountain loomed high and majestic, covered by trees in the distance. It stretched north and south for miles on the other side of the Hudson River which flowed in the valley below them. The trees mesmerized Walker. They were beginning to surrender their green summer foliage to autumn's magnificent hues. Fiery oranges, crimson reds and golden yellows tipped the tallest branches. They transported Walker into a different world. Together he and the boy were starting a new life. Kirk seemed to feel the same way.

"Wow, what's that?"

Walker looked up into the sky to where the boy pointed. In the distance, two bald eagles circled in the air. They soared high above the trees on a small island in the center of the river. Each was approximately thirty inches long with a wingspan of five or six feet. Walker suspected they were only about five years old. Suddenly the right talon of one locked with the left talon of the other and they began spinning round and round like a cartwheel flying with increasing speed straight toward the earth below.

"Are they going to kill each other?"

"No, they are actually courting each other. Just before they hit the ground they will fly apart."

"Oh my gosh! That is totally amazing."

"Yes, it is amazing. Those are bald eagles. They are pledging their absolute commitment to each other, expressing that they are willing to die one for the other. It's a true act of dedication and loyalty." Then Walker noticed black feathers on the tops of their spiraling heads. The reality of what these birds were slowly sank in. The scene became even more spectacular!

"But look, Kirk, at their heads. Scientist genetically altered some eagles several years ago to grow slightly larger with each generation. The mutant birds didn't reproduce in captivity so they were released into the wild. These must be their offspring!"

Suddenly they were distracted from this mesmerizing sight. Recklessly leaves rustled on a twelve-foot wide precipice about fifteen feet below. Walker looked down to see a pit-bull crawling on its belly toward the shelter of a bending tree. Its head and left shoulder dripped with blood. Immediately Kirk positioned himself to drop down over the edge of the wall.

"Wait," Walker cautioned. "Let's try to find safer way." At the other end of the overlook the wall decreased to only about two feet. They jumped over the wall and carefully made their way to the injured animal. Walker slipped three times in the process but the boy scrambled down with renewed energy and youthful agility.

"Wait for me!" Walker warned. When he finally reached level ground Walker approached the dog with slow guarded steps, palms up.

"Take it easy, boy, it's alright." His steadied his voice and spoke softly. You never knew what to expect from an injured animal. His gaze never veered.

"Kirk, just stay back until I check him out." The dog remained docile as Walker looked him over. His ear hung by just a corner and his back was severely lacerated by teeth bites in several places. The worst one exposed the bone.

"Bring me my backpack, Kirk." The boy obeyed immediately. He ascended to the top almost as quickly as he came down and retrieved the backpack as ordered.

"Can we keep him, Doc?"

"Let's see if we can patch him up first." The dog lay patiently while the doctor worked his craft. He cleaned the wounds and glued the skin together wherever possible. When Walker finished he had little hope that the ear would remain intact. The dog was so mauled he doubted he would survive the night but at least the wounds were clean now. If he had the will to live he just might make it.

"So, can we keep him?'

"I don't know, Champ. He's in pretty bad shape. He looks like he hasn't eaten in a while and we only have one bag of trail mix left."

"He can have my share. I don't like trail mix much anyway." He couldn't resist the dog's forlorn eyes let alone the boy's pleading ones.

"Well, okay. Go get him some fresh water dripping off that cliff." He pointed to a seeping crevice that he noticed when they first arrived at the overlook. Kirk took the tin cup from Walker's backpack and ran across the road. He returned in five minutes, his cup full. The boy sat on the ground in front of the pitiful dog, carefully poured the water into his cupped hand. The whole time Kirk encouraged him, "That's a good boy, keep drinking. Doc says you're going to be alright and Doc knows what he's talking about."

Chapter Forty

Ten angels ushered the Rogues into Alex's apartment. No demons had followed them to this safe place. They had been fighting off demons for two days and they would not give up now. Their mortals were almost free. They were met by their old friend Jonathan.

Alex's angel Jonathan greeted them. "Welcome. You have arrived at an unfortunate time. Kasha is not here. He has fled with his mortal Nadia."

"Jonathan, will your man take up the cross?"

"I will convince him. This is Hakah. His charge is here too."

The ten angels briefly bowed their heads in recognition of the esteemed angel in their presence. Together they made an impressive team.

xxx

"Please, Mr. Lichtenstein, at least take the children." Desperation blanketed the man's face. He looked at his wife. "We can make the journey on foot but the children cannot."

"Yes," the other woman added. "We escaped arrest yesterday and we've been walking ever since. The children are tired and can't walk any farther. They must get away tonight."

"I can hide all six children in the van without a problem," Alex quickly agreed. Megan ached with compassion for these despairing people, but anyone who hid or otherwise helped Rogues could be arrested. She admired Alex who so unselfishly put himself at risk for complete strangers. She could never do it.

Suddenly, the doorbell rang again. All eyes shifted to Alex. Alex moved to the door and pressed the intercom.

"Who is it?"

"Officer Sandler," was the curt response. Everyone except Alex froze.

"Just a minute, please." Alex calmly answered. He crouched down in front of the children and said with great enthusiasm, "We are going to play a little game now. It's a very exciting game in which you are brave princess warriors out in the jungle. You are protecting all the elves in the kingdom by being very quiet. Don't say a word, or make a sound. Now hurry up little princesses and follow this beautiful queen." He indicated Megan who lingered in the corner trying to be as invisible as possible. Then he handed Megan the keys to Herb's van.

"I can't do this," Megan protested, her eyes pleadingly locked onto his.

"Yes, you can. You must. They have no other choice."

"But I don't know how to get to the farm."

"Just say 'Monroe' into the GPS. When you arrive someone will meet you there and take you to the farm." Alex herded them like little chicks to the back door. "Go quickly. I will keep the cop here as long as I can."

Megan followed the others quietly down the back steps. As she closed the outside door she heard voices in the apartment above. Herb's truck was parked next to the back door. Megan pressed the keys into the hand of the man.

"Here, you take them. I can't."

"No, that's impossible. When I get to the check point at Bear Mountain they won't let me pass. We will all be arrested."

Megan covered her face momentarily with her hands. "All right, get them into the van. There are built-in crates along each side in the back." Megan unlocked the rear doors and climbed in to help the girls hide.

The children clung to their parents and hugged them one last time. The oldest blue-eyed girl opened the left metal cabinet. She picked up her pint-sized sister, and then lowered her inside along with her backpack. She then took her other sister's hand, helped her climb in and then got in herself crouching down between them. The youngest started to speak when the oldest put her finger to her lips, winked her eye and noiselessly mouthed, "Shhhh."

Megan helped three brown-eyed sisters into an identical bin on the opposite side. She then closed both lids and put several empty baskets on top. When she climbed into the driver's seat the man waited outside her window. "Thank you so much and God be with you." She forced a weak smile. *He sure better be.*

Chapter Forty-One

In the seventh dimension, The Ancient of Days sat on His throne delighted by the sweet aroma of Megan's sacrifice.

In the sixth dimension, the Archangel Michael heard the man's command and elicited a host of angels to accompany Megan on her trip to the mountains. Hakah, Megan's angel, flew ahead of her and spotted the angel Justin hovering over his mortal Jeremiah Walker.

"Hello, comrade," Hakah greeted him.

"Does it go well with you, Hakah?"

"Yes, so well that I had to come and thank you for the prayer your mortal offered up for my charge. It came at a desperately needed point."

"Jeremiah Walker is faithful to pray for many mortals. What is the name of yours?"

"Megan Cameron Montgomery – as we speak she is on the road transporting six "unmarked" children to the safe haven."

"In that case, I would like to solicit your help." Justin, the mighty warrior, saw an easy way out of his dilemma.

"I would consider it an honor and a privilege."

"Do you see that man and boy down there? I need to get them safely over that bridge ahead. Maybe your mortal could be of some assistance."

"I think we could manage that." Hakah agreed readily. A glass bottle could be left in a strategic location.

xxx

At the overlook, Walker leaned his hips against the four-foot wall. He watched Kirk feed the pit-bull their last package of trail mix. The brindle dog had a massive head, a strong muscular body and short legs. Walker had discovered multiple scars on his young frame. He must have had had many previous encounters with hostile animals. The boy had been so careful and gentle when he carried the dog up the embankment. *Everyone needs a purpose in life. The responsibility of a pet is the perfect choice, the right decision.* Walker tried to convince himself that the dog would be an asset. He had considered abandoning the animal but thought better of it. What would that teach the boy; abandon those that are no longer useful or productive?

The pit-bull lay still now except for the thumping of his long tan tail on the ground. *I'm beaten and torn apart too, fella.* He patted the dog's head. Walker could empathize completely, but if he had a tail, it probably wouldn't be wagging. *Lord, I need to see your glory.*

Walker turned back around to face the river. The sun, a ball of molten gold radiated soft butter-yellow beams of light which lined the sky as it dropped down behind the mountains. Scarlet mixed with pale cherry-red tumbled over and around thick purple-blue clouds. It painted a glorious picture across an azure canvas. His muscles relaxed. It calmed him in a way no words could describe. Walker remembered the last sunset he had enjoyed in his beloved Samantha's arms. This one, not filtered through smog, was far more beautiful. But without Sam it was far less enjoyable ... until the Lord spoke.

"My son Jeremiah, focus on the living for in the living there is hope. A lion may be strong and mighty, a powerful force with which to reckon. But a living dog is greater than a dead lion no matter what the size. One day soon I will swallow up death forever. I will wipe away tears from all faces. But tonight I wipe away your internal tears forever." The gentle passionate inner voice whispered, "I love you, I love you," until in the stillness quiet reigned.

The warmth of Samantha's arms embraced him. He missed her more than he ever thought possible. He closed his eyes and saw her. She walked steadily away from him with light gay steps; a gait he clearly recognized. In the distance she lingered, turning to see him once more and then she disappeared forever into the clouds.

The colors slowly melted away but something much better replaced their glorious presence – peace and security. The sunset had been a tender love letter from the Lord signed by Sam. It compassionately sealed a closed chapter. He would cherish it forever.

Revitalized, Walker turned again to the boy and his dog. The dog appeared renewed as well for he and the boy played kick the can with an empty beer bottle. Kirk kicked the bottle back and forth like a soccer ball as the pit-bull tried to bite the untied laces of his partner's shoes.

"So, have you thought about a name for him yet?" Walker asked.

Kirk stopped dead in his tracks. The glass bottle continued to roll into the middle of the driveway.

"Yeah," he said as he sauntered over to the wall where Walker stood, "Neeko."

"Neeko," Walker thought about it for a moment. "That sounds like a good name for a dog. I'm sure he will like it."

"That *is* his name," Kirk said with confidence. "He whispered it to me."

Walker smiled at the boy and gave him a reassuring pat on his back. He could tell they were becoming very good friends.

The wind accelerated. Chilly mountain air gusted fallen leaves around them.

In the distance several hungry wolves howled.

Walker rolled down his sleeves.

Chapter Forty-Two

The room was filled with guardian angels. Each was confident. Their mortals were safe. Few demons dared to visit the Round Lake Community. When they did they were asking for punishment.

xxx

Nadia spoke to the townspeople about the program that she had developed for their children. When she finished, she asked if the parents had any questions. A hand went up in the back row.

"Yes, Carl."

"We've heard about the academics you plan to introduce to our children but what are your views about the return of Christ? Isn't it more important to increase their spiritual growth than their mental growth?" A ripple of agreement went throughout the crowd. Nadia welcomed the opportunity to share her opinion about that very topic. She took only a moment to collect her thoughts and then looked straight at her anxious audience and began.

"Dear friends, concerning the coming of our Lord Jesus Christ and our going together to be with Him, don't be confused or worried about what is going to happen. The antichrist has come with the power of Satan. He is a man of utter destruction. He exalts himself above all that is worshiped. He sits as god in the temple of God, claiming to be God. Don't you remember that the Bible told you these things would come?"

"So do you think Sixtus is the antichrist?" A woman in the front blurted out.

"Yes, I believe he is. All around us we see his lawlessness at work; but only until the Lord restrains him. God will consume and ultimately destroy Sixtus when He comes again for the final battle. Satan, with all his power, signs and lies will perish. God will send a strong delusion to all those who do not believe the truth, the truth that would save them if they had chosen to believe it.

"But remember, from the beginning God chose you and your families for salvation through belief in the truth. He called you because He knew you would give the glory to our Lord Jesus Christ. He alone deserves all the glory. Therefore, stand firm and hold onto your belief in Christ. Our God the Father has loved us and has given us hope through grace. Be comforted knowing that the Lord is faithful. He will guard you from Satan and his horrible schemes.

"I will be starting an adult Bible study next Tuesday evening at seven o'clock for anyone who wants to discuss it further. I would like to study the scriptures with you so that we can all become stronger. These are perilous times. We need to give God the glory because He is completely in control."

A father jumped up, shook his fist and shouted out to Nadia. "So what should we do? Just sit around and let Sixtus devour our families?"

"There are many Rogues who are defending their homes with guns and lethal weapons." Fire flamed through her veins. "But taking thing into our own hands ... how would God be glorified in that? I urge you to listen to the Holy Spirit. Remember, the Lord is our protector and shield." Her fist punched the air. "Like a strong steel barrier He defends us and keeps us safe. If we faithfully call on Him He will save us from our enemies. I thank God who gives us victory through our Lord Jesus Christ." She heard her voice escalate. Her open palm struck her chest. "Therefore, hold firm to your ideals, always do the work of the Lord, knowing that your daily tasks are not futile." The man sat back down, his anger dispelled.

She paused and searched their gaunt accepting faces. She took back control of her voice and softened. "Wisdom is better than strength, it is better than the weapons you carry. So, be careful how you live. Be wise. Every opportunity you have to do what is good do it, because these are evil times. We have no way to protect ourselves against Sixtus' army. We don't really know what to do except to look to God. The battle is not ours but God's!" Many heads nodded in agreement. She had convinced them.

"Remember how frightened Elisha's servant was when he saw all the troops, horses and chariots surrounding them? And how relieved he was when God showed him how the angels outnumbered the enemy? Have faith. We have the same number of angels around us." She paused for a while to let this fact sink in. Then she added.

"You must work well with your non-Christian neighbors and do what you can to build them up. Jesus didn't come to please Himself. But He suffered insults and pain from those who were against Him. So let's be a witness of Christ's love in the world. That will glorify Him."

"Amen," came from someone in the back row.

"The most important thing you can do is to find out what the Lord's will is for your life. That is what I am always telling my students. God has a purpose for each one of us and it is our responsibility to find out what that purpose is." The room fell quiet.

"Has God removed His hand from our nation?" A woman called out. Nadia exchanged glances with Todd. They had expressed the same sentiment to each other that morning.

"We must continue to pray. Revival is still possible." Nadia counseled.

After everyone left the schoolhouse Todd helped her put the chairs back. He looked at her with the proudest eyes she had ever seen.

"I love you, Nadia, my inspiring teacher."

"Whatever inspiration I have comes from God." She playfully poked his firm abdomen.

"You're an angel." He said and wrapped both arms around her.

Twenty minutes after Megan drove away with the children, Officer Sandler headed down Alex's front steps and Alex ascended up the attic steps, two at a time, to his bedroom. He immediately sat at his computer and emailed the children's arrival. His coded note read '6 BTL @ 9.5' (Six butterflies to land at nine-thirty).

Time ticked by.

No reply. *Where is he?*

Chapter Forty-Three

Hakah, Megan's guardian angel returned to her side. All had gone well. The glass bottle lay in the targeted spot. Now she must listen to him. Would she? That question forever loomed in the air.

xxx

Alex tried sending the message again, '6 BTA @ 9.5'. Still no response. *Where is everyone? Megan and the children should be arriving soon.*

Just before Megan had reached the foot of the mountain the sun went down. Complete darkness curtained around her. Then she saw what appeared to be an overlook on the left side of the road. Something told her to turn into it. She jerked the wheel and drove onto the gravel.

There was a slight pop under her left rear tire. She thought nothing of it.

I can't believe I'm doing this. I must be truly crazy. The fear that someone might spot the children and get suspicious had kept her driving. She wasn't sure how much farther she had to go before the bridge came up but she need to see if the girls were all right. She unhooked her seatbelt and climbed over the console to the cargo area. They had been so good and so quiet. Had they suffocated?

When she opened the lids, she saw that all were asleep except for the oldest. How precious they all were. Who in their right mind would ever want to hurt these little ones?

"What's your name?"

"Kaylie," the little girl answered. "My sisters are Emma and Madyson."

"Would you like to come up and sit with me, Kaylie?"

"Sure if you think it's okay."

"I'm sure it will be fine. When we get a little closer to the bridge you can climb in with your sisters again."

"Great, I've never ridden up front in a van before!"

"Well I'll let you in on a little secret. I've never driven a van before." *And I have also never hidden Rogues before!* They both fastened their seatbelts and Megan pulled out onto the road again. She drove around a sharp curve to the right and then one to the left. Suddenly, her high beams caught three silhouettes walking on the left side of the guardrail; a man, a boy and a dog. *Why are they walking in the dark on this dangerous road? They must be crazier than I am.*

Slowly she realized something was wrong.

She began to fight the wheel. The steering was sluggish.

She drove around the next bend, checked her rearview mirror then pulled onto the shoulder. Cursing up a storm she got out to check the tires.

"Looks like you have a flat." A calm male voice came up to the left back wheel. Megan whirled around and saw the man, boy and dog that she had just passed.

"Yes," she responded looking around as if she could find somewhere to escape. Her mind raced to Kaylie sitting on the front seat. "I must have run over something when I stopped at the overlook back there."

"Do you have a jack?" He asked politely.

"How the hell do I know?" Megan remarked in frustration. She saw the shocked look on the man's face and caught herself.

"I'm sorry it's been a long day." She rubbed her forehead and her ponytail brushed the side of her face. When she looked up again the man's eyes were locked on her. She saw something familiar. *I have seen those eyes before.*

"It's probably under the floor board in the back. Can you open it for me and I'll take a look."

"Um ... just a moment ... the keys ... are in the car." She went back to the front seat. What should she do? She clearly needed the man's help but what about the children? She motioned for Kaylie to crouch down on the floor. She grabbed the keys and went back. When she opened the rear door one of the girls woke up and began to cry. "Mommy," she called and pushed the bin open. Two more heads popped up in succession. Megan looked straight into the man's eyes again, fear gripped her.

"Are you smuggling children in your van or have they just been playing hide and seek?" He had a twinkle in his eye and a smile on his face. Megan finally recognized the deliriously heart melting taxi cab driver's eyes. She relaxed slightly. She knew he was probably a Rogue now too.

As he squatted next to the tire she recognized the wide shoulders and the hair pulled back in a ponytail. It didn't take him long to finish. Finally he put the jack away while she got the girls settled again into their hiding places.

"May we have a lift?"

"I'm not really sure where I am going but I was told it is safe for these children." Megan shared the only information she had. She couldn't say no to the guy, right? But what did she know about him? He could be a serial killer or something worse. She nodded and the three travelers climbed into the van.

"We were told about a safe place for Rogues in a community around a big lake; Round Lake in fact, not far from the other side of the river. It must be the same place."

She started the van and slowly pulled back onto the road. They rode for a short while then came up to a traffic light.

"Turn left in 200 feet ... Turn left," the voice on the navigational system commanded. Megan stopped at the red light. Turning left would take them over the bridge. On the other side the highly anticipated check point waited.

"Do you want me to get out?" Walker volunteered.

"Absolutely not. I can't do this alone."

"Kirk, put one of the girls in the left crate and you climb into the right." Immediately the boy opened both bins and Kaylie jumped out. "Remember our game," she whispered to the rest of the girls as she squatted down next to the youngest on the other side and hugged her tightly. Kirk climbed in with Kaylie's sisters then closed the lid behind him.

When everyone resettled and the light changed to green for the second time Megan made the left turn and drove at twenty-five miles an hour over Bear Mountain Bridge. Just before reaching the check point Megan pulled the elastic tie-back from around her ponytail. As her hair fell down around her shoulders she heard Walker take a deep breath. He dropped his head back on his seat and he closed his eyes. She focused on the daunting check point ahead thankful he could not observe her next course of action. She unbuttoned the second button on her blouse exposing a little cleavage.

When she pulled up to the booth she did exactly what she did best.

Charm and sensuality purred through her voice, "Good evening officer. It's a beautiful night isn't it?" The skinny short attendant obviously picked up on her vibes.

"More than the night is beautiful," he flirted back. "May I see your ID, please?" Quickly Megan reached her right arm through the open window causing her blouse to bulge in full sight of the gawking man. After he scanned her wrist, he took hold of her arm. He caressed it with his long jagged fingernails. Megan was repulsed but she didn't jerk away. Slowly she retracted it and the guard followed, stepping close to the van.

"Who is that?" He asked shining a flashlight onto Walker's face which remained frozen; his eyes still closed. Megan lowered her voice trying to suppress the revulsion of the guard's decayed breath.

"That's my boyfriend. I'm taking him home and if you don't disturb him I can be back in about a half an hour to continue our conversation." The man lowered the flashlight so that the beam landed directly onto Megan's chest and the exposed white lace. His hand began to slip through the open window towards her.

Megan heard a whimper from one of the children. The sound reverberated in her head. Had the guard heard it too? She glanced in the rear view mirror. One of the bins began to open.

She froze.

As if on cue, Neeko leaped from the back, clawing the console. Ears straight up his wild eyes focused on the open window. His bloodcurdling growl threatened through sharp ferociously clenched teeth. Gums bared. The guard jump back three feet, lost his balance and drop the flashlight.

Shaken by the frothing mouth next to her ear, Megan controlled her voice. "That's my boyfriend's dog. He doesn't like strangers. I'll be back soon." With a smile and a wink Megan pulled away from the checkpoint. She clutched the wheel to control her trembling. Adrenaline flushed every ounce of strength from her body but she kept driving.

"You sure are one brave lady," Walker said respectfully.

"The scumbag, I should have let your dog rip off his hand."

"Thanks for what you did. Kirk and I are eternally grateful."

"That's payback for changing my tire. Don't expect any more favors." It came out harsh. She didn't care.

"Would you like me to drive for a while?" Walker offered. Megan pulled the van to the side of the road rested her head onto the steering wheel. Sobs poured forth like a raging river.

"I don't know what I am doing here. I just can't do it any longer."

Walker got out of the van and before she knew it appeared on the driver's side. Megan opened her door and slipped onto the pavement. Her legs hardly supported her so she leaned her back against the van. She shook uncontrollably, crushed by her new unwelcomed responsibility.

"You're my hero and I don't even know your name." He spoke from the darkness.

"Megan, Megan Montgomery." Exhausted, she mustered up a weak smile. *Is this what it feels like to be a hero?*

"Well, Ms. Montgomery, it's time you take a rest." She willingly walked to the passenger side, relieved to pass him the wheel.

A chorus of crickets cheered her on.

Chapter Forty-Four

"Keep her away from him." Justin, Walker's guardian angel warned Hakah. "He is just beginning to heal. She will only bring him down."

"And what of her condition? She is teetering and needs all the help she can get."

"That's you job. Do it." Justin was not joking.

xxx

"You have arrived at your destination, on the right." Other than the occasional prodding from the GPS, silence controlled the van. Even the ever vigilant dog had taken his cue from the others and had gone to sleep. Walker pulled into the vacant parking lot of the designated restaurant. Whoever would be meeting them for the final part of their journey had not arrived.

Monroe appeared to be a sleepy town. It was only ten-thirty and the streets were already deserted. It was a far cry from the hustle and bustle of New York City. Right now Walker welcomed the calm and serenity. He turned off the engine. He stared at the lovely woman in the seat next to him, the beautiful bewitching woman that reminded him so much of Samantha. *How in the world did she end up on his road to freedom?* Admiration and compassion filled the very fiber of his being. This woman was more than he ever hoped to find in another living being.

He wanted to touch her face and gaze into her weary eyes but he knew this was not the right moment. She didn't need another advance from a stranger. *Advance – is that what I want to do, to make an advance?* The thought crept into his mind accidentally. He continued to gaze at her quiet sleeping face. *Yes, I do want to.* He had vowed to start a new life. Would this lovely creature want that too? He doubted it. Not with him at least. Slowly she opened her eyes and turned to him.

"How long have we been stopped?"

"I just turned the motor off."

Megan's agile body climbed over the console to check on the children. She didn't even disturb the sleeping dog. Walker enjoyed his view. She opened the metal cabinets where the children were hiding. All was quiet. Then she worked her way back to the front seat.

"I'm sorry I was so crazy back there. I really do appreciate all you've done to help me."

"You're the one that did all the work. I was just a passenger. It's funny how the roles got reversed."

"Yeah, so what happened to you? Did your SPIDER Card expire?"

"Yes, the last time you saw me was the last time I was legal. The boy and I have been running ever since."

"Is he your son?"

"No, but that's a long story."

"Well from the looks of things I'm not going anywhere." Walker proceeded to tell her of the events that led up to the moment they met on the road.

"So where is your wife?"

"She died eighteen months ago."

"Oh, I'm sorry. I saw your ring and just supposed she was still in the picture. Normally men don't wear a ring unless they have to."

"Maybe I'm not normal." Back on the overlook, Sam, the love of his life, had said good-bye. His unrelenting connection to her slipped away. *Sam is dead. I am not.* "I mean, we had an unusually fantastic marriage and when Sam died, I was lost. Until now I haven't had reason to remove my wedding band." Did he see hope in her eyes?

Tommy pulled his old gray Ford up on the driver's side of the van. He jumped out then took a step backwards when he saw a stranger sitting behind the wheel. He pushed his shoulders back. Megan stepped out immediately and came to greet him.

"Am I ever glad to see *you!*" She hugged Barker's neck. Embarrassed by this affection, he returned it with a half smile.

"Sorry I'm so late. There was a meeting at the school and then Tyler didn't check his messages until just before he went to bed." He looked sharply at the man and his voice became rough. "Nadia was expecting Alex and six children."

"The children are in the back. Alex got an unexpected visit from a cop just before he was to leave so we went to plan "B" – me." By that time the stranger had slipped out of the van and unlocked the rear door.

"The kids are probably still asleep. Hi, my name is Jeremiah Walker. My friends call me Jerry." Barker relaxed.

"Nice to meet you, Jerry." They shook hands firmly. Barker relaxed even more.

"I'm Tom Barker." When the boy and his dog jumped down to the ground Barker resumed his defensive stance.

"These guys helped me with a flat tire. I owe my life to them."

"I'll take a look at that tire in the morning." Barker said. His eyes never left the injured pit-bull.

Megan gently lifted out a girl and handed her to Jerry and then another to him. They managed to squeeze all of the sleeping girls into the back seat of his old Ford. The boy climbed into the passenger side up front.

"Be back in a jiffy."

Chapter Forty-Five

Hakah sat on the roof of the van, content. Megan had come through the challenge with flying colors. This mortal prayed for her once, maybe he would do it again. It might even be a match made in heaven but he was not counting his chickens ... just yet.

xxx

Megan chatted away easily with Jerry. Relaxed, she laughed with this man as if they had been friends for years. Before she knew it Tommy pulled his car alongside the van.

"The children are settled in at the farm house. Nadia said you should stay at the cottage tonight and then she will work something out better for tomorrow."

Ten minutes later, they drove onto the Philips' property. The gravel driveway crunched beneath the tires for about one quarter mile. An occasional stone pinged the car. Tommy pointed out the buildings. "That's the main house there on the right. And there, on the other side of that field is the new schoolhouse. It used to be the barn before the community converted it."

The car inched along until they arrived at a stone cottage nestled in the trees next to a huge lake. The water shimmered in the moonlight and smoke billowed from the house's chimney; a Hallmark card.

The night air was chilly. Megan rubbed her arms and shivered a little as they walked to the front door. Inside smoldering embers in the fireplace greeted them.

"I stoked the fire earlier this evening. There isn't any other heat in the building so I like to take the chill off the house before I go to bed.

"I'm sorry if we kept you up." Megan apologized.

"Naw, that's okay. I'm happy to do it. There are extra blankets in the closet there and a couple of pillows. Megan, do you want to sleep in my room? The bed isn't made but the sheets are clean."

"No, I think I'll just sit here by the fire for a while. I still need to unwind a bit." Megan hoped Jerry wasn't eager to go to bed either.

"There is an extra bed up in the loft and this couch opens up into one as well."

"Thanks, Tom, you have been very helpful. I think the fire is the best medicine right now." Jerry answered.

Bingo!

"Good night then. Sleep well. If you need anything just let me know. I'll be right through that door on the right and the bathroom is the door next to it. The kitchen is over there if you need a glass of water or anything. Sorry I don't have any hot chocolate but I can make you some coffee if you like."

Jerry glanced at Megan as if to ask her opinion. She shook her head and flashed him her sweetest smile. *He's considerate too.*

"No, that's fine. We are just happy to be in a safe place, and you have already provided that." The men shook hands then Tommy retired for the night.

Megan headed straight for the bathroom. Her bladder was about to burst. At the sink she washed her hands. *Boy I look a wreck.* She ran her fingers through her knotted hair. *Leave it to me. I meet the man of my dreams and I look like a dirty dish towel just run over by a truck.* She splashed water on her face, rubbed her cheeks hard with the towel, and then bit her lips for some color. She pulled her hair back into a ponytail and secured it with the elastic tie around her wrist. *Hopeless. Thank goodness the light out there is low.*

She returned to the living room. Jerry squatted next to the fireplace adding another log. The dog slept next to him on the floor. Even crouched down, she could see that he had a slim waist and a great butt. He stood up and caught her staring at him. In a self-conscious sort of way, he lowered his head and wiped his hands on his pants.

"Excuse me," he said and headed for the bathroom.

Megan stood by the fireplace and warmed her hands. There were three pictures on the mantle; one of an elderly couple, one of a younger couple and one of three children. She recognized Nadia in the last picture. She must have been around eleven with pigtails, no less, holding a ten inch fish on the end of a line. Her face beamed. On the right stood an older boy, probably Todd, who also displayed a prized catch. He was thinner then but still very handsome. In the center posed a lanky boy with no more than sticks for legs. That obviously was Alex; his half smile would always give him away along with his signature shirttail hanging out. Megan chuckled to herself; she had never seen Alex without his hair sticking up, a corner of his shirt untucked, or his collar turned under. He resembled an absentminded professor – in a charming way – with two left feet. But in the picture he stood straight and tall, about two inches taller than Todd, with his right arm draped haphazardly over Nadia's shoulder and his left arm wrapped around his best friend. He appeared to be proud of both these fishermen, as if *they* indeed were *his* trophies. How lucky Nadia was to have two fabulous men her life.

"Should we put some blankets on the floor next to the fire or will you be okay on the couch?" Jerry's warm quiet voice beckoned her from behind.

"I think the couch will be just fine. The fire is almost too hot when you get close." Or was it the heat of the moment that now flushed her cheeks?

They settled in on the sofa, Jerry with his arm on the back and Megan facing him with her long legs tucked up alongside her. She couldn't remember having a more conflicting night. She went from being a shaken, frightened, stoic lawbreaker to being a relaxed, comfortable, secure mound of clay waiting to be molded into whatever this man beside her desired.

Their eyes had been locked all night but she wanted their bodies to be locked as well. Didn't he want that too? Why didn't he touch her the way she so longed to be touched? *He is a real gentleman.* She knew it that night in the cab when he refused her overtures but didn't admit it to herself then. Yes, he was a gentleman in every sense of the word.

Slowly she turned her back to him, pressed herself into the pit of his arm and then stretched her legs out on the couch.

"Is this okay?" she asked sincerely. For the first time in a long time she wanted to relinquish control. She didn't want to play a game. She didn't want to fight a war. She merely wanted to rest and feel secure.

"Sure, as long as you are comfortable," Jerry breathed into her ear. Megan looked at him with renewed respect. *Maybe for a cab driver he isn't so dumb after all.*

Walker and Megan talked into the night. He wanted to take her into his arms and hold her tight but she seemed so fragile and vulnerable. He wanted her to trust him above all else. Trust was one of the most important elements in a relationship. Just maybe he could start this one out right. There was so little time left.

Finally Jerry slipped his arm down around her shoulders. Her head dropped back against his face. The scent of newly washed hair aroused him and he dropped his head back too. In a moment he heard heavy breathing from the stunning woman in his arms. Slowly, as not to disturb her, he kissed her gently on the forehead.

He didn't know what lay ahead but he hoped that it meant spending more time with this beautiful creature.

<>
O'ER THE RAMPARTS WE WATCH WERE SO GALANTLY
STREAMING

Chapter Forty-Six

Day 361

The angel Justin leaned over Walker's sleeping body and whispered, "Jerry, I know you have made plans for the work you want to do for the Lord, and they are good plans. But God is the one that directs your path. Look how He's brought you safely to the farm. Maybe it's here that the miracles will come."

xxx

Walker awoke to the smell of coffee brewing in the kitchen. He looked down at the sleeping angel in his lap, happier than he had been in months. He cradled her body in his arms as he slipped out from under her beautiful blond head. He didn't want to wake her. He took a pillow and blanket from the closet and tried to make her more comfortable. Then he joined Tom in the kitchen.

"Good morning Tom. We really appreciate you coming to pick us up last night. The boy and I left Manhattan six days ago. With several people's help, including you and Megan, the Lord has provided us with safe passage."

"He brought me safely here too with Nadia and Todd. Todd's grandparents started the farm and then passed it on down through his parents to him. There's a whole community of Rogues clustered around the lake and in the neighborhood between here and Monroe. We all work together, share what we can, and barter for the rest."

"It sounds ideal. I am a doctor, so I hope my services will be a contribution to the group."

"Oh wow, can we ever use you!" Tom poured Walker a cup of hot coffee and they both sat down to a bowl of oatmeal.

"Good." Walker smiled, grateful for the hospitality. Then he thought some more and his mood drastically changed. "But I am also extremely limited by the knowledge of man." He had prayed over and over for the power to heal miraculously but had not been granted that gift. When Sam suffered so much he prayed for such a healing but couldn't save her. Again he tried to shake the inadequate feeling. *I must get rid of everything that gets in the way, especially this sin which has such a firm hold on me. There is a race set before me and I know I must run it with determination.*

"However, I must keep my eyes fixed on Jesus. He didn't give up even when He faced death. He could have called His angels to save Him but He didn't. He died that disgraceful death because He knew there was no other way. He knew joy would follow and it did. He now is in His glory seated at the right side of His Father." Tom nodded his agreement.

Walker stirred his cereal. He raised his voice as if to encourage himself. "Sometimes I think of what Jesus went through; how He put up with so much disobedience and hatred from the world!" *I won't let myself become discouraged and give up.* The pep talk seemed to be working. He remembered how the Lord took care of him his last evening in Manhattan and all the hours since. His voice softened as he continued. "For in all my struggles, against every opposition, I haven't had to resist to the point of death like He did. I suppose if it came to that I would."

He thought of the young woman asleep in the other room. *But I will become weak if I don't resist the desires building within me.*

At that moment he heard the front door slam.

Irritated and annoyed, Megan slipped out. She had awoken to the sound of her knight in shining armor's voice coming from the kitchen low, calm and steady. She sat contently listening to their conversation with her knees pulled up under her chin... until what Jerry said sank in. *This man is a Jesus freak. Why did you send me a Jesus freak?*

She ran all the way to the main house. When she arrived, Megan knocked on the front door and the children answered it immediately.

"It's the Forest Queen!" they squealed to each other jumping up and down and encircling her with hugs. She dropped to the floor and relentlessly hugged them all back, clinging ... clinging ... clinging to what?

"How are my little princesses? Did you sleep well?" She fought back tears.

"Yes," Nadia approached with a dishtowel in her hand and her mother's apron around her waist. "They just woke up about five minutes ago. Did you get some sleep?"

"Yes, but not much. I met this wonderful guy on the road who really saved my life."

"Well, come into the kitchen and tell me all about him. I am just getting breakfast ready. You must be starved. I know the children are." Megan couldn't argue with that.

"So tell me all about your wedding. I am so happy for you! You must be ecstatic." Megan needed to plunge herself into this diversion. Talk of Jerry was too confusing and painful.

"Yes, Todd told me he couldn't wait any longer. Being in this house together and not being together is driving him crazy – and me too."

"What do you mean, Nadia?"

"Well, my room is up stairs in the front of the house and Todd is in the den down here. Todd wouldn't have it any other way."

"I can't believe you're engaged and you're not sleeping together!"

"No, we want to save that intimacy for our wedding night."

"You two are unreal. So when is the big day?"

"In two months, Thanksgiving day."

The six little girls had moved to the family room to play, Kirk sat quietly at the table sleepily finishing his breakfast, and Todd had gone outside to work the fields when the back door opened and the pit-bull charged in. The sight of his new pet completely woke up Kirk.

"Neeko," he exclaimed. The dog smothered his face with licks as the boy tightly wrapped his arms around his neck. "I thought Doc ditched you."

"Good morning. Come on in." Nadia welcomed them.

"Hi, Megan, Nadia, this is Jerry Walker. He's a doctor and has come fully prepared to volunteer his services."

"That's fantastic! Megan didn't tell me you were a doctor."

This second surprise almost knocked Megan off her seat.

"That's because I didn't know that little piece of information." Her sarcasm oozed. "Well, you never can tell with these professional types." Megan's voice was ice. Last night she thought that maybe, just maybe she had found a man she could finally trust, one with whom she could finally abandon all and build a life. But that dream had been shattered, dashed to smithereens with the rising of the sun.

"I have to leave." Megan announced abruptly. "Tommy, can you please take me to the van. I need to get back." She stood up, gave Nadia an extra special hug and headed for the door.

"I can take you," Jerry volunteered.

"Whatever," Megan's flippant response elicited a surprised response from everyone, especially Jerry.

"Kirk, stay here with Neeko. I'll be back in a bit." Jerry took Tommy's keys and followed her out.

Chapter Forty-Seven

Hakah looked hard at his counterpart Justin and begged. "She needs your mortal's influence, his strong belief in the Word."

"Yes, but if he engages with her, he treads on thin ice. He must not team with those who do not love the Lord, for what do the people of God have in common with the people of sin? How can light live with darkness?" Hakah knew it was true. This male mortal must be obedient.

"Be persistent with her." Justin tried to console Hakah.

"I will, but her head is too stubborn and her heart is too hard."

xxx

"You lied to me." Megan accused him, riding on her fury. He stopped dead in his tracks. Megan continued walking without looking back, "So when were you going to tell me that you're a doctor and not a freakin' cabdriver?" Her sharp words came from the depths of her soul. She stomped all the way to Tommy's Ford, climbed in the passenger side and slammed the door.

In the rear view mirror she saw him sheepishly approach the car. She had him squirming and wanted to keep it that way. He eased in behind the wheel. Megan stared straight ahead and glared at a spider crawling up the front window.

She didn't know what had come over her. Why was it so important that he be honest with her? What made her think he would be? No man before had ever been. *I wanted to know everything about him; what makes him think the way he thinks, what makes him feel the way he feels, what makes him do the things he does. But why, what difference does it really make? He's no different than the rest.*

The engine started with the turn of his key. "I am a doctor, a surgeon exactly. But for the past two years I have been doing research at Columbia University. When my discoveries led to suspicions about the kind of poisonous chemicals that are floating in the air I was commanded to take the "Chip." They ordered me to pledge my allegiance to Sixtus and his ever controlling government. When I refused, my top security clearance was revoked and I was out of a job. In addition, I was banned from practicing medicine ever again ... I'm sorry if I misled you."

Keeping her anger under control Megan responded, "Listen, I get it that you want to rebel against the government. I'm not too crazy about Sixtus myself at this point, but you didn't tell me you were a Jesus freak on top of it!" Megan saw something flicker deep in his eyes. Was he hiding something more? Her sarcasm screamed, "So when were you going to let me in on that little secret?"

"It isn't a secret, Meg." Jerry didn't look at her. "I knew I should have told you the night I gave you a ride in my cab. I wanted to tell you but just couldn't."

They drove the short distance in silence. When Jerry stopped the car, Megan jumped out and stalked over to the van. She heard his feet shuffle a distance behind her until she got to the driver's side. She searched in her bag for the keys.

"I guess I must have them," he said, disappointment oozing from his pores. "Please don't leave. I have something to tell you."

"All right, but make it quick. Alex must be worried sick about me."

"Alex?" She had him. *He thinks I have a significant other.* She waited as long as she could to answer. She wanted to torment him. Should she lie? She decided against it.

"He's Nadia's brother – his tenant loaned me the truck." She indicated the sign on the side of her vehicle.

THE MARKETPLACE

"Oh, yeah," he sighed. Relief relaxed his face a little. She loved it. He stepped in front of her, boxing her in with her back against the van. One hand was on either side of her shoulders. He seemed to be bracing himself rather than locking her in. Then he began.

"When I was in medical school, I became very amazed at the intricacies of the human body; the way skin heals itself, the exchange of air through the lungs and blood, the complexity of the eyes. The sheer miracle of life and birth alone was enough to make me a believer. So I determined that there must be a God, a creator, an author of life." Jerry took a long breath. Megan's anger began to subside.

"Then I met Samantha. She was in med school also, specializing in emergency pediatrics. She was in one of my early physiology classes. I don't for the life of me know why, but she asked me to study with her before the final exam. The professor of that class was particularly tough. He prided himself in failing 60% of his students each quarter. But he was the best professor at Columbia. Everyone knew that if they passed his courses they could get through anything. Anyway, Sam and I studied together that night and almost every night after that until graduation."

"So when did you start dating? You must have become a couple somewhere along the line."

"Yes, but not right away. We had studied together for two semesters before I got up the courage to make a pass at her."

"Boy, you're really fast."

Jerry began to blush. He looked at the ground. Then he continued. "She was the one who had it all together. We had been out for a light dinner and then I walked her home. I had wanted to kiss her for months but she never encouraged me. I figured she wasn't interested. Finally I decided that if she rejected me I would just let her go and move on. I leaned down to kiss her ..."

Jerry had gradually leaned closer and closer to Megan. *Kiss me. You know I want you to.* He just might ... but instead he backed away.

"And ..." Megan encouraged.

"And she put her fingers on my lips to stop me."

"Wow that must have cut you to the quick."

"It did, but it was the best thing that could ever have happened. It was the beginning of a new life for me. She said, 'Jerry, you are the most wonderful man I have ever met but I cannot be unequally yoked.'"

"What the heck does that mean?" Megan asked.

"That's exactly what I asked her. She began to explain to me that she could never accept me as a romantic partner because of my beliefs. She knew I believed in God. We had had many discussions about the subject. She explained that believing in God was not enough, even the devil did that. I told her I believed in Jesus too. But still that wasn't enough. I had to love Jesus and desire to follow Him. I had never thought about loving Jesus before. It was a new concept to me."

"How can you love someone you have never seen?" It was a statement more than a question.

"That was my point exactly. She told me I needed to read the Bible and that Jesus would speak to me. Then I could get to know Him and love Him the way she did. Then we would not be unequally yoked."

"Nadia gave me a Bible to read." Megan confessed.

"Have you started to read it?" His words were eager.

"Well, I did read it yesterday morning – before all this." He searched her eyes for more. Instead, she clenched her jaw and tossed her hands up. "But I didn't hear anyone speak to me."

"I know it is hard in the beginning. After a while, when you get the hang of the language it becomes quite engaging. Sometimes when I read it now, the words seem to be printed in red. They jump off the page at me. Then I know God is speaking and I want to listen. But you can't hear God speak if you don't belong to Him.

"Any way, I discovered through all this that Jesus is more than worthy of my unending love and devotion. He loves me more than I could ever love Him. I know that when my heart is broken He gently heals it. If I fall down, He graciously helps me up again. When I get into trouble and I wait for Him, He faithfully saves me. He always hears me when I pray. Even without asking, He defends me from my enemies. And when I'm in the dark, the Lord Himself is my light.

"I know you don't trust me, Megan, and you have every right not to, but I must warn you. God has marked the evil nations and the time is coming soon when He will stand up and accuse them. Then He will pour out His fiercest anger and wrath upon them and the earth will be devoured with the fire of His jealousy."

Chapter Forty-Eight

Hakah pressed into Megan forcing her shoulders down. "If you live your life for yourself you will die and lose it; but if you lose your life for Jesus you will find it again and live forever. What would you profit, Megan, if you gained the whole world and then lost eternal life? What do you desire that could possibly compare with the treasure of an eternity of bliss?"

Justin, Walker's guardian angel, informed Hakah, "If she does not obey but instead rebels, then The Ancient of Days will rage against her. To unbelievers the salvation message is foolishness but to those who are saved it is power."

Salt poured into the Hakah's wound.

xxx

Megan wasn't sure she wanted Jerry to continue his conversation but she hoped he could somehow dispel the additional heaviness in her heart.

"Lately, Megan, I have been having terrible nightmares. I see nations waging war against each other, and earthquakes and famines. We are going through that now, but these are only the early stages of the suffering ahead. Soon we all will be in great danger. We Christians will be dragged before courts and executed simply because we believe in Jesus. As you can see, everyone hates us just because we don't bow down to Sixtus. But all those who endure to the end, without renouncing Him, will be saved. And that's the good news!

"But in the end there will be horrors that have never been seen since the beginning of God's creation. And unless the Lord intervenes, not one soul in all the earth will survive. But He has promised to shorten that time of calamity for those who love Him."

Anger crept back into Megan. "Are you trying to frighten me now?"

"It's good to be a little afraid. Fearing God will give you wisdom. I just want you to understand, Megan that your time on this earth may be very short and the decisions you make now will last for eternity." She could tell he wanted forgiveness but it seemed like a crazy way to ask for it.

Why hadn't he told her any of this before? Now that she thought about it, she *had* done most of the talking last night. She had almost been condescending supposing him to be just a cab driver. He never flinched or objected to her manner. She could see now he played her for a fool ... maybe even laughed at her expense. No, she didn't feel forgiving. She needed to be in control. She needed to steal back the control he had over her.

"I have one more thing I must tell you. I hope you won't think I am headed for the psychiatric ward." Momentarily he dropped his eyes to the ground, took a breath and then began.

"Megan, God sometimes speaks to me in dreams. I had one last night about you."

"Was that a nightmare too?" She immediately regretted her words when she saw the hurt in his sincere heart-melting eyes. She softened. "Okay, tell me about it."

Slowly he began.

"I had a vision last night from the Lord
He gave it to me so you could see
How deep is the love of the Father for you
And to show you how lovely He sees you to be.

I saw you, shining as a radiant star
I saw you, happy with who you are
I saw you, longing for heaven above, yet
I saw you, thankful for a life that you love
I saw you, thankful for a life that you love.

How He wants you to see you are precious to Him
Though your life is not always what you had planned
His vision for you is a reality
He can bring it to pass by His powerful hand.

I saw you, forgiving those who bring you to tears
I saw you, freed of sadness and fears
I saw you, running to Him with your pain, and
I saw you, choosing to trust once again
I saw you, choosing to trust Him.

I saw you, smiling with the joy of your King
I saw you, rejoicing, giving thanks in all things
O, I saw you, delighting in the good you can do
Finding all that you need in His deep love for you
All that you need in His sweet love for you, O, He loves you.

O, believe it, He sees you, He knows you.
He hears you, He loves you.
I saw you, shining as a radiant star
I saw you, happy with who you are.
O, He loves you." [ix]

Megan could no longer look at him. She pushed him away from her and turned to open the van door. Jerry gently slipped the keys into her left hand and ever so briefly held it. She jerked her hand away and opened the door. When she climbed in she saw three bedraggled people walking around the corner.

"Look," Megan exclaimed. "Those are the little girls' parents." Their tired bodies revived and their worried faces brightened when they saw Megan and the van. Megan ran to meet them and hugged each one.

"The children are safe! That man over there will take you to them." She led them back to where Jerry stood. She feigned happiness, as if nothing at all had passed between them. Jerry looked lost, his eyes pleading. Then he participated in the charade, smiled at the people, introduced himself and shook hands. Megan climbed into the van.

"Good luck," she said to Jerry and drove away. She never looked back.

Chapter Forty-Nine

In the sixth dimension the Archangel Michael stalked. His frustration and impatience with the human condition grew. Their ungrateful state infuriated him. He ranted, raved and bellowed.

"... And now, you rich people listen to me!" He knew they would not but yet he continued. "Weep and moan over the miseries that you encounter. Your riches are rotting away. Your gold and silver will be covered with rust which will not plead your defense. Instead they will eat your flesh like fire. You have piled up riches in these last days. The cries of those you have cheated to get them have reached the ears of Almighty God! Repent or be dammed!"

xxx

Sixtus slammed the phone down. *Incompetent people; a simple request and you'd think I had asked for her head on a plate. All I want is to know her every move; where she lives, where she goes, what she eats, how she spends her money and her time. Is that such a difficult task?* His obsession with Megan Cameron Montgomery increased every hour since she turned him down two days ago. He had watched the lingering admiration for him completely drain from her innocent eyes. At the time it didn't matter to him. He had witnessed that many times before but he always got what he wanted. It just meant the woman might not enjoy it. A little fight always made the act more exciting. But Ms. Montgomery had gotten away. He hated her rejection but her spirit tantalized him.

That similar lively spirit also drew him to New York. The city's hard beating pulse thrived on success and power. He loved this city but could no longer enjoy its pleasures. The air had become too contaminated, admittedly by his personal orders. However, he did not regret poisoning it. It was a necessary hazard.

His hermetically sealed car waited for him in the underground passageway leading out of the city. In less than an hour he would board his plane heading back to New Babylon. He did regret having to leave Megan Montgomery behind. Would he have invited her to go with him? Probably not. *I will have her though one day. I will.*

Alex's heart slowed when he saw Herb's van pull around the corner onto the street next to his building. Megan would be in the back parking lot in just a minute. Relief washed over him. He had only gotten word early this morning that she and the children had arrived safely at the farm. That gave him a sleepless night. In two minutes her footsteps sounded on the back stairs and he ran to the door to greet her. His heart sank when he saw her. She clearly had been crying.

"Megan, is everything all right? The e-mail said you arrived safely. Did something happen on the return trip?"

"No, everything is fine." She struggled to smile. "I just miss Nadia, that's all. They are getting married in two months and most likely I won't be able to come to the wedding."

"Two months, that's a long way off. A lot can happen between now and then. Maybe you could fly back for the big event. I'm sure she would love that and I would like it too. We could ride up there together." His attempt to cheer her up seemed to work.

"Is that grilled cheese that I smell?"

"Yes, indeed it is, made to order." He jumped up. He had found the key to success.

"I haven't had a grilled cheese sandwich since I was ten. Now that's real comfort food."

"I was just getting ready to check out the late afternoon sky. Why don't you go upstairs and I'll bring the sandwiches up. Want some pickles?"

"Sure, why not?"

Ever since she walked in the door Alex had that puppy dog "I want to please you" face. Had she not made that life-changing trip last night to Round Lake, she would have enjoyed his flattering attention.

When Megan got to the observatory, she plopped herself down into Alex's desk chair. A violin case leaned against the wall on the floor, next to her feet. The last time she discovered a violin in the house Alex practically attacked her in an uncomplimentary way. She wondered what the big deal was. So when he came into the room with two sandwiches, a bowl of pickles, two glasses filled with ice on a tray, and a bottle of vodka under his arm, she asked him.

"Alex, why haven't you played your violin since your father died? Nadia says you play really well."

"My father forced me to play as a boy. I never really enjoyed it all that much. When he passed away a huge burden lifted. The violin released its hold on me."

"I know. I have some issues with my dad too but I can't believe you don't enjoy creating soothing music. Please play something for me."

"No, Megan I'd rather not." Megan knew if she put enough sweetness into it she could persuade him. She smiled shyly and dropped her head. That usually worked.

"Please, please with sugar on top," she cooed.

"No, Megan, maybe some other time." Megan tried to make her disappointment evident. *I am really losing my touch.*

Alex pulled the hair back off her face and looked longingly into her eyes. She could tell he wanted to cheer her up but for some reason he just couldn't play that silly violin. Instead, he poured them each a tall glass of vodka.

"Let's eat these sandwiches before they get completely cold."

They ate in silence. Then Alex asked, "How is Nadia? Have they really set a wedding date?"

"Yes, Thanksgiving Day. She is so excited she's beaming already. She found Todd's grandmother's wedding gown up in the attic. It fits her perfectly!"

They chatted into the night. There had been no fights as usual. The stars were particularly bright and were a never ending topic of discussion. He told her of a major earthquake he suspected to occur in South America. This was the first she had heard of it. Usually the media got first wind of these things from the government agencies. Maybe she would get lucky and be assigned to it.

Then Megan lazily asked Alex about the train schedule for the next day. Her flight back to Chicago left LaGuardia Airport at eleven-fifteen in the morning. Alex tried to convince her to stay an extra day or two but she couldn't. She had to be at work on Monday. Besides she had to get away, to get back to normal. How could she get back to normal? Normal no longer existed.

Megan meticulously folded each item before she found a place for it in her bag. Each one conjured up a memory that drained her energy and left her breathless. The red suit and lace top was still crumpled up on the floor of Nadia's closet where she had flung it after the encounter with Sixtus.

She left it there.

She would never wear it again. Nothing would ever be the same again. Jerry's words began to haunt her.

"O, believe it, He sees you, He knows you." Stop, Jerry, stop. *Get out of my head I don't want to hear any more. "He hears you, He loves you."*

Megan refused to believe it. She took out the Bible Nadia had given to her and began to read John 3:16. "For God loved the world so much that He gave His only Son so that anyone who believes in Him shall not perish but have eternal life. God did not send His Son into the world to condemn it, but to save it."

Megan fell asleep with the Bible in her arms and a heavy weight on her chest.

<>

GAVE PROOF THROUGH THE NIGHT THAT OUR FLAG WAS STILL THERE

Chapter Fifty

Day 333

The earth's crust, made up of many huge plates, moved ever so slowly over partially melted rock. Five-hundred miles beneath the earth's surface, off the southwestern coast of Argentina, three crustal plates violently overlapped.

Hakah flew over Megan stirring the murky haze that gradually engulfed the room. He screamed at the top of his lungs to no avail. Finally he resorted to physically moving her bed.

xxx

Megan woke with a start hitting her head on the headboard. The bed of her hotel trembled then began to jump across the room as if dancing to a silent tune. Suddenly the silence broke into a roar. The musty smell of plaster filled the air as parts of the ceiling began to crumble down on her thundering head. The pane from her fourth story window shattered spraying glass and some form of dust into the room. Screams came from everywhere including her gut.

Megan groped in the dimness for the light. No electricity. *What's going on? Had there been a bomb?* She felt her way over to the chair where she left her multi-pocketed traveling pants and shirt the night before. She pulled them on and touched the bulge on her leg. Phone and passport secure. Her eyes slowly became accustomed to the eerie post dawn light. She stumbled over her shoes, put them on, and then edged to the door. In the hallway people were running in every direction bumping into each other and crying. Low emergency lighting barely illuminated the smoke filled walkway. *Think. Think. Where is the nearest exit?* She remembered turning left off the elevator when she arrived at the Hotel Plaza Grande in Quito, Ecuador yesterday. *Go right.*

The entire floor began to sway. Megan fell into the wall as a serving cart charged unattended past her. Plates of food crashed to the floor and she almost went down with them. Many people, mostly in night clothes, congregated around the elevator. A woman caring an infant with two other small children at her side entered the mob beside her.

"The stairs are safer." Megan yelled to her but the woman's confused and frightened face didn't acknowledge her. She obviously didn't speak English.

"Vamos amigos – pronto!" The old western movie line was all she could think of. She pointed to the stairs and the woman seemed to understand. Megan grabbed the toddler up and took the other child's hand. She pushed through the crowd and hoped the mother followed.

Others began flooding down the stairs as well. She had gone down two flights when suddenly the railing pulled away from the wall. An old man fell three steps to the landing in front of her. Grabbing for help he pulled two women down with him. The women scrambled to their feet but the man lay curled up in pain. He called, "Ayuda! Ayuda! Por favor!" Megan thought to stop and help him up but instead tightened her grip on the children as a wave of bodies forced her past him. His voice, muffled by the chaos of jumbled expressions, eventually faded to silence. *I can't believe this is happening!* The child in her arms cried and wiggled. He wanted to get down. She clung to him harder and fought to keep from falling herself.

Plaster began to crumble from the walls. Glass crashed in the distance. Megan's breath was shallow. The ash stung her throat and penetrated her lungs. She wished she had a scarf to cover her mouth. When Megan reached the bottom floor she searched the stairs behind her for their mother.

Only a sea of strangers.

Suddenly the grip of the older child loosened. She ran to a man. "Papi!" He whisked her up into his arms. He buried his worried face into her neck covering her with kisses. Then he jabbered something to Megan. She pointed to the stairs just as his wife came into view. "Gracias," he said, took the toddler and pushed through the crowd to the rest of his family.

Megan worked her way from the lobby to the front steps. The park-like Presidential Plaza was transformed into a snow covered nightmare. But it wasn't shiny glistening snow. It was dead dirty ash from the Pichincha caldera. The volcano was smoldering and about to erupt. The ground shook again. From the other side of the plaza the noise of twirling helicopter blades competed with the piercing screams around her. Then a voice, more deafening than them all chimed in her left ear.

"Move forward. Don't turn around." His tobacco breath nauseated her. But it was the barrel of his gun, in the small of her back, which pushed her over the edge. She felt her knees give way. His fingers, squeezing her arm, held her up. Her fingers became numb from his grip. *Is he for real? If I run will he really shoot me?* But how could she run she could barely walk? His long strides directed her toward the waiting helicopter.

Megan's heart pounded in her chest even louder than the whirling blades above her which pulled her hair in every direction. Both doors of the cabin were open. The President of Ecuador, Eduardo Verdugo and his wife Natalia, were entering from the other side. President Verdugo's face was calculating. Hers bore a rigid gentleness.

"Climb in," the man at her back commanded. Megan obliged. As soon as her last foot left the ground she turned around to see her assailant. She only caught the left side of his face before he disappeared into the crowd. He had a nasty dark mole over his eye.

President Eduardo Verdugo commanded her attention. "Good morning Ms. Montgomery. I see we meet sooner than scheduled." He had a dry sense of humor. "I trust your visit to Ecuador has satisfied your expectations." His tone turned bitter.

"The excitement is overwhelming. I must tell you though I have no intentions of going anywhere without my cameraman Frank."

"I see." He paused for a moment his eyes quizzical. "We must take off now or the ash will keep us grounded."

"Then I'm getting off." Adrenalin empowered her.

"You have two minutes, Ms Montgomery, two minutes." he yelled after her.

She believed him.

Her knees buckled as she dropped to the ground but she regained her balance in a second. Smoke filled her lungs. She coughed repeatedly and cupped her hand over her mouth and nose. *Frank, Frank where are you?* Her eyes teared from the smoke as she scanned the crowd. Almost blindly she ran toward the hotel. Swarms of people created chaos around her. Silt and smoke burned her lungs. Her nostrils swelled. Breathing was next to impossible. Police baring weapons corralled people into buses. One directed Megan toward a line.

She reluctantly moved in that direction.

Then she spotted him. Good old Frank, filming the scene from his first floor balcony.

She broke free from the police line and waved her hands violently over her head pressing through the crazed mass of people.

"Frank," she yelled repeatedly. He still filmed. "Frank!" Finally he put the camera down. "Hurry, Frank, we have to go!"

"Where are we going?" He asked in his usual layback tone.

"Away from here. Now get your rear end down here right now!" They worked as a team but she called the shots. He swung his camera over his shoulder, leaped over the railing and dropped to the ground.

"Run!" she shouted over the commotion. He obliged.

A policeman pushed her toward another line but she shook her head and refused. He blew his whistle and shouted after her in Spanish. Megan press onward toward the helicopter.

Natalia Verdugo's urgent eyes called out as her hand motioned for Megan to hurry. The president's wife was yelling at the pilot. In seconds, President Verdugo pulled Megan into the aircraft. Frank was right behind her.

The chopper lifted off. Its tail boom dragged and swayed as they began to ascend, the small rotor sputtered as if it would choke.

Chapter Fifty-One

Thousands of angels, led by Hakah, began beating their wings symphonically in front of the helicopter. The steady rhythm created a strong southerly airstream.

xxx

The helicopter swayed back and forth then caught the miraculous wind that momentarily cleared the air and they were off. Climbing ... climbing.

Megan sank into a seat and attached the seatbelt. Her hands shook even harder than her knees. She exchanged a thankful glance with Frank. "That was a real rush." he whispered. Megan turned her attention to the president.

"Thank you, President Verdugo, for allowing us to vacate with you."

"On the contrary, Ms. Montgomery, we are the thankful ones. This helicopter was ordered for you."

Frank briefly looked at Megan. "WWBC must really love you! They expect a great story and I'm getting it for them. This footage is fantastic!" He leaned over the doorway his camera pointed downward.

Megan concentrated instead on the agitated president. Obviously his thoughts were somewhere else. Probably with his fellow countrymen left in the rubble far below. Then he gave his wife a reproachful glare. She responded, headstrong with a nod of her head. He turned away from his wife and starred at Megan. She felt the grief that poured from his eyes. His people were suffering. He was flying away.

"May I speak frankly with you Ms. Montgomery, off the record?"

"Sure, I welcome your comments." She didn't know what to expect. Mrs. Verdugo clearly wanted him to tell her something he didn't want to divulge.

"Be careful what you say, Ms Montgomery ... Nothing is at it seems." That was it? His intense eyes bore into her relating a deeper meaning. She wasn't getting it. Was he afraid of something or someone beyond these outrageous circumstances? Or was it anger instead?

"What do you mean?"

"One wrong word can sadly bring down a nation." He paused and looked at his wife. "It is like a jigsaw puzzle, Ms Montgomery. Do you like jigsaw puzzles?" He didn't expect an answer and focused his attention on her again. He continued. "You are a smart woman, you have most of the pieces, and today's event is just one more." He put his arm around his wife and looked out the window.

He implied that this botched evacuation had not been an accident! Reports were that Ecuador was far north of the fault line; it never should have been touched. Unless someone lied. She planned to get to the bottom of it one way or another.

Quickly they left the crying population behind them. The charging aircraft followed the mountain range south. Megan stared in horror as Frank filmed. Never before had she seen such devastation. They witnessed the edge of the Andes Mountains dropping straight into the Pacific Ocean. Everything west of the Andes, from Central America down to the tip of Argentina disappeared beneath the swells of rushing water. In some regions where copper, gold and silver mining were the most prevalent, the mountains themselves cracked away. Landslides of boulders and trees crashed into the sea forming smaller, unstable summits. Nothing in history compared to the devastation. Megan couldn't keep her eyes off the destruction below. Tears spilled down her face. She had seen more destruction in this one day than she had ever dreamed of seeing in a lifetime.

<>
"My God, rescue me from wicked people, from the power of cruel and evil people" (Psalms 71:4 GNT)

Chapter Fifty-Two

Day 303

Whole populations had completely washed away – Chile and Peru half gone, Nicaragua, Costa Rica, and Panama gone. Ecuador and Colombia hung on by a thread. It was the longest and deepest earthquake ever recorded in the history of the world. As a result a tsunami wall battered the coastline destroying everything and everyone in its path. There were no survivors between the Pacific Coast and the Andes Mountains. Over forty thousand, seven-hundred, sixty-three million people were presumed dead. The ripple affect traveled as far west as New Zealand.

xxx

Megan dropped the stack of mail she had clutched under her arm on the couch just before she collapsed next to it. Her trip back from Quito, the capital of Ecuador, had been a long arduous one. There were many delays and cancellations leaving South America. She was lucky to have gotten out at all. She pulled off her sneakers, propped her legs up on the coffee table, leaned her head back and closed her eyes. The last four weeks had been the most treacherous of her entire career.

Megan left the earthquake torn region of South America, when the United World Forces (UWF) began evacuating the nations west of the Andes – parts of Bolivia, Brazil, Argentina and Venezuela. Ojos del Salado, located on the Argentine/Chile border, the largest volcano in the world, plus some fifty other volcanoes scattered throughout the mountains were smoldering and suspected to erupt. Thick volcanic ash spewed into the air which drove people east as far as they could go. All air space closed; all aircrafts were grounded. Black ash clouds hung at an altitude of ten-thousand to forty-thousand feet. Lines and lines of traffic bottled up the small narrow roads leading away from the mountains. No one attempted to search for survivors on the ocean side because aftershocks continued to rock the landscape.

Going had been an exciting prospect but she witnessed far more than her heart could handle. As a result, the focus of her passion changed forever. Reporting the news now took a back seat. Of course the news needed to be reported quickly and accurately, but now objectivity no longer dominated the equation. Where was the UWC before the earthquake hit? Why had more people not been evacuated before the earthquake? She needed to get to the source of the crisis; to expose to the world the reason, to delve into the question of why so many lives were lost, and so many others were changed forever.

She sat on the sofa exhausted but completely unable to sleep. She tried to force the images of the profound destruction out of her mind, but they appeared to be seared on her brain. The voice of the old man crouching on the stairs shouted in her ears.

She decided to take a long needed shower. *Maybe that will help me relax.* In Bolivia she had purchased a few clothes and a new flight bag. She pulled it into her bedroom and emptied the contents on the floor. Her clothes reeked of sweat. She would deal with that tomorrow. She grabbed a fresh towel from the closet and headed for the shower.

Her bathroom was small but clean, like the rest of her one bedroom apartment. She would never complain about its size again. Most places where she slept the last several weeks had no bathroom at all.

The water flowed over her like streams from heaven. She lathered long and hard, scrubbing until her skin shone pink. She fought the temptation to remain there for hours and finally turned the water off. Revitalized, she dried herself and slipped into a soft white terrycloth robe. Even though it was only seven o'clock, she was ready to settle in for the evening.

Megan grabbed a can of chicken noodle soup from the cupboard and heated it up on the stove. She went to the coat closet by the front door and pulled a bottle of red wine from under some hats and scarves on the top shelf. It was the last bottle from a case she had bought almost a year ago from the liquor store down the street that since had gone out of business. She had been saving it for a special occasion but this was probably about as special as it would get. Besides, it might dull the mental agony, soothe her aching body and help her unwind enough to fall asleep. Megan poured herself a large glass.

Finally settling in on the couch again, she began to sort through over two months of mail. Bills and junk mail were easy to separate. What remained were three plain envelopes and one pink one with flowers on the back flap. She recognized the perfectly sculpted "teacher-like" handwriting on the pink one. No return address. She checked the postmark hoping to see Monroe, New York. Sure enough. Megan opened it carefully, not wanting to tear the beautiful envelope. She pulled out a note handwritten on cardstock.

My dearest friend Megan,

You are cordially invited to the marriage of
Todd Philips and Nadia Liechtenstein
Thanksgiving weekend

Love, Nadia

P.S. Please be my Maid-of-Honor!

She loved the sweet invitation and began to giggle. Because of all her stirring escapades, she had totally forgotten about the wedding. Immediately she sent Alex an e-mail. "Am coming to Nadia's wedding, will notify you of my ETA!"

Her mind raced. Tomorrow she would book her flight and clear her trip with the TV station. What better person to talk to about the recent earthquake than the expert, Alex Liechtenstein? She knew her boss would buy it if she only asked for a few days. Most of her colleagues were away on location covering disaster stories all around the world. But a few days would work. How wonderful it would be to celebrate Thanksgiving again!

Next, she curiously looked at the other three envelopes left in her lap. They were plain white with chicken scratch for the address. How did the postman even deliver them? Again, no return address, and the postmark – Monroe, New York! Her heart skipped a beat ... then several more!

She took the three envelopes and placed them in chronological order putting the oldest one on top. She pressed her hands together, interlocked her fingers and rested her chin on them. Closing her eyes, she took a deep breath.

They were from him.

She had tried to force him out of her mind the past few weeks but had been unsuccessful. Now the moment of truth – should she open the letters or immediately tear them up and throw them away?

Alex' heart pounded in his chest when he read Megan's message. He wasted no time passing the information on to Nadia through his internet contact. In five days, she will be here! His heart sang as he busied himself around the apartment. Nadia said there was nothing like fresh air to perk a place up.

The brisk evening wind swished through the apartment blowing papers everywhere as he opened all the windows. He'd pick them up later. More important things pressed on his mind. What to do next? He went into Nadia's bedroom, the place where Megan last slept, and pulled off the sheets. Before he had been reluctant to rid the bed of her scent, but now! He decided to wash his sheets just before she arrived – one never knew!

He picked up the phone and called down to Herb in the store below, "Hi, my friend, would you by any chance have an opportunity to get some fresh cherries?"

Chapter Fifty-Three

Mammoth amounts of energy suddenly released under the earth's crust. On this day, seismic waves caused millions of earthquakes measuring 2.8 to 3.5 on the Richter scale to erupt all around the globe. Three seismologists took note of this activity but dismissed it as some rare occurrence. It was, however, the beginning of the end.

xxx

Megan took one large gulp of wine and recklessly ripped open the first plain envelope. What the heck, he has already ruined my life. What more damage could he do?

Dear Megan,

    I hope this letter finds you well. Nadia gave me your address. Please forgive me if I am out of line by writing you. I just wanted to update you on the beautiful little girls you rescued. You can't imagine the wonderful reception that awaited their parents when I drove them back to the farm. It would have brought tears to your eyes. It almost brought tears to mine. Kaylie, her sisters and her mother, are staying in the main farmhouse until their father, Leo arrives. There is no word from him yet and we are worried he may have been arrested. They all asked me to send you their love.

    Kirk has also settled in quite nicely. He is living in the farmhouse with Nadia and Todd. Nadia has given him several textbooks to help him catch up to his school grade level. He is taking it all in like a sponge. But what he seems to be soaking in even more is the love that Nadia and Todd have for him. He truly has found the perfect home. One of my patients exchanged two horses for my services. I gave them to Kirk and he readily adopted them.

    Neeko is healing quite nicely though his ear, as I suspected, never reattached. I had to remove it completely. He sends a happy wag and a mighty bark. He misses you as we all do.

Sincerely,
Jerry

    It took several minutes for Megan to process all that she had read. *Oh, I hope Kaylie's father has arrived by now.* Then she read the final line again. "He misses you as we all do." *As we all do – does that mean you miss me too?* She couldn't wait to tear open the next letter.

Dear Megan,

    I pray all is well with you. Everyone here is excited about the upcoming wedding. It is on the way to becoming the event of the year. A man in town gave me a used car as payment for my services. Tom is working on it now to make it roadworthy and non-traceable. It will be a wedding gift to Todd and Nadia from the two of us. If you want, it can be from you too. (Without you, I would not be here at all.)

    The enclosed drawings are from the little girls. They insisted I send them to you pronto. You are, after all, their "Forest Queen" and they are almost your biggest fans.

    Still no word from Leo, we know he is in God's hands. As King David wrote to his son Solomon, "Be strong and of good courage; do not fear or be dismayed, for the Lord God – my God – will be with you." (1 Chronicles 28:20)

Everyone sends their love,
Jerry

    Megan shook all the little drawings from the envelope. Some were on colored paper. Some were cut in shapes of circles, and hearts. One had rice glued all over it. Each had a picture of six little stick figures holding hands with one large figure in the center. They each signed their own name and added Xs and Os.

    Without a doubt, these were the most precious children in the world. Megan wondered whether she would ever get pregnant again. She arranged all the drawings in a line on the coffee table. *I have to get some picture frames for these. They would look great mounted on the wall across from the kitchen table.*

    She read again the letter from Jerry. Her heart ached for Kaylie's family. *I wonder if God really is with her father.* A pang of guilt crossed her mind. She had not read Nadia's Bible since she had gotten back from New York over two months ago. She got it from the table next to her bed and then she sat back down on the couch.

    She tried to find the text Jerry had quoted. It took her a few minutes then she read where it left off, "He will not leave you nor forsake you, until you have finished all the work for the service of the house of the Lord." *What if Leo has finished the work he had to do for the Lord? What then?*

    She read the second letter a third time. Everyone sends their love. *Why can't you just say it, Jerry? You love me and you miss me!* She couldn't keep a huge smile contained as she opened the third letter.

My Dear Megan,

    It has been several weeks since I have written you last. Frankly, I would not find it difficult to write everyday but I am sure you would not want to read all the thoughts that come into my mind. So let me tell you a little about what is happening here.

Nadia teaches a Bible study Tuesday and Thursday nights. Each week the number attending grows. She is an inspiring and knowledgeable woman with incredible insight into the Word of God. There are about thirty-five that attend on Tuesday and another fifty on Thursday. The people come from Monroe and other surrounding towns. Through her, God is touching them and changing them forever.

Yesterday Kaylie's father, Leo safely arrived at Round Lake. It was perfect timing. We all see how faithful God is. His word says, "Then shall the virgin rejoice in the dance, and the young men and the old, together; for I will turn their mourning to joy, will comfort them, and make them rejoice rather than sorrow." (Jeremiah 31:13)

The joy that He brought to the whole community is a foretaste of what the wedding will be like. I hope you can come. It is only ten days away. It will be a day of joy and pure celebration. We all would be blessed to see you again, especially me.

Love,
Jerry

There it was in black and white, "Love, Jerry." Megan took her fingers and gently moved them back and forth across his signature. She guessed it had taken him a bit of time to print each letter. *I'm so glad you did, my doctor friend. I never could have deciphered your longhand.*

So who was this man with the scratchy penmanship? He clearly was a doctor, a Christian, and a Rogue but what else? Who else? She decided it was worth finding out. She poured herself another glass of wine, pulled her feet up under her robe and read the three letters again.

<>
AND THE ROCKET'S RED GLARE,

Chapter Fifty-Four

Day 298

Hundreds of black rat colonies erupted from the ground. They foraged the rice paddies and cornfields of South East Asia and South America. Within hours they had rampaged and obliterated all the crops. The flood of rats increased to over six million and continued to spread northward pushed by demons of every kind. They devoured every plant in sight – ninety-thousand metric tons of crops destroyed.

Rats that originated in Coega, an area in the Eastern Cape of South Africa, carried the bubonic plague. They began to wipe out huge human populations. Previous attempts to exterminate them only partially addressed the problem. Most of them were mutants that reproduce at a rate of fifteen thousand per month. Famine and disease ensued.

xxx

Sixtus sat next to the swimming pool at his private home on Arwad, a small Syrian island located in the Mediterranean Sea about two miles west of Tarsus. He had inhabited the Fortress of Arwad, the ancient island citadel, shortly after its elaborate renovation two years ago. The location, not far from the mainland, satisfied his occasional need to "get away."

Alone, Sixtus enjoyed the cool fresh air, a tall glass of jasmine iced tea and a long awaited time of solitude. He had just finished a two-hour workout in his fully loaded customized gym. His body was pumped up, strong and virile; his mind was strung high on adrenaline. Generally, he had to work at relaxing. It never came naturally.

He stared at his teak chess set. Little in the world relaxed him as quickly as a game of chess, especially when he played against himself. The challenge came when trying to find a way to outmaneuver his most detailed plan of action. He held the black queen gently in his right hand, fingering her crown and contemplating his next move when the phone rang. Briefly, the much-welcomed call interrupted his tranquility. The curt and professional voice on the line reported.

"Sir, Megan Montgomery arrived in New York City at six-ten AM local time. She then boarded a train for Katonah, NY. She apparently has a boyfriend,

Alexander Liechtenstein, who lives there. Together they crossed the Bear Mountain Bridge at nine, twenty-three AM. I should have their final destination for you soon."

"Good work, Azimi." He paused to absorb completely the implications of this new piece of her ever more interesting puzzle.

"Alexander Liechtenstein... That name sounds very familiar to me."

"Sir, you have read several of his articles relating to the current galactic phenomenon."

"Ah, yes. Follow up on this Liechtenstein character. I want to know everything you have on him." Sixtus closed his eyes and smiled. In his mind, he pictured the lovely provocative Megan Montgomery very, very slowly, undressing herself before him. Relaxation slithered through his pores!

As soon as the door closed behind him, the cool morning breeze threatened to eliminate all trace of the floral scent from Al Adams' nose. He put his head down to smell the sweet aroma coming from the white box that he held. Using the front door of Fancy Florals was foreign to him but he no longer owned the flower shop. Today he was just like any other customer picking up his order. His emotions ran high, both nostalgia and anticipation. He glanced back one last time at the establishment where he had spent the last forty years of his life. Who knew what the next forty might bring?

The Lord found a buyer for his store and the money hit his account exactly two weeks ago. With those funds, he bought a log cabin kit. The thought of building a house from the ground up daunted him somewhat, but at the same time exhilarated him. Daunting had never stopped him from starting a new project before. He didn't see any reason for it to get in the way now.

The cabin kit had been delivered last week to a plot of land deep in the woods behind Alex's farm. Spanning 4,000 square feet it would far exceed the needs of only one person but Nadia assured him there would be no problem filling it. New Rogue families were arriving at the lake every week. Too many years alone had made Adams sullen so he looked forward to having company again.

Adams put his truck in gear and headed toward Round Lake. Another chapter closed and a new one opening. He would arrive just in time for Nadia's wedding.

Chapter Fifty-Five

All around the world, climate change drastically altered mosquito ecology and habits. One particular gigantic swarm of African Bush Mosquitoes left their breeding place unchecked and unstoppable. They infected over five-million people then crossed into the Saudi Arabia transmitting the diseases of West Nile, Dengue Fever and Encephalitis. Countless victims died a merciless death.

xxx

Many people were afraid to celebrate Thanksgiving because Sixtus had banned it. But this celebration served a dual purpose; Thanksgiving and the wedding of the most in love and the most loved couple on Round Lake.

Tom Barker pulled up to the farmhouse with Alex and Megan in the car. He knew Nadia would be happy. She flew out the front door. Her face lit up. Her beauty overwhelmed him. She wrapped her arms around her brother.

"I was so worried you wouldn't get here in time."

"Yeah me too, but we made it and that's what counts." Nadia gave Megan a quick hug, then took her hand and led her into the house.

"We have work to do, Megan, and lots to catch up on. Alex, will you help Tommy and Todd finish setting up the schoolhouse for the reception and then be back here by eleven-thirty?"

"Anything for my little sister," he winked at Megan.

"Thanks, oh and Tommy could you check to see if there is any more ice in the freezer? I think they might be able to use more in the cooler."

"Sure thing, anything else you need me to do?" He wanted to make this day perfect for her even though it made minced meat of his heart.

"No, nothing I can think of right now. Thank you so much for all your help, Tommy. You're an angel."

Barker watched Nadia flit up the stairs. He and Jerry Walker had spent the last two days cleaning the cottage next to the lake from top to bottom. It wouldn't be a real honeymoon for them but at least it would be a quiet place, even for only a few days, where the two of them could start their new lives together. Barker began to tremble when he thought of Nadia and Todd sharing their lives together ... forever. He forced himself to think about the ice.

Noise and activity surrounded Barker when he entered the schoolhouse with the ice. Last night he had helped transform it into a banquet hall. There were five rows of tables, seven-deep, two on one side of the room and three on the other. They left the center open – a dance floor. Barker had built a small platform in the left corner for the "band." Five teenagers had been practicing dance music for the last three weeks. At the back of the building, Nadia's desk had been moved to the right corner and a head table had been set up. An old beautiful white linen tablecloth, hand embroidered by Todd's grandmother, draped over it. On the sly, Nadia's students had made red construction paper hearts and colorful crepe paper flowers. Barker had strewn them all over the table. The perfect wedding for the perfect lady.

Today, however, moved forward without him. No one asked for his help. Community members scurried around doing what? He had no clue. Bows dangled from chair backs. Napkins, plates and cutlery turned up. People buzzed and bounced him around like ping pong balls begging to be wacked. How much more could be done? One guest practically ran him over.

"Careful, coming through, hot food!"

The food tables were covered with the typical Thanksgiving Day fare. One creative man arrived at four o'clock that morning to roast one of his own pigs! Everyone brought a dish. Everyone had an agenda. Everyone except him.

Barker carried the ice to the beverage table in the front left corner of the room. Next to it, on a small square table, sat a perfectly shaped, beautiful pink cake that Kaylie's mother had created. On the top were five hot pink carnations, a donation from Al Adams. It was the most beautiful cake Barker had ever seen. He hoped it tasted as good as it looked. He could really go for something sweet in his life. Somehow he didn't think he would find it here.

With about fifteen minutes to kill, Alex entered the farmhouse hearing laughter and general bustling throughout the rooms above. Three families now shared this house with Todd and Nadia. They all got along amazingly well. They never argued. They lived in perfect harmony. The children slept either on the floor or on cots in their parent's bedroom. The kitchen, living and family rooms were shared by the group. All pitched in to do whatever work needed to be done. Everyone who lived there cherished it.

He could never do it.

Alex sat down on the couch and then noticed his father's violin hanging on the wall next to the fireplace. It drew him.

"Nadia would be ecstatic if you would play it at the reception." Todd's entrance startled him. "We have someone playing a violin during the ceremony but I know a concert from you would be a special gift to her."

"It is such short notice and I haven't prepared anything." Alex hoped he sounded convincing but by the sad look on Todd's face, he doubted it.

"It would really mean a lot to her – and me too."

"Sorry." Disappointed in himself, he looked at the floor and shook his head. *What a lame excuse.* But he couldn't. Try as he might he just couldn't. He still couldn't even play his *own* violin. He shoved his hands in his pockets. Todd rested his hand on Alex's shoulder.

"That's okay, Buddy, I just wanted you to know it would be an honor."

Nadia looked in the full-length mirror at the image before her, holding the bouquet that Mr. Adams had brought her. It resembled the one her mother had made for Nadia the night of her first ballet recital. Had Mr. Adams remembered? He probably did, he had a gentle thoughtful style. The magnificent scent of white roses and her favorite – fuchsia carnations brought her back to days gone by. *Oh, Mama, I wish you could be here to share this fabulous day with me. I miss you so much.*

Nadia studied the woman staring back at her in the mirror. She had dreamed of this day many times but never quite believed it would come. She wore a gown more beautiful than she could ever have imagined. It fit snuggly around her curves until just below her knees, where yards and yards of fabric then billowed out to create a full long skirt with a flowing three-foot train. The square scalloped neckline of lace fanned up behind her tanned neck. The sleeves continued the lace down her slender arms and ended in a widow's peak at the back of her small hands.

Her mind wandered to her first dreams of marriage, to silly dreams of walking down the aisle with Tommy. She had practiced her new signature on discarded bags, receipts and scraps of paper – Mrs. Tommy Barker. *Stop pining over a childish romance that never was and never would be. Poor Tommy, his face never lights up any more and he rarely smiles. Something must be seriously troubling him.* She checked herself and refused to think of him any longer. *Today I will become Mrs. Todd Philips and that is more than any woman could hope for.*

Megan came up behind her. "Why the solemn face? Smile, you are getting married!" Yes, the happiest day of her life.

Megan took a simple satin edged veil and attached it to the top of Nadia's head with the elephant comb she had given her. Then she led her over to the bed.

"Please sit down, I have something for you." Megan presented Nadia with a colorful shopping bag. "Go on, open it. I found it at a second hand shop in Chicago. It was the only one they had." Nadia pulled a large coffee-table picture book from inside the bag. A genuine smile erupted.

"Oh, Megan, it's beautiful!" She ran her fingers over the embossed letters of the title, "America the Beautiful." Slowly Nadia opened the book and began to leaf through pages and pages of awesome and majestic photos of the best sights in her beloved country. She stopped when she came to a picture of a cloud covered Grand Canyon. It spanned two pages. Her hand slowly caressed the image. Mystery and wonder played out on those pages which displayed depth and power, strength and might. It was the perfect symbol of God's bountiful love.

"I always wanted to go to the Grand Canyon," she whispered, barely audible.

"Well, there's nothing stopping you now."

"Yes, I suppose you are right." She answered with a sigh knowing full well it would never happen. Nadia ran her hand over the picture again and then closed the book.

"This is the best present ever," she said clutching it tightly. "Thank you so much."

Megan beamed.

Someone knocked at the door.

"Are you ready, Nadia? You said you wanted me here at eleven-thirty." Megan checked the clock next to the bed. It was time.

Chapter Fifty-Six

Angels filled the sixth dimension over Round Lake. Weddings were celebrations they enjoyed most. It couldn't have been a more beautiful autumn day. The leaves had almost disappeared from the trees completely. Like arms, their branches reached up to praise God as if singing a Hallelujah chorus. The sun shimmered on the water which dressed it with diamonds. It was a magnificent backdrop for the perfect wedding.

xxx

Megan abhorred receiving lines and since she didn't know any of the guests, she went immediately over to the buffet tables. Her eyes searched the crowd for Jerry. His head towered six inches above the other attendees. He was not difficult to find. Not a hair out of place, but pulled back into a tight ponytail at the nape of his broad neck. He looked more like a wrestler than a doctor. The sleeves of his dark blue dress shirt, clearly designed for a smaller man, were rolled up just enough to expose his strong tanned forearms. He was talking to Tommy when suddenly he glanced up and his eyes shifted to hers. A warm friendly smile instantly broke out on his face.

Megan couldn't help but smile back but he had caught her gawking. Embarrassed, she stared at the floor. *Now what?* She forced herself to focus on the man behind the food laden tables. She thought it a very odd place for the minister to be, actually serving people as they went through the line. As maid-of-honor, Megan had done practically nothing except hold the bride's bouquet. *If he can dish up mashed potatoes so can I.* She joined him behind the table.

"It certainly was a beautiful ceremony, Pastor Williamson."

"Yes, Nadia and Todd planned a unique and memorable celebration."

"I have never seen a wedding quite like it before. The main focus seemed to be on acknowledging and thanking the people most instrumental in shaping their individual lives."

"Yes, and now they plan to focus on God shaping their lives together."

"I've been thinking a lot about God lately, Pastor. It seems like a huge risk not to join the World Wide Church and yet you seem to be very at ease not worshiping there."

"I'm not so concerned about religion. It's my relationship with God that is important." His apparent conviction stunned her. Wasn't religion the whole point? There was that idea again about having a relationship. She answered with her usual response.

"I'm not very good with relationships. Except for my friendship with Nadia I've never had one that worked."

"Relationships are dependent on two parties, what they each hope to get out of the relationship and what they are each willing to put into that relationship. God is someone who wants to have a relationship with you. He will pursue you until you completely reject Him. He loves you right now even if you don't love Him."

The concept was very foreign to her.

"My advice is, don't put your trust in people. They will try to persuade you through their own philosophy or deception. Read God's word for yourself and you'll find out."

"I've been getting that advice a lot lately."

"Well, maybe God is trying to tell you something. You need to fix your eyes not on what you see, but on what you can't see. What is seen is temporary, but what is unseen is eternal. Take a look at Nadia and Todd over there." The newlywed couple shook hands and embraced every person that passed in front of them. Gently Todd put his arm around Nadia's small waist and pulled her to him.

"They aren't concerned about religion. Keep in mind God looks at the bottom line; do you love Him or not love Him, do you know Him or not know Him, do you want Him to use you or not use you? Anything that takes away from or clutters these basic principals is a religion designed by man not God."

The pastor merely increased her frustration. He continued to talk but Megan no longer listened. She smiled and greeted people as they filed in front of her holding their plates out for sweet potatoes and green bean casserole. Some asked about her job and how she knew Nadia. Others asked how she liked the ceremony, or the weather. They were quirky and hometownish but sincere. One woman tapped the top of her hand, leaned in, gave her a knowing smile and commented how well she and Alex looked together. Oh yes, that love/hate (hate emphasized) relationship? *If she only knew.* But everyone here welcomed her with open arms. Nadia fit into this crowd completely.

Tommy approached her station with Jerry right behind him. Her heart raced even faster than her mind. When they stopped in front of her, she greeted them like the others, with a smile.

"Hi, are you guys enjoying the wedding so far?" She saw the sad look on Tommy's face then looked to Jerry for a possible explanation.

Jerry answered, "My friend here has seen better days but it's been perfect for me. You look quite lovely in green, I might add." Though she fought it, she couldn't contain a big smile. His voice caressed her heart like a soothing song.

"It's turquoise actually, but thanks." All her prepared, well thought out witty lines escaped her.

"See you later, I hope." Jerry said as he helped himself to some sausage stuffing and turkey gravy.

"Yes, but I have to sit at the head table. Maid-of-honor duties you know."

"Of course, this is their day after all." She tried to see behind his words but could not.

After everyone finished eating, the band began to play. Al Adams pushed himself away from the table and stood up. The conversation quieted.

"I would like to announce the first dance of the evening and introduce to you for the first time, Mr. and Mrs. Todd Phillips." Nadia and Todd danced as if they were made for each other's arms. Eyes glued together, they rocked back and forth.

When the song was over, Al invited the best man and maid-of-honor to join them on the floor. Alex looked relaxed and "together". How surprising! Every hair combed in place, his tie perfectly matched his suit, his shirt neatly exposed in only the right places – a picture of perfection. He acknowledged Megan's approving glance and winked.

Megan took Alex' hand then he spun her around and led her into the center of the room. Quite amazing! He glided her like Fred Astaire across the floor. He completely controlled her movements including spins and dips. Applause burst forth occasionally. Megan didn't remember the last time she had so much fun. She loved to dance and her partner sure knew how. *I guess he doesn't have two left feet after all!*

Chapter Fifty-Seven

In Colorado, left parched by record heat and drought, dry timber burst into flames. It pulsed relentlessly blazing and consuming more than 200,000 acres of forests wildlife and homes. It left very few people thankful.

xxx

It sucked that Thanksgiving was no longer a holiday. There were very few holidays celebrated and he used to get that one off. Well if he had to be miserable, he planned to make others miserable too. Officer Pruitt was a third generation cop. Ever since he could remember, he wanted to be a cop and, just like his father and his grandfather before him, he had always planned to die a cop. But now he wouldn't give a rat's ear for the job. It had changed drastically in New York City the past three years. Gone were the days when he actually protected the public. The street gangs handled that now. They had carte blanche to badger, bully and pursue anyone and everyone, so much so that the average Joe was afraid to step out of line.

In a way, it was a good thing but Pruitt resented the fact that they had stripped so much of his power. He was left to supervise the gang activity. Supervise! Hell, he wasn't a supervisor he was a cop, or had been.

Pruitt printed out a list of all the "unmarked" whose SPIDER Card would expire within the next six months. The street gangs usually got to the Rogues before he did, so he played with the "unmarked" before their time ran out. It gave him great pleasure and some simple satisfaction to harass and stalk them during their final months of freedom. It was important to keep a very close eye on the "unmarked" because often they would flee before they became illegal. They seemed to have a specific location to run to and he was determined to find it. He hadn't made one single arrest since he was reassigned to this precinct almost two months ago. He hated it.

He hated them. The "unmarked" were the worst of the worst, clearly ungrateful for all that Sixtus had done for the world and them. They were ignorant as well. *That's what they are, ignorant, ungrateful traitors.* And too much money had gone down the tubes when they escaped through his watch. When he arrested one, or gave information that led to the arrest of one, he was given a bonus worth three months salary. The stakes were high and he was missing out.

Pruitt glanced down the list. Since the computer crash, he preferred dealing with hard copies rather than relying on cyberspace. As a result, he always printed out six months at a time. He grabbed his third cup of coffee for the day and leaned back in his swivel chair wondering which SOB he would torment that day.

Suddenly a clumsy rookie careened around the corner knocking Pruitt's elbow. Coffee flew down his newly pressed uniform and all over his desk. *Imbecile!* Pruitt jumped up and took a swing at the greenhorn who ducked causing the punch to land against the cubical wall. Pruitt cursed and rubbed his hand.

He didn't notice that some of the coffee landed on his freshly printed list smudging one of the names at the bottom – Jordan Crane, night manager at Docker's Pharmacy.

The boy named Jordan Crane sighed and rubbed his full belly. This Thanksgiving celebration topped them all. For the past several years, he had spent that day minding the store which remained open since it was no longer a national holiday. This year Docker decided to close for the day. He never had any sales on that day anyway.

The boy named Jordan had never been invited to Mr. Docker's home before. He wanted to stay and talk more with his boss but the tired look on Mrs. Docker's face told him it was time to go.

"Thank you so much for the wonderful dinner, Mrs. Docker. May I help you with the dishes?"

"You'll do nothing of the sort. You two men just sit and relax a bit."

"No, I really should get going. I don't want to intrude on your holiday any longer."

Mr. Docker walked him to the door. "Thanks again, Jordan, for the book."

The boy named Jordan figured he owed his boss a lot. Mr. Docker had really taken a big chance hiring a rebellious kid off the street. Jordan wanted to give something back but he only owned one valuable thing; the pocket Bible that Kirk's Aunt Rachel had given him. Jordan had taken up reading it at the store instead of comic books. It only took him one week to get hooked – then nothing could stop him! That Bible had changed him even more than Mr. Docker had.

"You gave me a chance for a better life here on earth, Mr. Docker, and I can never thank you enough. Read that little book and you'll have a better chance of life after you *leave* this earth." The boy named Jordan knew, without a doubt, the effect it would have on his boss. Mr. Docker just stared back at him. A big question mark sat on his face.

"Read it, you'll see."

Mr. Docker just shook his head.

The boy named Jordan planned to head north in about six months to a safe haven for Rogues. By then he would be a Rogue too. He prayed that this good man and his wife would join him.

Chapter Fifty-Eight

By nine that evening, the lingering wedding guests had completely restored the schoolhouse to its original order. Those remaining had moved to the farmhouse. Most of the angels left with their mortals.

xxx

Alex checked the time. They needed to get back. He pushed away from the kitchen table where a chess board sat with only a few pieces left on it.

"Well, Kirk, you're getting good at this. You'll be beating me on a regular basis if I don't watch out."

Kirk beamed. "Thanks, it's really pretty simple once you figure it out."

"Yes, it's the figuring out that's been a problem for me. You're one smart cookie."

"It's a good game. Can we play one more?"

"Not tonight, Kirk, I need to get home." Kirk frowned. His shoulders slumped almost down to the table. He had developed a pretty impressive chess strategy in only a few hours. The kid had a lot going for him and Alex liked him a lot.

"We'll play again." The boy's face lit up.

"Promise?"

"Promise, but now I have to hit the road." Nadia entered carrying a tray of empty glasses.

"Nadia, I'm sorry but I've got to get back to Katonah. It is hard to account for long days away like this." Alex hated to leave but he wanted to cross the bridge before ten o'clock. Crossings after that became more suspicious. It had been a wonderful day, the wedding, the reception, dancing with Megan. She laughed and smiled the whole day. No arguments. Why did they usually argue? She always pushed his buttons and frustrated him so. Today he was pretty sure he had made great progress and hoped it would continue through the end of the weekend. He gave his sister a hug.

"I understand. I really am so happy that you were able to come and stay as long as you did. Thank you, Alex, for giving me away. I'm sure Papa would have been proud."

"Of course he would have been proud. Look at the beautiful woman you've become." He looked around and spotted Megan sitting on the couch. "Megan, are you about ready to leave?"

"Oh, I'm sorry, Alex, I won't be going back with you tonight." She got up and walked over to him. "Al Adams asked me to drive his truck back tomorrow after he finishes unloading it. He wants the final record to show that it returned to Katonah. That way it may disguise his disappearance for a little while at least."

Alex glanced over at Walker who had been sitting next to Megan. His anticipation of spending a romantic weekend with Megan crumbled. She gave him a big hug and kissed him on the cheek. On the cheek no less – a real slap in the face. There go those buttons again!

"Thanks so much for everything. I'll see you tomorrow night. I shouldn't get back too late."

Stunned and weak-kneed Alex ran his fingers through his hair. He clung to her eyes searching for some glimmer of expectation, some tiny indication that that he could look forward to more from her when she returned. But he saw nothing, only beautiful green tantalizing eyes smiling back at him, eyes that he had fallen helplessly and hopelessly in love with.

"Alright then, don't rush and drive carefully." He managed to harness his anger and disappointment. Nadia hugged him one last time and walked him to the door where Todd stood waiting to shake his hand.

"You did a fine job, brother. Take good care of her."

"You know I will. And thanks so much for being my best man." Their hands pumped up and down followed by repeated pats on the back. Todd shook Alex's hand once more and said, "Success doesn't come by our own strength but by God's power. God has a purpose for each one of us and every problem in our lives has a reason. I think that reason is so that we can move on to victory and become better men."

Victory my eye ... I will never be a better man.

It had been a stellar wedding; Alex's best friend had become his new brother, his sister was gloriously happy, but the emptiness in his heart ripped him to pieces.

Tom followed quickly behind him.

"I'll give you a lift to your car." Outside Tom remarked, "We are like two lonely wrenches in a toolbox. We hold the nuts, work the bolts and when everything is together and working well, we're thrown back into the box again."

Alex agreed. Silently they rode into the darkness. Alex couldn't wait to get home to his bottle of Gray Goose.

During the day, the temperature had gotten close to eighty degrees but with the sun down now, the temperature had plummeted. Walker slipped one of Nadia's sweaters around Megan's shoulders as they left the house. They followed the bridal path from the farmhouse down to the lake. Flower petals still lined the edges. Neither spoke.

"So, do you have a lot of patients now?" Megan broke the silence.

"Yes, mostly people from Monroe though. The community here at Round Lake is generally in good health."

"Do the people from Monroe know you are a Rogue?"

"We don't discuss it, but they know. They give me goods, like the car for Todd and Nadia, in exchange for my services. It works out pretty well all around." He hesitated hoping not to put his foot in his mouth again. Walker wasn't sure if he should speak about it but it had been hanging over his head for weeks. He learned from arguments with Sam that he must apologize. Get it over with, the sooner the better.

"Look, Megan, I am really sorry I didn't explain to you that first night that I was a doctor."

"It's okay. I have gotten over it."

"It somehow seemed irrelevant. I guess I never expected to have a relationship with you."

Megan looked surprised, "And do we? Do we have a relationship?" A chill crept into her voice.

"I was hoping for one at least."

"I think it's best if we don't talk about it." He had blown it for sure. There was silence again. A calm breeze refreshed the air. The moon glowed bright. When they approached the lake, a choir of tree frogs serenaded them.

"I have never been in such a peaceful place," Megan said. They stared for a long while at the gentle ripples on the lake as it lapped against the shoreline. Walker spotted a wooden bench in a clearing off to the left. He took out his handkerchief and spread it on the seat so that Megan would not soil her dress and motioned her to sit down.

"You expect me to sit there? Not on your life." Megan put both hands on his shoulders and playfully commanded, "Sit." Once he obliged she immediately planted herself in his lap. "Now that's much better," she laughed. Her lips beckoned him as she spoke. He knew if he kissed her, he would forget who he was and where they were. Her arms clutched his neck. At times, she would rock her head back and forth and her long sweet smelling hair would brush his cheek. Her scent drove him wild. His desire to devour her grew as her cheerful laughter, like a shot of adrenaline, quickened his heart. He fought the temptation that aroused him.

Hours later, after Megan poured out her heart concerning the devastation she experienced in her recent trip to South America, they sat quietly with their arms wrapped around each other, staring into the water. The implications of her experience had a profound impact on both of them and silently they escaped into their own thoughts.

Suddenly a car crunched on the gravel as it approached. Walker recognized the sound of his wedding gift. Gradually it slowed to a halt in front of the cabin about fifty yards from where he and Megan sat. Quiet laughter from the lovesick couple filtered toward them as Todd easily lifted Nadia into his arms and carried her over the threshold.

The man in the moon smiled down.

Nothing would be more perfect for any of them than this.

<>

THE BOMBS BURSTING IN AIR

Chapter Fifty-Nine

Day 297

The Lord looked with spite on the Middle East. "Would I be roaring like a lion if I had no reason? Indeed the reason is clear. In fact I am getting ready to destroy you. You must be punished for your sins against My people. A trap does not snap shut unless it is stepped on; your punishment is well deserved. The alarm has sounded – listen and fear! For I, the Lord, am sending disaster into your land."

xxx

The sun rose high in the Middle East as Sixtus approached the six-hundred gallon aquarium build into the wall of his game room. The fish inside swam to his hand when he touched the outside glass. He smiled as he dropped a live white mouse through the top feeder. The water quickly churned. Blood trickled into the ten-foot long tank as five piranhas nibbled at their helpless victim. They started at the stomach, disemboweling their prey as it frantically attempted to claw back to the surface.

"Just a little snack, my friends," Sixtus crooned as his finger followed the frenzy. Spellbound by the kill taking place before him, the phone rang seven times before he answered.

"Good afternoon, sir. I have the report you requested on Alexander Liechtenstein."

"Excellent, Azimi, brief me."

"Alexander Liechtenstein, age 38, freelance writer for several publications, self educated astronomer and meteorologist, living in Katonah, NY, son of Russian immigrants and sister to Nadia Liechtenstein, a high profile activist against your régime. She is actually more noteworthy than he is. She disappeared about two months ago when her SPIDER Card expired."

"Any history on his travels to that town in upstate New York?"

"Yes, sir. His monthly travel statements account for several trips there each month. He owns, or rather rents to the owner of a grocery store, who makes regular deliveries to a restaurant in that town – Monroe. It appears to be strictly legitimate. Do you want me to dig any deeper?"

"No, that will be sufficient for now. I do want you to continue to monitor his activity going forward, especially any connection to Ms. Montgomery – visits, phone calls, emails, texting, that sort of thing. Keep me updated on an ongoing basis."

"Yes, sir."

Sixtus clicked off the receiver. *So lover boy is a scientist and a landlord. I like that. She appears to have good taste.* No trace remained of the white mouse that, only moments ago, had struggled for its life behind the three-inch-thick glass that separated Sixtus from his ferocious pets. He smiled again. *In due time nature always takes its course.*

Sixtus boarded the yacht that would return him to the mainland. He spoke abruptly on the phone to his Secretary of Affairs.

"Azimi, I want Ms. Montgomery to be permanently living in New York. Provide a reporter position for her there at the UWBC television station. Make it an offer she cannot refuse."

"Yes, sir, right away."

That should make her very happy. Ah yes, and ultimately very beholden to me.

Barker and Mr. Adams worked as quickly as possible to unload Mr. Adams' truck. The quicker they emptied it and got it back to Monroe the better.

"Well that just about does it, Tommy. Thanks for your help."

"I was glad to do it, Mr. Adams." Barker had a deep respect for this old man. Mr. Adams had been a big part of his life while his family lived in Katonah. Barker usually worked at his parent's service station on weekends, but sometimes after school, he would unload trucks for Mr. Adams when the flower deliveries arrived. Nadia would often be there in the back room doing homework while her mother worked out front. Barker cherished the moments that he spent in the large refrigerator. He always took his time, slowly emptying each carton and placing the flowers on the appropriate shelf. Nadia's mother told him he would freeze his fingers off because he spent so much time in there, but he didn't mind. From there he got a perfect, unobstructed view of the girl that had captured his heart. Behind huge glass doors, he could see Nadia sitting straight and tall, her sleek brown hair swishing around her beautiful face, concentrating hard. He liked the way she would make funny faces when confronted with a difficult math problem or something she didn't quite understand. Occasionally she would look up and catch him starting at her. Shyly he would beam with embarrassment and she would graciously smile back at him. Her smile had a way of making him melt even in that refrigerated room.

"Funny how things work out," Mr. Adams brought Barker back to the present.

"I always thought you and Nadia would one day end up together. You looked so enamored with each other when you were young." That comment renewed Barker's pain. His heart dropped down to the pit of his stomach.

"Yeah, well, time has a way of changing things. Anyway, Nadia was always too classy for me."

"You underestimate yourself, my boy." Barker knew he had not but he just let it go. Together they carried the last of the boxes and put them in the clearing next to the logs that occupied the left half of the open field. It was the perfect spot for a log cabin right next to a huge cherry tree. Barker would have loved to build a house for Nadia.

"It seems you have become a master mechanic, Tommy."

"Yeah, I can fix anything they bring to me." Engines were like jigsaw puzzles to Barker, a thing of beauty, intricate and complex. Each peace enhanced the loveliness of the whole. Each groove fit snuggly into the neighboring groove. No room for error or misalignment. His machines also had their own personalities – like woman but much less complicated. Engines needed to be handled with care but were a lot easier to deal with – all the pleasure without the pain.

"Right now, I am overhauling two old clunkers on the side. I hope to get them running without a computer board by the end of the month."

"Well, Tommy, if you have an extra one I'll take it. Megan is going to drive my truck back to Katonah."

"We'd better get going then."

Megan awoke with the crow of a rooster cutting off her sweet dream. The sun crept up behind the trees but she had a hard time opening her eyes. A truck crunched on the gravel road outside her window. The delicious aroma of coffee drew her from the bed. Quickly she pulled a pink lightweight turtleneck over her head and zipped up her jeans.

Al and Tommy were just walking in the door when she sauntered, still half asleep, down the stairs. She found Jerry in the kitchen cooking oatmeal and toasting bread. Fresh squeezed orange juice filled a pitcher on the table. He really looked fantastic with his hair curling around his ears and almost down to his shoulders. Unshaven he had a scruffy, woodsy look that caused her to melt in her tracks. *Any woman would die for his long thick lashes.*

"Good morning everyone," Al exclaimed cheerfully. "Did you all sleep well?"

"Yes, the little sleep we got was great." Jerry smiled at her and she eagerly returned it. They had talked out by the lake until almost two AM discussing everything from the earthquake in South America to the owls hooting in the trees. Then the inevitable question again. Have you been reading your Bible? Megan stiffened slightly at the thought of it. *Why did he have to bring that up again?* The night had been going so well. But there it was and there it would always be until she gave him the satisfactory answer. An answer, in all honesty, she could not give. Yes, she had been reading her Bible but no, her mind had not been changed. What role did logic play in the scriptures? Jerry claimed that when a doctor reports that, "recovery exceeded expectations," it really means it has defied all scientific logic. It implies that some form of miraculous element aided the healing process, but does that really mean a God element? She experienced more confusion than ever.

They had walked back to the house in silence ... hand-in-hand, but in silence. Her mouth curled up as she recalled his sweet kiss on her forehead. She had hoped he would follow her up to Nadia's bedroom but as she suspected he didn't.

In a few minutes, she would head out the door, on her way back to reality, and nothing seemed to be resolved. He had written down the address of one of his patients where she could send him letters. She had reluctantly agreed to write him on a regular basis. She hated conveying personal thoughts or emotions, especially on paper.

For about twenty minutes, the four of them chatted quietly, not to wake the rest of the household. Then unwillingly, Megan got up to leave. "I'd better hit the road. It's almost eight and I don't want to get stopped when I cross the bridge." They all said their good-byes. Jerry walked her to the truck and lifted her suitcase into the back seat.

"Have a safe trip home. And write. You promised to write."

"I will." She wanted to blurt out that she would gladly stay with him if he only asked. She would quit her job and hide away with him forever. But instead, she only added, "Take care, Jerry."

"There is not much here to get me into trouble." He laughed. Something suspended between them. *Please say something more.* She longed to crawl inside his head. Get inside his soul. Her eyes searched his, hoping desperately to see in them what obsessed her heart. They came up empty. One last hug held them close for a ballooned moment. Then Megan broke away, climbed into the truck and drove off, her eyes glued to the rearview mirror. *Parting is such sweet sorrow.*

Chapter Sixty

At midnight, Megan finally rested her head on the pillow in Nadia's old bedroom in Katonah. The past two days had been enchanting and she hated to see them end. Last night jumped vividly into her mind as if it had happened five minutes ago. She decided she might even be falling in love but she wasn't sure what that actually meant any more.

Megan still didn't understand why this "God" thing was so important to Jerry. *Why doesn't he just go with his emotions?* She sensed he had strong feelings for her but he fought them ... held them in. *Why would God stand in the way of his happiness?* She closed her eyes and imagined herself sitting on his lap again, his rough face scratching against her cheek. *He really should grow a beard. At least then, he wouldn't have those stubbles all the time.* She laughed quietly to herself. As if that would make any difference to her at all.

She faintly heard Alex banging around in the kitchen on the other side of the apartment. Most likely he was getting ice for that last little bit of vodka. *He was so sweet to get me those cherries and to spend all that time tonight answering my endless questions.* Megan held a new admiration for him. She vowed to call him weekly to get his take on current storm systems and geological developments. The man was a genius and she planned to pick his brain as often as he would let her.

Poor Alex must have had a very traumatic experience when his father died. Tonight when Megan asked him to play his violin she thought she had broken through. There had been a long hesitation before he shook his head no. *One day I'll get him to play for me.* Her thoughts continued until she slowly drifted off to sleep.

<>

GAVE PROOF THROUGH THE NIGHT THAT OUR FLAG WAS STILL THERE

PART FOUR:

Condemned

Chapter Sixty-One

Day 183

The steamy waters off the California coast failed to nourish its underwater population. Patterns changed. Cannibalism reigned. Disaster was in the making.

xxx

Humming a tune that he remembered from his childhood, the boy named Jordan sat at Grand Central Station in a train bound for Ossining, NY. His funds wouldn't take him any farther north.

Last night the Dockers gave him a farewell dinner. He could still taste the delicious lasagna and sweet apple pie. Mr. Docker had thanked him three times for the little Bible Jordon had given him at Thanksgiving. Jordan repeated the words Doc had said to him. "God rewards those who seriously try to find Him."

Now the boy named Jordan was headed for a new life. Where it went he didn't know. He bounced a little in his seat. Next chapter? Walking in faith, a little bit like Abraham when God told him to leave for parts unknown.

Officer Pruitt printed out a fresh list of the "unmarked" whose SPIDER Cards were about to expire. A new name jumped to the top – Jordan Crane, night manager at Docker's Pharmacy. *Where in the hell did this guy come from?* Pruitt fished his old list out of the trash. Sure enough, there it was, Jordan Crane, smudged and wrinkled under a large coffee stain at the bottom of the page. Immediately Pruitt pulled the name up on his computer, zeroing in on the last three months. Scanning the list, he saw nothing of significance until the last two entries dated this morning.

- Purchased a train ticket for Ossining, New York
- Boarded a train in Grand Central Station at 10:37 AM

He had hit the jackpot! Crane was on the run – headed north. He immediately placed a call to the Ossining police station, and then he alerted the United World Peace Forces (UWPF). This would definitely warrant a reward and he intended to cash in on it. He climbed in his cruiser and headed north.

Chapter Sixty-Two

In the sixth dimension Michael the Archangel sent a messenger to Kasha, Nadia's guardian angel. "Be on guard. This is a perilous day. Her freedom is at stake."

xxx

The signs of spring were all around. Nadia awoke to the meadowlark's sweet song and her precious husband's gentle breathing beside her. She watched him as he slept. His sandy blond hair was disheveled and sticking up in spots. His handsome face reflected peace and serenity. His features were so flawlessly striking that she never understood why he found her attractive. She sighed. Their life together was abundantly blessed and completely perfect.

Katie Westerly and Mrs. Pierce, the mayor's wife, were in the Civic Center just putting the last of the food trays out. In a few minutes the cafeteria would be filled with people, mostly "unmarked" and definitely hungry. Every day they served lunch to families from the surrounding communities. They had created more than a soup kitchen. It constituted a safe place, where people congregated to fill their bellies and their spirits.

The music was Mrs. Pierce's idea but Katie enjoyed it more than anyone else. After the noon meal, someone would bring out the guitar or harmonica and everyone would sing. Katie led the praise songs and others that cheered the heart. She especially enjoyed seeing the children dance and play games of tag and catch.

When Dr. Jeremiah Walker entered Ossining, NY over six months ago, he actually changed the town forever. One month later she and Mrs. Pierce had a chance meeting. She heard about the encounter he had with Mrs. Pierce and her son in the Italian restaurant. That started a chain of events that spread like wildfire.

Katie discovered that she and Mrs. Pierce both shared the same burden, to help the "unmarked," so they put their heads together and began a call line that ran from Dobbs Ferry up the Hudson Valley to the safe haven. It worked like a relay where Rogues were passed off from driver to driver until they reached Alex's apartment in Katonah. He then would smuggle them safely into Monroe and Tom Barker would drive them the last leg to Round Lake. All the other drivers alternated so the risks were minimal. Each driver would take the Rogues to the end of their safety zone where they could go without being suspected. Mrs. Pierce, with all her political ties, met with church directors and mayor's wives all the way up the line. So far, they had successfully transported seventeen families, all of which made it safely to Monroe and the Round Lake community.

When Jordan arrived in Ossining, he saw a sign over the Civic Center that read "Free lunch daily 11:00 – 1:00." That was a welcomed sight. After he had filled up on hot soup and pasta salad a woman sat down on the seat next to him.

"Hi, my name is Katie. I don't think I've seen you before. Are you new in town?"

"Yea, I'm really only passing through."

"Where are you going?"

"I'm not really sure." Throwing caution to the wind and wanting to spread the good news about Jesus, Jordan could not contain the excitement he had. Out of pure innocence he said, "I'm just going where the Lord leads me."

"Well maybe I can help you get there." Katie offered him passage to the safe haven. She drove him first to her house.

"This is a great home you have. I'm used to the city. I have never seen such a beautiful garden!"

"Come on in. I'll show you where you'll be going." She spread the map out on the kitchen table. "It's not really too far. You will be passed from driver to driver until you get to your final destination here at Round Lake." She pointed to the spot circled in red. She made a few phone calls and then packed him a sandwich.

Fifteen minutes later they backed out of her driveway.

Officer Pruitt and an Ossining policemen interviewed a woman outside the Ossining Civic Center. Yes, she had seen a man of Jordan's description. He had left not long ago with Katie Westerly.

Moments later the officers arrived at Katie's house. No one answered the bell so without hesitation they he broke down the door. On the kitchen table was a map of New York State with Round Lake circled in red. Officer Pruitt immediately notified the UWPF.

"The perpetrators are headed toward Round Lake, a few miles west of Monroe." Pruitt smirked. What a reward he would get for this one!

Chapter Sixty-Three

In the sixth dimension, a legion of angels hovered over the Round Lake Schoolhouse. Their swords clashed ferociously with the demons who tried to penetrate the hearts of the innocent children. Their wings pounded and thundered an almost deafening sound. Tired of the fight, one-by-one the demons retreated waiting for a more opportune moment to steal the children away.

xxx

Nadia dismissed the teenagers. Their classes began at seven-thirty and ended at noon. They were by far her most challenging students and kept her on her toes, a place she loved to be.

The younger children started to filter into the school at twelve fifteen and Nadia happily greeted each one individually. Kirk and his dog Neeko were the last to arrive and took their usual places in the back.

Nadia pointed toward a glass canning jar with holes punched in the lid. "Can anyone tell me what this is?"

Emma's hand shot up and Nadia called on her. "It's a chrysalis with a caterpillar inside."

"You are exactly right, Emma. Does anyone know how that caterpillar got inside the chrysalis?" Slowly Kirk raised his hand. Happy to see him volunteer, Nadia acknowledged him.

"He built the chrysalis around himself."

"Thank you, Kirk that is also right. Female butterflies lay their eggs usually on the bottom side of leaves." Nadia proceeded to explain the process of metamorphosis. She encouraged the younger ones to stand up and twirl around like caterpillars spinning their new home.

"Brianna, do you think that the caterpillar in this chrysalis knows that one day soon he will become a beautiful butterfly?" The child stopped her spinning dance and playfully tried to balance herself.

"No, I guess he doesn't even know he'll become a butterfly."

"I think you are absolutely right. All his life he ate and ate and ate. Then one day he just chose to stop. That decision ended his life as a caterpillar and he hasn't eaten since. And once he made that decision nothing could stop him from spinning that chrysalis. Do you think that was a good decision?"

"Yes," Brianna said. "It is much better to be a butterfly than a caterpillar."

"But you said before he didn't know he would become a butterfly." Brianna looked completely puzzled. Jaelyn eagerly raised her hand.

"Jaelyn, do you have something to add?"

"It's the same thing that happened to me when I gave my life to Jesus. Beforehand I didn't know what I would become but now I see how wonderful it is! All the bad ugly parts about me have disappeared." Nadia was delighted that Jaelyn made the connection so easily and explained it so simply.

"That's absolutely correct. When you give your heart to Jesus you no longer recognize yourself; you become far more beautiful and free."

"Did you know that we can't change on our own? Without God's help it is impossible to change. He gave us His Spirit to show us the way because, as Jaelyn said, when we give our hearts to Jesus we do become someone new like this caterpillar. We now wear wings and live with courage for Jesus. It's not what we see that is important, like the wings of a butterfly, but who we believe that is important, and that's Jesus. His love for us takes us higher than any butterfly can go.

"Good Friday is in three weeks. Who knows what that is?" Many hands went up all around the room.

"Kaylie, can you tell us?"

"It's the day that we remember when Jesus died."

"Yes, that's right. His love is so deep that he wanted to take the punishment for all our sins. He will always love us because His love lasts longer than anyone of us can live." One-by-one the children began to ask questions and one-by-one Nadia answered them. She loved their curiosity and wished that Kirk would participate in the discussion but he only listened silently.

Suddenly Kirk's complacent face changed. He sat up straight in his seat then slowly stroked Neeko who began to growl.

Sixtus smiled when Azimi called.

"Yes, I agree with you. It sounds like you have found the ultimate snare in Liechtenstein's maneuvers. I want you to raid Round Lake. His sister must be there and who knows how many others. I'm glad you made the connection between his sister's disappearance and all his trips to Monroe. Keep a vigil eye on him. His SPIDER Card will expire at sometime as well and I want him out of the picture forever."

Chapter Sixty-Four

Fifteen demons had received the call. Their mood was less than enthusiastic. Monroe was a town with which they were familiar. They had often been defeated there. They cursed and complained as they reluctantly escorted the UWPF troops to this destination.

xxx

Normally Tom Barker's customers pumped their own gas but when Mrs. Nelson pulled up to the station in her forty-year old Plymouth, he met her at the pump. At ninety-two, Mrs. Nelson could barely see over the steering wheel and her feet barely reach the pedals. But her mind was as sharp as a whip and she always greeted Barker with an engaging friendly smile. This afternoon was no different.

"Hi, Tommy, how is the best mechanic in town?"

"I'm fine, Mrs. Nelson." He laughed at her exaggerated compliment. "How are you?"

"Not bad for an old lady." She paused for a moment while he put the nozzle into her tank. "Do you by any chance know anything about air-conditioners? Mine is on the fritz and that Berry Hopper is so lazy, he never returns my calls."

"I'll stop by later this evening to look at it. How about six thirty?"

"If you come at six I'll have a chicken in the oven and I'll make your favorite biscuits."

"How can I turn down chicken and biscuits?"

An armored tank and two open camouflage trucks filled with UWPF drove toward them. Their foreboding presence poisoned the atmosphere. People moved inside and closed their curtains. A boy on a bike stretched his fist high in the air to flag his approval as they passed by. An officer riding in the lead truck motioned for his driver to stop.

Barker and Mrs. Nelson exchanged solemn glances.

"Hey kid. Do you know a teacher named Nadia Liechtenstein?"

"I know a teacher that the kids at the Round Lake School call Ms. Nadia."

"Get in boy and show me where that is." One of the soldiers riding in the back of the truck reached down to hoist him up.

Barker darted a pleading look over to his boss. He received a sincere affirmative nod. Mrs. Nelson said, "That's enough gas for today, Tommy. Run like the wind and may God go with you." He returned the nozzle to its cradle.

Without checking for traffic he dashed across the street and sprinted to the abandoned church around the corner. Three years ago the church practically burst with parishioners. Before membership in the United World Church (UWC) had become mandatory that is. Now the beautiful building and its bell tower were only used when miscellaneous groups, like Nadia's Bible study, periodically met there. When she used the building, the locals merely looked the other way. They preferred to go with the flow. It was too dangerous to rock the boat. The New World Order had become the established way of life, but in their hearts they secretly rebelled. Most, but not all the town's people sympathized with the Rogues at Round Lake and admired them for their courage and strong convictions.

Barker's mind raced to the farm. How many would they catch? He didn't dare think of that now, he just knew he must warn them. He found the hidden church-office key then fumbled with the lock. Moisture made it stick. Once inside the musty room he caught his breath and slowed until his eyes adjusted to the dark. There was the supply closet. Next to it was a lever. Barker pushed up with all his strength but it didn't move, refused to budge. Their freedom was up to him and he was failing them. Frantic, he looked for something, anything he could use to wedge under the lever. Where was his toolbox when he needed it? He spotted a stapler on the desk, grabbed it, forced it under the handle and pushed. The switch flipped. Twelve melodious gongs, each of a different tone, rang out from the bell tower above. It warned all those on Round Lake that their hiding place had been discovered.

Nadia, winding down her last class of the day, heard the bells in the distance. She knew this was not a drill. Kirk had the gift of discernment, that's why he reacted so strangely. That's what she had seen on his face – the presence of evil. Her brain went into overdrive.

"Alright children, remember we were talking earlier about butterflies? Well right now we are going to play the Butterfly Game." They had rehearsed the exit drill many times so the children knew exactly what they should do. Promptly they scampered over to the cabinet that Tommy had built to conceal the hen door. Orderly, all the children scurried through the hollow cabinet, out the tiny opening and dashed across the exposed yard to their designated hiding places in the woods.

"Fly little butterflies fly!" Nadia called after them.

"I didn't do it. It's not my fault." Kirk looked pleadingly at Nadia. "I didn't call the police."

"I know, Kirk. Don't worry. Everything will be all right. God creates only the best circumstance for those that give the choice to Him." Nadia gave Kirk one last hug before he and his dog disappeared through the disguised exit.

"I love you," she called as she closed the door behind him. Then Nadia pulled back the carpet that covered the door to the cellar below her desk. Carefully she carried Mary, the ten year old with cerebral palsy, down into it.

"Be as quiet as you can no matter what you hear above you. It's all a part of the game," she whispered to Mary who clapped her hands, happy to be included in the action.

"Remember, butterflies don't make a sound."

Nadia closed the trap door over Mary's head and then tugged at the rug to return it to its former position. Blood thrashed through her veins as if expecting to explode. With inhuman strength she lifted and dragged her desk back over the rug. All was perfectly set. The little girl would be safe.

Nadia charged toward the supply closet where she and Tommy had cleared the bottom shelf for this very purpose. As she crouched down to climb in, Megan's elephant comb began to dislodge from her fine silky hair. Every morning when she secured the comb, she said a prayer for Megan. Constantly throughout the day, it would slip and constantly she would respond with a prayer for her friend. This time, however, she prayed for herself.

"Lord, you defend me and protect me at all times. You keep evil away from me and constantly save my life. Your eyes are on me at this very moment guarding me. Thank you, my Lord."

Chapter Sixty-Five

Kasha bent down to touch Nadia's comb, to keep it from falling to the ground.

"No, Kasha," came the command from the Prince of Peace.

"But her prayer, Lord, Nadia's prayer for safety, we must answer her prayer."

"Her every word pleases My heart. I have answered."

xxx

Just before Nadia closed the closet door behind her, the ivory comb slipped to the ground. The brazen rumble of the military convoy arrived outside. Several soldiers jumped out of the trucks and entered through the side door. The schoolhouse remained quiet with no visible signs of inhabitants. Nadia's heart pounded. She did not move.

"So where are they?" The officer grumbled.

"I don't know. They are usually still in class at this time. I know because they usually go two hours longer than we do." She didn't recognize the young boy's voice. Steps scuffled over the dirt floor and approached her hiding place. The thunder of Nadia's heart seemed to echo throughout the metal chamber. She covered her mouth to stifle it.

"What's that in the dust?" The man barked.

"It looks like some kind of hair comb." Another voice answered.

"Open that cabinet." The order came.

They had found her. What should she do? Her legs, weak from crouching, suddenly sprang to life. She crashed out of her hiding place, slammed the door right into the intruder's head, and raced past the commanding officer who seized her arm.

"And where do you think you're going, Miss Liechtenstein?"

The stairway at Al Adams' new house needed some final touches. Only a few more pieces of molding ... Todd heard the church bell warning in the distance. He dropped his hammer. *Nadia's in the schoolhouse with the children.*

Lightening soared through his legs. He took a shortcut through the dense trees, breaking branches and catching briars in his hair. His chest heaved but he couldn't stop. He arrived at the farmhouse breathless but bounded two steps up at a time to his bedroom closet where he kept his hunting rifle. Hands trembling, he loaded it. *I wonder how many of them there are.* He raced back down the stairs and out the front door. He sprinted as quickly as he could to the schoolhouse praying all the while that the children got away and that Nadia was safe. He saw the UWPF vehicles parked on the right side of the building. Todd quietly approached listening for any sounds from within. Sadly, he heard Nadia's voice.

"My name is Nadia Phillips. I was married last November."

A gruff man replied, "It makes no difference Ms. Liechtenstein." Todd decided to go in through the front barn doors. If he could catch the soldiers off guard, maybe Nadia could get away. Carefully, without a sound, he slid the two-by-four from the bracket that secured the large doors. With one hand, he pulled the left door open.

"Nadia, run!" Todd looked longingly at his beautiful bride. Drained of color, features frozen, he hardly recognized her. Fear gripped her eyes as they met his. She reached toward him. Almost instantaneously, flashes of light exploded from three machine guns. The noise was deafening. A powerful force through him back, he was down. He had failed. *I'm sorry, my darling Nadia, I'm sorry.*

Nadia broke free of the colonel's grasp and lunged for Todd. Another soldier knocked her to the ground and handcuffed her behind her back. He dragged her to her feet and through the side door then loaded her into the bed of a truck.

"Look for other Rogues, there must be more of them." They drove to the farmhouse and three soldiers ran inside.

Please, Lord, they all must be gone. They returned empty handed. Nadia smiled. They drove down the pathway to the cottage by the lake but it was empty too.

Nadia glanced toward Mr. Adams' log cabin. Miraculously wildflowers and thistles, weeds and grasses of all sorts sprang up through the ground hardened by human feet. This growth, within five minutes, completely camouflaged the pathway to Al Adams' log cabin.

She closed her eyes. *Thank you, Lord. They'll never find him.*

The motorcade threatened the quiet town of Monroe with the defeated sight of Nadia chained on her knees. Sorrowful eyes peered at her through sheer curtains. They were the sympathetic ones. The hateful ones glared at her and jeered. Unashamed she held her head high however a shroud of death stole her usual smiling features. The wooden floorboards drew blood and pounded splinters into her knees. A young boy yelled, "Traitor!" and hurled a rock that hit her squarely in the head. Blood trickled down her face. She felt nothing. It didn't hurt. Nothing would ever hurt again because her life had already ended and was lying in a pool of blood at the Round Lake Schoolhouse. At the moment of his death she knew without a doubt he had been the love of her life. Her only real love.

Sixtus beamed like a Cheshire cat when he got the report from Azim. One more Rogue disposed of and this one apparently had been quite influential. *Well Mr.*

Liechtenstein, so much for hiding your little rebellious sister. And as for Ms.
Montgomery, you will not have her either.
   "Azimi, why haven't you been successful in contacting Ms. Montgomery?"
   "She isn't returning my calls, sir."
   "Well, try again!" The irritation exploded from him.

Alex drove into the silenced town. Not one person lingered on the street or waved
as he and his most recent delivery, Jason Crane, drove through. There were no
other cars. Monroe appeared deserted. Alex didn't know why but it gave him an
eerie feeling of fear and mourning. Death enveloped the air.

Catcalls and whistles from hardened criminals threatened Nadia as the armed
guard escorted her to her jail cell. Only on rare occasions was a woman
temporarily placed in a men's prison. The Sullivan Correctional Facility, only
about twenty-five minutes from Monroe, had a minimum-security annex but it was
completely full so they incarcerated her in the maximum-security section. More
than eighty-five percent of its occupants had committed violent crimes and sixty
percent were serving life sentences. Gradually the rude whistles turned to scoffing
taunts.
   "Traitor!" yelled Samson, a two-hundred eighty-five pound mass of muscles
and sweat who waved his fisted arm back and forth between metal bars.
   "Traitor!" echoed Kite his tattoo covered sidekick. Abruptly the whole pod
became agitated and their angry voices clamored around her.
   Finally, locked inside her own cell, Nadia sat on her cot clutching her knees to
her chest. She closed her eyes and pictured Todd just before his bullet riddled body
dropped to the ground. Again, she saw his unending love, his devotion, and his
sacrifice. She finally allowed herself to cry at the loss of her brave faithful
husband. Uncontrolled sobs clutched at her innards. Then suddenly, for the first
time, she felt the miraculous movement of their baby within her. Like a butterfly
she fluttered her first, "Hello!" *Oh my sweet child what do I have to offer you?*
   "An everlasting tomorrow," Jesus answered.
   Eventually the angry calls around her brought her back to reality. Nadia
focused on the Lord and took courage. She began to sing, quietly at first then with
full vibrato, "Amazing grace how sweet the sound ..." Slowly, the verbal
altercations began to cease. One inmate screamed, "Shut up b----!" Yet another
responded, "Let her sing."
   Nadia's voice rang out loudly at the fourth verse, "Yes, when this heart and
flesh shall fail and mortal life shall cease, I shall possess, within the veil, a life of
joy and peace."

As soon as Tom Barker sounded the alarm, he headed to the farm. By road, it was
about seven miles. By crow, it was closer to three. He opted for the shorter route

but said a prayer that he wouldn't lose his way in the thick foliage. He crossed over seven streets through alleyways and private yards. By the time he reached the edge of the woods he was panting hard. He knew his pace would naturally slow down once he reached the trees.

The fresh new springtime growth concealed any trace of a path he might have recognized. Prickles from wild raspberry bushes pulled at his jeans and ripped his shirt. He didn't even pause. His mind was focused on one thing – getting to Nadia. *Nadia, Nadia, oh please, Lord, please.*

As he wound his way deeper into the woods, the ground vegetation became scant, the trees denser. He couldn't distinguish any of them. He just followed his instincts in a westerly direction. Then in the distance, he saw human movement around a huge oak tree. He stealthily inched closer. It was Leo and his family. Barker finally had his bearings. He greeted the family with hugs and pats on the back. Leo was calm. His wife cradled the children in her arms like a sparrow protecting her chicks from a storm.

"We heard gunshots!" Leo whispered.

Barker, wild with new rage, charged toward the schoolhouse.

"Be careful." Leo called after him.

Barker advanced with a rebellious stride to the front of the building. Todd's lifeless body dominated the blood stained ground. Petrified, his legs refused to move. He couldn't bear to see his lovely Nadia lifeless as well. He tried to catch his breath but his heart pounded so hard it was impossible. Cautiously he peered inside but the classroom was empty. A wave of relief blanketed his already heavy shoulders. Hoping against hope he dashed to the main house – empty too. He raced back to the schoolhouse and knelt in the dirt next to his dead friend. Barker's chest heaved. His anger and fear exploded into tears.

Jesus consoled him. "Do not be afraid for I am with you. Do not be grieved. I am your God. I will strengthen you; I will help you; I will make you victorious."

With new resolve, Barker entered the schoolhouse. A beam of light streamed through the skylight over Nadia's desk covering it with sunshine, a brutal trick to cheer him. He refused it. The open cabinet gave the true verdict.

He remembered the flag that he and Nadia had rescued from that same empty space. His eyes swept the room and there it still stood majestically in the corner where together they had placed it so many months before. Could his heart sustain the pain? He went directly to it. He gently caressed the red striped fabric. He remembered Nadia's tears at first sight of it. How much blood had been shed for it, for American soil and for freedom that seemed forever lost? Shaking internally, he raised the flagpole from its stand, marched defiantly out the door and into the east field. With all his strength, he violently waved the flag high in the sky boldly yelling repeatedly through sobs, "God bless America! God bless America ..."

<>

OH, SAY DOES THAT STAR SPANGLED BANNER YET WAVE

Chapter Sixty-Six

Day 165

"Stop the trumpeters before they destroy my kingdom!" The order came swift and direct from the devil himself. A myriad of demons scurried in a fury to the distant most point of the sixth dimension where the seven angels with their seven trumpets had stationed themselves. Each angel with three sets of powerful wings held a shophar. They stood tall and majestic knowing they held the power to destroy in their hands. Their wings beat strong and hard, so hard, the demons could not get near them.

xxx

Kirk and Neeko had moved deep into the woods with Mr. Adams and Doc Walker. Mr. Adams was okay but the Doc got on his nerves. Doc was chopping wood when he and Neeko slipped out of the cabin and headed to the farmhouse. He knocked before entering. Kaylie and her sisters were sitting on the floor playing a board game.

"Hi Kirk, do you want to play?"

"No, I was just looking. Have you guys done your homework yet?"

"Yeah, Mom said if we got it done before three o'clock we could go down by the lake. But it is too cold so we decided to play a game instead."

"Alright then, I'll catch you later." The girls returned to their game and Kirk let himself out. He wasn't sure what he was looking for ... but something was missing and he needed to find it. He walked to the schoolhouse looking at every stone on the way.

His life stopped the day Todd died and they arrested Nadia. They were like parents to him. His real mother died when he was only five years old. She was Jewish. Everyone said he got his determination from her. She always told him he could be anything he set his mind to. He had set his mind on becoming a veterinarian.

People said he got his good looks from his Irish father who wasn't actually a father at all. Patrick McCartney had provided money for groceries and a roof over their heads but little more. It was his older brother Pete that really raised him. Pete had always taken care of him, defended him and watched out for him. Pete even took a beating for him from time to time and often kept Kirk out of trouble.

His brother taught him how to read and write – the most valuable lessons of all. He loved to read and the hunger to learn burned deep inside him. Every chance he got, he would sneak into the library on 42nd Street and go to the science floor. There he could escape to any part of the world from inside the human body to the far corners of Africa. He missed the library and it was all Doc's fault. That life and those dreams had changed forever when he left with Doc. He never would become a vet now.

Maybe it wasn't so bad leaving the city. At least he didn't have to worry about his dad finding him. The last time he saw his father he had charged into the apartment cursing, crashing into furniture, pounding on everything like he needed to bust out of a cage! He came at Kirk, murder in his eyes, swinging a beer bottle. Pete tried to step in between them but pow – his father's strong punch smashed Kirk's face. Kirk flew across the room – knocked out cold. When he woke up his father was gone and his brother lay dead on the floor next to him. He ran away that night ... and ran and ran. He never went back. He was afraid his father would come looking for him but he never did. For years he had wished his father would die or at least go to jail. But now Kirk didn't care anymore.

Why do the people I love all die? I *must be very bad.* Kirk crossed the meadow. The schoolhouse loomed ahead. Parts of the huge weathered doors were completely ripped away by bullet holes, the dirt still black and bloody. He entered through the side door. Whimpering, Neeko trailed behind him.

Again Kirk searched for what? Then he spotted it in the dust. His heavy legs scuffed his shoes across the floor to the supply cabinet. He sank to the ground. There it was, her ivory elephant comb lodged in the dirt. He wiped it clean with his shirttail. He traced the outline with his finger and stroked it gently like he would a helpless kitten. He had seen it every day in her beautiful hair.

It was his fault they arrested her. If only he had left Neeko behind to protect her. If only he'd helped her hide the girl, she would've had time to hide. If only... If only...

Tears streamed down his face. No matter how hard he tried, he couldn't hold them back. Neeko, his only true friend, sat next to him. His coarse wet tongue mopped Kirk's face. Suddenly his tail began to wag but the faithful dog never left his master's side. Doc had entered the schoolhouse and slowly approached.

"She is a good teacher and a very brave woman." Doc said in a slow steady voice.

Kirk wiped his nose and eyes on his shirtsleeve. "What do you know about it?" He scowled.

"You're right. I don't know much about her or you. I only see the sullen quiet that surrounds all your actions. You must be very angry."

Kirk refused to look at the man.

"Trust in the Lord, Kirk, there are many things we don't understand, things we're never meant to understand."

"Where was He when Miss Nadia was arrested?" Kirk exploded.

"God works inside of us first to shape us and to help us to grow. Then He works on the outside to shape and change our circumstances." After a long silence, Doc put his hand on Kirk's shoulder. "You'll be all right."

Kirk briskly shrugged out from beneath the large hand. *Nothing will ever be right again.* Clutching the precious comb Kirk stood up and his devoted dog followed.

"You don't know nothin'. Just leave me alone," Kirk bolted from the schoolhouse, the place he had learned to love but now brought his deepest pain. He ran as hard as he could to the only place that comforted him – the meadow where his horses grazed.

Chapter Sixty-Seven

Megan's angel Hakah was glad the air controllers had some sense. It would have required a whole army of angels to keep this flight safe.

xxx

Megan needed to get away. The stress of Nadia's arrest was more than she could handle. She had no idea how Alex was standing up so well. She was grateful to get this assignment in Israel but it had not come without hitches. This was the third one. Her flight had been diverted to Istanbul, Turkey due to a treacherous storm brewing. It was six AM and she had a seven hour layover. Megan couldn't see wasting seven hours in the airport of one of the most historic cities of the world so she did the most logical thing a reporter would do. She left Frank, her boring cameraman, sleeping on an airport bench and took a tour.

Her guide had been incredible. His knowledge limitless. She picked his brain the entire time. His final comments were in the Hagia Sophia Museum, a church turned mosque, turned church again. "Feel free to walk up to the balcony for a better view. The passageway on the left goes up and the one on the right comes down." Megan was mesmerized by the beautiful tile domed ceiling.

"Will you take my picture?" she asked the guide handing him her cell phone.

"Of course," he agreed. He snapped the shot then handed the phone back.

"Thank you so much. It was a great tour. May I have your POS?" She keyed in a sizable tip and swiped her wrist. It was well worth it. She had learned so much and on top of it, it had kept her awake for the last leg of her trip. She needed to be back at the airport in two hours. She had plenty of time to check out the balcony.

Her high heels clanked and echoed against the marble stones as she ascended the steep winding ramp. A rank odor of sweat sifted through her nostrils. She was tempted to sniff her own armpits but decided the odor came from persons unknown. Once at the top, she took two pictures then looked at the picture her guide took. He was in it. How could it be? She went to the railing and looked over, searched the sparse crowd. He was nowhere in sight. Then she heard the click of heels on the marble ramp. Mole Man was coming.

Huge marble pillars supported the mammoth ceiling above her. She could hide behind one of them. No, he would find her for sure. Several people admired pictures of mosaic sculptures against the walls. Surely he wouldn't accost her in front of a crowd. Who was she fooling? It wasn't a crowd, just three isolated tourists. She could run. He would catch her.

   She went back to the three foot railing overlooking the museum. On the other side was a narrow service platform suspended fifty feet above the ground. She pulled her skirt up six inches to get over the railing then drop to the platform. She crouched down just as his footsteps reached the balcony ... then they stopped. She heard him meander from one pillar to another. Her heart pounded in her chest. He came to the railing two feet away from her and looked down. She pressed her body against the railing. She smelled his hot tobacco breath and thought she would puke. Slowly he moved away. Megan slipped her high heels off and peeked over the railing. He was talking to a woman on the far side of the balcony who sounded annoyed by his presence.

   Lightening zipped through Megan's feet as she sprinted over the railing and ran toward the up ramp. On her way down she almost dropped her shoes when she crashed into a romantic couple on their way up. Her heart pounded harder. She ran her hand against the wall to steady herself on the slippery stones. When she reached the bottom she stayed close to the outer wall finally making it through the huge wooden doors. Out in the hot morning air she put on her shoes and ran like a lunatic from the courtyard, through the turnstile to the main road. She hailed a cab and never once looked back.

Chapter Sixty-Eight

Hakah tucked his wings behind him and settled on Megan's shoulder. She was one of his biggest challenges but he wouldn't give the action up for anything. He just wished she was a little more responsive to his directions and proclamations.

xxx

Megan's flight from Istanbul to Jerusalem lifted off as scheduled. She would be there in two hours. Megan had no time to read Jerry's letter before she left home. Now she needed it to distract her from her morning pursuit. She pulled the letter from her purse. She had waited as long as she could before opening it. Somehow the anticipation heightened the pleasure she knew the letter would bring.

Dear Meg,

I hope you are well. The farm is so lonely without you. You fill my dreams; your eyes, your hair, your smile. Your laughter possesses my waking hours and your scent still lingers in the air. Every day I look forward to a letter from you but I know you are busy. The little girls ask about you daily. They want you to come for a visit too.

Life here is tremendously different without Nadia and Todd. Kirk wanders around aimlessly at times. He studies very little and spends most of the day with his horses. I have a growing concern for him.

We have three goats now that the children love to milk. The chickens are reproducing with the help of a neighbor's rooster. And the egg supply is nonstop. I make a mean omelet if you care to join us!

Todd did an amazing amount of planting before he died. Leo is working the land but it's a lot to stay on top of. Al Adams and I help out as much as we can. Tom taught me how to use the bailer. Don't laugh; I actually managed to finish the east field in less than a week. Obviously my talents are put to better use in the healing field.

Jordan, the young man who arrived the day Nadia was arrested, is working at the local pharmacy. He is able to get all the medical supplies that I need. It makes my job servicing the rogue community a lot easier.

Mandy has taken Nadia's place teaching the children. They all love her. I have taken over Nadia's adult Bible study classes. I can't say her students love me that much. I tend to admonish where she tended to encourage. The truth is the truth. I don't soft peddle it. Sometimes it is not so well received.

And how about you? Are you keeping up on your Bible reading? It is more important than you know.

Words can't express the emptiness I feel in your absence. I pray you will be safe in all your travels. Stay out of trouble if you can. And please write!

God bless you.

Love,

Jerry

"I can see how you're all just one big happy family." Her sarcasm aroused the man sitting next to her. He looked over at the open letter on her tray table. She turned her back to him.

O, Jerry, don't you know how busy I am? I've been chasing everything from dust storms and fires to flash floods and droughts. There are so many disasters around the world. My job occupies all my waking hours. I have no time. No time to visit and no time to write. There certainly had been no time to read the Bible. Besides Nadia had underlined so many passages it was distracting. Too many ideas jumped out at her. She had no time to sort them out. She was tired, so tired.

"I wish you could come to me." Megan whispered into the letter. She read it again then closed it up and held it next to her chest. She tried to steady the tremble in her fingers. A cough welled up deep inside her. *I must be coming down with something. I can't afford to be sick now.* She popped a cough drop in her dry mouth then closed her eyes but when the face of Mole Man appeared in her head she immediately opened them again. There would be no sleeping on the plane today.

Chapter Sixty-Nine

In the sixth dimension the demon Baleful flew as far above New Babylon as he could and still see the chaos below. Serpentine followed him. "If the Ancient of Days does not destroy them, they will destroy themselves." Baleful bellowed.

"It is all happening just like it says in the Bible. Satan told us he could change the ending." Serpentine was distressed beyond consoling.

"Satan lies. He does not tell the truth because there is no truth in him. Whenever he speaks a lie, he speaks from his own nature, for he is a liar and the father of lies." Baleful admitted condescendingly.

"But not to us, not about this." Serpentine whimpered.

"You are a bigger fool than the mortals. Don't you know Satan lies to everyone about everything as long as it suits his purpose?"

xxx

Sixtus sat in his New Babylon office in the presence of three advisors. The heat released from the powerful man's anger rivaled the heat outside on the street. His secretary buzzed him.

"General Fowler is here to see you."

"Don't you know I am in a meeting?" He barked.

"He says it is a matter of utmost importance."

"What is it this time?" Silence met him on the other end. "All right, send him in."

Abruptly Fowler entered the room. All eyes turned to him. The three sitting across from Sixtus relaxed at the intrusion.

"So what is this matter of extreme urgency that could not wait?"

"Sir, the scorpion drones have malfunctioned."

"What exactly does that mean, Fowler?"

"It means that three-million miniature drones, full of poison, have entered the atmosphere and are heading for unspecified targets."

"As we discussed, I authorized the scorpion drones to be filled with a poison to eradicate the wild animals and deadly rodent swarms that have invaded the populations. What in that scenario has changed?"

With a white handkerchief that he took from his back pocket, Fowler wiped the sweat that dripped from his shaved head down to his chin. He took a deep breath and continued.

"Well sir, there was a drone systems failure. It's as if they have taken on a mind of their own. They are not attacking their designated targets; instead, they are infecting only humans. This will cause people to feel tormented. They will begin to hallucinate and imagine their skin is crawling with insects. Their agitation will become maddening and most will be suicidal."

"Is there no way to neutralize them or call them back?"

"No, sir, I have tried."

"Well, try harder! I have put you in charge of implementing the most aggressive programs I have created. I thought you were capable of doing that effectively and successfully."

Sixtus glanced at Ashtoreth sitting in the corner. Her look was nonchalant and knowing. He responded with a slight nod. "Take care of it!"

General Fowler saluted Sixtus. "Yes sir, at once. One more detail, sir. They are headed this way. The trajectory indicates they will arrive here," he paused to look at his watch, "in exactly seven minutes." Fowler turned to leave the room.

"Lock down the building!" screamed Sixtus. All his advisors fled the room and scrambled to help seal the building. Ashtoreth locked the door behind them. Within minutes, as Fowler predicted, one-inch long camouflaged scorpion-like drones pelted the bulletproof windows of Sixtus' office. Try as they might, they did not break the glass.

<>

"Locusts came down out of the smoke upon the earth, and they were given the same kind of power that scorpions have. They have tails and stings like those of a scorpion, and it is with their tails that they have the power to hurt people for five months" (Revelation 9:3, 10 GNT)

Chapter Seventy

Day 150

Moufid braced himself. He angled into the powerful wind that thrashed against his body. Lightning flashed in the distance and thunder immediately followed. He was a cryptologist and history professor at the University of Cairo specializing in Egyptian antiquities. He moonlighted as a tour guide which paid much better.

"Sir, I don't think it is wise to take off in this severe weather." Moufid shouted above the storm and the rumble of the private jet they were approaching. Senator Blackstone was an old client, turned friend, who came to Egypt every year around this time to reminisce and learn more about the history of Moufid's beloved country. Moufid was not only a walking history book, but he had an easy way of speaking and his western style made him the favorite guide of many educated tourists. Once inside the plane, violent hail pelted hard against the aircraft. The ground trembled beneath them. The plane, though sitting stationary, rumbled and bumped as if it were taxiing down a battlefield.

"We are not cleared for takeoff, sir." The pilot reported to his boss, who had nicely settled in his seat with his fingers around a cold bottle of Fosters. Senator Blackstone was gazing out the window when suddenly his careless cavalier attitude changed. Moufid followed his gaze and saw what transformed his friend's demeanor.

"Oh my ...!" Profanities flew. "I want this plane off the ground immediately!" ordered Blackstone.

Instantaneously the pilot's eyes practically left his head. The engines started and accelerated in record speed. Miraculously the pilot outran it. The wheels left the runway only seconds before the ground split open beneath them. Hail continued to pound the aircraft leaving dents on every surface. Sheets of blinding rain masked the destruction below them. Quickly the jet climbed to a safe altitude and circled around Cairo following the base of the rupture. As they approached the towering pyramids, the last of the Seven Wonders of the Ancient World, Moufid witnessed the Great Pyramid of Khufu topple, like a house of cards, into the earthquake's belly. Four-thousand years of history, buried forever.

xxx

"How can we know what you say is true?" Kite, a burly man with tattoos covering 90% of his body, called out.

Divine intervention delayed Nadia's trial. Every day since her arrest over one month ago, she taught her fellow prisoners about God's promises. Every question led to a discussion about the Lord's life, death and resurrection. Many hearts softened through her words but skepticism remained high. Today the topic revolved around forgiveness.

"Talk is cheap," Solomon chimed in. "Actions speak louder than words."

"Jesus was arrested and imprisoned just like you. And then they sentenced Him to death. Do you know what His reaction to that was?"

"No, what?" challenged the tattooed man.

"Forgive them, Father! They don't know what they're doing." Silence from the inmates. Nadia continued.

"He died to set you free. Although my body is in chains today, my spirit is free and can never be controlled by mere men. My husband died for this same freedom and every breath I take is a testimony of that freedom." She beamed. "Jesus is the source of my life. That source will forever live in me long after my body is no more."

Megan washed the breakfast dishes. Every fiber of her body laughed when he suggested she stay in Nadia's old room until she found an apartment of her own. She loved her move to New York. It brought her one step closer to the coveted anchorman position. Had this not been such a crucial time in everyone's life she would be completely swept away. But now with Todd's brutal killing and Nadia's arrest everything had a bitter taste to it. Plus the drone stings were driving her increasingly crazier. She even caught self-disciplined Alex intermittently scratching them while he was engaged on the phone. Then he hung up.

"Ramsey said there is virtually nothing we can do to help Nadia. He has seen many cases like this before. It seems traitors are not entitled to any form of defense representation. They must confess and comply or be deemed guilty and sentenced accordingly."

"I can't believe there is nothing we can do. Maybe we should get another lawyer." Megan suggested.

"No, Ramsey is the best. I trust him and believe he's right."

"What will the sentence be?" She clung to the tiniest bit of hope.

"Ramsey also reminded me that the courts consistently use Sharia now to determine "God's will" in most cases. It provides what they consider to be "moral guidance." Alex dropped his head and ran both hands through his hair. "That means they may rule for beheading."

Megan lost her breath. That's impossible! How could all this be happening to her precious friend?

"Which god do they consult for that moral judgment? Nadia is not a traitor. As a matter of fact I have never known a person more dedicated to their country." She seethed indignation.

"Sixtus doesn't see it that way, nor does the UWC. Anyone that refuses to take the mark is outside the law. Ramsey said there are very few exceptions."

"So there's nothing we can do?"

"Outside of convincing Nadia to take the mark, I don't think so."

"She will never take the mark, Alex, I know her." Megan contemplated one additional possibility.

When Megan arrived at work she automatically went into overdrive, cleared up a few loose ends from the day before and then made the call.

"Good afternoon, Ms. Montgomery. It's so nice to hear your voice again." Nausea rushed her stomach at the sound of Sixtus' voice. He continued without skipping a beat. "I am very happy to see you on television now and then. Your reporting has brought a new style to the New York team. Congratulations on your promotion," He cooed. Megan ignored the compliment.

"I am calling to ask your help on behalf of my friend, Nadia Liechtenstein. She has been arrested."

"What would you like me to do?"

"I would like you to intervene and pardon her."

"What? And set a bad example for the rest of the ungrateful conniving traitors in this world?" He gave out the most evil laugh Megan had ever heard.

"However, I would like to get together with you the next time I'm in New York." Megan clicked the phone off, outrageously miffed there was no receiver to slam down in his ear!

Chapter Seventy-One

A rush of foul air filled the courtroom. Five-hundred demons led by Satan himself entered. Gloating, Serpentine announced to everyone within earshot, "See I told you we would get her sooner or later."

"Well, don't expect any medals. She has eluded us for the last seven months and has in that short time been instrumental in loosing over 50 captives to The Ancient of Days." Satan loathsomely remark.

Kasha surrounded Nadia with his powerful wings and whispered, "There are many homes where the Almighty Father lives and Jesus has prepared one of them for you. When you are ready He will take you there."

xxx

Alex had been sitting in the courtroom all afternoon encouraged by the fact that most of the cases so far were for traffic violations and domestic disputes. *Maybe Ramsey was wrong. This court is for minor infractions. Nadia's case will surely be treated lightly as well.*

At exactly 4:47, a huge apish guard escorted Nadia into the courtroom. Her small body shuffled back and forth uneasily, constrained by the shackles on her ankles. Her hands were cuffed behind her back. Alex's insides churned.

The bailiff announced, "People vs. Nadezhda Lyudmila Liechtenstein." Her strong jutting chin was raised high as she stood confident before the judge. Ceremoniously the judge leafed through her file.

"Miss Liechtenstein, you have been charged with directing and teaching in an unauthorized, illegal school. How do you plead?" Alex thought the judge's gaze would bore right through her.

"Guilty, your honor. I cannot work in a federal school where the children have become a ward of the state and brainwashing is the main stay. Children need to know how to survive in this world. That's what I want to teach them. In addition, I admonish them to be honest, trustworthy and productive citizens. This is contrary to the UWC curriculum, which by the way is full of lies."

Alex cringed when he heard Nadia's testimony. *Please, Nadia, don't be so antagonistic. Just answer his questions respectfully.* Alex ran his fingers back and forth through his hair.

"Your plea has been accepted. Your comments will be purged from the record. Your second charge is that of treason. I order you to take the "Chip" and pledge your allegiance to Sixtus III and the United World Commission."

"You order me to deny the Prince of Peace, who is the very reason for every breath that I take. If I denied Him and worshipped Sixtus I would be cutting out my own heart."

"Don't you see that your life is in my hands? Take the mark, Ms. Liechtenstein, sign the allegiance and I will set you free."

"No, don't you see, your Honor, my life is in the hands of One far greater than you."

The judge pounded his gavel. Alex and the entire courtroom jumped. "Your impudence is out of order! So, where is this God of yours? If He is so great why doesn't He save you?"

Nadia squared her shoulders. The chains around her ankles rustled, as if the onlookers needed to be reminded who the prisoner was.

"He already has saved me and He can save you too."

"You are wrong Miss Liechtenstein, I will live without Him but you will die, you will die very soon. Nadezhda Lyudmila Liechtenstein I hereby sentence you to death by beheading for acts of treason against Sixtus III and the United World Commission."

Nadia briefly closed her eyes. "I will always be ready to speak out boldly for Christ. I will always be an honor to Him, whether I live or whether I die. Living means opportunities to share Christ with others, and dying – well, that means being with Christ." She said each word emphatically, "And that's better yet!" She looked squarely at the judge. "So I thank you, your honor and praise the Lord because soon I will see His blessed face."

"Stop this insolence!" Judge Hamas repeatedly pounded the gavel. The entire courtroom ignited in an uproar.

"Silence!" he shouted over the crowd. "Schedule the execution immediately."

As the guard led Nadia out of the room, she looked straight at Alex. Her eyes were pleading. *Don't feel remorseful for me, Nadia. It's you that will be dying soon.*

He dropped his head, afraid she would detect the soul eating rage that consumed him. "I'm sorry, Alex, I'm sorry," she called out to him but her words fell on deaf ears.

<>
O'ER THE LAND OF THE FREE

Chapter Seventy-Two

Day 146

"You are the sweet aroma of Jesus." Kasha imparted to Nadia. "That fragrance infuses life inside these prison walls."

To the demon Sinister, it was a deadly stench. He fled without a word.

жжж

Breakfast was over and a large group of inmates circled around Nadia to listen to her final Bible teaching. Every day drew new seekers curious as to what this bold little woman would say. Every day the Holy Spirit engulfed her. Solomon, the unchallenged leader of the pack, asked a question that Nadia knew burned on most of the prisoner's hearts.

"Why didn't God help me when I was in trouble?"

"Let me tell you what happened to Jesus' followers." Nadia related the facts about the disciple's experience with Jesus walking on water then calming the stormy sea.

"When did the storm stop?" She questioned.

"After they asked Him to get into the boat?" Kite volunteered.

"That is exactly correct. They had to invite Him into the boat in order for Him to calm the storm. You must invite Him in also. He is a gentleman and doesn't force Himself onto anyone or into anyone's life. When the boat is rocking, you must ask Him to take the helm. You must trust Him and completely step away. Then you will see how quickly He will come to your aid."

"Liechtenstein, you have a visitor." A guard interrupted their discussion.

Saturdays were visitations days. The only exception was prisoner execution day. Alex had come every week since Nadia's arrest. This was Monday his fourth visit. He sat across from Nadia in row "A" by the big windows that overlooked the Neversink River Valley and far reaching foothills of the Catskill Mountains. This very room made Sullivan Correctional Facility a desired jail. If you were lucky enough to get one of the tables in row "A," you could easily imagine that you were in a luxurious country club.

Alex wasn't interested in the view. He was only interested in spending as many precious moments with his sister as he could. The conversation with Nadia flowed easily and lightly. He avoided any controversy. He filled his sister in on the progress Megan had been making at UWBC. Her fan club had grown like flies on a pool of honey.

"That doesn't surprise me." Nadia said, "She's very talented and has a magnetic personality. Has she had any luck in finding an apartment in the city?"

"Yes, but she only recently moved to the city completely. It seemed to be working out fine for her to take the train from Katonah every day." Alex couldn't keep from smiling at the thought of Megan in his apartment.

"Well I'm happy for both of you." Alex felt his cheeks flush. He looked at his hands clasped lightly on the table that separated them. His insightful sister had picked up on his vibes. She knew him almost better than he knew himself.

"Alex, you know that Papa loved you." Of course she would bring that up. It was as if she had waited all morning to proclaim it.

"You say that but I'm not so sure." She always managed to make him examine his own "hot spots". She crossed her arms and leaned on the table toward him.

"You must accept it as fact – just because I say so."

"Just because you say it doesn't mean it's true."

"It is true, Alex, you just can't see it. You're limited by your memories and you only remember the bad times." She was right. When he thought of him, he only rehashed the times when Papa disapproved of him or was disappointed in him for one reason or another. Nadia continued.

"Papa thought you were the perfect son. He *wanted* you to be perfect because you excelled at everything. He pushed you because he knew you would succeed and he wanted nothing less than success and happiness for you."

"Well he sure had a funny way of showing it."

"Maybe he didn't know how to show it. I saw it. I saw it all the time. He looked at you with such pride, as if he didn't think it possible that he could father such a fantastic being." Alex looked toward the window.

"Why can't you accept the fact that God created you and He doesn't make mistakes?"

"You can believe that if you want but I think your whole idea of God is foolishness. You think if you take a stupid mark that God will never forgive you and that the rest of your life will go down the tubes because of it. It really makes me mad, Nadia that you just don't take the "Chip" and be done with it."

"It's more than just taking the mark; it's aligning myself with the Antichrist, accepting his fate for me not the fate that God planned for me. Alex, pray that God will send His Holy Spirit to open your eyes so that you will know Him and see His light. Then you will feel His great power within in you and the victory He has waiting for you. He has called you to an existence far better than Sixtus could ever offer you."

Alex pushed his chair back away from the table to increase the distance between them. She still made no sense to him.

"What you hope for is a waste of time. Your life is about to end senselessly and you still think that He will somehow save you."

"It doesn't make any difference when I die. I still will never renounce my Lord Jesus. My hope is that someday you will have the same faith; that you will be certain as I am of the things we can't see. I have hope even when there's no reason for my hope. My faith is strong therefore everything is possible for me.

"Alex, I know you don't understand this but I firmly believe that those who belong to God will live again. Their bodies will rise again! Those who have been buried will come alive and sing for joy! God's light of life will once more live in their bodies. Please don't try to take my hope away." Her face sank and her shoulders slumped.

Alex was sorry for bringing her down and tried to think of something that would redeem himself. He moved back towards the table and leaned forward. They were forbidden to have any physical contact though he desired to put his arm around her. When they were kids and she was sad, he would wrap his arms around her shoulders and squeeze tightly until she yelled, "Stop!" It would make her laugh every time. He wished he could do that now. He spoke quietly which drew her close.

"The people in the town of Monroe have become even more sympathetic toward the Round Lake community. In the beginning, they hid many of the Christians in their homes. Now that the UWPF have left the area, most of the families have moved back to Round Lake. They all send their love."

Nadia's face lit up. He felt the force of her smile.

"I knew the Lord was at work in the hearts of the people. He is working here at the prison too." Her beautiful face, warm voice and loving spirit burned into his heart.

Chapter Seventy-Three

Kasha hovered over Nadia at a loss for what to do. Jesus came to his side and reassured him. "You did all that was required. It is her time now."

xxx

"It will be quick." Nadia's executioner said as they stood waiting for the doors to open.

"God bless you," she answered.

He stared ahead. During the previous three intense weeks she had spent valued time with her fellow inmates. The officer at her side overheard many of those discussions. When she was gone would he remember the lessons, understand God's plan for his life?

The doors of the execution cell opened then thundered shut behind her announcing to the rest of the prison the beginning of the end. Alex was seated on the other side of the glass. Without a word or even a glance, the guard strapped her to the block. It was cool and hard on her back. Two florescent lights on the ceiling buzzed slightly and blinded her. She squinted then turned to the guard.

"It's not your doing." She whispered. He lifted his head. His sorrowful eyes searched hers. "God forgives every grievance. If He does, I do too." He looked away again.

Typically an execution provided brief entertainment for the prisoners. Final last breath proclamations from the death chamber would waft through the air ducts. In the past weeks hellish curses and fearful groans – some remorseful, some defiant – had reached Nadia through those ducts. Convicts in their cells either rejoiced or condemned. Reputations either flourished or bit the dust. It all depended on the way a man died.

During her incarceration Nadia had spoken many words of grace, mercy, forgiveness and love. But her dying words may have more impact than her living ones. All were listening ... expectant ... attentive. Some would want to hear words of condemnation for her captors. Others would want a prayer. Instead she raised her voice and proclaimed a statement of admonition, "Fear God and give Him glory!" She shouted.

Then she sang her final song, not for herself but for them – to remind them of God's passion and loyalty, that no matter how fiercely the storm raged around them, God would be with them. Her strong alto voice, resounding with conviction belted out, "My eyes have seen the glory of the coming of the Lord ..." Through the air ducts the inmates rumbled the chorus back to her.

"Glory, glory Hallelujah ..."

The entire jail resonated with their heartfelt song. It drowned out the buzz of the laser which cleanly and swiftly severed Nadia's head from her shoulders.

"... His truth is marching on."

The prison walls waited for Nadia's second verse. Her silence clamored the reality that her body no longer breathed. Hardened criminals dropped to their knees with tears in their eyes and prayers on their lips.

Nadia heard a voice ripple her name as if through water. Could it be? Ecstatic she looked toward the direction of the sound. A blinding light compelled her to shield her eyes but she refused to, she dare not. She would not even blink for fear the magnificent sight of her glowing Savior would disappear. Jesus slid His arms beneath her and lifted her from the execution block. His massive strength made her body feel weightless, but no ... She actually floated, outside her body, within a tingling atmosphere.

"My Lord and Savior." She didn't recognize her own voice.

"Yes, we are finally here together, I have longed for this day." He gently reassured.

"Why did you wait so long? Why didn't you come for me sooner?" Nothing from her former life mattered only that she stood now, face-to-face, in His presence. Bursting with blissful exuberance Nadia embraced her new existence wholeheartedly. Her body, light and released of all constraints, rejoiced. It was completely and unequivocally free!

"Look." He pointed down to the weeping prisoners. "They are the reason. They will be coming soon as well because you told them about Me. Within the confines of those prison walls the shackles just fell off of over two hundred captives."

"Solomon and Kite?"

"Yes."

"My execution guard too?"

"Yes, their souls are all released from prison. They gave their lives to Me all because an obedient young woman loved her Lord and refused to deny the truth."

Chapter Seventy-Four

Kasha tried to shake the emptiness inside. Nadia no longer needed him. As he flew through the sixth dimension, Baleful and Serpentine followed, mocking him.

"Where is the promise of His coming? We thought your Prince of Peace was coming back!" The demons flew next to Kasha then circled around him. They cackled and harassed the saddened angel. "As far back as we can remember His creation has not changed. They will never change. You know He just lied in order to give them false hope."

"You are the liars. You distort the scriptures to your own destruction. The Ancient of Days gave the Prince of Peace authority over them and He has given them eternal life. Satan's power cannot destroy them." Kasha raged. "And like dead flies you can even make perfume stink."

Boldly Kasha flew off into the distance.

xxx

Alex drove mindlessly away from the jail that stole Nadia's life. The echo of her melodic voice thundered in his head ... The smell of her burning flesh nauseated him.

He relived it over and over.

Within twenty minutes, he found himself in front of the service station in Monroe where Tom Barker worked. Since Nadia's arrest Tom had disconnected the GPS's and rigged up manual operating systems on seven cars that had been donated to him. He had already sent them out with drivers to spread the word about Nadia's arrest.

He appeared to be was working on one more when Alex approached.

"Hi buddy."

Tom abruptly stopped. His face reflected Alex's agony. A storm blustered in Tom's eyes. Without a word, his fist pounded through the garage wall. Tools clanked to the floor around him. Uncaring, he sank lifeless onto the floor. Unchecked tears rolled down his face. Alex crouched next to him. Tom's head slumped to his knees. He shared Alex's sorrow. It was too great to bear alone. Then Alex heard Tom, ever so quietly, take courage and begin to pray.

"Dear Lord,

When all is dark, when all is painful
You bring me hope, though all hope seems gone
When I'm confused, when life falls around me
You are my Rock that shall never be moved
You never change

You bring beauty from ashes, turn mourning into gladness
Restorer God, I trust in your plan
You bring the healing, you remain faithful
My eyes are on you; let me never be moved

When I'm afraid, when walls close around me
You shine your light, your presence is there
When I am weak, whenever I stumble
Your hand is near, guiding my way
You are my Strength" [x]

Then Tom, as if he could contain himself no longer, yelled with conviction from the top of his lungs,

"You bring beauty from ashes, turn mourning into gladness
Restorer God, I rest in your plan
You bring the healing, you remain faithful
My eyes are on you; let me never be moved."

Numb, Alex drove home, through normal traffic which was oblivious to the event that so devastated him. He passed through a malevolent world completely unchanged by his loss. How could it be?

In his apartment he poured himself a Gray Goose and downed it. He poured another and downed it too. He sloshed the last of the bottle into the glass and went to his room. He tripped over a sneaker and almost spilled half his drink and cursed profusely.

He sat at his desk breathing hard. Then he ripped opened the Bible that had belonged to his mother. His father's letter slipped to the floor. First he stomped on it hiding it from his sight. He sat motionless starring into oblivion. What difference did it really make? What did it really matter? Nadia's words haunted him. *Papa thought you were the perfect son.* He slowly bent down to retrieve the letter. Reluctantly he read the smudged words on the faded page.

"I know I'm not a good father to Alex, but how does a man show love to his son? I hope that someday he knows just how much I really love him. He makes me so proud." Trembling, Alex refolded the letter and closed the Bible around it. He pushed his chair back knocking over his violin case. His gaze burned a hole through it. Finally he opened it and took his violin out. He gently fingered the strings. The day his father gave him this instrument was the last time Alex ever saw pride on his father's face. That day, Alex had won the Junior Regional String Competition. Alex was proud of himself that day too – that day so long ago.

"Oh, Papa, I don't think you are proud now. I have failed you one last time. I couldn't save her. I'm so sorry. Nothing makes any sense." He nestled the violin under his chin, took a long breath then put the instrument down. Alex lovingly returned the violin to its case. *What is the use of trying? The entire world is doomed.*

Alex shook his head as if to deny his internal struggle. Then he spoke slightly above a whisper. "Lord, all my life I protected and guarded her. In the end it wasn't enough. I never should have let her go away with Todd."

Alex took a gulp of alcohol and wiped his mouth on the back of his hand. He opened the Bible again and began to read with resolve. Suddenly the words jumped off the page at him. *"Be strong! Be Courageous! Do not be afraid of them! For the Lord your God will be with you. He will neither fail nor forsake you."*

He drained his glass and threw it across the room.

Nadia's body was burned and her head was hung in the center of Monroe as a deterrent for anyone else who wished to believe as she did. But it had the opposite effect. The sight of her dangling head compelled fifty-three more people to rebel against Sixtus and give their lives to her Lord.

<>
AND THE HOME OF THE BRAVE

Chapter Seventy-Six

Day 89

Hakah flew in wide circles over Megan's dangling head. Demons flooded the area but none paid particular attention to her charge. Something else was in the air but he could not put his finger on it. Trouble was ahead – he could feel it.

xxx

Megan had checked and rechecked her sources as usual before she accepted this assignment that brought her one hundred miles west of Budapest, Hungary. The false information flying around the world sometimes made her head spin. Not that she would ever refuse an assignment because of it (that would set her way back in the reporter pecking order) but she wanted to have her facts right. This time her facts were wrong. Dead wrong. Matyas Aradi wasn't a brutal bloodthirsty terrorist suppressing the Hungarian government as she was lead to believe. He was not even a spiteful mercenary. He was a twenty-four year old rebel leader trying to keep the country side safe for his people. Her interview was ending with little to show for her efforts. Maybe she was here for a different reason. She believed nothing happened by chance.

"Is there one last thing you would like to say to the world, Mr. Aradi?" She held the microphone in front of the scruffy young man. His formerly preoccupied eyes gazed powerfully into Frank's camera.

"The race is not won by the swift, nor is the battle won by the warriors. Food is not procured by the wise or wealth by the discerning. Favor does not fall on talented men. Time and chance rule over them all. Man does not know his time; like fish caught in a treacherous net, and birds caught in a snare, so the sons of men are ensnared at an evil time when it suddenly falls on them. Whatever your hand finds to do, do it with all your might; for there is no activity or planning or wisdom in Hell where we are going."

Then he abruptly turned and walked away disappearing into a swarm of fellow soldiers.

"As you can see, these men are fighting for survival. They are the hope of this western region of their war torn country."

Hope? Megan turned off her mic. It was too much. She was tired, so tired. Maybe the young rebel was right. The more she dug the more she realized the fate of the world spiraling out of control. Famine, fires, floods, disease, hurricanes and earthquakes – when would it all stop? Would it ever stop? She longed for one of Matt Haven's abandoned human interest stories.

"I'll meet you at the bus, Frank. I'm going for a walk."

Frank waved her off as she headed away from the park that was now empty of spectators. After three weeks of rain, the sun finally began to peek through the clouds. Three children ran past her chasing a dog. She almost felt like smiling. Deviscer, Hungary was actually a very charming little village at the foot of the Bakony Mountains. She followed the road to Harshfa Street and made a right. The flap of a blue and white awning in front of a bakery drew her attention. She stopped to refresh herself in its cool shade. Racks of baklava in the window case tempted her. Inside two old men sat dunking scones into their coffee cups. It was too inviting to pass up. She was about to open the door when a little boy tugged at her elbow. His dark eyes were large, round and playful. His clothes were worn but clean – his knees visible through the holes in his jeans. He stood about three-foot six and clutched a staff in his right hand.

"Miss, Miss, come." He was laughing now. "Come, come." *He speaks English!*

This was a human interest story she couldn't pass up.

She followed him over the cobblestone street. Megan briefly looked around for Frank but he was nowhere in sight so she filmed the boy with her phone. In ten minutes they were out of town on a dirt road surrounded by farm land. Megan had a rough time keeping up with the boy; as usual she wasn't wearing the right shoes. *Blasted, when will I ever learn?* The muddy path sucked at her heel. She gripped it tightly with her toes.

Farther and farther from town they came to a wooden fence. *Where is he taking me?* He slipped under it quickly then waited for her on the other side. He called out and immediately three little lambs circled around him.

"Wait," she yelled after him. But he didn't seem to hear. He charged toward a rock formation in the distance, his playful friends bleating after him. Staff in hand, he spread out his arms like a bird in flight, zigzagging through the meadow. He was delightful to watch. Then he mounted a huge boulder at the edge of a precipice and waited for her. His staff continued to whirl around his head.

Megan laughed and out of breath called to him.

"Where are we?" No comment. "What is your name?"

"Bertok is my name. I am a raven! I protect my sheep! This is my rock!"

"I can see that," Megan said as she approached, slowly catching her breath. The rock was sheltered by a huge sycamore tree. Sweat poured off her body and soaked the bodice of her sleeveless yellow cotton dress. Her chest heaved sporadically from the climb but it was wonderful to be out in the open. Free as it were like the boy and his pets. She welcomed the refreshing shade. The lambs playfully jumped and called out to their shepherd.

Megan began filming again. The boulder was on the edge of Torna Creek which twisted back and forth snaking its way to Ajkai Timfoldgyor, the neighboring aluminum processing plant.

The three animals and the boy jumped here and slid there about fifteen feet down to the swelled creek bed. All four drank from the rushing water. Megan painstakingly followed them one craggy step at a time. When she reached the bottom she sniffed the air. It smelled musty not like a fresh water spring should. She couldn't quite put her finger on it but it was almost metallic. The baby animals didn't seem to mind; they pranced at the edge of the water then ran up stream. Bertok danced behind them. Megan followed at a distance catching all the action on her phone.

A shrill siren blew in the distance.

Through the camera lens Megan suddenly saw, Bertok wave her to go back. *That's strange.* Then she heard it – from around the bend, a red tide of sludge barreling toward them. The boy bolted after his sheep passionately calling their names. Frantically Megan wedged the phone into the case around her waist never taking her eyes off the hopeless scene in front of her.

Megan heard another siren. Then another.

The three little lambs finally listened to their master. They bleated and ran, overtaking the boy, even charging past her toward the slope they came down. Megan screamed and ran toward the boy but froze when the eighteen-inch wall of toxic sludge pulled his feet out from under him. His arms flailed and reached out to her. His staff flew to the ground. His big eyes pleaded as he slipped under the lethal mass. She was too far away. She couldn't save the young shepherd boy who laid down his life for his sheep. A frightened cry escaped from him just as the breath was crushed from his lungs.

Megan turned and ran but there was no time to return to the hill where they came down. The wall of sludge grew deeper and denser as it approached. She had to go up and go now! The terrain above her was rough and steep. Her fingers scratched the rocks searching for a grip. Finally, she placed her foot on a solid crag and heaved up. Was she high enough?

She heard the roar of the toxic waste as it rushed below her. Its heat crept up her bare legs.

She reached up looking for another spot to grip when his face glared down at her from above the crest of the ledge. Mole Man!

"Who are you?" She shouted hysterically practically gagging from the stench of the mud.

"Vladimir."

"Why are you here?"

"Orders." She got another firm hold and raised herself up another ten inches.

"Whose orders?" Couldn't he explain himself a little more?

"Sixtus" Her fear and frustration sent her into a rage.

"I don't need a babysitter!"

She immediately regretted those unguarded, sarcastic words because what followed she deducted was a punishment! A stone broke away from under her left foot which then dangled freely in the air. She scrambled to find another footing but nothing stuck. Her body slammed hard against the bluff. Her knees scraped a bolder and burned as her shoe hurled into the powerful mass below. She tightened her grip but it was useless. Her tensed body slowly followed her lost shoe down the slope. She looked for a rock to hold onto but it was too late. Her already torn fingers just dragged the cliff.

Mole Man reached down and grabbed her left wrist. She pressed her knee into the gravel and stones managing to hoist up enough to grasp his other outreached hand with her right. As the flood grew higher on the embankment Megan scrambled up to safety.

"Not babysitter – bodyguard," was Mole Man's stoic response.

<>

"... A third of the water turned bitter, and many people died from drinking the water, because it had turned bitter." (Revelation 8:11 GNT)

Chapter Seventy-Five

Day 68

Michael brought his most recent agenda to the God head. "Ashtoreth is claiming that the world will no longer see war and the famine will cease. Also that Sixtus will bring lasting peace to that place."

"Yes, I am aware of her boasting. She will meet her end. Those who believe her will suffer from her sorely infected wound. They will stalk the streets because of hunger. They will die by the hand of man and no one will be there to bury them." The Father's voice was moved with compassion but He could only state the truth. "They will be consumed by their own wickedness."

xxx

Ashtoreth, her hair pulled straight back into a bun, paced back and forth by the pool at Sixtus' home on the island of Arwad. The rats could not reach them there and the water appeared less contaminated. Her open, brightly colored cotton robe swished back and forth across her body. Her tiny black bikini beneath it exposed most of her shiny sleek skin. Sixtus, easily distracted by her beauty, could not keep even the slightest train of thought on their conversation. The sores on her arms and neck had not healed. They didn't detract from her beauty but they did indicate that her mystical powers were limited or diminishing.

"What do you mean you have everything under control? Nothing can be done to save the river!" She shrieked. For hours, over one-hundred million tons of liquid waste from three adjacent processing plants oozed from their storage reservoirs, devastating everything in its path. Homes, bridges, stores and factories, all destroyed. A mile long, three-hundred yard wide wall of toxic red sludge moved toward the Danube at increasing speed. No amount of poured concrete had been able to stop it. When it finally reached the river, all fish died instantly by record high doses of mercury and arsenic. Every spring and waterway in its path also turned into a fiery bloodbath. Shouts of fear and panic reverberated all along the Danube. Warnings not to even touch the infected water flooded the airwaves and the internet.

Sixtus paused for a moment, blinked, and then remarked with confidence. "There have only been 700 deaths due to the sludge in the river. I think we have contained it fairly well."

"I don't care how many useless people died. I can't even get a blasted glass of clean water and you say, 'everything is under control.' That's a lot of bull and you know it." In a hissy fit she whipped the robe close to her body and tied it tightly at the waist. Her eyes like lasers tore into his mind.

Sixtus tried to console her. "I have a crew of experts cleaning the waste from the river. I am sure the rains will come and refill the Mediterranean. In any event it all should be filtered enough to drink in two weeks."

"Two weeks!" she screamed even louder. "I could be dead by then. And if I go, I swear, you are going with me."

"Well, my darling, if you had not gotten rid of Fowler we might not be in this position right now."

"Don't blame that one on me, Mr. President. You gave the order."

"Yes, indeed I did. You have me there." Why did she keep pressing him? He nervously flicked his right thumb with his forefinger.

"But you can't expect me to know exactly what is happening everywhere at all times and at the same time. I am not ubiquitous! You are the one with the telepathic powers. You should have anticipated this disaster!"

Ashtoreth stopped pacing, marched over to the table where he sat, pressed her fists firmly on it and leaned into him. "What I want to know is, what are you going to do about it? Not just about the toxic waters – I'm talking about the control of the world that is slipping away to the powers above. We are losing ground and I don't like it. Where are your powers to destroy?"

She paused as she panted then stomped away. "You can suffer as long as you like here in this putrid hole. I'm going to New York."

Sixtus merely stared at her as if she was not there. He had already tuned out her raging complaints.

<>

"... O horror! horror! How horrible it will be for all who live on the earth when the sound comes from the trumpets..." (Revelation 8:13 GNT)

Chapter Seventy-Seven

Day 13

Fire blazed all around. Blacktop bubbled. Some melted through bridge scaffolding. Some secured airplanes to the tarmac. Burned bodies, both animal and human, peppered the landscape. The fire of the sun and stars was so intense that in no time, they and all other heavenly bodies melted from the heat. An angry voice roared.

"The present heaven and earth are reserved for fire, judgment and destruction. God is a consuming fire."

Walker woke with a start. His body drenched in his own sweat. He breathed hard. He had overslept. It was a poignant start to the day.

xxx

Megan was back in Israel, this time reporting good news. She hoped she and Frank would wrap up and get out before the storm hit. In the mean time, she eagerly reported.

"This is Megan Montgomery reporting live from Jerusalem. As you can see behind me, the crowd is in an uproar over the death of the two so-called prophets that have been predicting gloom & doom for this region. The people are rejoicing in the streets. The tension that has gripped this city for the past three and a half years has exploded into an amazing celebration ..."

Sixtus disconnected himself from the electrifying events that were happening outside his hotel penthouse window. People were cheering and shouting over the death of the two biggest thorns in his side. From day one, they had threatened him. How many times had his henchmen tried to kill them only to die themselves instead? Finally Sixtus triumphed over them. They were no more. Now, their dead bodies would rot in the streets before he would allow anyone to remove them.

He flipped on the TV to see how the media covered it. There she was, beautiful, poised, intelligent, articulate and provocative. Immediately he contacted Azimi.

"I want Megan Montgomery to be an anchorman at UWBC – No, not Chicago, you idiot in New York! And I want it effective immediately!" *There is hope yet again for the world!*

<>

"... A third of the earth was burned up, a third of the trees, and every blade of green grass." (Revelation 8:7 GNT)

Chapter Seventy-Eight

Day10

The Middle East had just survived the the fiercest storm on record. It had rained all night and into the next day. Lightening struck all power lines, leaving millions without electricity. Hoards of lethal demons converged on the Middle East and as the waters rose, looters ransacked unsecured buildings – chaos ruled.

Intense heat followed the torrential rain. The two dead prophets still remained on the ground, rapidly decomposing. The odor nauseated all those who passed by but no one was authorized to remove the murdered men.

God approached the prophet's rotting corpses and breathed His life-giving breath into their lungs. Miraculously they stood up, their grey flesh restored. Gabriel, God's ever faithful messenger, called out to them from above. "Come here."

The two risen men ascended joyfully into heaven. Their evil accusers watched them go, and then frantically ran to hide in their homes. Suddenly the ground began to tremble and breakaway. That earthquake took seven thousand lives in one day and the survivors praised God.

xxx

Alex gazed intently through his telescope. He made a few more notes on his laptop and then closed the hatch. Beads of sweat dripped down the back of his neck from the stifling heat. Drained of energy, he went to the bathroom and stepped into a cool shower.

When he returned to his bedroom he retrieved his last clean polo shirt from the laundry basket on the floor. Nadia used to fold his shirts and put them in drawers. He was lucky to get them washed. He had no time for folding.

His violin case sat on the floor next to the laundry basket. His thoughts went immediately to Nadia's last words to him. *You know Papa loved you. You are limited by your memories.* He removed the violin from its case. *Please help me to remember the good times.* He raised the instrument to his chin. Someone banged at the door several times at brief intervals before the sound penetrated his thoughts.

"Alex, Alex, it's me. Are you there?" At the sound of Megan's voice he hurried down the steps to the back door and flung it open. He hated the fact that she had moved out completely.

"Megan, you're here! When did you get back to New York? Due to the storm, I thought for sure you got stranded in Jerusalem." They briefly exchanged kisses on the cheek.

"I got back last night. I was lucky, my flight left just before the clouds rolled in. I can't stand being so out of touch with you."

"I know but they tapped my phone and tampered with the lock on my e-mail. I don't trust any communication now." He didn't try to hide his sorrow over Nadia's death.

"Alex, what is wrong?" He couldn't say the words.

"I'm so sorry, Alex. I'm so sorry."

Together they wept. The void in his heart was too big to express. He was thankful she didn't press him for details. The silence buffered the stress.

In the distance a whistle blew from the 9:40 express train.

Life around him continued.

His stood still.

"I have some good news," she volunteered.

"You got the promotion?"

"Yes, Alex. You are looking at UWBC's new Day Break anchorwoman!"

"Congratulations!" He scooped her up into his arms and twirled her around glad to have something good in their lives.

"Thank you, you crazy man, now put me down! Here, I brought you something." He obeyed her immediately and Megan proudly held out a tall rectangular box wrapped in green and white paper.

"What is this, you get a promotion and I get a present?"

"No, silly, haven't you heard? The two prophets are dead!"

"Is that cause to celebrate?" What was she thinking?

"Of course, everyone is celebrating. Don't you see all your worry and talk of dooms day is over. The two prophets are dead and nothing has happened. The world is still here and better than ever. They say it is even going to rain here too, and end this terrible heat wave and drought. Go on open it." Alex obliged. It was a bottle of Grey Goose.

"Wow, where did you get this?" Vodka, along with almost everything else, had become a scarce commodity.

"I have my connections," she replied coyly.

"Black market," Alex deducted. Megan laughed and headed for the kitchen.

"You get the glasses; I'll get the ice."

Alex went to the bar, chose two highball glasses and poured the clear tantalizing liquid into them. Megan called to him from in the kitchen.

"Not much in the refrigerator, but at least you have ice." She returned to the living room, ice-bucket full. She dropped three cubes in each glass.

"It's like an oven in here. You really should put on the air." Taking one of the ice cubes she lifted up her hair and rubbed it on the back of her slender inviting neck. The gesture melted Alex's insides. He caught himself staring.

"Since I have no more legal funds, Herb down stairs pays for my electricity along with the store's. Air-conditioning requires a lot of electricity. I can't put that additional burden on him. Plus they may begin to question a higher bill. Lately all his expenses, transactions and inventory are being regulated. They know exactly how many cans of beans he has on each shelf. He still brings me groceries as often as he can."

"I'm not a big fan of the UWC but I think you should just bite the bullet and take the "Chip." Her face scrunched up a little just like it always did before she got angry.

"What for, air-conditioning?" Now his dandruff was up. "No, Megan, I promised Nadia I never would. This is one promise I am going to keep."

"Alex, you're getting more like Nadia every day. This is not some childish game or act of heroism. This is a matter of survival. How long do you think you can go on like this?" Animosity thundered through her voice.

"I take one day at a time. I am fine, really I am." He bridled his temper. Her fumes were rising.

"Oh, you look really fine. Judging from the lack of supplies in the kitchen you could look this fine for maybe another twelve hours ... at least!"

"Let's not fight." Alex raised his glass to toast, "To your promotion!" She hesitated then flashed a sweet smile.

"To a better life," As she lifted her arm Alex noticed crusted red boils on her wrist. He took her soft arm in his hand.

"These don't look any better. In fact they look worse. Have you been to the doctor recently?" Megan yanked her arm away.

"They aren't nearly as bad as the drone attack. And, yes, I have been to my doctor," she pouted. "And she said it's completely normal. Everyone with the "Chip" is getting them. After a while the boils will dry up and eventually go away."

"These don't look like they are going away. I think ..."

"It's my fault they're still there." She interrupted, her defenses up. "I keep scratching and picking at them. They make me crazy."

Chapter Seventy-Nine

In the seventh dimension there was a great altar and under that altar were the saints martyred because of their faithful witnessing. They shouted to the Lord, "How long will it be before you avenge our deaths?"

"The time has come." He answered.

The whole earth shook. Dead bodies arose from their graves. Completely intact, filled with new life, they ascended up into the sky. The living "unmarked" faithful believers around the world followed close behind including all those at Round Lake. They soared up, up, and up into a whirlwind that carried them safely away. It was not a dream.

The sixth dimension exploded with a choir of angels who began to sing.

"Your name is glorified forever
Your might will never be destroyed
Your love covers us with mercy
Your power has won the victory

And we praise your name
We exalt you forever
Holy Lord, there is no one else like you
Praise you, God, you are holy and worthy
Mighty in power, we proclaim your name

There is no one else like you, holy and worthy
We exalt you; you have power and glory forevermore"[xi]

xxx

Suddenly Alex's apartment turned pitch black. Megan groped for Alex in the dark. He turned on a lamp.

"Boy it got cloudy fast," she said.

"That's like no cloud that I've ever seen before. I've got to see this."

They ran up the stairs. She flicked the switch to open the hatch and he went straight to the telescope.

"I don't understand it," he said. "It's as if the sun and the moon are gone! It's incredible. I can't ..."

"Let me see." Alex stood up keeping his eyes glued to the lens. Megan grabbed his seat.

"What could have caused it?"

"I don't know."

When Alex finally let her see, light streamed in again through the windows.

"Oh, Alex, Alex!"

"What is it?" Megan sat back away from the telescope – stunned. Alex leaned over her shoulder to look.

"Nadia was right. Jesus has come for them. They are all meeting Him in the sky!"

"Here we are, live in New Babylon, with Sixtus III. He will give a press release regarding the extraordinary phenomena that occurred around the world only moments ago. Here is President Sixtus III."

Sixtus sat behind the desk in his private office. He had allowed one reporter from UWBC to record his statement. He flicked his thumb. Ashtoreth paced back and forth in the far corner. Her eyes like lasers dug into him. Would he disappoint her?

With a controlled steady voice he announced, "You can all rest assured, my people, that you are safe. I have been in contact with the space ship Zartec for the last month. I have everything under control. As I have commanded, the unmarked traitors have been beamed up and removed forever by Zartec. Do not worry. You now will forever be at peace. Thank you for your attention."

After a brief pause, Sixtus barked at the news reporter. "Turn that thing off and get out of here ... now!"

Satan breathed heavy and hard into Sixtus' ear. "I am sick of all this mindless prattle. The highway to hell is broad, and its gate is wide enough for all the multitudes that choose the easy way. It is only a matter of time. I want to know the names and locations of all those remaining who are still unmarked. If they were not believers before the rapture, they surely will be now."

Within minutes Sixtus had Azimi on the phone.

"Yes, and get me a list, by location, of all those who as of yet are still without my mark."

"Yes, sir but the computers have been down for over an hour now."

"I don't care how long the computers have been down." Sixtus screamed. "I want that list on my desk - now!"

Alex abruptly turned off the TV as soon as the announcement was over. Megan watched as he filled his glass with vodka for the third time and in one gulp drank it down. He began to fill her glass also when she raised her hand to stop him. He paced back and forth rage building with each step. A storm thundered in his eyes. She had never seen him like this before. It almost frightened her.

"He is such a fool." Alex roared. "The unmarked have been beamed up! Where did he ever get that spacecraft garbage? The rapture has taken place and he is trying to explain it away with this lame Zartec story."

"What is the rapture?" Megan interrupted cautiously almost afraid to speak.

"Nadia said that Jesus would come back to take the elect, meaning the unmarked believers, to heaven with Him before His final judgment of the world." Smoke came out his ears.

"Megan, I'm going to Round Lake to see if it's really true."

Immediately Megan thought of Jerry, the love of her life. "I'm coming with you." She grabbed her purse and followed him out the door. Surely Jerry wouldn't have left her. Surely he would be there when they arrived.

They took the van and drove as quickly as possible. They dodged deserted cars on the road. People were out on the streets looking into the sky. There was chaos everywhere. It was all too bizarre to comprehend.

Chapter Eighty

Michael and Kasha hovered high above Sixtus' office.

"You heard him, Michael. They all are in extreme danger now. What can we do?"

"It has already been done. Gabriel purged all earthly records of the remaining unmarked from their system."

"But Alex is not a believer yet!"

"Kasha, Kasha, you forget, God is the blessed controller of all things. It is not for us to decide."

"But Nadia's many prayers for Alex. Surely they will not go unanswered."

"Yahweh is an awesome God who is faithful in all His ways. It is not for us to judge. He gives mercy to those He chooses to receive mercy."

Below them Satan shouted in triumph, "Now that He has taken His morbid followers, I have total control of the entire human population. I have the power, glorious power. I will reign forever!"

The Archangel Michael flew down to his side. "Fear God, and give Him glory, because the hour of His judgment has come."

"I will survive. It is my destiny." He spit the words out as if they choked him.

"Satan, you try to deceive even yourself. Your time is short," Michael put his sword to Satan's throat.

"Temper, temper," the devil scoffed.

"Be careful, Michael," Kasha cautioned. "You cannot touch him until the allotted time. When it comes, the Lord of Hosts will send His mighty warriors to slaughter Sixtus and his nations. On that day the bondage of God's people will be revenged."

xxx

Finally, Megan and Alex arrived at Round Lake. All was quiet. A peaceful quiet. An unsettling quiet. When Megan entered the farmhouse, she hoped to see the "little princesses" on the floor at play but they were not. Her heart sank as she ran into the kitchen. There was no one there. Nadia's apron hung on a hook next to the stove. There was a mound of vegetables half chopped on the butcher block table. A cleaver rested on the floor next to it.

"You search the house, Alex. I'm going to the cabin." Megan darted from the farmhouse and ran toward Al Adams' place. She almost missed the path because a new growth of wild flowers heavily concealed it. Finally, she recognized the area and slowly wound her way through the dense woods. Eventually she emerged into the open area. The stillness overwhelmed her. The beautiful house was empty. *He can't have left me. I know he must still be here ... The cottage by the lake; he must be there.*

She took a shortcut through the woods then stopped when she saw it. The water shimmered as usual in the distance but there was something different. Slowly she approached, afraid of what she may find ... or not find there. She opened the front door, everything was still ... surreal. Suddenly the tea kettle whistled. She didn't think. Her legs just brought her, as if in slow motion, to the stove where she turned off the flame. It was true. He was gone. They were all gone. In the silence she lashed out.

"How dare you leave me, Jerry Walker! How dare you go with them! I gave you my heart. You had no right to take it and then leave me like this." Anger turned to tears. She collapsed on the floor in the kitchen and abandoned herself to the sobs.

"I'm leaving!" Megan exploded into the farmhouse playroom. She approached Alex sitting on the couch. His back was to her. It was odd he didn't respond. Only when she stomped up to him did she see Kirk. His eyes bulged. Catatonic and motionless, he clutched Neeko's neck. Compassion took over but Megan's mind went blank. She stunk at consoling.

"They all went up into the sky." Kirk finally cried out. Alex turned to her and whispered very quietly. "I found him crouched in the corner."

"I know, Kirk. We saw it too. It's all right, you are safe now." Megan attempted to calm him.

"No, I'm not!" He shouted back. "Jesus took them and now it is too late for me. It's too late." His whole body limped lifeless, hopeless. Megan understood exactly what the boy meant. She thought the same thing. Alex's glance agreed. Megan cupped Kirk's hands in hers and knelt on the floor in front him.

"It's all right, baby. You'll see everything will be all right." Her confidence in that statement waned the longer they sat there in silence. Finally she stood up.

"Let's go, Alex. There is nothing more we can do here." Fear froze Kirk's face.

"We can't leave him." Alex responded boldly.

"Of course not, we'll take him with us. He can stay with you in Katonah." She desperately needed to get away from this place. She couldn't breathe. Her world had collapsed.

"No, you go. I need to spend some time here. We'll come in a few days. I just want to get my head straight first."

"Have it your way. I'll wait for you at your place."

"Thanks, Megan, you're a real trooper but I am sure they'll need you at work tomorrow. Go home. I'll let you know when I'm back." Megan kissed them both on the head and slipped out the front door. The hot air suffocated her.

Kirk finally fell asleep on the couch next to Alex. They had both been too tired to eat but now it was approaching seven o'clock and Alex's stomach began to growl. He went to the kitchen and found the refrigerator full of fresh fruits and vegetables. There was even a plucked chicken marinating in a pan. He turned on the oven, then spotted Nadia's apron on the wall. He took it down and put his own hand over the little fingers painted on the pockets.

"Why does it have to be like this? Oh, Nadia, how did you know things would end up this way? They have all gone to be with your Prince of Peace, haven't they? It all happened so quickly. I want to follow Jesus but I don't know how!"

Chapter Eighty-One

Satan and Serpentine arrived at the farm hoping to find more unmarked victims. They heard Alex cry out. Satan fed Alex more lies.

"If you don't know what to do, then simply do nothing, Alex, just do NOTHING and you will always be in my kingdom. I am the Prince of Darkness. I can give you Megan ... on a silver platter if you like. All I ask is that you follow me!"

Jonathan, knowing his physical power was no match for Satan's, flew down to surround Alex with his wings. The guardian angel pleaded with his seeking mortal, "Don't you know that the penalty for sinning is death, but the free gift of God is eternal life in Jesus?"

"I just want to give you pleasure," Satan coaxed, "pure sweet pleasure."

"Don't listen to his lies. For true happiness you must accept The Prince of Peace as your Savior and King."

"He can't help you now. Only I can help you. I can give you a poison so sweet, so irresistible."

"No, Alex, listen to me. Your heavenly Father longs to help you. You know that if you asked your earthly father for a fish, he would not give you a snake. If hardhearted sinful men know how to give good things to their children, wouldn't your heavenly Father be even more certain to give good gifts to you if you asked Him? Ask and you will receive; knock and He will open the door to you. When man turns to the Lord the veil is taken away."

xxx

The smell of chicken began to waft through the house as Alex walked back into the living room. Oppression and hopelessness weighed him down as he trudged over to the wall where his father's violin hung.

"Oh, Papa, Papa, help me." Alex collapsed on the couch and buried his hands in his face. "Oh, Lord," he began to pray.

"Are You there?
Are You truly there?
Do I believe? Have I deceived myself?
I feel the doubt, the rising cloud
That seeks to drown out the flame in my heart.

There are days
There are days that all flow
There are days when I fear I do not know
If You are real
If You truly are the God that I know and believe
And love so much

Pull off the veil that blinds my eyes
Cast off the weight that covers my heart.
Send in Your light, Your piercing, knowing,
So revealing, holy Presence, O God!

Let me know, give me faith
Do I know? Give me faith
I know I believe, yet give me faith
I know, just give me faith."[xii]

"Pull off the veil, Lord." Alex repeated the cry. "Pull off the veil! Forgive me for my stubborn pride. I am deeply committed to doing your will. Jesus, I know you died for me and if you can still use me, in any way, I want to serve you as my Lord and Savior." He had spoken from the bottom of his heart. He could do no more.

In the fifth dimension, the Lord Jesus washed His cleansing blood over Alex's soul. God's everlasting light shone where only darkness reigned before. The veil over his eyes disintegrated. A supreme sense of peace and wellbeing filled Alex.

"Papa, I love you."

The forgiveness poured out. He went directly to his father's violin, took it down and stroked it ever so gently. He lifted the precious instrument and, with newly released abandon, began a sweet melody that sprouted directly from his heart.

<>

"At that time two men will be working in a field; one will be taken away, the other will be left behind. Two women will be at a mill grinding meal; one will be taken away, the other will be left behind. Watch out, then, because you do not know what day your Lord will come." (Matthew 24:40-42 GNT)

Chapter Eighty-Two

Day 8

In the seventh dimension, the euphoria far exceeded all his lofty expectations. Jerry Walker approached Jesus. The glory of His presence was so overwhelming; Walker had to bypass his own thought process to get his words out. Walker needed to shout over the chorus of rejoicing angels but only a stranger's whisper left his mouth.

"My Savior Lord Jesus, why did you allow my country to perish?"

"Its destiny was in their hands. If they, as a nation, had humbled themselves, prayed, sought Me and turned from their wicked ways, I would have heard them. I would have forgiven their sin and healed their land." His voice boomed as He continued. "If they, as a nation, had not rejected Me, I would have moved over them. I would have touched them. Any nation that denies Me is no longer Mine."

Jesus just confirmed what Walker already believed. The next question had no such obvious answer. His mind fought the words. How would the Lord receive his plea? There was only one way to find out.

"May I return?"

"I know your heart. You cannot save her. The answer is NO!"

"But, Lord, I love her. She needs me. I should have done more."

"My love for her is greater than yours." He said softly. "She needs Me too but she has chosen neither of us. There is no more you can do."

xxx

Alex could not contain his joy. He desperately wanted to share his decision about Christ with Kirk but the boy was too distant. He had almost completely shut himself away from the world. He only let Neeko break through.

"Hey, Kirk, what do you say we go fishing?" The boy had to do something. He couldn't sit around and stare at the walls for the rest of his life. Kirk sat silent only for a minute.

"Ok." It was the first word the boy had spoken since Megan left two days ago.

At the shed they collected all the fishing gear they could carry. Alex and Todd had often fished together when they were boys but only Todd had caught any.

They meandered down the path with gear, a big bucket and a dog wagging his tail. When they got to the lake Alex pointed out a sizable splash in the water.

"Boy that must be a big one! Striper, don't you think?"

"Yes, I suppose it is. Todd said these waters are full of them. He caught three the week before ..." Kirk cut his sentence short. Alex didn't want to stop this new flow of conversation so he quickly continued.

"Todd was the best fisherman I ever knew. He caught sixteen in one week when he was just about your age. He broke his own record."

They fished in silence for about an hour. Then Kirk got a nibble.

"Hey, buddy, reel her in!" Alex shouted and the conversation flowed freely. Kirk caught six strippers and three bass that afternoon. Alex caught none. It gave them a good reason to laugh. Alex had fried two of the bass up in a pan, seasoned with salt and pepper. He wasn't much of a cook but when men were hungry it didn't matter. And they were really hungry. When their plates were clean and their bellies were full, they went out on the back porch to enjoy the sun fading down behind the trees. They sat on an old wooden swing that Todd boasted had been made by his grandfather. It made a squeaking sound as they swung slowly back and forth. Kirk finally broke the silence.

"Where do you think they all went?"

"Jesus came and took them up to heaven."

"Why would He want to go and do that?"

"I'm not sure. Maybe there are a lot of bad things that are still yet to happen in this world and He didn't want them to suffer through them. He loves them very much."

A long silence followed. The boy began to draw with his finger on the arm of the swing. "I guess He doesn't love us like Nadia said, otherwise we would be with them too."

"Well I don't think that's quite right. I think He does love us like Nadia said. I just don't think we loved Him back. If we don't believe in Him and we don't accept what He did for us then there is nothing more He can do." The boy looked intently at Alex so he continued.

"Just imagine what it would be like if you did something to break the law. Say it was something really bad." Kirk looked grave as if he were about to admit to a crime.

"You mean if I killed someone or something?" Alex hesitated. Should he press the boy?

"Kirk, did you kill someone?"

"Naw ..." He dropped his head. Alex was sure Kirk wanted to say more. He didn't so Alex continued.

"Yeah, say you killed someone and you were about to spend the rest of your life in jail. Then someone comes along and says they are willing to take your punishment. They agree to go to jail for life instead of you."

"Well that wouldn't be fair. If I killed someone I should suffer the consequences. Miss Nadia said we always have to suffer the consequences of our actions. My father killed my brother. I think he should go to jail." Suddenly it all made sense. Alex put his arm around Kirk. The boy's shoulders were tight. Now what? He decided to proceed with the example.

"And Miss Nadia was right. But just imagine that this other person *could* take your place in jail. Would you let him? Not your father's place. He must make his own decisions."

"Well sure, I guess. But why would he be willing to do that?" Kirk's face was blank. Alex couldn't get a reading.

"Because he loves you that's why, and that is exactly what Jesus did for us. When He died on the cross, he took all the punishment that we deserve for our sins." Alex paused for a moment to let that sink. Then he asked another question.

"What would happen if you decided not to let that person go to jail for you?"

"That would be a pretty dumb thing to do."

"I know it would be, but what would happen?"

"I would have to spend the rest of my life in jail."

"Exactly. The same happens to the people who don't accept the sacrifice that Jesus made on the cross. They must spend the rest of their lives in darkness and when they die, they go to hell." Kirk dropped his head again.

"I don't want to go to hell."

"Neither do I. That's why, after Megan and I came up here to be with you, I accepted what Jesus did for me."

"But I'm not sure I believe in Him."

"Well, I wanted to believe in Him and when I really tried God showed Himself to me. Now I know Him, I trust Him and I have been reading His word every day. And I have to say that my soul is truly glad because of Him."

"Even with Miss Nadia gone?"

"Yes, even with her gone. I know that I will see her again one day. Because I know that my Redeemer lives and I know that after my body dies, I will see God!" Kirk's eyes popped open wide.

"Yes, I will see Him not as a stranger, but as a friend! Jesus is coming back again, Kirk. This time I'm going to be ready for Him."

"I want to be ready for Him too." The boy quietly answered. Alex began to pray with Kirk, first that he might know God better, then that God might forgive and cleanse him and last that God might direct his path. When they were finished Kirk's body was completely relaxed for the first time.

"Could we pray for my dad too?" Alex identified with the boy.

"Of course. Let's pray for him too."

Chapter Eighty-Three

Four angels stood at the four corners that encompassed the earth. By God's divine order, they firmly held back four winds that had the power to damage the earth and the sea. Another angel carrying the seal of the living God called out to them in a loud voice.

"Do not harm the land, the sea or the trees until I mark with this seal the believers from the twelve tribes of Israel. There shall be one-hundred and forty-four thousand of them. This seal shall protect them from the final disasters." The angels stood by waiting to mark the very last two – Alex Lichtenstein and Kirk McCartney. The final devastation was not far behind.

✗✗✗

Megan stepped off the subway car and instantly a wall of stifling heat hit her. Droplets of sweat formed on her scalp as she laboriously climbed the steps to the street. The thick heavy air weighed down her already sullen mood, the result of another grueling day at the TV station. The only news these past few weeks had been bad news, too many disasters in the world. Too many floods. Too many droughts. Too many fires. Too many animals (and insects) gone wild. She determined before she left for work this morning that she must forget the bad and move forward to the good – whatever that may be. But another dismal day dashed that hope. Could there be no more good in the world?

Once out on the street the air began to move around her slightly and breathing became somewhat easier. She slipped her jacket on, not for lack of warmth but for protection. Since she moved to New York City, her skin suffered dreadfully from the air. Hundreds of people died weekly from the mutant bacteria that plagued the big cities. Many believed it was bioterrorism. Panic gripped the people until Sixtus provided free medication, injections once a week, which miraculously saved thousands of lives every day. *At least he is doing something good in the world.* Megan also put on her sunglasses. Allergy season had stretched to all twelve months. Like so many others, she continuously suffered from some form of prickly heat, a side effect from the weekly injections. Her exposed skin turned red and constantly itched. The long sleeves helped a lot.

She had gone only one block north on Lexington Avenue toward her apartment when a black limousine drove slowly next to her. Finally it turned the corner and stopped directly in front of her as she stepped off the curb to cross the street. The front seat passenger window opened slightly.

"President Sixtus requests the pleasure of your company," the rider said.

Megan ignored the invitation and instead of crossing the street abruptly turned the corner and began walking east. The vehicle followed closely. She defiantly gave the finger to its surveillance camera. Megan's phone rang and she answered. It was Sixtus.

"Good evening, my dear."

"What do you want?" she snapped.

"I want you to get into the car. I have a lovely dinner table here set for two."

"What makes you think I would want to have dinner with you? You are a terrorist." She threw that out to get his reaction. *Maybe he will hang up and leave me alone.*

"Manipulating a few terrorist here and there. Controlling a few wars ..." She cut him off.

"You mean you were behind all those wars?"

"A gentle push, my dear, that's all it took – arms in the right hands, stirring up the rebels. Believe me, that's all it took."

"You are a mercenary."

"No, I am a savior." Pride filled the boast.

"You activated and squelched wars just to impress the world?"

"It worked, did it not? Besides, someone needs to control the masses. You are a bright girl. You should know that. Society understands that the world must work together to keep peace and freedom for all. I am the ultimate solution for the betterment of humanity."

Her blood boiled as she heard him chuckle.

"You also poisoned cities around the world then conveniently rode in on a white horse to 'save' them with medication." She didn't wait for him to comment. She accused again.

"So what about the earthquake in South America? Why didn't you evacuate sooner and more wide spread? Or was it a matter of economics? Too costly to save lives?" Contempt oozed.

"You are mistaken on that one. I had a score to settle. Besides, I believe in letting nature take its course. Over population is a problem these days. Nature has a way of evening things out. Don't you agree, Ms. Montgomery?"

Appalled, Megan stomped away.

"You, Mr. Shining Knight, what else have you manipulated for your glorification?"

"You know too much already, my dear. Trust me; you don't want to know more."

"You are right!" she yelled at the top of her lungs. "I don't want to know any more about you, you ..."

"It's all for their own good," he cooed.

She raised her hand to shut off the receiver in her ear.

"Don't cut me off." She detected irritation. Then calmly he continued, "There are so many plans for your future that I want to discuss. I have a very interesting proposal for you."

"I am doing just fine. I don't need you to plan my future. Any proposal from you I would certainly turn down."

"Ah, Ms. Montgomery, but you have already accepted my proposal."

"What do you mean?" Caught off guard she slowed her pace.

"Well how do you suppose you got where you are today? You can't possible imagine you suddenly got your position here in New York on your own."

Punched in the gut, she realized the implication. Each promotion, first to New York and then to anchorman *had* come rather abruptly. Could she have been so foolish to believe it was on her own merit?

"Get into the car, my dear, or your job will disappear as quickly as it came."

"I don't care if you take my job. I am not interested in your sordid little fantasies."

"Well consider this fantasy – Alexander Liechtenstein arrested for treason. I took care of his little sister; I can take care of him too." Megan stopped dead in her tracks. The limo pulled up next to her.

"I thought that might get your attention. Now please get in the car. My driver will see to it that you arrive here safely."

The front seat passenger jumped out and opened the back door, his pistol was clearly visible.

Megan reluctantly climbed in. It locked immediately.

Chapter Eighty-Four

From the sixth dimension Hakah yelled, "Turn back Megan, You don't need to do this! God will take care of Alex." He could see she would not be deterred. "You are brave and strong. I will be with you."

xxx

From the basement of the building Megan entered the elevator that would deliver her to the dreaded fifth floor.

"Swipe the security panel. You have clearance and may come to visit me at any time." His voice was sweet and alluring as it came through the elevator speaker. Megan did as she was told and the doors closed quietly behind her. There was no turning back.

When the doors opened again, she inched her way along the corridor to his private quarters delaying the inevitable as long as possible. The air was cleaner and breathing became easier within the confines of that upper floor. She contemplated her next move, eyes glued to the carpet. She hadn't noticed the color before. Red, scarlet red. *Probably conceals the blood stains of all his victims.*

At the end of the hallway she stopped. In front of her loomed the mammoth French doors that led to the final walkway. The last time she passed through those doors, she was running away, running to a safer place, away from the lion's den. She desired to be in that safer place right now.

Oh, Jerry, why did you leave me?

Again she swiped her wrist and the doors opened. Her heart pounded loudly in her ears as she went around the corner and towards the slaughter house. As she approached the two guards stationed outside the president's apartment, she pulled her hair straight back into a pony tail and secured it with the scrunchy that she carried in her purse. Then she took a tissue and wiped the lipstick from her mouth. If he wanted her he would have to have the bare bones.

One guard opened the door to Sixtus' suite while the other winked and gave a knowing grin. Her flesh began to creep as if thousands of spiders were crawling on her. She lowered her eyes and stepped over the threshold into the den of vipers. Immediately she was greeted by fresh exhilarating air. It was the first truly fresh air she had breathed since she had moved to New York.

"Come in, my dear. I'm so glad you could join me." He met her at the door, took her sweaty limp hand and kissed the back of it. His crisp white shirt, open at the neck, contrasting his dark skin reminded her of the reason she was once so attracted to him. He led her over to a table set for two. A sigh of relief silently left her lips. At least Ashtoreth was not there.

"May I offer you a glass of Champagne?" Without waiting for her response, he poured a glass of the chilled bubbly wine. She accepted it without reserve. It would ease the pain of what she knew would inevitably follow.

"Where is your goon?" Megan asked. His eyebrows closed over his nose. "Mole Man."

"Ah, yes, you have met my friend Vladimir. When you go to unsafe areas you need protection."

"Well then, he should be here. Being around you is the most unsafe area in the world."

"Megan, you hurt my feelings. I want only what is best for you."

"Then leave me alone."

"I can't do that, my dear, you obviously know too much."

Megan said little throughout dinner. There was no need. Sixtus mainly talked about himself and his narcissistic magnanimous exploits. Red wine followed the Champagne. White followed the red. Her senses were dulling and she was fine with that.

Oh, Jerry, why did you leave me? I could be dining with you right now. I could be drowning in your eyes and longing for your touch. Oh, Jerry, how I love you. How I miss you. Why can't we go back?

She didn't hear the front door open nor was she aware of Ashtoreth's presence until the prophetess firmly stroked her shoulder. Megan looked up with a start.

"Ashtoreth, we are delighted to see you." Sixtus smiled and began unbuttoning his shirt. "You remember Megan. She has decided to participate in what presumes to be an exhilarating evening."

Megan's stomach began to wretch. Dizzy, she quickly she stood up pushing her chair into Ashtoreth. "Excuse me," she muttered and made a dash toward the powder room. She got there none too soon. Her dinner, nonstop, made its way into the toilet. At the sink she wiped her mouth and splashed water on her face.

Images from the past rushed into her mind. Long lost images which she had fought to forget. Images of her voyeuristic father and his likeminded girlfriend, both drunk, their garments discarded, playfully removing the clothes from her newly developed twelve-year-old body. Their hungry appetites were routinely satisfied at her fragile, innocent expense until one night two years later she had the courage to slam a cast iron skillet into her father's head. He never touched her again.

Now, the sex triangle nightmare was back, haunting and rearing its ugly head.

Megan looked at herself in the mirror. *Do what you must do.* Determined not to falter, she finally mustered up the nerve to return to the living room. Ashtoreth was laughing with a drink in one hand and her other hand on the zipper of his pants. Her soulless expression that could scar and maim bore down on Megan.

"Come, come, come," Sixtus beckoned her. "The fun is just beginning!" With cheerless resolve she joined them. *Alex still has a chance after all. For me it is over. I'm already damned.*

<>

"The fierce anger of the Lord will not turn back, until He has performed, and until He has accomplished the intent of His heart; in the latter days you will understand this." (Jeremiah 30: 24 NAS)

PART FIVE:

The Return

Chapter Eighty-Five

Day 7

A hoard of demons swarmed the sixth dimension above Captain Steinway of the SS Amity. It was his last assignment. His fleet consisted of five battleships and three aircraft carriers. Conscientiously, he had patrolled the better part of these waters during the last thirty years. They were the best thirty years of his career. His wife anticipated his retirement much more than he did. He always missed her smiling face and gentle touch on his long days at sea but in retirement he would miss much more. He would miss the men. He would miss the command. He would miss the ship but most of all he would miss the sea.

The ocean was particularly calm that day. White caps topped occasional waves. They were three days out and not a whale in sight. He would miss the whales too.

Suddenly a warning came from the radar deck below.

"Something of mammoth size is in the sky over the starboard." Steinway looked to the north. Before he could react, a meteor plunged into the water three hundred feet away. Within moments, the swells swallowed them all.

xxx

Megan stood in front of the microphone reading the latest report that had just come on the monitor during the morning news. Shock paralyzed every muscle. The tension at the UWBC studio in New York was thick. She had a hard time shaking the sickening feeling left by Sixtus and his lioness the night before. Megan had taken the opportunity to slip out while they were taking showers. They had ten PM flights for New Babylon. *May they be gone from my life forever!*

"Only report the relevant information. The rest will be dealt with discretely, as necessary," Richard Rockman, the producer brought Megan back to the Day Break set.

"And what part of this information is irrelevant?" Megan was appalled at the explicit instruction to distort the news. She was also itching to rebel in any fashion possible.

"This order comes from the top." Rockman, with tempered anger, responded.

"Three ... two ... one ... you are live."

"The guided missiles have FAILED to deflect the meteor Eras. As predicted, it has plunged into the Pacific Ocean destroying all forms of life in that sea. Seventy-five foot tidal waves are consuming the West Coast of the Americas and the coast of China. All islands have disappeared. I repeat. All islands have disappeared. No ships are reported to have survived.

Half way around the world, Ashtoreth had her long legs wrapped around Sixtus. They were slowly waking when she turned on the TV and caught Megan's bulletin. Sixtus abruptly sat up knocking Ashtoreth sleepily onto her side.

"She defied my direct order."

Ashtoreth sat up. Her grogginess gone, it finally registered.

"What does she think she is doing? People already are beginning to question your competence and authority," she quipped.

"There is unrest and skepticism arising but no one is questioning my competence, Ashtoreth. And they better not question my authority."

"Excuse me, Mr. President," Ashtoreth smirked at his conniption. "*I* haven't ruffled your feathers, *she* has. You have complete control over cyberspace, education, banking, commerce and the military. You apparently have no more control over the media. She must suffer the consequence of her disobedience."

"Not just yet. I have something in mind for her myself. Get Azimi on the phone for me. The world is getting far too rebellious. This must stop and I want it to stop immediately."

Ashtoreth knew what he had in mind for Megan. It was not what she would do. She would eliminate the woman entirely but Sixtus was not so ruthless. Clearly he was becoming dangerously attached to the wench. There was a price to pay for disloyalty. Sooner or later, Megan Montgomery would pay that price.

<>

"... Something that looked like a huge mountain on fire was thrown into the sea. A third of the sea was turned into blood, a third of the living creatures in the sea died, and a third of the ships were destroyed." (Revelation 8:8-9 GNT)

Chapter Eighty-Six

Day 5

The Eurasian and American plates, two of the Atlantic Ocean's crust began to diverge beneath Iceland's Katla caldera. The ground shook. Mammoth amounts of lava pushed through and melted the snow and ice above the six mile wide volcano. It significantly poisoned agriculture, destroyed property and killed both livestock and humans. Three-hundred million tons of toxic sulfur spewed into the air in a dense ash cloud.

"Iceland had less than an hour warning. Europe fared better but a high pressure system coming in from the north is sweeping over the area, sucking the thick air down. Red haze covers the sky. Crops as far away as Scotland are burned. Birds and fish have not survived. As winds pick up, the evacuation continues as far west as Austria. These sporadic eruptions may continue over the next ten months. Continue to listen for the emergency broadcasts in your area for further instructions. Remain calm above all else." Similar reports reverberated all around the world.

xxx

It was Saturday afternoon and Megan had actually slept in for once. She now sat comfortably with her feet up on the coffee table in her New York apartment. It wasn't a large apartment but it certainly was an improvement over her Chicago studio. Her furniture was sparse; a rose covered loveseat, a wooden block coffee table and an antique floor lamp in the living room, bed and dresser in the bedroom. Simple stuff. She kept promising herself a shopping spree but found she had very little energy and even less interest. The kitchen however was packed to the gills with pots and pans and every kind of gadget. She loved to cook but had no time for that lately either.

She sipped on her second cup of coffee. The New York Times headline screamed FIRE BURNS THE WORLD! She pushed the paper to the floor. No more gloom and doom. Instead, she opened again her last letter from Alex. At least that held some shred of hope. She knew it would be wiser to sever ties with him completely, but ultimately she couldn't do it. He was such a dear. He constantly warned her to keep her distance from Sixtus. She never told him about the threat Sixtus made on his life or their recent encounter.

Being with Sixtus meant keeping him away from Alex. In doing so, she hoped she was finally doing something a little noble even though it was actually very evil. She was numb to Sixtus' affection and completely blocked out the touch of Ashtoreth.

Megan rubbed her eyes. Even with the air-conditioning and purifier, the air was thick and dusty. Fumes from the Iceland volcano were moving fast. She had heard rumors they might even evacuate on this side of the ocean. She scratched her thigh. She had more allergies than she could count. Thankfully the purplish rash that had been bothering her for the last month or so was finally almost gone. The yellowish ring around the outside had already disappeared completely.

Suddenly Megan stood up, collected her letter and her bag and went to the door. *I must be insane to stay here. I need to go see Alex. He is the only bright thing left in my life.*

In no time, she was at Grand Central and on a train headed for Katonah.

"Sir, I am sorry to wake you but you said you wanted to be notified the moment Ms. Montgomery went to Katonah. She left for there on the 3:57 train, local New York time."

"Good job, Azimi. I want you to set up some kind of a disturbance there so that she will think twice about returning. Tell Vladimir not to touch her. But make her know I mean business."

"Yes, sir, I will get right on it."

Megan drove Nadia and Todd's Chevy up the farmhouse driveway. Megan had probably used this car many times more than the newlyweds. Without a tracking system, going from Katonah to Round Lake required no monthly reporting.

She parked by the main house. The sun was setting. Stillness enveloped the farm except for the constant hum of the windmill in the east field and the crickets waking up all around her. She picked her way from tree to tree taking full advantage of the few final rays of light filtering sparsely through them. Eventually she emerged from the woods. The log cabin was silhouetted in the dusk. Smoke billowed through its chimney. What a welcoming sight! *Alex must be cooking dinner.* If heaven on earth existed, this certainly was it.

Sure enough when she opened the door, Alex, donned with Nadia's apron, bounced up and down singing a tune and frying fish on the wood burning stove. Kirk was setting the table and laughing at his mentor's attempt to bring music into the room. All action suspended when Megan entered except for the charging force of Neeko that practically knocked her on her fanny. Then Kirk shouted and threw his arms around her waist. Alex waited in the background for his turn to embrace her.

Megan and Kirk chattered nonstop throughout dinner. After every morsel of food vanished from the plates each took a job cleaning up. When the work was done, Alex ordered Megan and Kirk to sit down in the family room. He then proceeded to take his father's violin from the wall. Megan couldn't believe it!

"You're gonna' really love this." Kirk whispered into Megan's ear. Megan smiled and squeezed his hand. Alex winked at Kirk and began the most beautiful piece of music Megan had ever heard. His fingers ran up and down the instrument like lightening, vibrating the strings as needed. The bow seesawed back and forth at the same speed. His body bobbed and swayed with the tempo, revealing the emotion that swelled up within him. Finally, the beat slowed and the melody ended, leaving his audience breathless.

Megan jumped to her feet and clapped like a little child seeing a performance of Cinderella for the first time. What had made him do what she could not? She didn't care. She wanted to hear him play again.

"Alex, play some more!"This time the bow hopped and popped over the strings with a rhythm that couldn't keep their feet still. Kirk jumped up and pulled Megan up behind him. They danced and danced until they both dropped with laughter onto the floor. Melody after melody delighted her. She couldn't remember when she had a more wonderful time. Her cheeks even hurt from smiling so much.

The evening passed much too quickly. Kirk eventually headed off to bed, but not before Megan reassured him that she would still be there in the morning.

Chapter Eighty-Seven

Hakah shook his head. Was there anything he could do to convince Megan of the truth? Jonathan saw the hopelessness on the other angel's face.

"You have done all you can, Hakah. Don't let her discourage you. Remember what the Ancient of Days said?" Hakah raised an eyebrow at this young angel quizzically as if he could tell him anything he didn't already know. Jonathan's knowledge surprised the weathered angel.

"There will be difficult times in the last days. There will be weak women who are burdened by the guilt of their sins and driven by all kinds of desires, women who are always trying to learn but who can never come to know the truth. Your mortal may be one of these."

Hakah refused to believe it.

Serpentine laughed as he flew into the room. In a rage, Hakah grabbed him by the tail and flung him ruthlessly against the wall. Daggers protruded from the demon's eyes but Hakah was not deterred. He continued to pummel the demon's body. When Serpentine spoke again Hakah charged for his throat. Serpentine gasped and choked as he chanted, "Megan Cameron Montgomery, release your spirit to ..." Hakah cut his statement short.

"Don't listen to him," the angel pleaded. "Your time is short."

xxx

Megan watched Alex as he put the fiddle down and strategically positioned himself on the sofa next to her. He really had changed; his tension and insecurity – gone. He would never cease to amaze her.

"Can you stay awhile?" Hope rang clear in his voice.

"I have to be back at the station on Monday. I was hoping you might let me move into your apartment in Katonah. It would be an easy commute for me and the air is much cleaner than in New York."

"You can stay there as long as you like but you don't *have* to go anywhere. You could stay here with us. We're self sufficient. It's secluded. No one even knows we exist."

She couldn't bear to look into his sorrowful eyes. Her shoulders slumped and she focused on the carpet beneath her feet. She must say what she came to say. She must be firm. She had to protect him. She breathed deeply before she spoke.

"No, Alex, there is nothing for me here. I have to go back," she lied. "I have my work."

Alex stared at her blankly so she tried a different angle. She mustered up a light and flippant tone but cotton choked her throat and rocks weighed down her heart.

"I finally have a position of power at the station. People even recognize me on the streets. You can't imagine how that makes me feel." Alex looked surprise so she continued to milk it.

"I'm not going to quit and walk away from the best thing that ever happened to my career. Without my job, I have nothing – I am nothing." There it was. She said it. She hoped it would be enough to satisfy him, to keep him from pressing her more. His invitation to stay tempted her beyond belief but she knew, for his sake, she couldn't.

Several moments passed. His sad puppy expression almost melted her.

"You have me, Meg ... and Kirk. We need you. Besides, what good does it do to have this powerful position if you are rotting away both inside and out?" He paused, moved closer to her and searched her eyes. She knew he was looking for a more meaningful response, an argument that she didn't have.

"I'm not rotting away!" Her relaxed posture suddenly stiffened.

"Maybe not, Megan, but don't you feel sometimes like you are running from the truth?"

She couldn't keep her voice from rising. "Absolutely not, you are the one who has run away seeking your ultimate truth. I already have my answers. The truth is I am well fed, I have a good job and I'm happy."

Alex persisted. "Are you? Are you really happy?"

Thunder from the heat rumbled in the distance. Megan stood up and walked over to the open window. "I would be a lot happier if the rain would bring a little relief from this heat."

Outside the window she saw a tall sturdy tree glowing in the moonlight – a cherry tree. The sweet ripe cherries beckoned her to stay. She tore her gaze away and turned to Alex whose face cringed. She lightened her tone. "Alex, must there be a source of truth for everything? What is true for you may not be true for me."

"Truth is truth. It cannot change, and if it did then it would become a lie no matter how you try to disguise it."

"Alex," she pleaded, "Nadia's death is proof that even the holy have no peace in their lives. If there is something that I've learned from all the tragedy and chaos of the past three and a half years, it's that life is for the living. We must take whatever we need to preserve ourselves and leave the rest to the fools who think that by helping others they can somehow benefit themselves."

His head sunk down. He did not look at her or speak. *Say something. Be angry. Curse me. Something!* His silence deafened her. She walked over and sat next to him. She strained to hear his muffled voice.

"So you think Nadia was a fool?"

"Alex, I didn't mean that, you know how much I loved her." This was going all wrong. She hoped he would just accept what she said and leave it. She put her arms around him and kissed the side of his head. They cried and mourned once more.

Fifteen minutes passed before Alex spoke again. "God has a definite purpose for your life, Megan, and He expects you to fulfill that purpose before He returns. And He will return." Alex took her hands in his. Calmly he spoke,

"When the time has reached her fullness
And the trumpet sounds the call,
Jesus will appear in glory,
King of Kings and Lord of all
Every nation under heaven
Every ruler, great and small
Every man, woman and child will see it all

Then a sound will start to swell
From every corner of the land
All together, with one voice
And under one command
Even those who never knew Him
Will declare His name
Eyes open wide in wonder, they'll proclaim

He is Lord; He is Lord
Every tongue will confess, He is Lord
At the name of Jesus, every knee shall bow
Every tongue confess, He is Lord

The Lord of all creation
Will come to call His own.
The ones who loved Him with their lives
Longing to come home
As His bride is standing ready
He will greet her face to face
And she'll drop down to her knees and praise
He is Lord; He is Lord
Every tongue will proclaim He is Lord."[xiii]

"And what makes you so high and mighty, Mr. Know-It-All?" Megan jerked her hands away from him and planted them on her hips. Alex dropped his head and silently moved over to the violin that now lay on the coffee table after their evening of jovial entertainment. He stroked it gently then hung it back in its place.

"The reason I couldn't play the violin, Meg, was because I couldn't forgive my father. In his eyes, I was a failure – or so I thought." It was Megan's turn to be surprise. He charged ahead not skipping a beat. "It was only through experiencing God's love that I was able to forgive my father."

"No amount of love will ever enable me to forgive my father." She reacted without even thinking. Adrenalin still coursed hot through her veins. Alex' eyes were soft and warm. She wanted to jump into them.

"When you don't forgive, you build walls around yourself. You're tortured." His response was gently not judgmental.

She knew the walls, she felt the torture but she couldn't forgive.

"Anyone who accepts Christ is a new being; the old leaves, the new takes over. All this is done by God who, through His Son, changes us from being His enemy to being His friend."

Megan's mood softened. "Alex, I don't deserve His friendship or even yours for that matter."

"None of us *deserve* it, Meg. That's the whole point. He gives it just because He loves us."

"But you don't know what I've done." She said almost inaudible. She forced from her mind the image of herself lying in bed between Sixtus and Ashtoreth. Alex pulled her face up to his and held it as if it might break. She thought he would kiss her but he didn't.

"It makes no difference what you've done. If you confess and believe, Jesus will do the rest. God hates sin but there is no boundary to His goodness, mercy and love."

It was more than Megan could handle. "I'm sorry, Alex, I just can't be who you want me to be."

"It's not what I want you to be but what God wants you to be."

"I'm not so sure there is a god, but if there is He made me the way I am."

"He made you with a hole in your heart, a hole that only He can fill."

"You are absolutely right, Alex." He had hit the nail on the head. She fought his words. "I do have a huge hole in my heart. But I don't trust God or want Him anywhere near it. I don't want anyone near it, including you!"

She had done it. She had severed the tie. He would cut her loose; let her go, leave her alone now ... alone now for what? She turned her back on his wounded face. "I'm going to bed." His meekness infuriated her. He had changed ... really changed.

"Sleep with the angels!" His remark caught her off guard and she glanced back at him. The depth of his smile penetrated her heart. Despite what she said, he still loved her. She had to look away. *How can you, Alex, how can you?*

She stomped up the stairs.

A refreshing gentle wind swept over Megan as she lay fidgeting on the bed in the guestroom. *There always seems to be a breeze on Round Lake. I guess that's what makes the windmill work so well.* She recalled the day she and Nadia went to that hardware store to purchase it. "Oh, Nadia, have you been reborn in your brother? He is so much like you now. I can't help but love him. He is much stronger than I could ever be. Sometimes I feel so weak, too weak to stand up. I'm, so afraid I'll fall."

Megan stirred and turned in the bed. She scratched the welts and scabs that resulted from the scorpion drone attack. She went over again and again in her mind her conversation with Alex. If what he said was the truth, it was a hard truth, a truth too hard to believe. Exhaustion overcame her and eventually she fell into a fretful sleep.

Sixtus III personally called the commanders of the ten remaining armies around the world. "I know your troops are suffering and supplies are limited but I entreat you to arm every man alive. Yes, civilians as well. I have emailed you the treaty I want you to sign. It gives me power over you only briefly. It is of utmost importance that we unite as one. You have not failed me in the past. I expect you will not fail me now."

<>
"A third of the human race was killed by those three plagues; the fire, the smoke, and the sulfur." (Revelation 9:18 GNT)

Chapter Eighty-Eight

Day 4

"Stop tormenting her." Hakah hissed to Satan who was hovering over Megan. "What does it gain for you to take one more?"

"Don't you know I have come to steal, kill and destroy? Besides, what does it profit her to serve your God of wrath when she can be her own god? The real question is why do you care? The Ancient of Days doesn't love you or any of the angels the way He loves that cursed human race." He was angry.

"Satan, could it be that you are jealous?" Satan's piercing eyes darted back and forth.

"Jealous of mankind, jealous of that mindless species, nothing could be further from the truth!"

"They are not mindless. They are fashioned after the great Creator Himself. Unlike you and me they have a soul."

"That is just a rumor." Satan scowled trying to disguise his uncertainty.

"No, I have seen it. It can be foul and blacker than death or alive and radiantly beautiful."

"It makes no difference to me. I do not need to be like them or the Ancient of Days. I am a god just like He is. Join me, and you will be a god too!"

"You are a sad and pitiful sight, Satan. You were the most beautiful angel of all, but you threw it away. No, I have no use for you or your kingdom. I would rather be a servant in Yahweh's kingdom than a god in yours.

So the seventh mighty angel brought his trumpet to his lips. The sound bellowed throughout the sixth dimension shaking even the remotest areas. Loud voices began to shout, "The time has come to destroy those who destroy the earth!"

xxx

Megan sat in Alex's Katonah apartment with her knees drawn up under her. She munched away at the bowl of cherries Herb had just delivered. They comforted her. *Herb is such a dear. He always thinks of me.* Food and other commodities were so scarce that every exchange was moderated. Households with more than two vegetable plants in their gardens were required to register them and pay a tax. Many tried to hoard and hide. Often air surveillance exposed them. Their punishment? Hefty fines or even jail sentences. Herb took care of her no matter what the risk.

Thanks to him she also had Faith to keep her company. Faith had belonged to Nadia, but Nadia left the dog with Herb when she moved to the farm. Now Herb let Faith stay upstairs with her. Faith wagged her tail and Megan scratched her new pet's ears. Through sputters and racking coughs she laughed. *For the first time in my life I get a pet and even though that ugly rash is gone, it still appears I'm allergic!*

Finally she settled down with a glass of iced tea. Her phone emitted a four tone beep. She had an e-mail. It was probably Sixtus. She never answered his phone calls so lately he resorted to cyberspace. She refused to let him interrupt her serene moment. Or maybe it was Frank ... lazily she opened her inbox. *Oh, Alex you shouldn't risk a transmission!* Without hesitation she opened it.

Dear Megan,

When you were here yesterday I didn't tell you about my life changing encounter – my battle with God. Remember, Megan, how I kept asking you about the truth? Well, I have found the ultimate truth. I have found that it is not *what* I believe that counts, but *who* I believe. You don't have to believe me, but it's very hard not to believe an all-knowing faithful God. I don't know why I never saw it before, but His identity screams to us through the world He created. Just think about it for a minute the next time you look at the sky. We know there are over one-hundred billion stars in our galaxy alone. And, not one of them is missing or out of place. That's not an accident or freak of nature. It can't be! An awesomely powerful God *must* be in control. There is no other rational explanation.

Nadia was right. The Prince of Peace is that God. He not only created it all, but He totally encompasses it all, and at the same time, is right here inside of me. It's an amazing miracle that I cannot explain or even adequately describe. I tell you, Megan, if you have the true living God present, inside of you, what else can matter? Nothing, no matter how grand or how plentiful, can compare with that.

I don't know why all of this destruction is happening around us, but I do know that God is trying to get our attention. Believe Him, Megan. He *is* the truth. With Him I have peace, true peace – perfect peace. Put your life in the hands of the one true Almighty God. He will heal you with His forgiveness and mercy.

Please, Megan, whatever you do, don't give up. I miss you dearly.

Much love,
Alex

Mice like beings agitated her stomach. She had heard it before from Nadia but refused to believe it could be true for herself. She began to read his letter again when Faith's head shot up. Her ears pointed like a sphinx. She growled then ran to the back door.

"What is it girl? Is something there?" Megan suspected a rodent probably moved in the stairwell leading to the store. "I know you are a great hunter, but let them alone for the evening. You can go hunting in the morning." Then the terrier began to bark wildly.

"It's alright, Faith, come here." Megan's voice became shaky when she heard some shouting in the store below. She went to the door and opened it a crack.

"Herb, are you there?" She only heard muffled groans.

"Herb, are you alright?" She opened the door a little more and brave Faith bolted through it barking as loudly and ferociously as she could. Megan flung the door open and called, just above a whisper, "Faith, come here. Come here, girl."

Next, she heard men shouting then a pained, "Stop, please" from Herb. Then a gun exploded.

Silence.

Immediately, she stepped back and quickly, without a sound, eased the door shut. She leaned against it. Her mind went wild. Panicked, she searched for her phone. She had had it when she was reading Alex's letter but where was it now? Not on the coffee table, not on the couch, not under the blanket.

Faith barked fiercely behind the locked apartment door at the bottom of the stairwell.

Steps scuffled from the store through the hallway toward the exit. Megan listened for a moment. *Are they leaving?* Her heart drummed savagely. A deafening thud echoed up the staircase. They were ramming the door! *Where is that phone?* She pulled the cushions from the couch. *Got it!* Hands trembling, she dialed 911.

"I heard gunshots. They are coming for me." She whispered into the phone. "I'm above the market, in Katonah!" The phone went dead. Had her call gone through? She began to dial again.

Faith barked violently then whimpered when they crashed through the door. The gun rang out again. Faith was silent. Megan eased open the door to Alex's loft and silently closed it behind her.

No one picked up the emergency line.

She held her hand over her mouth to muffle another cough. Her chin dropped down to her chest. She closed her eyes. His pleading, brave face appeared, haunting her again as it had so many times in her dreams. It was the Hungarian boy she could not save. His actions were pure. His decision was definitive. Shepherd for his sheep. Death for life. Sacrifice for the disobedient. Love that knew no bounds. It was real. He was real. It knocked the breath from her.

Jesus, are You real too? She crouched on her knees in the dark. *Jesus!* She could hardly breathe. *Forgive me for all. Forgive me if You can and save me.*

Wash over me, Holy Spirit, flow
Floodwaters come, flood my thirsty soul
Cleansing waters flow on through,
My heart's open to You
Wash over me, Holy Spirit, flow

You're holy, You're worthy,

Flood through me, have mercy
O, You're holy, You're worthy,
Flood through me, have mercy[xiv]

Her simple prayer reached the seventh dimension. Instantaneously His miraculous healing blood emptied like a river from His veins and poured into the fifth dimension. It pierced the wall around Megan's soul and washed it clean; no more black tar, no more noxious rot, no more crusted stones, no more oozing puss, no more feeble white wash. What remained was a pure white soul glowing from a brilliant internal light. The light had finally arrived; His redeeming light, His holy light indwelling the hole in her heart designed only for Him. His Holy Spirit entered her being never to leave her again.

A host of angels began to sing as the sixth dimension rejoiced over her new birth.

She felt supreme peace. A gentle internal voice reassured her. "I took out your stony heart of sin and gave you a new heart of love. Divinely I chose you and abundantly blessed you. By My love you are adopted, by My grace you are redeemed and through My mercy you are forgiven."

"Thank You Jesus," she mouthed, eyes pressed shut.

She knew she would survive.

But what now? They were crashing around in the apartment. What did they want? One of the intruders spoke.

"Come."

Megan recognized the thick accent of the titillating conversationalist. It was Mole Man. A brief silence was followed by thumping steps descending the back stairway. They were gone.

Slowly she turned the doorknob and opened the door. Across from her, written in black marker on the wall, was the warning, "DON'T CROSS HIM AGAIN."

<>

"Peace I leave with you; My peace I give to you; not as the world gives do I give to you. Let not your heart be troubled, nor let it be fearful." (John 14:27 NAS)

Chapter Ninety

Day 3

From the seventh dimension, Jesus announced to the seven angels, "Pour out the contents of your bowls upon the earth. Then they will see My anger is real."

xxx

Megan and Pete, one of the techs who worked sound, were the only ones at the TV station. Many stopped coming after the scorpion attack. Today the rest called in sick due to the dreadful sores around the "Chip."

The fewer people around the better. She would have to be quick. On and off. Pete turned on the sound system and camera. Her heart raced as never before. Usually she felt so at ease before the camera. Not today. Not with what she had to say. What she was compelled to announce to the world.

The Day Break theme song began ...

"Four ... three ... two ... one ..." Pete gave her the "live" sign.

"Good morning and welcome to Day Break." Piercing pain shot through her head as the teleprompt signaled her next line. 'Another deadly earthquake rocked the San Andreas Fault this morning at 5:57 EST. California has been severed from Garberville to Browley. The Costal and Transverse Ranges are no more. The World Geological Survey says ...' Megan ignored the devastating words on the monitor. An inner calm took over.

"I am so happy to be here. It is the dawning of a new day. I bring you this Tuesday morning a startling update. Upon my diligent research, I have concluded that the sores that emerged on everyone are a direct result of God's judgment on the earth." Pete's bulging eyes told her she was crazy but she continued.

"Those who have received the mark of Sixtus will drink the wine of God's fury which He has poured full strength into His cup of rage. The time is now." Pete made a chopping signal across his throat. She sat gripping her chair for support. Her body was weak and on fire. She had been denying it for days but she knew the infection had won. She plowed ahead.

"You can, however, be redeemed by dying in the service of the Lord. New Babylon is soon to fall! Therefore, worship Jesus and you will be set free!"

Pete cut to a commercial. "What is wrong with you?" He shouted. "You're dead." Her head pounded.

"You mean like drop dead beautiful or dead in the water?"

"No, like deader than a door nail. I mean it Megan. This is serious."

"I know, thanks my friend. I will never forget you." She blew him a kiss and, with little energy left, stumbled out the studio door where she immediately plowed into Frank coming down the hallway.

"Hey, doll, where you going? Shouldn't you be in front of the camera?"

"Yeah well, I'm in a bit of a jam."

"What did you do now?"

"I'll tell you on the way. Right now I need to get out of the building."

Megan filled Frank in on her morning broadcast as they rode down in the elevator.

"They will be looking for you. Probably locked down the whole building by now. Do you have a plan?"

"No not for this. I guess I didn't think things through clearly."

"What else is new?"

When they reached the first floor instead of going left to the front lobby, they turned right, ran down a long corridor then ducked into a storage room marked "Employees Only".

"Now what?" Megan huffed and puffed. Her body ached and her knees began to tremble.

"Is there a more secluded exit?" Frank questioned.

"Yes, but we have to go down three flights of stairs. I think it goes to the service garage."

"Let's do it!" Frank slowly opened the storage door slightly. "The coast is clear." He whispered.

"I can't believe you just said that!" His humor encouraged her.

Megan darted out before him and continued left stopping at another door. She waved her wrist over the POD and turned the doorknob. It opened. They hadn't locked down her ID yet. Megan and Frank raced down three flights of steps before the sound of voices coming from the underground garage made them stop just short of the service entrance. One of the two bays was open. Two men who had finished unloading a paper supply truck sat on a wooden bench. An older man checked the merchandise in. The burley driver was dressed in navy overalls with a green shirt. Engraved on the pocket was his name, Kenny. Kenny leaned against the wall smoking a cigarette.

Megan tried to suppress a cough that had been tickling her chest but had to let it out. Her breathing sounded like a wheeze. Her legs weakened.

"You OK?" Frank looked at her.

"Yes, of course." She tried to be convincing but she was glad he took her arm. "Now what?" Megan whispered in desperation.

"Just follow my lead." Frank said with confidence as he casually led her through the exit and into the garage. "Hey, where are you two going?" A tall gray-haired black man holding a manifest blocked their way. "We were looking for the employee parking lot and I made the wrong turn." Frank said matter-of-factly.

"Aren't you that TV lady from the news station?" Kenny had spotted Megan hiding somewhat behind Frank.

"Yes, we didn't mean to intrude. My friend here wanted to show me his new car. I told him this wasn't the right way but he insisted."

The black man gave them a disapproving glance. "No intrusion, ma'am, just please be more careful next time."

"Yes, sir we will, for sure. God bless you and have a great day."

"Don't know if I will but I'll try." He responded adding afterward, "Crazy people, they look smart but got no sense at all." Kenny agreed with a nod and put his cigarette out.

Megan and Frank walked briskly across the parking lot and up the ramp. When they finally emerged onto the street, they shook with laughter and disappeared down an alleyway.

"So what are you going to do now?" Frank sobered up.

"That's where I need your help."

"Sure, anything, just name it."

"It may be a bit risky for you."

"Risky is my middle name – shoot."

"I know you've always wanted to live in Manhattan. Would you consider moving into my apartment?" She held out her key to him.

"Are you suggesting ...?" he said with a sly grin on his face.

"No, you idiot, I'm moving out but I don't want the authorities to know that until I'm long gone. If you move in, they will see that the place is still occupied."

"Awe shucks, I thought we might have something going on here that I wasn't aware of. I would consider it an honor to take over your apartment. But that doesn't seem very risky."

"Here is the risky part." She lowered her voice to a whisper though there was no one around to hear her. "I want you to buy a train ticket for me. If I buy it they will know for sure I am on the run."

"That's no problem. You just tell me when and where and I am there. Megan, do you think this is the end of the world?"

"No, but I think Jesus is coming back to judge the world and you have to believe in Him. That's all I know."

Megan coughed again. This time uncontrollably. It felt like her insides were erupting. Her head was on fire. The energy drained from her body as if through a hole in her ankle. She needed to get to Alex.

Sixtus abruptly flipped the TV off in the bedroom of his New Babylon location hoping Ashtoreth had not heard the broadcast. To no avail. Enraged, she immediately emerged from the bathroom and stormed, "That is it. She is finished!"

"I will take care of it." Sixtus remarked solemnly.

"Like you did the last time?" She was livid and he knew it.

"No, not like last time."

"See to it or else I will do it myself."

"I will take care of it." He yelled back. He would not give her the satisfaction. Without hesitation he went to his office and made the call. *What a shame, my pretty, what a shame.*

"Vladimir, dispose of her." His voice was emotionless.

The trip to Round Lake was long. It was all she could do to keep her feverish mind alert and concentrated on the road ahead of her. When Megan arrived at the cabin Alex and Kirk were playing chess. Neeko was sprawled out on the floor. *What a perfect father Alex would be.*

Kirk gave out a cheer when Megan eased her way through the front door. "Is there enough room at the table for one more?" Like cupid's arrow, Alex's eyes leaped from half a room away. Her heart melted.

At last all her strength gave out. She slumped to the floor coughing. She felt the phlegm fill her mouth and spill into her hand which then dropped lifeless to her side. She didn't need to look. She knew it was full of blood. Her mind no longer processed what was going on around her until Alex lifted her easily in his arms. Her pounding head rested lightly against his cool neck. She was finally home. In that moment she realized she had truly found enduring love.

<>

"... Terrible and painful sores appeared on those who had the mark of the beast and on those who had worshiped its image."

(Revelation 16:2 GNT)

Chapter Eighty-Nine

Day 2

Satan, surrounded by his legions soared to the edge of the sixth dimension. He scowled, growled and spit. The demons following him trembled from his obvious rage.

Michael the archangel met him there. "Do not think for one minute that you can escape His judgment. After all, He already defeated you when He died on the cross. Your sentence is yet to come."

Satan groaned when the angel approached. "I am the conqueror. I have ruled the earth with an iron hand. Look at how many times I snatched away what He sowed in their hearts, when they heard but did not understand. How many times did I blind the minds of mortals to His gospel? Oh how I love prowling about like a roaring lion, seeking someone to devour. I devoured more than He saved."

"They were destroyed only because they believed your deception, which camouflaged your hideous identity and your coming defeat. They believed your lies and did not search for the truth. Now the book of life is closed. Your time is short."

"I am sick of your monotonous chatter. I will forever control the earth. It was my past, is my present and will be my future. Michael, you only know what your Master has told you. I know more than your little mind can possibly conceive. Trust me, you will see."

"Trust you? I cannot. See your future? That is for God to decide but what is written does not bode well for you."

Satan unshaken did not waver or tremble. He merely flew off into the distance followed by his fearful cohorts.

xxx

Sixtus stood before the UWBC microphone in his New Babylon office. Ashtoreth was at his side, her beauty mesmerizing and luring. Sixtus had one last card to play and that would put him on top of the game. He looked straight into the camera and with calm authority announced, "All males over sixteen are called to arms. You have responded to your leader's plea in record numbers but now we need you all. Ashtoreth and I need you *all* to fight the final battle. Then peace will reign forever.

There *will* be no more fighting; there *will* be no more enemies. You *will* be free forever."

The broadcast went instantaneously around the world. Men and boys from all races and nationalities responded and gathered; compelled to support their controlling, prevailing, and formidable leader.

Vladimir sat in the driver's seat of a black sedan parked across the street from Megan's apartment building. He pulled his collar up around his neck and pulled his baseball cap down over his large forehead. He wanted to look like a typical New Yorker but merely succeeded in hiding the black mole over his left eye. No one had seen her since her incriminating broadcast the day before. She would have been arrested if she were caught leaving the city. No records indicated that she had. She appeared to be holed up in her apartment. He had seen lights and other activity through the front window.

He didn't want to kill her in her apartment. He liked things neat. Dispose of the body completely. Unfortunately the boss was impatient. Vladimir had to do it tonight.

He waited until traffic passed then he got out of his car and sprinted across the street. He entered the brownstone and found himself in a well lit hallway lined with mailboxes and call buttons. He pressed the one marked M. Montgomery 4-G.

A man answered. "Who is it?"

Vladimir remained silent. He pressed another button. He got the same response.

A woman about as wide as she was tall, with short brown hair entered the building carrying a grocery bag in her right arm. A huge duffle bag hung over the left. Never looking up she retrieved her mail then sideswiped Vladimir as she shuffled passed him. Without a word, she approached the inside door and, after fumbling between curses, opened it with her key.

Vladimir took two steps toward her with a ten inch switchblade pointed toward her back. He hated messes but there seemed to be no other alternative. He had a job to do. He was not a killer at heart; however he had known others who were. Their eyes changed when the talked about the assassinations they had performed. No he was not like them. He merely followed orders and sometimes that included murder.

Suddenly this little round gnome's cell phone began to ring. She fumbled some more and juggled her mail angling through the door as her foot lodged it open. Clearly distracted she began to speak, "Hey."

Vladimir took one step closer to the door and flung his cap to the floor just before the door closed. Without looking back the woman started up the stairs. She turned toward him when she reached the first landing. Vladimir quickly glanced at the call board as if looking up a name. Her heavy footsteps continued up the stairs.

He pushed the wedged door open with his foot, immediately retrieved his cap and slid through the opening. He had learned to be light on his feet, even for a man of his size. He arrived on the fourth floor without making a sound. Apartment G on the right. He was not adept at picking locks but this was an old building. He hoped for an old lock. It was. His plastic card did the trick.

Frank had just plopped his TV dinner on the table when the buzzer sounded. He went to the door and pressed the button.

"Who is it?" He was annoyed. When would the pranksters give up? Street gangs often wanted to scare apartment dwellers but he wasn't scared. This time though he had a funny feeling. It was a haunting feeling that he couldn't shake.

He went to the bedroom and opened the window. A cloud of toxic hot air blasted him in the face. He looked down the fire escape to the alley below. It was quiet. What did he expect? Was he becoming paranoid?

Still, Frank waited in the bedroom for a good fifteen minutes. As he waited he leafed through the Bible Megan had left next to her bed. "For God so loved the world that He gave..." *This is ridiculous. My dinner is probably cold by now.* Yet something still held him back. He opened the bedroom door slower than he expected. His body was cautious though his mind was not.

Then he heard it.

Footsteps in the outside hallway.

Someone fiddling with the lock.

Frank's breathing began to intensify. *My camera!* It was on the kitchen table. As he sprinted from the bedroom to his camera the front door quietly swung open. He flung the camera over his shoulder, turned and bolted for the bedroom. He never looked back. In a flash he disappeared through the window and down the fire escape.

Good for him. Vladimir held the switchblade firmly. *I really don't like messes.* The woman was no where around.

He sat down and ate the cold TV dinner.

He needed to switch gears. Devise a new plan. The woman must be found.

<>

"For God loved the world so much that He gave His only Son, so that everyone who believes in Him may not die but have eternal life." (John 3:16 GNT)

Chapter Ninety-One

Day 1

The blistering heat and relentless drought seared much of the world. Baked soil strangled vast amounts of trees. Withered crops produced little harvest. Arid, desert like conditions ravaged pastures where cattle grew emaciated. The perfect formula for disaster brewed over the Pacific Ocean. La Nina emerged creating mammoth tornadoes, deadly tropical storms and monster hurricanes.

The burning sun ignited massive relentless wildfires. Thrashing flames destroyed thousands of homes abandoned by shocked and grief-stricken people. The fires drove wildlife from the mountains into the valleys in search of food. Black smoke engulfed areas miles and miles from the intense blazes.

Overgrazing and deforestation combined with the massive draught caused the deserts to expand in Saudi Arabia, Sudan, Egypt and Mongolia. In one day, sandstorms dropped twenty tons of sand over each of their cities.

The globe became a torch and pandemonium reigned. People cursed God.

xxx

Vladimir drove to Katonah in search of the illusive butterfly. As he suspected she was not in the abandoned apartment. She must be at Round Lake but in the past all searching for survivors had come up negative there. Alex Lichtenstein appeared to have disappeared into thin air as well. He would search there one more time.

Vladimir shuddered as he entered the tattered town of Monroe. Burned buildings peppered the landscape. Weather torn stores and homes lined the streets on every block. It was not unlike most of the villages he had already passed. He stopped his car in the parking lot of the restaurant Lichtenstein noted in his travel reports. An Italian looking woman met him at the door. Her eyes averted his.

"To stay or carry out?" Her voice was shaky.

"Stay." He was equally as curt. She led him to a booth in the back near the kitchen and dropped a menu in front of him.

"May I get you anything to drink first?"

"Beer." She walked away and returned two minutes later with a glass of draft so weak it resembled piss water. He smelled it before he drank. It was cool but tasteless. It would do to quench his thirst.

"I'm looking for my cousin Alex Lichtenstein. Do you know him?"

"Yes." She refused to look at him.

"Have you seen him lately? Do you know where he lives?"

"No, I haven't seen him. He doesn't live around here."

"Could he be at Round Lake?" That made her look up.

"No, sir. No one has lived there for quite some time." Her voice lost any trace of friendliness that had been there before.

"Can you direct me to it?"

"Go down two blocks; make a right, drive two miles, turn left. The road winds around but will eventually take you there. Do you want anything from the menu?"

"No, what do I owe you?"

It was dark by the time Vladimir left the restaurant. The woman's directions were not good. He drove for half an hour before he happened onto the road out of town. His tires crunched on the gravel road as he passed the sign that read, "Phillips Farm." Three deer crossed in front of his headlights but all else was quiet. A red haze covered the sky hiding any trace of star or moon light. He didn't know when he had ever seen such a dark night. It was too dark for his liking.

City lights kept the night bright in New Babylon where he lived now. When he was a boy there were no city lights, only the stars and moon which were so bright no street lights were necessary.

He approached an old farm house. It was not locked. He took a mini flashlight from his pocket and went in.

Alex raised a spoon of soup to Megan's parched pale lips. She needed liquids but could barely swallow. Her eyes had lost their emerald hue. Her life was slipping sway. If only he could exchange his for hers. He would gladly defend her against armies even slay the devil for her but try as he might, he could not heal her.

"Please Lord, heal her." She had only moved slightly since he carried her up to her room last night. Her cough steadily grew worse – harsher, louder, more blood. He had nothing for it except tea and a bit of honey. As night fell, her fever rose, he didn't need to measure it. He could see it in her glassy eyes he could feel it through her sweat drenched clothes. He had given her the last two aspirin this afternoon and her temperature still climbed. He had replaced the cold washcloth on her forehead every fifteen minutes or so but she needed something more. He decided to search the old farmhouse. He had already taken what was in the kitchen but maybe there was ibuprofen or something in the medicine cabinets in the upstairs bathrooms. It would be old but maybe still good.

"Kirk, come and stay with Megan." He called to the boy. "I'm going to the big house."

"Don't go," Megan weakly whispered.

"I'll be right back. I'm going to look for something to lower your fever." Alex kissed her forehead. Its fire warmed his lips.

Alex briefly thought about going into town but by now the pharmacy would be closed and he knew no one would open their door at night. As he crunched through the dense woods he tried to remember any other remedies that Doc Walker used on his patients when their temperatures were high. He couldn't recall any. *Lord, please help Megan. Don't let her die.*

When he emerged from the woods he noticed there was a light on in the farmhouse family room. He would have to speak to Kirk about turning lights off when he left a room. He wondered how long that one had been burning. His boots echoed on the wooden porch as he approached the back door. It was locked.

He walked around to the front of the house but stopped abruptly when he saw a strange car parked there. He ducked back out of sight when he heard the front door open then peeked around the corner. A tall well built man emerged. He didn't look military so why was he here? A thief? Alex doubted it. His instincts kicked in, he had a very bad feeling. The big guy was definitely looking for something ... or someone. The intruder got into his car and slowly drove toward Alex. He pushed his back against the side of the house. Headlights swept past him moving slowly down the gravel road to the cottage by the lake.

Would he come back? Alex didn't know. He made a dash for the front door and went straight up the stairs to the master bathroom. He opened all three drawers. No meds. He went to the other bathroom down the hall and pulled at the mirror above the sink. It was jammed. He pulled harder and three bottles, a hair brush and a cap crusted tube of toothpaste fell out clanging to the floor.

The gravel crunched on the driveway. The trespasser was back.

Alex flipped off the light. Had the man spotted it? Suddenly the floor beneath his feet began to tremble. Caught off guard he grabbed hold of the sink. It began to shake as well. He held it tight then felt it wrench away from the wall. Alex dropped to the floor which was shaking violently now. Dust from the ceiling dropped all over him as it began to crack open. He heard the three bottles of medicine from the cabinet bounce around on the floor and he fumbled for them in the dark. He found all three and slipped them into his pocket.

The front door crashed open. From the earthquake or the man he didn't know.

Pots and pans made a racket in the kitchen. Cupboard doors banged and dishes clanked and clattered to the floor. Alex heard a thump then a thud. The intruder cursed loudly. Had the man fallen? A moan followed.

Alex stopped briefly at the top of the open stairway. Adrenaline kicked in. It was warm and gave Alex the confidence he needed. Slowly, knuckles white, Alex gripped the railing. He went down one step at a time making himself as light and as quiet as possible. He wished he had worn his sneakers rather than these clunky work boots. His heart pounded but he controlled his breathing. He remembered sliding down this banister with Todd when they were just kids. Should he do that now? The last time he tried it he landed on his back side at the bottom. Better walk.

The entire house was shaking now. The free standing staircase Todd's grandfather built so long ago, partially broke away from the joints at the top and bottom. The railing, no longer stable, swayed under his weight. He lost his balance, careened down on his side and slid over the edge of the step. He dangled from railing not knowing whether to hold on or jump free to the ground. His split second decision to let go came too late. The banister plunged Alex eight feet onto the floor. The fall was not bad but the debris that followed bruised his shoulder and knocked his head silly. He heard the moan, this time louder, coming from the kitchen.

Alex took an accounting of all his parts. No broken bones. He freed himself from the rubble and dashed for the hearth that separated the family room from the kitchen. Not knowing just where the other man was, he crouched down next to the stone smokestack. Again the moan and a shuffle. Alex peered into the kitchen. The man was on his feet. Blood poured from his head.

The earthquake stopped.

An aftershock would surely come. Alex needed to get back to Megan and Kirk. He sprinted across the ten feet of once open space, now covered with railing parts, ceiling debris and broken boards, to the front door. Loose on its hinges, it squeaked opened. He slipped out then darted around the corner.

He stopped to catch his breath.

The front door opened briefly then closed again. Alex sank down to the ground. *Thank you, Lord.*

Steam rose from the streets of New Babylon. The heat was unbearable. Suddenly every twenty feet, lightening began to strike. A cataclysmic charge of gases hurled to the earth from a solar storm. Multiple electric shocks resulted in deafening thunder. Houses burned. People died. Anguished screams rang louder than the thunder itself.

The ground began to tremble and then to open. The magnitude ten point five earthquake split the city into three parts. All structures leveled. Every island vanished, the mountains disappeared – nothing remained. Nothing, except a few surviving inhabitants who cursed God. And they were then deluged by hail.

Sixtus did not despair though the elements destroyed the world around him. He rallied his armies. Together they poised for battle in a place deemed Armageddon.

In the seventh dimension, a voice shouted and the sound reverberated through the air, "The end has come. It is done!"

<>

"Then I saw three unclean spirits that looked like frogs. They were coming out of the mouth of the dragon, the mouth of the beast, and the mouth of the false prophet. They are the spirits of demons that perform miracles. These three spirits go out to all the kings of the world, to bring them together for the battle on the great Day of Almighty God." (Revelation 16:13-14 GNT)

Chapter Ninety-Two

Jesus Returns

"One-thousand sixty days have passed. Are you ready to judge the living and the dead?" Jesus, the Prince of Peace, waited to take His place on the throne. He looked down on the flaming earth. Fire lapped at forests, fields and homes on every continent. The entire world burned. Little escaped the blaze.

"As you command, my Father."

"I see your hesitation. I know how much you love them."

"Your will is perfect and just. I am ready." Jesus gathered His mighty army. Starting in the East, Jesus slit open the sky and peeled it back like a scroll. Miraculously the vapor that separated the sixth dimension from the earth's atmosphere disintegrated. Angels poured through and bounded among the clouds which ultimately dissipated entirely along with the preexisting sky.

xxx

Sixtus, armed and surrounded by his battalions stood proud, confident he would succeed. In the distance, far above him, he saw a crack which began to open the sky. The armies trembled. Sixtus stood the course. Hundreds of stars dislodged and fell as the fissure widen. Gradually the sky expanded, completely exposing every kind of spirit.

Satan appeared at his side, prepared for the fight. Sixtus recognized him immediately.

"I am certain of victory." Sixtus stated.

"We shall prevail." Satan answered.

Ashtoreth stood between them, joined their hands and raised the cry. The battle of Armageddon began.

Sixtus fought with more power than he thought he possessed. Jesus' mighty warriors fought courageously but it didn't last long. Sixtus pushed them back, Victory was his. Then one single word thundered.

"Stop!"

Jesus wore layers of crowns on His head. His brilliant white clothes, dipped in blood, demanded vengeance for those previously slain. All warriors froze. Try as he might, Sixtus could not move. He searched the crowd for Ashtoreth. She too stood motionless.

"Your power is useless," Satan raged but he too was cemented to the ground.

A majestic archangel stood on the darkened sun and shouted in a loud voice to all the birds in flight. "Come, you feathered avengers, gather together for God's great feast. Eat the flesh of generals, commanders, and soldiers, the flesh of all these people great and small!"

A great roar rippled toward Sixtus – thousands of wings beating. First the birds soared around his fallen soldiers feasting on their eyes and entrails. Then they picked the bones clean.

Sixtus, deafened by their screams, watched as the birds devoured the living. He then locked his gaze on the Living Savior. Jesus took the false prophet, Ashtoreth, and threw her still alive into the lake of fire that burned with sulfur. Angels threw demons into the lake also, where the fire never burns out. Even from a distance Sixtus felt the heat. Then Jesus came to him. Sixtus squirmed in raging fury but could not break the hold Jesus had on him.

"Go!" That one word controlled a might force that flung Sixtus into the pit as well. Down, down. Burning, burning. The lake of fire, now heavily fueled, burned into the fifth dimension and licked up all the souls anguishing there.

Flames consumed the remains of the great city of New Babylon which created a black smoke that went up forever and ever.

Chapter Ninety-Three

The sky continued to open, rolling back the veil. The sound of God's coming was like the roar of rushing waters and the whole landscape lit up displaying His glory. "Praise God! Salvation, glory and power belong to Him! His judgments are true and just," boomed the sky.

He spoke individually to every person alive that had not gone to the battle. He dissolved the veil between them and their unique "space" in the fifth dimension. The contents of their souls poured onto them physically. It surrounded them like a blanket and then absorbed into their viscera through their eyes, ears, nose and mouth. Their brain, lungs, heart, and stomachs were filled with the substance that would eternally sustain them.

The state of their soul determined the outcome. Some screamed in horror. Some withered then writhed on the ground and cursed God. But others glowed with delight and renewed power.

Jesus continued west touching everyone.

xxx

An eerie bluish-green light woke Vladimir as it streamed through the shattered window next to where he lay. At first he thought it might be a distortion caused by last night's residual haze. Then as he looked up, reflex dropped his mouth open. He tried to get up. Instantly his body ached reminding him of the knock to his head and the nasty fall from the quake. He pushed his way through the front door. His optics scanned the sky – or what was left of it.

He finally appeared. Swarms of angels surrounded Him. A compelling force dropped Vladimir to his knees. The light that emanated from the apparent apparition was so bright it surrounded every object and dispelled every shadow. The light drew his face upward. It warmed him, going beyond the surface skin, burning through his eyes and into his heart.

Suddenly their eyes connected.

Fearfully Vladimir perceived Him to be the Christ, who they called Jesus. His voice, like a razor, cut through the atmosphere. Vladimir heard it but could not understand it.

Instantly the air soared around the awestricken man like a wind tunnel. It ripped at his clothes. The pressure pushed on his chest crushing the breath from him. The veil that separated him from his "space" in the fifth dimension dissolved. All was instantly quiet, soaked in torment. The putrid muck and slime from his soul clung to him and painfully sucked itself into his body. The morose filling was unearthly and beyond his depth of understanding. He reeked with its odor and slumped to the ground under its weight. For a moment he thought he would suffocate as it filled his lungs. His heart would surely explode from the pressure.

The Savior's voice, though distant, was crystal clear. "Your judgment has come."

Help me.

Jesus drew near. His countenance softened with compassion, seemingly on the verge of tears. Vladimir's arms were weak as if hundred-pound weights pinned them down. With all his might he reached up until he saw Jesus' blood drenched robe. Vladimir recoiled. Jesus bent closer and passionately whispered, "I never knew you."

Slowly Vladimir's body began to equalize as the vile substance assimilated.

"What have you done to me?" His voice screeched as if coming from a stranger.

"I have done nothing but release the barrier to your soul. You have done it to yourself. Every human still alive on this day is the same. Your souls live inside you now, be they wretched and dark filled with human thoughts and deeds, or pure and bright filled with My grace and mercy. You will live forever, Vladimir, dwelling on the sustenance your soul provides."

"I merely obeyed orders," Vladimir sheepishly confessed, but Jesus had already departed.

Megan stirred slightly then a memory sparked. She clutched the bed tightly recalling how, amidst Kirk's frantic screams, it had danced over the floor the night before. But the earthquake had long passed. The cabin had shaken wildly but had remained structurally sound. Her hands relaxed.

Through long lashes she saw Alex asleep on the chair next to her bed. How gallant he was. His peaceful expression encouraged her, though his blood crusted nose was swollen. Probably broken. His eyes slowly opened and that worried look returned.

"You don't look so good either." She said barely audible. His puppy dog smile returned as he rubbed his shoulder. Did she detect a limp? At her side he gently rested his hand on her forehead.

"Fever's down." His face relaxed and he smiled again. Megan tried to sit up but her energy was spent. Heavy, her eyelids dropped down.

All was dark.

She drifted.

Far off Alex shuffle to the window. His cheerful voice brought her back.

"Megan, you've got to see the incredible sky." She barely heard his soft voice. He returned with renewed energy to her bedside. Carefully he swept her up into his arms.

"All I want is Jesus." It came out raspy and quiet. She could not open her eyes but draped her arms heavily around his neck. It was cool against her face. *How I wish I could stay with Alex forever.*

Once outside, she breathed a little easier. The air tingled against her skin. She limply rolled her head back.

"Open your eyes, Megan, this is amazing!"

She knew she was dying so what was the point? But she obeyed him dutifully. Through tiny slits, she observed the sky. Though still dark, it sparkled in a way she had never seen before. The haze reflected some unknown source of light.

"I wish I had my telescope. But even with it I don't think I could explain what is happening." There was fear in his voice so she opened her eyes completely. The sky was parting at the apex of a falling star! A great light replaced the shimmering night.

"The Light of men vindicating His people." Alex whispered. Clearly, amazement had swallowed his fear but his body stiffened around her.

She saw the dripping blood on her Savior's garment, the cleansing blood of the Lamb that was slain. She tried to stand up but instead Alex dropped to his knees clutching her even tighter. The Lord's soft gentle voice spoke directly to her but she didn't understand the words. Alex finally put her down. Had he heard the voice too? She leaned limp against him. Suddenly a tornado like force surrounded them.

Then she felt it.

The veil that separated Megan from her soul dissolved. An entirely new atmosphere engulfed her. Slowly her body filled with an incredulous phenomenon. Her breath tingled as it entered her nostrils and filled her lungs. Her arms and legs appeared to have been washed in stardust. Her body was revitalized. The infection was gone. She felt strong once again.

It happened in a moment.

She looked at Alex. He had experienced the same. His face glowed with an indescribable smile and radiance. She felt her lips part and her cheek muscles rise to her ears.

He cradled her face in his hands. "Marry me," he commanded. His breath was so sweet, like irresistible cherries.

She answered him with a passionate kiss on his welcoming lips. *Yes, Alex, I will love you forever.*

Jesus knew their hearts. His eyes were warm and consenting. Gently He placed a hand on each of their heads and proclaimed, "I bless this union to the end of the age."

Then He was gone.

Megan basked in His residual glory with her beaming husband by her side.

A loud uncontrollable laugh from inside the house broke the tender moment. Kirk, who had been sleeping up stairs, had obviously met his maker. *Thank you, Jesus, for your saving grace.*

.

<>

"And you can be sure that if the owner of the house knew the time when a thief would come, he would not let a thief break into his house. And you, too, must be ready, because the Son of Man will come at an hour when you are not expecting Him." (Luke 12:39-40 GNT)

"God did not choose us to suffer His anger, but to possess salvation through our Lord Jesus Christ, who died for us in order that we might live together with Him, whether we are alive or dead when He comes. And so encourage one other and help one other, just as you are doing now." (1 Thessalonians 5:9-11 GNT)

Epilogue

Megan and Alex spent their honeymoon in the cottage by the lake. Soon after, Jesus returned. He took Megan, Alex and Kirk to the home where they would reside with Him in their glorified state for a thousand years.

The earthquakes continued at Round Lake and the rest of the earth followed by waves of torrential rains and then devastating droughts. Vladimir was condemned to roam the corrupted land for a thousand years, never able to satisfy his perpetual hunger.

<>

"He seized the dragon, that ancient serpent - that is, the Devil, or Satan - and chained him up for a thousand years ... They that had not worshiped the beast or its image, nor had they received the mark of the beast ... ruled as kings with Christ for a thousand years." (Revelation 20:2, 4 GNT)

How Beautiful

How beautiful
    the eyes to see
    of the One who adores me.
How beautiful
    to hear His voice
    and know He calls me.
How beautiful
    to taste His mercies
    for they are new each day
    like the rising of the sun.
How beautiful
    the heart that broke for me
    and the love that was its undone.
How Beautiful
    the wounded hands
    that call to me still.
How Beautiful
    the feet that brought
    Him to me.
How Beautiful
    the Savior to know
    God's love in Him
    makes me whole.

By Lynda Amundrud

A Message from the author:

Jesus loves you and desires to have you spend eternity with Him. He is the only mediator we have with our heavenly Father. If you desire to have God's life giving blood cleanse your soul and bring your spirit to life, say the following prayer:

Dear Father in Heaven,
Thank You for sending Your Son Jesus Christ, the sacrificial Lamb, to shed His blood on the cross on my behalf. I am sorry for all my sins and acts of disobedience against You. I give my life to You. My desire is to please You in all things and to follow You the rest of my life. In Jesus' name. Amen.

If you prayed that prayer with a sincere heart your soul has been cleansed. You can be sure that Jesus will never leave you and you will have everlasting life with Him in heaven.

What to do next?

- Tell someone that you have given your heart to God (a loved one, a local pastor or me*)
- Read the Bible everyday starting with the gospel of John
- Find a Bible-believing church in which to grow and worship

*If you contact me at **www.PatriciaBortz.com**
I will be in prayer for you and will help you find a local church.

The following Bible scriptures were taken from the Good News Translation (GNT) and the New Standard American (NSA).

All songs by Elizabeth Graham are from her CD "LONGING" which may be purchased through the following web site:

http://www.cdbaby.com/cd/elizabethgraham

She may be contacted directly at: **eg@elizabethgraham.net**

---

[i] © 1999 by Elizabeth Graham "You Gave Your Hands"

[ii] © 1999 by Elizabeth Graham "Come Lord Quickly"

[iii] © 2002 by Elizabeth Graham "God is Good"

[iv] Psalm 119:96-98,105 (GNT)

[v] © 2000 by Elizabeth Graham "Longing"

[vi] Colossians 3:1-4 (GNT)

[vii] 1 John 5:4 (NAS)

[viii] Revelation 22:7 (GNT)

[ix] © 1990 by Elizabeth Graham "Sandy's Song"

[x] © 2000 by Elizabeth Graham "Beauty from Ashes"

[xi] © 1999 by Elizabeth Graham "Your Name"

[xii] © 2003 by Elizabeth Graham "Are You There?"

[xiii] © Copyright 1998 by Elizabeth Graham "He Is Lord"

[xiv] © 2002 by Elizabeth Graham "Flow"